E. V. Thompson was born in London. He spent nine years in the navy before joining the Bristol Police Force where he was a founder member of the Vice Squad. Later he became an investigator with BOAC, worked with the Hong Kong Police Narcotics Bureau and was Chief Security Officer of Rhodesia's Department of Civil Aviation.

Over two hundred of his stories were published in what was then Rhodesia, and he returned to England committed to becoming a full-time writer. While pursuing this goal he supplemented his income with a variety of jobs, from sweeping floors in clay works to working as hotel detective in London. He then moved to Bodmin Moor, the powerful background for *Chase the Wind*, published in 1977 and the book that won him the Best Historical Novel Award. Its success has been followed by many other historical novels, including the acclaimed saga of the Retallick family and the popular Jagos of Cornwall ser...

Lewin's Mead

E. V. Thompson

HEADLINE

First published in 1996
by HEADLINE BOOK PUBLISHING

First published in paperback in 1996
by HEADLINE BOOK PUBLISHING

10 9 8 7 6 5 4 3 2 1

ISBN 0 7472 4823 0

Phototypeset by Intype London Ltd
Printed and bound in Great Britain by
BPC Paperbacks Ltd

HEADLINE BOOK PUBLISHING
A division of Hodder Headline PLC
338 Euston Road
LONDON NW1 3BH

Lewin's Mead

BOOK ONE

BOOK ONE

Chapter 1

When the bell sounded in the entrance hall of the crumbling chapel, the pupils of the makeshift school rose in a body and fought to be first out to the street.

In Fanny Tennant's class, more than thirty boys and girls aged between eight and fifteen stampeded for the door, ignoring her half-hearted call for them to leave in an orderly fashion.

At the doorway the youngsters pushed, pulled and jostled each other. One boy, obstructed by a girl a couple of years his senior, seized her by the hair and hauled her head back painfully. Ignoring the obscenities she shrieked at him, he retained his grip. Then, with a final heave that sent her tumbling to the ground, he scrambled past her.

Seated behind a high desk at the front of the class, Fanny watched the scene with despondent resignation. She should have brought the children to order. Made them leave the classroom with at least some semblance of decorum. Exerted her authority over them.

On any other day she would have done so, but not today.

This had been one of those days that was best forgotten. She had woken with a shocking headache that would not be shaken off. Then much of the morning had been spent unsuccessfully tramping through the reeking alleyways of the Lewin's Mead slum in search of a young child who had not been seen at the 'ragged school' for more than a week.

Eliza Gardener was one of her favourites and a promising pupil. Fanny wanted to learn the reason for her absence.

Few men or women who did not actually reside in the back streets of Lewin's Mead would have dared venture

3

here. Policemen were known to have entered the warren-like slum twice only.

On the first of those occasions they were in sufficient numbers to wage a small war if the need had arisen. They had entered the maze of streets in order to arrest an escapee from a prison hulk who had murdered more than one victim.

When, a few weeks later, two policemen had entered the dark alleyways in close pursuit of a robber, both constables had been set upon and killed.

Despite this, there was not a single resident, drunk or sober, who would have laid a finger on Fanny Tennant. Although not yet able to open the door to the outside world for the children of the appalling Bristol slum, she had at least shaped a key for them.

At her ragged school Fanny had given a sense of pride to children who would otherwise never have known the meaning of the word. She felt it was vitally important for the pupils of the Lewin's Mead ragged school to have some-thing in their day-to-day existence they could rely upon.

Her headache had persisted throughout the day. It would have been wiser had she not come to work this evening, but there was no one else available to take the class.

When the children had finally fought their way through the door, she counted the pencils deposited in haste upon her table by the class monitor. There were four missing. Four pencils, new only that day.

Fanny shook her head in despair. It was her own fault. She should have counted them before allowing the children to leave.

Sometimes she did not know why she bothered trying to educate such children. It seemed an impossible task. Every one of them was too dirty, unruly, or just too plain dishonest to be accepted in any other school.

Here, in a near-derelict chapel that had been disused for many years, she worked hard to give such children a glimmer of hope. An opportunity to achieve something outside their miserable existence. To show them that life had more to offer than poverty and dishonesty.

Fanny threw the pencils in the drawer in an angry gesture. She wondered whether the effort and long hours she put in at the school served any purpose at all. Whatever she, or any of the other helpers, did was ultimately to no avail. Every one of the ragged school pupils would eventually be convicted of robbery, thieving, prostitution, or worse, and was destined to spend most of his, or her, life locked inside a prison cell.

She had no doubt they would show far more interest in whatever they might learn there than in anything *she* could teach them.

Fanny pulled herself up short. This was the very defeatist argument put forward by the many opponents of the ragged school system. An attitude shared by some of the children themselves. It was an argument she was constantly fighting against.

She realised she *must* be feeling low. She would need to pull herself together and decided the answer might be to have an early night.

Fanny had slept badly the night before. In fact, she had not slept really well for some weeks. A feeling was beginning to creep up on her that life was passing her by. It left her with a discontent she had never known before.

She paused in the hallway and looked at herself in the full-length mirror in which the pupils were encouraged to study themselves and improve their appearance. She saw a small, slim woman in her late-twenties, with long, reddish hair, pulled back and secured in what she herself would describe as a 'severe' style. She was not unattractive, Fanny told herself, but she looked tired. Extremely tired.

Perhaps this was the problem. She was too exhausted by her work at the ragged school to enjoy a social life.

Outside the old chapel building, Fanny waited for two of her fellow teachers who were following her out. Husband and wife, they passed by in frosty silence, with no 'Good nights'.

Both were under notice of dismissal – for failing to maintain discipline in their classrooms. Mary Carpenter, the almost legendary Bristol-based reformer who had been the founder of the school, had signed their dismissal notices. It had been as a result of a report submitted by Fanny.

She had denounced them for countenancing the standard of behaviour she herself had experienced in her own classroom that very evening.

Turning the key in the lock, Fanny remembered what she had been subjected to during the lesson. Marbles flicked at her from the back of the class. A steady erosion of her authority which had culminated at one point in a fight between a girl who was defying her and another who took Fanny's part.

Still thinking about it, she tucked the key inside her purse and set off for the cab rank around the corner, in Stokes Croft.

'Good evening, Miss Fanny. May I have a word with you, please?'

A tall figure in dark clothing stepped from the shadows of a nearby doorway, touching his fingers to a shiny, black hat that made him loom even taller than he was.

'Hello, Ivor. You startled me for a moment. I'm not used to seeing policemen in doorways around here. I hope you've had a better day than I.'

Fanny had known Constable Ivor Primrose for some years. He was one of the few policemen sympathetic to the aims of a ragged school and had done much to help Fanny and Mary Carpenter on numerous occasions.

'I've had better days, Miss Fanny. I'm afraid the reason I'm here isn't going to improve yours very much, either.'

Fanny's heart sank. 'Oh! Is it something that will keep until tomorrow?'

'Quite frankly, no, Miss Fanny. I wish I could go home tonight and forget about it altogether. But I can't, so I want to see someone caught for it, and the sooner the better.'

Fanny frowned in annoyance. 'You are talking in riddles, Ivor. What has happened, and how do you think I might be able to help you?'

'A street urchin – a young girl – has been found dead, Miss Fanny. Assaulted and strangled, according to the path-

6

ologist. A lady came to the police station early this morning. Said she'd been stopped in the street late last night by a "creature". A woman with painted face and bold ways.'

'You mean a prostitute, Ivor?'

'That's right, Miss Fanny. She told the lady she was to come to the police station and tell us to make a search of the derelict houses down by the river. The ones where the Irish were staying a year or two back. She said that when we found what was there we should look for the girl's step-father, because "he did it". Those were her very words, apparently. Well, we went there and found this young girl's body, like I said.'

Fanny was puzzled. 'It's very sad, Ivor, but surely it's quite straightforward. You have the girl's body. Now you need only go and arrest her stepfather. I can't see how I can be of any help to you.'

'Ah! Well, the trouble is that we can't put a name to the girl. Until we do we can't arrest anyone. The superintendent said I should come and find you. To see if you can identify her.'

Fanny looked at the grim-faced policeman in open dismay. 'You mean . . . you wish me to go to the mortuary and identify this poor girl?'

'I wish there was another way, Miss Fanny, but you know most of the children who live in Lewin's Mead. I waited until you finished school until I spoke to you. I knew it wouldn't go down too well with some of your pupils if you were seen talking to me.'

This was true enough. Almost every one of the children in her class had an undetected crime or two upon his or her conscience. If it was known she had been talking to a constable there would be many empty seats in her class-room tomorrow.

'When do you want me to go?'

'Right away, Miss Fanny. The superintendent, the coroner's officer and the mortuary attendant are waiting in the Quakers' Friar mortuary right now.'

It was the last thing Fanny wanted to do tonight, but she knew there was no way of avoiding the gruesome task.

Nodding to the tall policeman, she said, 'All right, Ivor. Let's go there now.'

The mortuary was in an ill-lit courtyard not very far from the ragged school. It was a cold, forbidding building. Not a place she would have visited had she not been in the company of Ivor Primrose.

Three men were waiting for her inside the hallway of the building. Two were policemen and were looking decidedly uncomfortable. Only the mortuary attendant was cheerful.

'Ah! You're the lady who's come to identify our little street urchin, are you? I'll tell you one thing, she's a sight cleaner than she was when she was brought in here, that's for certain. The pathologist did a good job on her. Thorough, it was. Afterwards he stitched her up as neatly as though he was making a silk purse for a lady.'

While the mortuary attendant was talking, the small party walked through to another room. There was a smell in here that caused Fanny to wrinkle her nose in distaste. To one side of the room was a large marble slab, on which lay a tiny, sheet-covered form.

Before Fanny even realised what was happening, the mortuary attendant had drawn back the sheet revealing the head of a small child.

The pallor of death served to accentuate the bruises and abrasions on one side of her small face.

Fanny drew in her breath in an involuntary expression of horror.

'You know her, Miss Tennant?' The prompting came from the police superintendent who had been watching her expression closely.

Fanny's eyes clouded over with tears, but she nodded her head. 'Yes,' she whispered. 'Yes, I know her.'

Fanny had found the girl she had been seeking in Lewin's Mead that morning. The girl on the mortuary slab was Eliza Gardener.

Chapter 2

'Are you all right, Miss Fanny?'

Outside the Quakers' Friar mortuary once more, Ivor asked the question anxiously.

Fanny had made the official identification of Eliza Gardener. She had also been able to tell the police superintendent the name of the man suspected of killing her, and the place where he worked.

She was unable to shut out the memory of that poor, bruised and bloodless face. But she nodded. 'I'll be all right tomorrow, Ivor. Just for tonight I'll grieve a little for Eliza. There's no one else who cares enough to shed a tear for her.'

It was a sad truth. Eliza Gardener had never known her real father. It was doubtful whether her mother could have identified him with any degree of certainty.

Then, when Eliza was eight years old, her mother had married Charlie Stock, a coal-heaver employed on the jetty at Welsh Back. Less than two years later, Eliza's mother died. Since that time Charlie Stock had brought a variety of women to the basement rooms that constituted Eliza's home.

Most of the women left after no more than a week or two, refusing to put up with the violence to which they were subjected at Charlie's hands. Because of this, Eliza's fortunes fluctuated wildly, dependent upon the whim of her stepfather's woman of the moment. It was a recipe for disaster, but no more so than the conditions faced by a hundred or more children who existed in similar, or worse, situations in Lewin's Mead.

9

At the end of the road, Fanny turned left instead of taking the road which would have led to the cab rank in Stokes Croft.

When Ivor Primrose expressed his surprise, she said, 'I've decided to walk home, Ivor. I feel I need a little time before I have to face anyone else.'

'Then I'll walk along with you, Miss Fanny. If you don't feel much like talking I'll follow some way behind you, but the city at this time of night isn't the place for a young lady to be walking alone.'

Fanny's inclination was to argue with the constable, but she knew he was right. She gave a wry smile. It was ironic that she was safer in Lewin's Mead than in the more 'respectable' parts of Bristol.

'Walk with me, Ivor. I'm pleased to have your company. It's just that I need to think of a white lie to tell my father about being late home. If I tell him the truth, he'll try to persuade me, yet again, that I should give up my work at the ragged school.'

'At times like this I'm inclined to agree with him, Miss Fanny, but I doubt if the school would be able to carry on without you and Miss Carpenter.'

The two walked on in silence for a while before Ivor asked, 'Have you seen anything of our young artist friend recently, Miss Fanny?'

'Fergus? No, I was thinking only yesterday that I haven't seen him for some weeks. Have you?'

'I haven't seen him since he was on his way home from London and the prostitute was murdered in the house where he and young Becky live.'

Fanny remembered the incident which had shocked the whole city. A prisoner had murdered a guard in an escape from a prison hulk and made his way home to Lewin's Mead. He had then killed the prostitute after holding her and the unfortunate woman's landlady hostage. The man was patently insane. This had been the occasion when the police entered Lewin's Mead in strength.

The siege of the house had ended when the man fell from

the window of the room occupied by artist Fergus and his wife, Becky.

'I was speaking to Charlie Waller, landlord of the Hatchet Inn, recently. He said Fergus could be making good money there if only he'd put in an appearance. It's not only seamen who want portraits of themselves. Many Bristol men have been there asking for him. His fame has spread far and wide.'

'I heard from London that his visit there was hugely successful,' said Fanny. 'But I have seen neither him nor Becky since his return.' She had intended calling on them long before this. Time seemed to pass all too quickly. She was also somewhat hurt that Fergus had not contacted her since his return.

Fergus Vincent was a very talented artist who had come to Bristol's Lewin's Mead when he was invalided out of the Royal Navy with an injured leg. He painted the misery and the poverty of the people of the slums with a vivid realism that had seized the imagination of thousands who viewed his work.

Recognising the very real talent he possessed, Fanny had introduced him to people able to help his career as an artist. It had not taken long for his talent to capture the attention of those who were influential in the art world.

Before long Fergus was being fêted by all and sundry and had made a couple of journeys to London to fulfil commissions and arrange exhibitions.

Unfortunately, somewhere along the way Fanny had fallen in love with Fergus, although it was something she had admitted to no one. She had been devastated when he suddenly married Becky, a young waif he had befriended in the Lewin's Mead slum.

Nevertheless, Fanny had continued to do all she could to further Fergus's career. It was she who had arranged his most recent trip to London.

'I'll try to get news of him over the next day or two,' promised Ivor.

'Don't put yourself out too much, Ivor. He's an artist, remember. When he's working, neither time nor friends

11

mean very much to him – and he has Becky.'

'No doubt you're right,' agreed the big policeman. 'All the same, I'd like to know that all is well with him and Becky. I like them both . . .'

At that moment there was a sudden eruption of noise from a public house farther along the street in which they were walking. Amidst the hubbub there were many raised voices. There was also the unmistakable sound of smashing glass.

Ivor sighed. 'I'm sorry, Miss Fanny, but I had better find out what's going on in there.'

More glass was broken inside the building and suddenly people began spilling out on to the street.

Ivor stepped into the road to stop a passing hansom cab. As the vehicle came to a halt, the policeman said to Fanny, 'I think you'd better be catching this, Miss Fanny. The city is a bit lively tonight.'

'I'm not for hire,' protested the hansom driver. 'I've been out since five o'clock this morning and I'm on my way home.'

'So you may be,' said the policeman. 'But you'll go via the home of Alderman Tennant. In case you're inclined to argue I'll remind you that he's chairman of the Watch Committee. He's the one who'll be considering renewing your licence next month.'

The driver of the hansom cab grumbled, but his protest was more subdued now. A moment later he climbed down from his seat to help Fanny inside the vehicle.

'You'll be home in no time,' said Ivor, kindly. 'Try to forget about what you've seen tonight. It's not going to bring the poor child back. If her stepfather is the guilty party you can be quite sure he'll pay the penalty for what he did.'

'Thank you, Ivor.' Amidst renewed uproar outside the public house, she added, 'Shouldn't you be there, putting a stop to the disturbance?'

He glanced in the direction of the public house where two men were locked together in combat, wrestling on the ground watched by fellow customers.

'It won't hurt to give them a minute or two. I recognise

12

both the men who are fighting. There'll be more noise than blows coming from them. I'll let those about them enjoy it for a few minutes more. By then both the men who are doing battle will be pleased to have me stop them. If they haven't had too much to drink, a word or two from me will be enough to bring them to their senses. If they've been drinking heavily I'll take them to the police station and tomorrow they'll appear before a magistrate charged with being drunk and riotous. Seven days in prison should be long enough for them to sober up and reflect on their foolishness.'

Saluting Fanny, Ivor Primrose signalled for the hansom cab driver to whip up his horse and be on his way.

Chapter 3

Fanny was having breakfast with her father the morning after her unhappy visit to the mortuary when a servant came in to the room. After apologising for disturbing them, she told Fanny there was a police constable outside who wished to speak to her.

Alderman Aloysius Tennant frowned in annoyance. 'Tell him to come back later in the morning. Miss Fanny was out until nigh on midnight attending to ragged school business.'

Turning to his daughter, he added, 'I've told you before, Fanny. It's high time you gave up your work at that school. You've spent enough years there. I don't want you to end up like Mary Carpenter. She's an admirable woman, but her good works have come between any chance she might have had of finding a husband and raising a family. That's not what I want for you. It's not what your dear mother would have wished, either.'

His last sentence was intended to circumvent any argument Fanny might make. Her mother had died many years before, leaving Fanny to revere the dim memory that was all she possessed.

The Alderman's ploy was only partly successful. Fanny did not argue with him. Instead, she spoke to the maid.

'Has the constable told you why he is here?'

'No, miss – but he told me to tell you it was Constable Primrose.'

Fanny deposited her napkin on the table in front of her and rose to her feet immediately. Ignoring her father's disapproval, she said to the servant, 'I'll come and see him right away.'

14

Ivor Primrose had taken off his tall, shiny top hat, but he was still large enough to dominate the hall of the Clifton house.

'Come in, Ivor, we'll talk in the library. It must be something serious for you to call on me so early in the morning. You can hardly have had any sleep.'

'There was little sleep for any of us last night, Miss Fanny. It was as busy as any I can remember.'

'Have you arrested Eliza's stepfather?'

'Yes, thanks to you. He's in the cells right now. When I left him he was sobbing his heart out and swearing that he'd never meant her any harm.'

Accepting a seat in a leather armchair, Ivor looked up at her. 'But I'm not here about Eliza. When I returned to the station last night a woman named Iris was there. She'd been arrested for prostitution – and not for the first time. She lives in the house where Fergus has a room.'

Ivor had Fanny's full attention as he continued, 'I asked her about Fergus and Becky. The question seemed to surprise her. She said she thought everyone knew that Fergus hadn't been seen in Lewin's Mead since the night there was all the trouble in the house.'

Fanny was startled. 'But . . . that was two months ago! Where is he?'

'No one knows, although there was some fuss about us going in to try to arrest Alfie Skewes. Perhaps his landlady, Ida Stokes, blamed him for what had happened, him coming back when everything was going on.'

Fanny was not sorry to learn that Fergus had apparently left Lewin's Mead. The Bristol slum was a totally unsuitable environment for such a promising artist. However, she could not understand why he had failed to inform her of his new address. She was the link between Fergus and the art world of London.

'Does anyone know where he and Becky have gone? Why hasn't he told me? There are a number of exhibitions in the offing . . .'

'Fergus didn't take Becky with him. Apparently he's gone off alone, without saying anything to anyone.'

15

'Becky is still in Lewin's Mead? Fergus has *left* her?'

Fanny found the news hard to believe. When Fergus had first risen to fame in the art world, he had been prepared to risk all he had and all he hoped for, because of Becky. She had always meant more to him than even his work.

'Where is the woman who told you about this?'

'Probably on her way to prison. She's been convicted and sent away for fourteen days.'

This seemed to rule out the possibility of Fanny's speaking to Iris and having her confirm what Ivor had just said. But she still found the news difficult to accept.

'I just can't believe that Fergus would go off and leave Becky. Why?'

Ivor shook his head. 'I've told you all I know. If I hear any more I'll tell you, but it's taken two months for this information to reach me. Unless Fergus gets in touch with someone here . . .' He shrugged.

'Yes . . . yes, of course. Thank you for coming to tell me, Ivor.'

'What will you do now?'

Fanny had already reached a decision. 'Go and see Becky. I'll do it this morning.'

Fergus and Becky had a room in Back Lane. It was one of the worst of all the alleyways that extended like the tunnels of a warren in this, Bristol's most notorious slum.

As she walked along the narrow, garbage-strewn street, Fanny wondered, as she had on many occasions, why Fergus had chosen to continue to live here. It was, perhaps, understandable while he was gaining the trust of the inhabitants. He had wanted to paint them at home, at work, in birth and in death. Happy or distraught. But there had been no reason why he should continue to live here once his talent was recognised.

When Fanny reached the house she was seeking, her arrival was witnessed by Ida Stokes. The owner of the house, she occupied a ground-floor front room. There was very little that went on in Back Lane that was not witnessed by the blowsy, overweight woman.

Coming from her room as Fanny entered the house, Ida said, 'Hello, dearie. Is there something I can do for you?'

'I've come to see Becky. Is she in?'

'I expect she's still in bed at this hour of the day. Not that I'm one to interest meself in the comings and goings of me tenants. As long as they pay their rent on time they can do as they please, as far as I'm concerned.'

Eyeing Fanny, she said, 'You're the one who runs that school in St James's chapel, aren't you?'

'That's right.' Fanny made her way along the gloomy passageway, heading towards the stairs.

Behind her, Ida Stokes sniffed her disapproval. 'If you was to ask me I'd say that giving schooling to them as lives in Lewin's Mead ain't doing 'em no favours, dearie. All it does is give 'em ideas above their station in life. When they find that such learning don't put shoes on their feet, nor meat in their bellies, they feel let down. Turn to doing what they'd have done anyway. They take what they want from them who have more than they need. The only difference is, they've learned fancy names for what they're doing. If that's all that learning does for anyone it's got to be a waste of time, ain't it now?'

Climbing the uncarpeted, rickety stairs, Fanny thought ruefully that she had heard the same argument put forward, if rather more eloquently, in the houses of her father's friends, in Clifton and beyond.

She wondered how members of both vastly differing communities would view being allied in this way. In fact neither side had ever put forward an argument to cause her a moment's doubt about what she and others like her were trying to achieve.

Fanny firmly believed that only by educating *both* sides would they ever eliminate slums such as this.

She arrived on the first floor to find a number of half-naked and incredibly dirty children staring at her through the uneven gaps between the banisters. Some of the children were small enough to fall through if they were not very careful, but Fanny knew better than to try to point this

17

out to their mother, Mary O'Ryan – even were she in the house.

Fanny smiled at the children but received only blank, faintly hostile stares in return.

There was a door open on the next floor with a bundle of belongings standing inside. Fanny guessed this was the room belonging to Iris, the prostitute who had been arrested the night before.

Finally, a narrow, flimsy staircase brought her to the door of the attic room that had been Fergus's studio before his marriage to Becky, and to where he had taken his young bride.

Fanny knocked twice before she had a reply in a voice thick with sleep.

'Who is it?'

'It's Fanny Tennant. Can I come in?'

As she spoke, Fanny tried the latch but it seemed the door was bolted on the inside. It was something that was unheard of in this neighbourhood where nobody stole from each other.

'No . . . it's not convenient.'

Fanny couldn't be certain, but she thought she could hear low voices in the room. It puzzled her. Was it possible that Fergus was in the house after all? Perhaps he was hiding from the world for reasons of his own? There was only one way to find out.

'Please yourself, Becky. I'll sit out here on the stairs until it *is* convenient.'

There was more whispering inside the room and now Fanny was convinced that one voice was definitely a man's.

'Wait for me at the ragged school. I'll come and see you there,' Becky's voice came to her through the door.

Fanny was not willing to accept this suggestion. If Fergus was hiding from something, or someone, she wanted to know what it was.

'I've had experience of some of your promises, Becky. If it's all the same to you I'll wait here until you come out. You might as well come sooner than later. I can stay here all day if need be.'

18

There was more whispering inside the room, then silence and Fanny settled down to wait. She hoped she would not have to remain on the stairs for too long. In spite of what she had told Becky she would not wait for more than an hour. Even that would seem longer. The smells rising from the remainder of the house were particularly unwholesome.

Suddenly, there was the sound of a bolt being drawn inside the room. The door opened and a man came rushing out. He turned his face away as he squeezed past Fanny on the dark stairs and she did not have a clear view of his features. However, one thing was quite certain. It was not Fergus. The artist still had a severe limp as a result of his naval injury. He would not have dared to take the stairs at such a speed.

Fanny rose to her feet and entered the sloping-ceilinged attic room.

Becky was shrugging herself into a dress. Not yet twenty, her body was still that of an immature girl. Lifting her long, black hair free of the dress, she looked at Fanny defiantly. 'Well, now you've seen what I'm doing you can go back and tell Fergus that I've had a man in our room. You can tell him that he's only himself to blame. I need to live and he's sent me no money.'

Fanny's sorrow was tinged with sympathy, but it was for Fergus, not for Becky. 'So it's true, then? Fergus *has* left you?'

Becky was startled. 'You mean . . . You didn't know? He's not with you?'

'I haven't seen Fergus since before he went to London. I wouldn't have known he was back had they not told me at the ragged school that he had called there on his return, looking for you. Don't you know where he is?'

'He's just gone away for a while.' Becky looked at Fanny aggressively. 'He's . . . painting. That's where he is. He just forgot to leave any money in the house, that's all.'

'Do you have any kindling here?' Fanny became suddenly practical. 'If we get a fire going I'll make us both a cup of tea and you can tell me exactly what's going on between you and Fergus.'

'I've told you. Nothing's going on,' replied Becky, defensively.

'I doubt that, Becky. Fergus thinks the world of you. He'd never have gone off and left you with no money and not saying where he's gone.'

'He might not have done before he met all your grand friends, with their talk of exhibitions, and everything.' Becky was defiant now.

'I heard he had an argument with your landlady on the night you had trouble in the house.'

'They had words, yes. So what? He didn't need to go off without telling me where he was going – or you either, by the sound of it.'

'It certainly isn't like Fergus,' admitted Fanny. Still looking at Becky speculatively, she asked, 'But where's that kindling?'

'I haven't got any,' replied Becky, churlishly. 'Nor no tea, neither.'

It was quite apparent she did not want Fanny in her room, asking awkward questions. But Fanny was not so easily dismissed.

'Where were you when Fergus returned from London, Becky? You obviously weren't in the house.'

For a moment, Fanny thought she was not going to receive a reply, but she met the other woman's defiant gaze and it was Becky's glance that slid away, uncomfortably.

'I was out, with my friends. Well . . . I didn't know when he'd be home, did I? I couldn't be expected to sit up here on my own for weeks at a time, waiting for him to come home when he felt like it.'

'He was working, Becky. Making money for both of you. These friends you were with, were they women – or men?'

'That's none of your business!' Becky flared up angrily. 'And no one asked you to come up here today. If you hadn't poked your nose into our business, taking Fergus off to meet all your grand friends, he might be here with me now.'

'Fergus has a rare talent, Becky. You couldn't have kept it hidden in Lewin's Mead for ever. It belongs to the world.'

'So it might, but Fergus belongs to *me*.'

For a moment Fanny imagined a hidden meaning in the fiercely made statement. She dismissed it immediately. She had always been very careful to conceal the way she felt about Fergus, especially from Becky.

'That's true, and I'll do my best to find him for you.' Opening the small purse she had tucked in a pocket of her coat, she took out some money. 'Here's twenty-five pounds. That should keep you in food and rent for a while. It's money that was sent to me for Fergus. Money for some of his paintings that have been used in a magazine.'

It was a lie, but Fanny knew the truth of it would not be questioned by Becky.

She took the money without a 'thank you' and Fanny turned to leave. She was halfway down the stairs before Becky called after her.

'If you find Fergus before I do, you can tell him he should come straight home. You can tell him I've got some news for him. Important news.'

Chapter 4

Fergus Vincent sat alone in an enclosed compartment as the sprawling new suburbs of Bristol were rapidly left behind. The train was bound for Plymouth, but its destination was a matter of no importance to Fergus. This was the train that had happened to be standing in the station at Bristol's Temple Meads, when he arrived there on foot from Lewin's Mead.

It was an exceptionally slow train. Calling at most of the small stations along the way, it was not due to arrive at its destination until six o'clock the next morning.

The slow progress would suit Fergus. He needed to try to gather together his confused thoughts. With all that had happened to him in recent months, he should have been confident of an exciting future. Instead, his world had been brought crashing about his ears in the last few hours.

The world he had worked so hard to build during some very difficult years . . .

Fergus had always been a talented artist. When he left his home city of Edinburgh to join the Royal Navy he had continued to sketch and paint. It had provided him with a useful source of extra income. Officers and men were eager for sketched portraits to send home to families they might not have seen for years.

Then came the serious accident when his leg was crushed as he boarded an Arab slave ship off the North African coast, from the man-o'-war on which he was serving. The weather was rough, he lost his footing and his ankle was trapped between the two vessels.

He was fortunate not to have lost the leg. As it was, his sea-going career was brought to an abrupt end. But he still had his art.

Making his way to the Bristol slum of Lewin's Mead, Fergus sought his early tutor and lifelong friend, only to learn he had drunk himself to death.

In the slum where his friend had died, Fergus discovered tragic subjects for his sketch pad and the work became a crusade.

Thanks largely to Fanny Tennant, Fergus's work was brought to the attention of those who were influential in the art world and he soon became in demand.

By now, too, Becky occupied a very important place in his life and he was deeply in love with her.

Becky was a true product of the slum. An unloved, unwanted orphan who had never known a surname. She had survived only by using all the means at her disposal at every stage of her young life.

Theirs was a romance that shone like a bright beacon of hope for the slum-dwellers in this, the poorest district of Bristol. Yet, in the end, the evil influence of Lewin's Mead proved too strong for them.

No doubt the break-up of their marriage would come as no surprise to many who had tried to persuade them to move from the slum. Fanny had been particularly vociferous on the subject.

It had been a stubbornness in Fergus that had kept him in Lewin's Mead in the early years. Depicting the misery of the men, women and children who lived in the narrow and dirty alleyways had brought fame and a comfortable income. His reluctance to leave his fellow slum-dwellers amounted almost to guilt. It was as though by living elsewhere he would be deserting them.

Now his loyalty to Lewin's Mead had cost him his home, his future – and Becky.

It hurt Fergus deeply to remember her as he had last seen her. Returning to Bristol from an important visit to London he had expected to find her at home. Instead, he had finally located her in a public house. Laughing and half-drunk, she sat with a man's arm draped about her neck.

Twice before she had resorted to whoring, but this time he could not forgive her. On the earlier occasions there *might* just have been an excuse for her conduct, but not now, when life was so much easier for them.

Seeing Becky in the public house had left Fergus feeling sick and quite unable to cope with the situation.

His bags, packed for his London trip, had been left in the attic room at Back Lane. He simply returned to the house, picked them up, and headed for the railway station . . .

The train had been slowing as it approached yet another station. Now it drew alongside a platform lit by a line of yellow-flamed oil lamps and came to a juddering, clanking halt. At the front of the train steam escaped from the boiler as though the engine was exhaling in a giant sigh of relief.

The platform became a scene of feverish activity, captured in the flickering light of the station's lamps.

People left the train and mingled with those outside. Through the window Fergus witnessed farewells, and some joyful reunions. Watching the latter made him feel empty inside.

The door opened unexpectedly and a young girl, perhaps some ten years of age, was pushed into the compartment. She was followed by a tall young woman who wore an expression that seemed to express disapproval of the world in general.

Entering the compartment, she fixed Fergus with an unsmiling glance. 'Are you travelling in this compartment alone, sir?'

When he assured her he was indeed travelling without companions, the woman replied, 'Then you'll have no objection to sharing the compartment with a young lady and her governess.'

This time it was a statement, not a question. However, the woman had at least explained her relationship with the rather pretty little girl who smiled up at Fergus as she settled herself in a window seat opposite him.

A porter brought two small travelling cases and placed

24

them on the leather-upholstered seats before adjusting the wicks on the oil lamps in the compartment. This done, he informed the governess that her trunks would be perfectly safe in the guard's van during the journey to Plymouth.

She thanked him and handed him two penny coins, holding them pinched between thumb and forefinger.

When the door had closed behind the porter, the governess took off her bonnet and that of the young girl and laid them on a seat. She then tidied the little girl's clothing.

Outside, a whistle was blown and the train jerked into motion. As it got underway the young girl looked directly at Fergus and said, 'I'm Sarah Cunningham. What's your name?'

'Sarah! It is extremely rude to ask such a question of a perfect stranger,' the governess admonished her charge.

'Yes, Miss Bell,' replied Sarah meekly, but the smile she flashed at Fergus belied the spirit of the apology.

'It's quite all right,' he said. 'We'll be sharing the carriage for some hours, so we might as well introduce ourselves. I'm Fergus Vincent.' It was a relief to think about something other than his own situation.

Miss Bell nodded her head in tight-lipped acknowledgement of his introduction. Her expression indicated that she did not approve of such familiarity.

'That's a funny suitcase.'

Sarah pointed to a flat canvas artist's pouch propped up against the back of the seat beside him.

Fergus gave the inquisitive young girl a wan smile. 'It's not a suitcase. I'm an artist and it contains some of my sketches. Here, I'll show you.'

Before the stern-featured governess could object, Fergus lifted the canvas folder to the floor in front of him. The space it had occupied on the seat beside him was immediately filled by the small girl.

As he undid the ribbons tying the folder, the girl chattered happily. 'What do you paint? I like painting flowers. I painted a horse once, but I don't think it was very good. My grandfather said it looked more like a kitchen table with a plum pudding falling off one end.'

Fergus smiled again, more warmly this time. This young girl was proving to be a tonic. 'I expect my horses would look like that too, I haven't painted very many of them. But . . . here, this is a sketch of some birds feeding on the windowsill of the room where I live . . . Where I once lived. Here's another of a man selling live chickens.'

Soon Sarah was engrossed in the paintings and sketches until, suddenly, she jabbed a finger at one of his sketches and cried, excitedly, 'That's my great-uncle George!'

Despite her determined aloofness the governess had been craning her neck in a bid to view the sketches. Now she leaned forward openly and looked closely at the sketch pointed out by Sarah.

It was one of a series Fergus had made for the last portrait he had painted in Oxfordshire, whilst on his way home from London. His sitter had been Lord Carterton.

'So it is!' Miss Bell looked at Fergus with a less jaundiced eye as she exclaimed, 'Now I know who you are! You're the painter who has been recording life in the Lewin's Mead slum. I went to an exhibition you held in Park Street, in Bristol. I am honoured to make your acquaintance, Mr Vincent. I believe that what you are doing shows great courage and an uncommon concern for your fellow men. May I too glance through your folio?'

Now Miss Bell had lowered the barriers between herself and Fergus, she chattered almost as incessantly as did Sarah and Fergus learned a great deal about them.

Sarah's mother had died some years before. Her father was a Royal Navy captain who had only recently returned from service in the Crimea. Whilst home on leave he had been recalled to take command of a new 74-gun ship of the line. Captain Cunningham and his ship were due to sail for China within the week.

The captain had sent word for Miss Bell to bring Sarah to Plymouth immediately. He wanted to enjoy his daughter's company during his few remaining days in England.

Miss Bell complained to Fergus about the problems of travelling with a child at night, but declared there had really been no alternative. She had very little time at her disposal.

26

She also spoke of Lord Carterton. He was indeed Sarah's great-uncle. They were both in the habit of spending holidays in the great house in Oxfordshire where Fergus had painted the peer's portrait.

Now Fergus had been given the backgrounds of his fellow travellers, Miss Bell turned the conversation towards his own life. He was grateful for the intervention of Sarah, who asked suddenly, 'Could you draw a picture of *me*?'

'I not only can, but *will*,' declared Fergus, readily. 'Go and sit where you were before and I'll sketch you.'

He had earned a living sketching seamen in dockside public houses in Bristol. They were impatient men and he could have completed the young girl's portrait much more quickly than he did. But he was in no hurry. Whilst he was concentrating on his work, Miss Bell did not expect him to make conversation.

By the time the sketch was completed, Sarah was having great difficulty staying awake. She livened up briefly when he handed her the sketch, but it was the governess who waxed eloquent about it.

'It is wonderful, Mr Vincent. A truly extraordinary likeness. I wonder . . .?' She hesitated. 'I do not have a great deal of money, but might I possibly purchase the sketch for Captain Cunningham? He could have it framed and hung in his cabin. It would be a constant reminder to him of his daughter.'

'I made the sketch for Sarah. It's a gift. A "thank you" for your company.'

Miss Bell was effusive in her gratitude. Fergus was relieved when she said she would read a story to Sarah, whose eyelids now appeared to be more closed than open.

As the girl sat leaning against her governess, Fergus thought they made a charming picture and captured the moment swiftly on his sketch pad.

Minutes later, Sarah was asleep. The governess laid her gently along the seat before covering her with a travelling rug.

Looking at the sketch he had just made, Fergus realised he had captured an expression on the face of the governess that was totally out of keeping with the image she had projected when she entered the compartment.

Without a word being said, Fergus handed the sketch to her. He felt embarrassed when he saw tears come to her eyes.

'This is an absolutely wonderful sketch, Mr Vincent. Quite wonderful.'

He was not certain whether the words were whispered in order not to wake her charge, or whether it was the result of the emotion she so obviously felt.

As the governess continued to gaze at the sketch, he said quietly, 'Please accept that too, Miss Bell. I hope it may bring you pleasure in future years.'

He only escaped the gratitude of the governess when he closed his eyes and feigned sleep. Occasionally he glanced across the compartment through barely opened eyelids. On each occasion Catherine Bell was gazing down at the sketch he had made of her and Sarah Cunningham.

Chapter 5

'Where are you staying while you are in Plymouth, Mr Vincent?'

The train had reduced speed as it neared its destination.

Miss Bell asked the question as she folded the blanket which had covered Sarah while she slept. This completed to her satisfaction, she placed it neatly in one of the small travelling bags she and Sarah had in the compartment.

'I haven't really thought about it.'

It was hardly a satisfactory reply. In response to a faint upward lift of one of Miss Bell's eyebrows, Fergus added, 'I came to Plymouth on the spur of the moment. I . . . I felt the need to get away from Bristol for a while.'

'Captain Cunningham has arranged for Sarah and I to stay at the Lord Nelson Inn. I believe it is quite close to the Royal Naval dockyard. You might do worse than stay there too. Captain Cunningham says it is very comfortable, and not too expensive.'

'I'm not certain of my plans yet . . .'

'Please come and stay there. I'll let you draw . . . *sketch* me again, as often as you like, if you do.'

The plea was made by Sarah. Fergus smiled. 'How can I possibly refuse an offer like that? All right. I'll see if they have a room for me.'

Sarah clapped her hands in delight and even Miss Bell seemed pleased. 'Then we might as well share a hackney carriage. Now, as we are travelling to the same destination, may I place the sketch you so kindly gave me in your folder? Perhaps Sarah's should go there too. They are both far too valuable to suffer the risk of damage.'

* * *

The Lord Nelson Inn was a very popular establishment. It appeared to be full, but Miss Bell's use of Captain Cunningham's name was sufficient to secure a very comfortable room for Fergus.

Although the sounds of a busy inn were all about him that morning, once the others had gone to their room Fergus felt very lonely. He had been away from Becky for the previous few weeks, but had carried with him the knowledge that he would soon be returning to her, in Bristol. He no longer had that consolation. He doubted if he would ever see her again. What they once had was over.

Finally, when Fergus could suffer the loneliness no longer, he took his sketch pad and left the inn. He walked to the bank of a stretch of the River Tamar, known as the 'Hamoaze'. Here he found a great many warships anchored in the wide channel of the tidal river. It was a stirring sight and soon he was hard at work sketching, his problems momentarily forgotten.

Most of the warships still relied upon sails for propulsion, but there was also a screw-propelled ship and, churning the water to foam, a paddle-steamer, performing duty as a tug.

A prison hulk was moored on the Hamoaze, closer to the shore. Fergus thought it a sad fate for what had once been a proud man-o'-war. There were iron bars at port-holes where guns had been run out to engage England's enemies. Other ports were heavily boarded up. Masts that had once carried heavy canvas sails had been cut away at deck level. Taking their place was a haphazard jumble of deck-houses.

Despite the disturbing presence of the prison hulk, Fergus found a certain nostalgia in painting warships. He had painted many hundreds during his service in the Royal Navy.

While he was sketching, an old man came along, leaning heavily on a stick. He stopped beside Fergus inspecting his work. Then he gazed out towards the hulk and remained silent for so long that Fergus felt obliged to say something to him.

'I didn't expect to see a prison hulk here. I thought they had all been done away with.'

'Then you thought wrong,' said the old man, ungraciously. 'There are still many hulks moored at Woolwich. Mind you, this one isn't an ordinary prison hulk. It's a Royal Navy hulk. A floating hell especially for sailors who've fallen foul of regulations – or a vindictive captain.'

'Do you think it's really that bad on board?' Something in the old man's voice made Fergus want to know more.

'I don't *think* anything, I *know*. I spent two years on one just like it. You'll have some idea what life is like on board if the wind changes. It's the foulest smell you're ever likely to come across. The stench of hopelessness and despair.'

'You were a crew man on a prison hulk?'

The old man turned to give Fergus a scornful look. 'Who said anything about being part of the crew? I was a prisoner. Two wasted years I spent behind the bars of a hulk. Two years of my life living out a nightmare. Sometimes I wake up in a sweat, believing I'm still there. I did my share of time in "the hole", too. That's a punishment cell, deep down in the heart of the hulk. They lower you down there by rope. It's as near to hell as I hope I'll ever come. No light, not enough room to lie down properly. All a man can do is sit in the straw all day with only the rats and the stench of the bilges for company. It's surprising what the mind conjures up after a day or two of that.'

'Why were you sent to the hulk in the first place?' Fergus thought it must have been something serious for a sailor to be sentenced to two years on a prison hulk by a naval court martial.

'Deserting in the face of the enemy, is what they said it was. Told me I was lucky I wasn't hung from the yardarm.'

'And did you . . . desert?'

'Me? I was a gunner's mate on the *Bellerophon* at Trafalgar, when we suffered more casualties than any other ship in the fleet. My crew was still firing our gun when every other on the deck had been silenced. Me, desert? I'll tell you exactly what I did to get two years on a prison hulk.'

The old man sat on the wall between Fergus and the Hamoaze and shook his stick in the direction of the hulk. 'I was gunner on a frigate in the Mediterranean when we engaged a French man-o'-war that was twice our size. By the time we'd finished we were both in danger of sinking. When the Frenchie came alongside, their marines and our boys fought a battle with no quarter given. I think they must have been sinking faster than we were because some of 'em was abandoning ship. Suddenly from my gun port I saw a woman in the water. A Frenchwoman, she must have been, drifting away between the two boats, shouting and hollering when her head wasn't under the water. Her clothes were billowing around her like a jellyfish. It seemed I must have been the only one to have seen or heard her. I jumped in and tried to save her, but the sea was a bit too rough. I couldn't find her, 'though I searched for long enough.'

The old man gazed away from Fergus, face muscles twitching as he relived the happenings of many years before.

'What happened then?' Fergus prompted.

The old man came back to the present and his shoulders sagged. 'We'd beaten the French and they'd struck their colours, but one of the officers had seen me jump overboard while the fighting was going on. I was clapped in irons until we got back to port. There I faced a court martial. By that time there were no Frenchies around to say whether or not they'd lost a woman overboard during the fighting.'

'And for that you spent two years on a prison hulk?' Fergus was appalled.

'That's right. I was never the same man again, for all that I spent another twenty years in the service.'

'Tell me about some of the other ships on which you served,' prompted Fergus. He had begun sketching the old man, with the hulk and the men-o'-war behind him. 'The happier ones.'

The old man recounted his experiences for more than an hour, during which time Fergus made a number of sketches. One day he knew he would incorporate them in a painting.

Eventually, the ex-prisoner rose stiffly to his feet from his seat on the low wall. 'It's been nice talking to you, son, but it's time I went home, otherwise my sister will have a search party out for me.

'I should have married before I left the navy,' he added.

'If I had, I might have ended up master in my own home. As it is I'm lower on her list than the cat. I swear she'd put me out at night if it wasn't for what the neighbours would say.'

The dejected old man went on his way, leaning heavily on the stick. It was a picture Fergus was able to capture on his sketch pad before he disappeared around the next corner.

Chapter 6

Fergus worked on for a while after the old sailor had left him, but before long he began thinking about his own troubles once more. Aware that he was not giving of his best to the sketching, he decided to call it a day.

On his way back to the inn, he heard the sound of laughter coming from a public house. Acting on impulse he went inside.

The long, smoke-hazy bar of the public house was crowded with off duty sailors and young women of the town. The reminder of Becky and the life she was now leading hit him like a physical blow. Turning about, he hurriedly left the public house before his presence had even been noticed.

Back at the inn, Fergus was walking across the lounge, engrossed in his own unhappy thoughts, when a young voice called excitedly, 'Mr Vincent! Mr Vincent!'

The next moment Sarah Cunningham ran across the room to take his hand, saying, 'We've been waiting for your return. Come and meet my father.'

They walked together across the lounge towards a sun-tanned man wearing the uniform of a naval captain. Beside him was Miss Bell.

Captain Arthur Cunningham rose to his feet and extended his hand in a greeting. 'I am very pleased to meet you, Mr Vincent. I would like to thank you for the splendid sketch you made of Sarah. It is already framed and hanging on the bulkhead in my sea cabin. It will be a treasured reminder of my daughter when I am far from home.'

Nodding towards the folder beneath Fergus's arm, he

added, 'I can see you have wasted no time in starting work in Plymouth. May I look at what you have been doing?'

Fergus was slightly taken aback by the unexpected request, but had no objection to anyone looking at his work. He handed the folder containing his sketch pad to Captain Cunningham.

Turning the pages slowly, the naval captain expressed his approval. 'These are good, Mr Vincent. Very good indeed. Catherine – Miss Bell has been telling me you are something of a celebrity. She also mentioned that you have painted a portrait of my uncle, Lord Carterton. Now I have seen some of your work it is easy to see why you are so much in demand. It also, I hope, provides an admirable solution to a problem presented to me by my fellow officers. Admiral Sir Cuthbert Mallory is due to retire very soon. He is temporarily occupying the office of Flag Officer, Plymouth, but for most of his life he has been an Admiral of the Red. I have been asked to find an artist to paint a portrait of him to hang in the Admiralty, in London. You would be doing me a very great favour if you would accept the commission.'

Fergus needed to think about the offer for only a few moments. The money he would be paid for the commission, added to that which he had already received from Lord Carterton, meant he would not need to worry about funds for a very long time to come. Besides, it might possibly prove an interesting task. He declared he would be pleased to accept Captain Cunningham's offer.

'Splendid! I'll try to arrange the first sitting for tomorrow afternoon, if that is convenient for you? But for now come and have a drink with me. We'll *all* have a drink – yes, you too, Catherine.' Captain Cunningham added the rider when the governess began shaking her head. 'After all, you have saved me a great deal of work by finding an artist for me so quickly.'

Fergus's first inclination had been to refuse the offer to have a drink with Captain Cunningham, his daughter and her governess. He believed Miss Bell would take the opportunity to continue questioning him about his life in Lewin's Mead. However, when the captain heard that Fergus had once served in the Royal Navy the talk was of ships, fleets, and foreign ports.

Eventually, Miss Bell said she needed to change Sarah into clean clothes before dinner. Fergus said he too had things to do.

'Of course,' said Captain Cunningham, graciously. 'But you *will* join us for dinner?'

Fergus had been watching Sarah during the time her father had been talking to him to the virtual exclusion of the others. He thought she was unhappy at being left out of the conversation Fergus was having with the father she so obviously adored.

'I think your time with Sarah is far too precious to share with a stranger. I look forward to speaking to you again tomorrow and to beginning the portrait of the Admiral.'

Fergus was doing nothing that evening so had a meal sent up to his room and worked on the sketches he had made that day at the Hamoaze.

Much later a note was sent to his room from Captain Cunningham. It thanked Fergus for his thoughtfulness and agreed he would have all too little time to spend with his only daughter. He ended the note by saying he would collect Fergus at two o'clock the following afternoon to take him to meet Admiral Sir Cuthbert Mallory.

Chapter 7

Fergus was awake early the next morning. Drawing back his curtains he saw there was a light mist hovering above the river, giving a ghostly appearance to the ships anchored there. He dressed quickly and hurried to the Hamoaze. He wanted to capture the composition of ships, mist and water before the sun rose sufficiently high to dispel the mist.

He had chosen his time well. The tide was well out and the mist followed the sinuous line of the channel, its touch softening the lines of the warships and the squat prison hulk.

Fergus worked for some time, only vaguely aware of an object that broke the smooth surface of the glistening mud, halfway between the shore and the water. He had dismissed it as a piece of partly submerged tree trunk, probably washed downriver by the current.

Suddenly his glance fixed on the 'tree trunk'. From the corner of his eye he had thought he detected a movement. He looked at it intently for a while. Almost convinced that it must have been a bird he had seen – he suddenly saw the movement once more.

With the movement came the revelation that it was not a piece of wood. He was looking at a man! What Fergus had seen was the weak movement of an arm.

There was a large expanse of smooth mud between Fergus and the prostrate figure and he had no way of knowing how deep it was. He looked about him seeking help and saw a boy of about twelve years of age, pushing an empty barrow.

'Boy! Quick – go and fetch help. There's a man out there, lying in the mud.'

Releasing the shafts of the barrow, the boy looked in the direction pointed out by Fergus and frowned, 'That's not a man. It's just a bit of old . . .'

At that moment there was another movement from the object. This time there could be no doubting what it was. A hand waved weakly.

The boy's face was suddenly drained of blood. He stuttered, 'I'll . . . go and . . . fetch my dad. I live just around the corner.'

The boy turned his barrow around and ran with it, the wheels' screeching proclaiming the urgency of his errand.

For what seemed an age, Fergus was at a loss as to what he could do next. Then he realised there was less mud between him and the channel than there had been when he arrived. The tide was creeping across the mud flats towards the feebly moving man.

Fergus deposited his painting gear over a wall in the tiny garden of a nearby house. Then he hurried down some nearby steps to a strip of shingle before stepping gingerly out on the mud.

He had not progressed very far before the mud was knee-deep. By the time he was two-thirds of the way to the trapped man it was halfway up his thighs. Each step became a major effort. Fortunately, it levelled out at this depth, but Fergus was increasingly aware of the limitations placed upon him by his crippled leg.

Before he had reached the now still form he heard a shout. The boy, two men and a woman were at the spot where he had been painting. One of the men shouted something at Fergus, then he and his male companions clattered down the steps to the shingle.

Fergus floundered the remaining couple of paces to the body. So muddy was it, that he was not certain whether it was a man or woman. He assumed it to be a man lying face downwards, head turned to one side.

The water was snaking closer across the mud now and

Fergus reached down to take the man's arms. He would try to pull him towards the bank, hoping the two rescuers would reach him before the water did.

Fergus located one arm, but when he pulled it clear of the mud he made a startling discovery. A shackle and chain linked one wrist to the other. When he checked, he discovered the man's ankles were similarly secured. He was an escaped prisoner! Most probably an escapee from the naval hulk moored not very far away.

Nevertheless, whoever the man was, or what he had done, he could not be left here to die in the mud of the Hamoaze.

Fergus began desperately tugging, sliding him awkwardly across the mud in the wake of his own slow and laborious progress.

It seemed he had made hardly any at all before the two men from the shore reached him. Both were large and strong.

One of them lifted the chains to show his companion, then, without a word, he swung the prisoner to his shoulder and began the laborious journey to the bank.

The other man stayed with Fergus, helping him through the cloying mud.

By the time Fergus reached the steps he was close to collapse. He was helped up to the road by some of the large crowd which had now gathered.

Someone had thrown a bucket of water over the rescued man's head, revealing the features of a youngster who could hardly have been out of his teens.

'What are you going to do with him?' gasped Fergus.

'What do you think we're going to do?' retorted the man who had carried the escaped prisoner to shore. 'There's a reward for escaped prisoners. Mind you, I don't know whether it's paid out for dead as well as live ones – and he's likely to be dead before the police arrive.'

'You'll be collecting no reward for him.' A man walking with the aid of a stick pushed his way through the crowd. Fergus recognised him as the one he had been sketching the previous day. 'He's a naval prisoner. They'll be quite happy to have him die so they don't have to pay for his victuals. You'll get nothing from them.'

'They'll need to pay me *something*,' protested the mercenary rescuer. 'I've ruined a good pair of trousers by going out there.'

'Then it's not going to do them any more harm if you carry him into my house. It's no more than a street away. If a man's going to die he should be allowed some dignity, at least. He'll have had precious little of that, out there on the hulk.'

The rescuer protested but was pushed aside by two women who heaved more water over the prostrate escapee. They then persuaded two men to place him in the barrow belonging to the boy Fergus had sent off to find help.

As the still form was borne away, Fergus recovered his paints and sketch pad and followed after the crowd. He too was caked in evil-smelling mud from the waist down, but there was nothing he could do about it immediately.

At the house of the old ex-naval man, the shackled escaped prisoner was laid on the flagstones inside the doorway. In the background, a woman whom Fergus took to be the ex-sailor's sister protested in vain.

'Shall I send for a doctor?' asked one of the women in the crowd which had followed the barrow.

'Only if you know one who's prepared to treat a man with these on, without sending for the police.' The ex-naval man rattled the chains hanging from the young man's wrists.

'The police have already been called,' replied one of the women. 'Harry Harris didn't believe what you said about the reward. He's hoping to get something out of this.'

'If you're thinking of getting a sketch of him you'd better do it quickly, artist,' said the ex-sailor to Fergus. 'And make it a good one. You won't often come across a man who's so desperate to escape that he'd go into the sea wearing shackles and chains and risk death on a mud bank rather than endure life on a prison hulk.'

Fergus had not even thought of sketching the man, but now the idea had been put to him, he decided to act upon it immediately.

40

He had only just begun the sketch when the rescued man's eyes opened. He looked about him in terror for a moment or two. Then, in a voice devoid of strength or emotion, he whispered, 'Where am I?'

'You're in a house in Stonehouse. You've just been rescued from the Hamoaze.'

The eyes moved once more, but the head remained still. 'Don't let them take me back. I don't want to die on a prison hulk.'

'You're not going to die anywhere,' said the ex-sailor.

'Yes, I am. Just like the others. But they went quickly. Cleanly.'

'There are others? More than one of you escaped?' The question was put by Fergus.

'Three of us. The other two were washed away in the dark. We misjudged the tide. It doesn't matter now . . . but I don't want to die on board. They'll put me in "the hole" again.'

For the first time, the man suddenly seemed to be in pain. 'I . . . I can't move my legs.'

'There'll be a doctor here soon,' said one of the women. 'Someone went for one while they were carrying him ashore,' she explained to Fergus and the ex-sailor. 'No one knew he was an escaped prisoner then.'

The prisoner closed his eyes once more and did not open them again until a doctor pushed his way through the crowd and into the narrow passageway.

Looking down at the young man, he frowned. 'How did he get in this state?'

Everyone spoke at once, but the doctor made enough sense of it to learn the circumstances of the young man's discovery and rescue.

'I'll have a look at him, but I want these taken off.'

He indicated the shackles around the man's wrists.

'I'll go and fetch a smith,' said the boy whose barrow had provided transport for the ex-prisoner.

The doctor carried out his examination swiftly and methodically. Then, with a suddenness that startled those watching, the young prisoner began to scream.

41

Standing up, the doctor said, 'I'm afraid this young man has broken his back. Something probably hit him while he was in the water. It's incredible that he's survived this long. All I can do is give him something to ease his pain.'

He rummaged in the large bag he had brought with him and mixed up a brownish mixture. When it was done, he lifted his patient's head and forced the mixture between the man's lips, not pausing even when he began choking.

As he laid the man down once more on the stone-flagged floor, two policemen made their way through the crowd to the house. Opening his eyes, the young man looked up and saw them. The fear on his face was something that neither Fergus nor any other artist could ever have captured. 'Don't take me back to the hulk.'

'It's all right, young man. You'll not be going back to the hulk. You have my word.'

The two policemen looked uncomfortable. 'You understand that we're obliged to take him into custody, sir? He'll stay at the police station to await the arrival of the naval authorities.'

Still crouching down, the doctor packed away his things in the leather bag. He took his time over the task. When it was done, he stood up and addressed the two policemen. Both constables seemed nervous. They were uncomfortably aware that the crowd outside the door were hostile to them.

'I am afraid this young man, whoever he is, is outside the jurisdiction of the naval authorities now, Constable.'

Fergus looked as surprised as the constables, but the doctor said, 'He is dead, and died onshore, not on a prison hulk. There will need to be an inquest and then he will be buried in consecrated ground, here in Stonehouse. All you can do now is ascertain his name, in order that it may be recorded on his tombstone.

The man who had carried the escaped prisoner to the shore had heard what was said and now asked, 'What about my reward?'

'Hopefully, it will be a great one,' said the doctor, preparing to leave the house. 'I believe great store is put on such things – in heaven.'

Chapter 8

When Fergus returned to the Lord Nelson and entered the
inn yard, his muddied state attracted immediate attention.
A servant intercepted him at the front door and guided him
to the servants' entrance. Here the inn-keeper met him and
heard his story.

The inn-keeper was himself an ex-naval man, and sympathetic to those who fell foul of the over-rigid code of
discipline imposed within the senior service.

A bath was ordered to be taken to Fergus's room.
Minutes later, servants were toiling upstairs bearing towels
and pails of hot water from the kitchen. Fergus's clothes
were taken away for laundering, with a promise that they
would be returned the same day.

Later, when he was soaking in the luxury of a hot bath, a
half-tankard of brandy was sent up to the room, with the
compliments of the sympathetic landlord.

Fergus took lunch that day with Sarah and her governess.
The inn servants had told Catherine Bell of Fergus's
morning adventure, but he had to repeat the details for her.
He also found himself being questioned once more about
his life in Lewin's Mead – and about Becky. To his relief, he
discovered that the governess had a great interest in ragged
schools. He was able to divert the course of her questioning
by telling her of the children he had met whilst giving
lessons at the Lewin's Mead ragged school.

He was eventually rescued by Captain Cunningham. The
naval officer arrived to take him to the office of the Flag
Officer, to commence his portrait.

For today, Fergus took only the sketch pad in which he

had recorded the events of the morning. He would buy a canvas and commence the actual portrait on his next visit.

Admiral Sir Cuthbert Mallory had a face that came close to the colour of the ensign he had flown as 'Admiral of the Red', and his manner was that of a bluff old sea dog.

Reluctantly following Fergus's instructions, he seated himself on a chair facing the window. As Fergus began sketching, the admiral grumbled, 'This is all a load of useless nonsense. Who wants a portrait of me, eh?'

'Your staff want it, Sir Cuthbert, so that you may be remembered with pride at the Admiralty in London. Officers will point to your portrait and say, "I once served with him." It's an honour, sir.'

'In fifty years' time everyone will walk past the painting, taking no more notice than if it were a piece of wallpaper. It's not as though I am Lord Nelson – although I am proud of having fought in his fleet. I was at Trafalgar, you know. A young, fourteen-year-old midshipman, I was then.'

Sketching busily while the admiral was sitting comparatively still, Fergus tried to keep him talking. 'You are the second man I have met in my two days at Plymouth who has boasted of having served with Nelson. The other man served as a gunner's mate on the *Bellerophon*.'

Fergus told the fiery old admiral of his first meeting with the ex-sailor, and of its sequel, only that morning.

Fergus's disclosure had the opposite effect to that he had intended. There was a break in the sketching while the admiral demanded to look through the sketch pad. It showed the old man, the prison hulk and the escaped prisoner who had died that morning.

Gazing at the sketch of the ex-sailor, Admiral Sir Cuthbert Mallory frowned. 'The *Bellerophon* went into action ahead of my own ship. She was in the thick of the battle and her gunners were the pride of the fleet. It's difficult to believe that one of them would one day desert in the face of a lesser enemy. As for the prison hulk . . . I knew it had been brought into port, but I assumed it had already left.'

Looking first at the sketch of the hulk, and then at that

of the dying escaped prisoner, the admiral, aggressive in defence, said, 'Are you one of those who say the navy has no need of such prisons, Vincent?'

'I've never held any strong views either way, Sir Cuthbert. I merely sketched what I saw.'

Handing back the sketch pad, the admiral frowned. 'You've done it well. *Too* damned well. All right, you enjoy sketching prisoners – I'll give you the opportunity of a lifetime. Leave the sketching of me until tomorrow. We'll go off and pay a visit to this hulk. See something of the conditions for ourselves. We'll not be made warmly welcome, you can be damned certain of that, but the ship's in the Hamoaze and is under my jurisdiction. I want to know how she's being run.'

The admiral stood up, happier to have something more useful to do with his time than sit still for an artist. 'Come on, now. If we don't hurry it'll be evening before we return and we'll end up wasting good drinking time.'

There was consternation on board the hulk when it became apparent that a pinnace flying the flag of Admiral Sir Cuthbert Mallory was heading for them.

Watching the flurry of activity as they approached the gangway leading from water level to the deck of the prison ship, Sir Cuthbert said to Fergus, 'What you've heard about prison hulks may or may not be true, but our visit seems to be causing a considerable stir.'

'It's the thought of having an admiral visit them, Sir Cuthbert. They'll be in a state of panic, above and below decks.'

'Then let's keep it that way, Fergus. Although, if things on board are all they should be, they have nothing to worry about. You seek out anything that's not in order and make a sketch while everyone is working hard to keep me happy. If there is anything I should see, let me know immediately.'

The crewmen of the pinnace shipped their oars and the bowman leaped from the boat to the gangway to make the craft fast.

By the time the last turn had been made with the securing

rope, the admiral was on the gangway. He made his way to the deck of the hulk at a speed that belied his age.

At the top of the gangway a hastily gathered party of sailors piped the senior officer on board and Sir Cuthbert acknowledged their efforts with a brief salute.

The admiral's visit had taken everyone on board the hulk by surprise. The ship's commanding officer was one of the last to appear. He came hurrying from his cabin, fastening the buttons of his tunic as he did so.

Bad weather in the channel had forced the hulk to be towed in to the Hamoaze on its journey to Woolwich from the north. There had recently been a great deal of criticism about the use of hulks as prisons for naval men. It had become a sensitive subject in the corridors of Whitehall.

During the voyage the question of the future role of hulks had been debated in London. The hulk at present in the Hamoaze would remain here until the Admiralty in London made a firm decision about those moored off Woolwich.

While the commanding officer gathered his senior men about him, crew members were sent scurrying to clean up those parts of the hulk where an admiral might expect to be taken.

As all this activity was taking place, Fergus made his way below decks in the wake of a small working party. Here was the accommodation for the naval prisoners. Rows of steel-barred cages extended on either side of a broad gangway. The stench was overpowering enough to make a weak-stomached man gag. It took some moments for Fergus to accustom himself to it.

Meanwhile, the working party, comprised of crew members, had opened a hatch in the side of the ship. From here they were lowering buckets on ropes to the river below. The water drawn up from this source was thrown across the gangway floor. At the same time other sailors were unshackling a double line of naval convicts who had been secured in the gangway.

The light was not good, but it was sufficient for Fergus to make a hurried sketch of the scene. As he worked he became aware that a young man, unshaven but otherwise fairly presentable, was watching him through the bars of the nearest prison cage.

'How long have those men been chained out here?' Fergus put the question to the watching man.

'Since we started our journey from the north. About eight or nine days, I suppose. Today's the first time they've been unshackled.'

The deck inside the cages was sparsely covered with soiled straw, now wet from the activities of the working party, but out here there was nothing and Fergus asked, 'What do the men have for bedding at night?'

The young prisoner gave a short, derisive laugh. 'Bedding? You're standing on it right now. They sleep on the bare deck. We'd have thrown 'em some straw, but there's barely enough to cover the deck in here. They at least have enough room to lie full-length. That's more than we have.'

The cages were desperately overcrowded. As the men newly removed from the corridor were pushed inside, the others shuffled back, complaining bitterly, to make room for them.

As the young man was squeezed against the bars by the new influx, he asked, 'Who are you, and what are you doing here?'

'I'm an artist. I've been commissioned to paint a portrait of Admiral Sir Cuthbert Mallory. While I was sketching him this afternoon I mentioned this hulk and a dying prisoner I found on the mud flats. He suggested we should come and look at conditions.'

'You found a prisoner . . . dying? Which one was he? There were three of them escaped last night.'

'They're all dead. The one I found was a young man, not more than twenty-two or -three, I'd say. He said the other two had been swept away when they leaped from the hulk. He must have been hit by a boat. A doctor said he had a broken back.'

The young man grimaced, as though in pain. 'His young brother was one of those chained outside. They should have escaped together but he couldn't release his shackles.'

'Hey, you, what are you doing here? Don't you know it's

48

against regulations to be talking to a prisoner?' A naval master-at-arms advanced upon Fergus, threateningly.

'No, I didn't know.'

'Who are you? You'd better have a good answer or you'll be inside with this lot until we've found out about you – and that might well take a few days.'

The master-at-arms was responsible for discipline on board the ship as well as possessing many other powers. There was no doubt he had the authority to carry out his threat. But Fergus held all the cards today.

'I doubt it. The admiral will come looking for me long before then. It might well be *you* who find yourself in the cage. I've no doubt there are many men in there who would enjoy that far more than you.'

There was a howl of approval from the prisoners, but the petty officer ignored the sound. 'You're with the admiral's party?' The master-at-arms looked Fergus up and down. He was not in uniform and was hardly dressed in the fashion of a gentleman. And yet . . . 'Who are you?'

'The admiral's artist.' It was only a half-lie. 'He's asked me to come below decks and record what I see. If you care to stand over there by the prison cage, I'll sketch you – and the prisoners too.'

'I don't want no one sketching me for any admiral. Nor for anyone else while I'm on this hulk, neither. You carry on and do what you want, but leave me out of it.'

The master-at-arms backed hurriedly away, to the glee of the prisoners.

'Is there really an admiral on board?' a young prisoner asked in disbelief.

'There most certainly is – and I don't think he approves of prison hulks. Tell me, is there any place he ought to see, that the captain might not show him?'

'Yes, the "hole". It's right down in the bilges. A man who's singled out for punishment is lowered down there on a rope, chained ankle to wrists so that he can neither stand nor lie down, even if there were room. For as long as he's in there he'll have neither light nor anything else. Young Johnny Kidd's been in there ever since we set sail.'

'Why?'

'The master-at-arms can tell you more about that than anyone, 'though you're not likely to get the truth from him. Johnny's the youngest and best-looking kid on here. The master-at-arms took a shine to him. Got him out of the cage to clean out his cabin, so he said. The next thing we know the master-at-arms is raving around like a lunatic and young Johnny is thrown in the "hole". If you ask me, he'll be there until he dies. Or until he's mad enough to forget whatever it was as happened in the master-at-arms' cabin.'

When Admiral Sir Cuthbert Mallory expressed a wish to see the 'hole' and the prisoners held there, the hulk's commanding officer at first feigned ignorance of such a place.

The admiral pointed out that telling a deliberate lie would render even the most senior officer liable to court martial. The warning was sufficient to jog the hulk's commander's memory.

'Perhaps you mean the punishment cell known as the "locker", Sir Cuthbert? I'll send for the master-at-arms. He is responsible for all disciplinary matters.'

When the man in charge of the hulk's security was found, the commander said, 'The admiral has been asking me about a punishment cell known as the "hole". Is that another name for the "locker"?'

'Yes, sir, I have heard it called that.' Fergus thought the master-at-arms's face had paled when he was asked the question.

'There you are, Sir Cuthbert,' said the hulk's commanding officer. 'I apologise for not being aware of the name by which it is known to the convicts. You may see it if you wish, but it is empty at present. I hope that while I am in command it will remain so.'

'I am given to understand there is a young prisoner by the name of Johnny Kidd there,' said Fergus.

The statement took the hulk's commander by surprise, but now he too observed the discomfiture of the master-at-arms and his next question was directed at him. 'Do you know anything about this?'

'Yes, sir.' The master-at-arms licked his lips nervously. 'The prisoner was causing trouble. When he became violent, I had him put in the "locker". I meant to tell you . . . it must have slipped my mind, sir.'

'How long has the prisoner been in the punishment cell?' The question came from the admiral.

'I think it was the day we set sail, sir.'

'Eight days and I haven't been informed?' The commanding officer's anger was genuine now.

'You can deal with your internal disciplinary problems later, Commander. I want to see this punishment cell immediately.'

The commanding officer led the party of officers and Fergus down to the deck below the one where he had been sketching. Here there was a small but heavy wooden hatch. When it was removed by a couple of seamen a narrow wood-lined shaft was revealed, leading down to the ship's bilges. A nauseating smell indicated that much of the filth from the prison decks had found its way to the bottom of the narrow shaft.

There was no ladder and the admiral called for a lantern to be lowered down the hole.

Fergus was beside the admiral as he peered into the hole. When the lantern reached the bottom of the shaft they could see a half-naked figure at the bottom. His hair was tangled and there was a stubble on his face that was not quite a beard. He was rocking himself to and fro with shackled arms wrapped about his knees. He seemed oblivious of either the lantern or the men watching him from the hatchway.

There was no ladder in the shaft. A prisoner would either be lowered or tumbled into the punishment hole. The mode of entry would doubtless depend upon his own behaviour, or the mood of those committing him to the primitive cell.

'I want that man brought up here,' said the admiral angrily to the hulk's commanding officer. 'Get someone down there – this minute.'

The prisoner took no more notice than before when a sailor who had been lowered into the 'hole' secured a rope about him and called for him to be hauled up.

Young Johnny Kidd resumed his rocking when he was hauled up and placed upon the deck beside the hatchway. He would have been unable to stand upright, even had he wanted to. A short chain, no more than eighteen inches long, linked his shackled wrists to the fetters on his ankles, forcing him to adopt a crouching position. The stench he brought up with him would have turned the strongest stomach.

Hardly able to contain his anger, Admiral Sir Cuthbert Mallory addressed the hulk's commanding officer. 'I want the shackles removed from that man immediately. Then you will personally supervise him while he is cleaned up. He will then be sent ashore to the naval hospital. His criminal file is to be sent to my office. In view of what I have seen, I intend having his sentence quashed. You will also send me a full report on the action taken against your master-at-arms in respect of this matter.'

Turning his back on the thoroughly chastened commanding officer, the admiral said, 'Come along, Fergus. I want to get the stench of this place out of my nostrils – and it's not the convicts I find hard to stomach.'

Chapter 9

The completed portrait of Admiral Sir Cuthbert Mallory was presented to him at a dinner in the Flag Officer's residence. Fergus had been invited, but chose to dine at the Lord Nelson Inn with Catherine Bell and Sarah.

He felt he would have found the company too grand at the official presentation dinner. The captain of every Royal Navy ship in Plymouth would be present. In addition, no less a personage than Admiral of the Fleet Sir James Stott was travelling from the Admiralty in London to be present at his colleague's farewell party.

Fergus was preparing for bed when there was an insistent knocking on the door of his room. He opened it to find a young and excited pot-boy outside.

'Sir, I've been sent up to ask you to come downstairs to the lounge. There's five admirals and nine captains down there! They're insisting that you come down and join them. The landlord would have come up to fetch you himself, but he used to serve on the same ship as one of the admirals and has just announced drinks on the house! It seems he made so much prize money when he was with the admiral he was able to buy this inn when he came shoreside. It's likely to be a lively party, sir.'

Fergus contemplated declining the invitation to join the party of senior naval officers, but quickly rejected the thought. It would be churlish. He had been very well paid for the portrait of Sir Cuthbert. The amount he had received was probably the equivalent of five years' wages for the average man and he had cause to be grateful.

Dressing once more, he made his way downstairs and

found a party in full swing. The landlord had cleared the lounge of all except the senior naval officers. Having come straight from the naval dinner, all were in their mess-dress uniforms. Fergus felt decidedly shabby in their company.

He was greeted enthusiastically by a jovial and red-faced Sir Cuthbert, who behaved as though they were old friends. Putting an arm about Fergus's shoulders, the retiring officer led him across the room to where Admiral of the Fleet Sir James Stott sat in an armchair, surrounded by glasses, bottles, and sycophantic post-captains.

'James, I want you to meet Fergus Vincent, the artist who painted my portrait. He was invalided from the Royal Navy some years ago and has since made quite a name for himself in the world of painting. Indeed, I'm told he'll one day take his place among the most important artists in the country.'

'He'll certainly never be short of patrons if his portraits continue to be as flattering to his sitters as yours is to you,' joked the navy's most senior admiral. 'Seeing what he's done for you, Cuthbert, I could almost be persuaded to sit for him myself!'

'I thought you had other plans for him,' replied Sir Cuthbert, mysteriously.

'So I have . . . So I have,' agreed the senior admiral, vaguely. 'But there's plenty of time to talk about that. Where's the landlord? Mr Williams, don't I remember you once played the concertina?'

'You have a very good memory, Sir James. As a matter of fact I have the very instrument in the cupboard, in the corner here. Would you like a tune, sir?'

'Of course I want a tune! Clear the women from the other room, sir, then you can give us a rendering of "The Blackbird Song". After that Sir Cuthbert can give us his special version of the song he learned in Gibraltar. The one about lobsters. Come along, Mr Williams, this is a party. Some music, if you please.'

The landlord of the Lord Nelson Inn took his concertina from beneath the counter, drew air into the instrument and began playing. Moments later the naval officers began singing raucous renderings of songs that were popular among all seamen who set out to sail the world from British ports.

It was the beginning of a party that went on for much of the night. So noisy was the gathering that, at two o'clock in the morning, the inn was raided by half-a-dozen uniformed policemen who rushed through the door to the cheers of the senior naval officers.

It took only a few minutes for the landlord of the inn to convince the sergeant and his constables that the admirals and captains were *not* drinking after hours, but were very welcome non-paying guests of the house.

Offering his apologies, the red-faced sergeant declined Sir James Stott's invitation for he and his men to have a drink with him and backed out of the inn, saluting to left and right as he went. The closing of the door behind the policemen was the signal for another loud cheer from the naval officers.

Dawn had broken before the party came to an end. The Admiral of the Fleet had sent one of the captains to tell his servant that he was ready to leave the inn. He would catch the early train to London.

One or two of the captains were patently the worse for their night's carousing. Fergus, who had drunk less than most, hoped they would not be required to take out their ships that day.

He was shaking hands with the Admiral of the Fleet, when Admiral Sir Cuthbert Mallory said, 'Isn't there a question you want to put to Fergus, James?'

'So there is. A good job I have you here to remind me, Cuthbert. Perhaps I should bring you up to London instead of allowing you to retire and rot away on that country estate of yours.'

Returning his attention to Fergus, Sir James Stott said, 'Do you have any commitments here in England, young man? Any family?'

The question almost caught Fergus off guard. For the past few hours he had been able to put Becky from his mind. Now he was being asked publicly to confirm or deny the action he had taken.

'No, sir. I have no commitments here.'

'Good. You are acquainted with Captain Cunningham, I believe?'

Fergus nodded. 'I met him through his young daughter. She's here to spend a few days with him before he sets sails for China.'

'Ah! Well, there's been a change of plan. He'll be sailing tomorrow in *Venus*, in accordance with his orders, but not for China. He's going to India. It seems there's trouble brewing there. We might need to put a Naval Brigade ashore to show the army how they ought to do things. I'd like an artist to go with them and provide a record of what goes on. Would you like to take it on?'

The offer took Fergus completely by surprise. It was some moments before he could marshal his thoughts and give the Admiral of the Fleet an answer.

It would provide him with a unique opportunity to use his talent in an unusual and exciting way. It would also take his mind off the painful parting with Becky. However, there was a problem which he believed had been over-looked.

'I would welcome the opportunity, sir. Unfortunately, you seem to be forgetting my injured leg. I doubt if I would be able to keep up with the men on a prolonged march.'

'Dammit, Vincent, no one's expecting you to *walk* anywhere. You'd have a horse or an elephant, whatever it is they ride there, same as Captain Cunningham and any other naval officers. You'll need one anyway, to carry your paints and easels and anything else you want to take. The navy will pay you a salary, of course. I don't know what it will be, I don't think we've ever had an artist as part of a ship's complement before, but we'll sort out something. What do you say?'

'I think it's a very exciting offer, sir. I'm happy to accept.'

'Good! Send back some sketches occasionally, just to let me know what's going on. We'll probably print them in the newspapers or something. It should be damned interesting. Wish I were going with you.'

The Admiral of the Fleet made his way to the door,

shaking hands with his fellow party-going officers along the way. Behind him, Fergus wondered what he had taken on.

He thought it might work out well. He would be far away from the heartache he had left behind in Bristol and it would give him time to come to terms with the break he had made with Becky.

He would send the money he had earned for Admiral Sir Cuthbert Mallory's portrait to Fanny, with a request that she give some of it to Becky, as and when she needed money. He would ask Catherine Bell to take it to Bristol for him.

Yes, accompanying Captain Cunningham on *HMS Venus* to India would suit him very well. By the time he returned he should have come to terms with life and be ready to make a new start in England.

BOOK TWO

BOOK TWO

Chapter 1

'Jesus! If this baby doesn't stop kicking me soon, I swear I'll find some way of kicking it back.'

Seated on the edge of the bed in Maude Garrett's room, Becky entwined her fingers beneath the distended bulge of her stomach and sat supporting it as Maude changed her dress.

'You make the most of it while it's still in there,' said Maude, ominously. 'Once it arrives it'll take over your life for twenty-four hours of the day.'

Maude Garrett had a five-month-old baby son. He had been born soon after her release from the Red Lodge, the experimental reformatory founded by Mary Carpenter in Bristol some years before.

'I'm not going to let it do that,' said Becky, positively. 'It'll just be such a relief not to be carrying it around in here all the time . . .' She gave a momentary lift to her heavily inflated stomach. 'I can't work or do any of the things I enjoy doing while it's like this.'

'You just wait, my girl. When you've a baby to look after it'll drive you mad with its needs. It never stops bawling. You think it needs feeding, but as fast as you shove something in at one end it comes out at the other. There's just no getting away from it.'

'You're getting away from it,' Becky pointed out. 'In a few minutes' time you'll be sitting in the Hatchet with a gin in your hand bought for you by a bloke who'll be panting to pay his money and get you home to bed. Look at *me*. I couldn't cope with a man, even if I found one fuddled enough to fancy me!'

'True,' agreed Maude, unfeelingly. 'But no man would fancy *me* for very long if there was a smelly bratling in the same room, squawling all night long. I *am* grateful to you for taking him off my hands for the night, Becky. I'll see you all right for it, I promise.'

Becky made no reply to either Maude's declaration of gratitude or the promise of rewarding her. Words cost nothing and Maude parted with them far more freely than she did her money.

'Have you heard anything of Fergus yet?'

'No.'

Becky tried not to show the deep unhappiness she felt about the loss of Fergus. It was not advisable to expose deep emotions to Maude. She had a nasty habit of using them against her 'friends' if ever there was an advantage to be gained by doing so.

'I've just got to accept that he's gone for good, I suppose.'

'Gone where?' persisted Maude. 'You must have some idea, surely? Has he gone off somewhere with his fancy friends?'

'Probably. Fanny Tennant at the ragged school told me she doesn't know where Fergus is, but I don't believe her. She's always had a fancy for him, herself. I wouldn't be surprised to learn that she's the one who turned him against me in the first place.'

Becky spoke bitterly, conveniently ignoring her own substantial contribution to the break up of her marriage.

'The likes of us are better off without having her sort poking their noses into our business . . .'

Maude used the tips of her fingers to tone down the colouring she had applied to her cheeks. 'When you get down to it, women like her are no better than us. Worse, even. We go out and get men because we need money to live. They'll take a man just because they fancy him. It doesn't matter to them whether or not he's someone else's husband.'

Having made this profound observation, Maude put the finishing touches to her make-up and turned away from the stained mirror which hung over a marble-topped wash-stand.

'Right, I'm off now.' With a pointed glance at Becky's distended stomach, she said, 'Don't do anything that I've already done, will you, Becky? Not tonight, anyway.'

Maude left the room to go about her 'business' without casting a glance in the direction of the baby son she was leaving in Becky's care.

Struggling heavily to her feet, Becky gathered up the child, saying wearily, 'Come on, Alfie, let's go upstairs and get you cleaned and fed for the night. I'd appreciate it if you were to let me have a bit more sleep than the other times I've taken care of you. Otherwise you and me's likely to fall out.'

Despite Becky's hopes baby Alfie was in a fractious mood that evening. He had been an unhappy child from the day he was born, and tonight he seemed to excel himself.

Becky was feeling desperately tired. She had found, particularly recently, that pregnancy was sapping her strength.

'Oh, Alfie, do stop crying, for God's sake! If you go on for much longer *I'll* have a screaming fit!'

Bending over the baby, it was immediately apparent to Becky that he needed his napkin changed yet again. In a moment of exasperation, she said, 'I don't know what's the matter with you, Alfie. That's the fifth time since your ma went out.'

She looked at the five squares of newly washed towelling, draped about the fire to dry. 'I've got nothing more up here for you to put on. You'll just have to wait while I see if I can find something for you in your own room. In the meantime, just SHUT UP! If you keep crying like this then you and your ma will be given notice to quit by Ida Stokes. Me too, most likely.'

Leaving the baby still crying, Becky made her way slowly and ponderously down the narrow, rickety stairs from the attic.

Maude Garrett's room was in a state of general untidiness, but Becky located a square of fairly clean towelling material for the baby. It was lying on the floor. Becky picked it up, but as she began to straighten again, she was gripped by a pain which caused her stomach to contract violently and left her gasping for breath.

Bent almost double, Becky gripped the back of a chair for support until the pain receded. She was not particularly alarmed, even though she had never experienced anything like it before. During her pregnancy she had suffered more aches and pains in various parts of her body than at any other time in her life.

The pain gone, Becky made her way back in the direction of the attic room. Baby Alfie was exercising his lungs in no uncertain fashion now, apparently furious at being abandoned.

Becky was halfway up the steep stairway when the pain returned. It was severe enough to bring her to a sudden halt. Hurriedly sitting down on a stair in the darkness, realisation of the cause of the pain came to her in a moment of sheer horror. She had begun her labour pains!

With realisation came a moment of terror. The baby was not due for another five or six weeks at the very least! She had also been led to believe that the bouts of pain would be well spaced out when labour begins. That they would only increase in frequency and intensity when the moment of birth was imminent. But the two bouts she had just experienced had hardly given her time to reach the attic stairs from Maude's room.

When this second bout subsided, Becky only just made it to the attic room before it returned once more. All thoughts of tending to Alfie's needs were forgotten. There could be no side-stepping the truth now. Her baby was on its way!

Becky sat on the edge of the bed where Alfie lay. She rocked to and fro, clutching her stomach with both hands. It felt as though a giant hand held her in its grip, trying to squeeze the baby from her . . .

In a brief interval between the pains she thought of Fergus. What would he do if he knew she was about to have his baby now? If only he were here . .

Suddenly, all the bitterness that had been festering inside

64

her since he left, fell away. She desperately *wanted* Fergus to be here with her, at this moment. He would know what to do. He would take care of her . . .

Somewhere beyond her own problems she became aware that baby Alfie's crying had reached a crescendo. She should do something about it.

But it was already too late. The spasm was taking over yet again. Time passed in a haze of pain. Nothing else was real – only a growing awareness that things were happening within her body over which she had no control.

Through the haze of pain she heard the voice of Ida Stokes.

'Can't you keep that baby . . . The Lord help us! Is it your time already? Get your clothes off, girl. Lie down on the bed . . . Here, give me that little Garrett brat. You can do without his noise at a time like this. We can *all* do without it. I'll see if there's anyone else in the house. You need help. More than I can give you . . .'

Ida Stokes helped Becky to lie back on the bed. At some time in recent minutes Becky's waters had broken. She was painfully aware that the arrival of the baby was imminent and began crying out uncontrollably.

At the foot of the attic stairs, Ida saw Iris, a prostitute who rented the room next to the one occupied by Maude Garrett. She was coming up the stairs with a seaman from one of the ships berthed in the city's docks.

'What's going on, Ida?' asked Iris, cheerfully. 'It's not often we see you all the way up here – and nursing Maude's baby too!'

'It's just as well for you and the others that I *don't* poke my nose up here too often, judging by the goings on.'

Ferociously, she shook the baby she was holding. 'I heard this one raising the roof and came up to find young Becky halfway to producing a baby of her own.'

'Becky? She can't be due just yet. Is she all right? Who's with her?'

'No one, but if you take this noisy urchin . . .'

Before Ida had finished talking, Iris was halfway up the stairs to the attic room.

'Hey! What is happening? Where are you going?'

The seaman's accent was that of one of the Scandinavian countries and he threw the questions after Iris, as she hurried to Becky's assistance.

'You've had all the fun you're going to get from Iris tonight,' said Ida, unsympathetically. 'Here, cop hold of this noisy brat for a moment while I go back up there and find out what's going on.'

The Scandinavian seaman recoiled from the screaming baby as though it had something contagious. Looking up the stairs, where Iris had now disappeared from view, he complained plaintively, 'I . . . I gave her money . . .'

Ida grinned wickedly. 'Then go upstairs and ask her to give it back to you. What you're likely to see will put you off whoring for the rest of your life!'

At that moment a new sound was added to the cries of Alfie. Upstairs, in the attic room, Becky began screaming.

The Scandinavian seaman waited to hear no more. Unfamiliar with Bristol, he had nervously accompanied Iris through the narrow alleyways of Lewin's Mead, fearing she might be leading him to accomplices who would rob him of the considerable sum of money he had on his person.

He went down the stairs at a run and fled into the night.

His hurried exit did nothing to solve Ida's problem of what to do with Maude Garrett's baby. By now she too had realised, as Becky had before her, that young Alfie needed to be cleaned up and have his napkin changed.

Ida's problem was solved when she reached the ground floor after laboriously making her way down the stairs. She met Maude Garrett entering the house.

Maude was clinging to the arm of a young man. She had to unlink her arm rapidly when Ida thrust the noisy, smelly bundle that was Alfie at her.

'Here! This is yours. You'd better change him quick, before he stinks out the house. While you're about it you can feed him too, or whatever it is you do to shut him up. And keep him quiet. If he has any more days like this one you'll need to find somewhere else to live. I don't care what you girls get up to in your own rooms, but I have other tenants to think about.'

Maude was bewildered. 'But . . . where's Becky? She was supposed to be looking after him for me.'

'Becky's busy bringing another young brat into the world. You'll need to find someone else to take care of this one while you're out picking up your fancy men.'

Turning to the man who had entered the house with her, and ignoring Alfie's screams, Maude said, 'I . . . I'm sorry. I'll sort this out. Just give me a few minutes.'

'You told me you were a young working girl. Fallen on hard times, you said.'

The young man looked at her accusingly, while from upstairs the screams from Becky rivalled those of the baby Maude held in her arms.

'I . . . Look, I can explain . . .'

It was too late. Even as she made the appeal the young man turned and hurried from the house, ignoring her plea for him to stay.

Left standing in the hallway holding her baby, Maude said petulantly, 'Damn! Damn you, Becky, for letting me down . . . *You* can shut up too, you noisy little sod!' She shook the baby violently. 'I can see what sort of a night I'm going to have with you!'

Chapter 2

When Catherine Bell delivered the small package entrusted to her by Fergus, she was deeply apologetic to Fanny about the length of time it had taken her to make the journey to Bristol.

'I told Fergus I didn't expect to be in Bristol for some weeks,' she explained. 'And he said it wasn't urgent, but I hardly expected it to be five months before I came here.'

She went on to tell Fanny that Sarah had contracted whooping-cough and been very ill. The young girl was well on the road to recovery now, but it had been a long and worrying time.

Fanny expressed sympathy with the governess, but she was somewhat bewildered. Why should Fergus send a package – or anything else – to *her*? When she opened the package and revealed a large bundle of banknotes, the governess sucked in her breath in disbelief.

'I . . . I had no idea what was in the package,' she gasped. 'Had I known I would have taken *far* more care and ensured that it was brought to you much sooner. The package has been sitting on my dressing-table since Sarah and I returned home from Plymouth. Fergus really should have told me . . .'

Fanny was hardly listening. She was reading the letter that accompanied the money. Partway through the missive, she looked up at Catherine sharply. 'He's gone to India?'

'That's right, with Captain Cunningham. He was asked to go, personally, by Admiral of the Fleet Sir James Stott.'

'How long will he be gone?' It was a foolish question, as Fanny realised the moment it had been asked.

'I really don't know,' replied Catherine. 'Two or three years, I expect. Possibly more. It's a very long time for Sarah to be separated from her father. She'll be a young lady by the time he returns.'

'Oh! This is very sad. Even Becky can't pass this off as a temporary separation,' said Fanny, unhappily. 'I wish it were possible for someone else to break the news to her, but it *isn't*. It has to be me.'

Catherine was looking at Fanny with a puzzled expression and she explained, 'Becky is Fergus's wife. I realised that something must have happened between them, but I thought it would quickly blow over, as it has before. It seems I was wrong this time.'

'I'm . . . sorry,' stammered Catherine. 'Fergus said nothing about having a wife. In fact, he was extremely reticent about his personal life. I was curious, of course, but on only a brief acquaintanceship I had no right to ask him questions of such a personal nature.'

She did not add that she had found Fergus attractive and had hoped they might meet again at some time in the future.

The two women were holding their conversation in the Lewin's Mead ragged school, where Catherine had found Fanny after first calling at her Clifton home. 'Does Becky teach here too?'

'Becky was once a pupil here,' said Fanny. She smiled understandingly at the embarrassment of the other woman, realising that Catherine also had fallen for Fergus.

'When Fergus painted the people who lived in Lewin's Mead, he lived among them. Becky was one of the urchins who lived there too. He fell in love with her and married her.'

'How very romantic!' exclaimed Catherine.

'Romantic, yes, but totally irresponsible. It was a marriage that was destined for disaster. They both *loved* each other, we could all see that, but Becky was brought up in Lewin's Mead, where there is, shall we say, a certain moral laxity? She knew no other way of life. She tried to change. She tried very hard. For a while, I thought a miracle might have occurred. I even asked her to teach here. But it wasn't to be, I am afraid.'

'Where is she now?'

'Still in Lewin's Mead. I'd better see about getting some of this money to her. Fergus has asked me to mete it out to her, a little at a time.'

'May I come with you to meet her?' asked Catherine, unexpectedly.

'Lewin's Mead is hardly a place to show visitors around. It is not something of which Bristol, or any other city, would be proud.'

'But *you* go there.'

'Only when I have to.'

'Some time ago I paid a visit to Bristol and saw an exhibition of Fergus – Mr Vincent's paintings, when they were in a gallery. In Park Street, I think it was. I found them most moving. I would like to see the place from which he drew such inspiration.'

Fanny's intuition told her that Catherine Bell's interest probably lay with the artist rather than the subject of his work. She sighed. What was it about Fergus that made him so attractive to women – herself among their number?

'All right. We will go now – but first I must place most of Fergus's money in the school safe. It might be a good idea to do the same with your bag. No one in Lewin's Mead has ever attempted to rob me, but there is no sense in putting temptation in their way.'

As the two young women set off together from the ragged school, Catherine Bell felt a quiver of excitement run through her at the thought of what she was about to do. She had led a very humdrum and sheltered life. The sort of life a children's nanny was *expected* to lead. Being unadventurous and reliable were two of the qualifications that had helped her to obtain the posts she had held in the past, but that was not how she saw herself. She would like to be more like Fanny Tennant. Taking risks by dealing with unpredictable and violent people every day of her life.

For Catherine Bell, visiting the Lewin's Mead slum would be the most daring thing she had ever done.

Chapter 3

Her visit to Lewin's Mead lived up to all her fears and expectations. The streets and alleyways were so narrow that even daylight seemed reluctant to enter the slum. Underfoot, the uneven cobbled footway was cluttered with rubbish and filth of every description.

Amidst this the two women passed at least two motionless forms. Thinking Fanny might not have noticed them, Catherine Bell pointed out the second. Fanny shrugged off the observation.

'He's most probably drunk. Even the poorest among those who live here seem to find money for gin. Mind you, most of what they drink would dissolve the pattern on a china cup. Heaven only knows what it does to their stomachs.'

Fanny was probably no older than Catherine Bell, but felt far more experienced and worldly-wise than her companion.

She was still talking to Catherine when a sailor staggered from the doorway of a grog-shop into their path. Swaying on straddled legs, he held his arms wide to prevent them from passing him by.

'Hey! You look a lot smarter than any of the other whores I've seen around here so far. How much do you charge – and tell me in good old Yankee dollars. I'll have none of this shillings and pence.'

The man's words and his accent gave away his country of origin.

Obliged to stop, Fanny said, 'I suggest you go back to your ship and save your money to spend when you return

71

to America. Have any more to drink in Lewin's Mead and you'll wake tomorrow with a thick head – but very little else.' She eyed the swaying seaman with undisguised contempt.

'Do you hear that accent, Charlie?' The seaman threw the question over his shoulder to another sailor who had appeared in the doorway of the grog-shop. 'Ain't she got the whores of Galveston beat?'

Taking an unsteady step towards Fanny, he announced, 'I like you, little lady. That's Charlie back there. He can have your partner. She's a bit too thin and cold-looking for my liking.'

Before Fanny could reply, the seaman standing in the doorway was grabbed from behind and pulled back inside the grog-shop. A moment later a number of tough-looking men spilled out on the narrow street.

One of them raised a finger to his coal-grimed forehead. 'Hello, Miss Tennant. Is this man bothering you?'

Fanny recognised the speaker. He was a notorious brawler who worked for the coal merchant who delivered fuel to the ragged school. She felt it advisable to play down the incident.

'Not really, but I think you should take him back inside – for his own safety. Better still, take him back to his ship.'

The coal-streaked man cast a contemptuous glance in the direction of the Yankee seaman before replying.

'Don't you worry yourself about him, Miss Tennant. We'll take care of him. I promise he won't bother you again.'

Before the American seaman had time to protest he was in the middle of a group of Bristolians, being bundled inside the grog-shop once more.

As the two women walked on, Fanny smiled at Catherine. 'This must be quite an experience for you. Are you all right?'

'Yes, thank you. I find it very exciting. Does this sort of thing happen to you often?'

'Very rarely. When it does there's always someone in Lewin's Mead to come to my rescue.'

'You must be very well respected here.'

'I've never really thought about it. I help them when and

if I can. My main concern is to educate children who otherwise would never see the inside of a school. I'm seen to be doing something for them. In return, they ensure I come to no harm here. It's their way.'

They were approaching Back Lane now and Fanny stopped to talk to a barefooted girl of about nine or ten years of age. Wearing a threadbare dress that was several sizes too small for her, the child sat on a stone doorstep.

'Hello, Millie. I haven't seen you at the school lately. It's a great pity. I really thought you enjoyed being with us there.'

The young girl shrugged with exaggerated indifference. 'It was all right. But my dad says that school's a waste of time for girls.'

'Oh, does he? Perhaps I should come along and have a word or two with him.'

Millie's indifference vanished immediately. 'No, you mustn't do that. If he thought that either Ma or me had been to see you he'd give us both another good hiding.'

'All right, Millie. I *will* have words with your father, but I will make quite certain he does not think that you or your mother have said anything to me. I'll merely say I haven't seen you at school lately and ask why. I'll do my best to persuade him that school is just as valuable to you as it is to a boy. Is he still pot-man at the Llandoger Trow?'

''Course he is. With all that booze all round him it's too good a job to lose. He'd work there for nothing if they wanted him to.'

As they walked away from the barefooted young girl, Catherine asked sympathetically, 'Is Millie typical of the children you teach in your school?'

'No, she is one of the luckier children. She has at least got a mother who cares about her. Most have no one at all.'

'That's very, very sad,' said Catherine, genuinely distressed. 'I sometimes feel sorry for my charge – Sarah. For much of the time since she lost her mother, her father has been away from home. But she has me and the servants, and we all love her. These children have nothing.'

'They have *less* than nothing,' corrected Fanny, grimly.

'Having *nothing* at least signifies a level starting point. These children were born in one of the worst slums in the country and they will never escape from it. If ever they set foot outside Lewin's Mead their dress – or lack of it – sets them apart immediately. They are watched and harried by policemen and shopkeepers. Driven away from shops and stalls and held responsible for every crime that takes place around them. Until recently the only hope they had of making a new start was to be transported for some trivial crime. Now transportation is coming to an end. It's a pity. It did at least give them an opportunity to make a fresh start, in a new country, upon their release.'

Fanny spoke with such bitterness that Catherine said nothing more for a while. Then they turned a corner and Fanny said, 'Here we are. This is Back Lane and the house that Fergus called home.'

Catherine looked at the house pointed out by Fanny. Most of the paint that had once been on door and window frames had long since peeled off, leaving behind wood that was rotting and discoloured. The ground-floor window nearest to them had patchwork panes of paper, cloth and glass in roughly equal proportions.

Remembering Fergus's neat and tidy appearance, Catherine was taken aback. 'He actually *lived* here?'

'It was his choice,' replied Fanny. 'Although in latter months I suspect it was because Becky would not leave. She is as fearful of the outside world as others might be of this place.'

The two women entered a dark and dingy hallway that led to a stairway. They were halfway up the first flight of stairs when a downstairs door swung open on noisy hinges and a querulous voice called, 'Are you looking for someone, dearies?'

'Hello, Mrs Stokes. It's Fanny Tennant. I've called to see Becky.'

Ida Stokes made a disapproving sound. 'It seems that half of Lewin's Mead is tripping up my stairs to see her, at all hours of the day and night. Pity she don't use the stairs herself, to come down here and pay her rent.'

'I don't doubt she will very soon, Mrs Stokes,' said Fanny politely, while grimacing at Catherine.

'What an *awful* woman,' said Catherine, softly. 'Who is she?'

Before Fanny could reply, Ida Stokes's shrill voice reached them once more. 'When you speak to her tell her to keep that baby of hers quiet. What with her and the Garrett brat, I wonder anyone has any sleep in this house.'

Fanny and Catherine had reached the second flight of stairs by now, but the landlady's words brought Fanny to a halt so suddenly that Catherine bumped into her.

'What baby, Mrs Stokes?'

But the acerbic old lady had already retreated to her room, still grumbling to herself.

As though Ada Stokes's words had provided a cue, a baby began crying in a room somewhere above the two women on the staircase. Fanny hurried up the remaining stairs to the second floor. Here it became apparent that the sound was from one of the rooms on this floor.

'Becky has an attic room,' explained Fanny. 'Up one more flight of stairs.' She led the way swiftly up a narrow stairway, Catherine followed her companion more gingerly.

The room came as a pleasant surprise after all Catherine had seen on her way through the streets of Lewin's Mead. It was out of keeping with the remainder of the house. Even its untidiness could not hide the quality of the furniture here.

Becky lay in the bed, looking pale and tired. Beside her, lying on top of a cotton quilt, was a small wrinkled baby. It wore clothes that had been made for a much larger child.

'Becky! Why didn't you tell me you were expecting a baby? I heard about it only a few minutes ago!'

Although Fanny was speaking to Becky, her gaze was fixed on the red, screwed up face of the baby lying beside her.

'Why should I have told you? Why should I have told anyone?'

Ignoring the aggression in Becky's questions, Fanny said, 'I don't think I've ever seen such a tiny baby. Come to think of it, I don't think I have ever before seen one who is quite so young. Is it a boy or a girl, Becky?'

'A girl – her name's Lucy – and before you ask me, she *is* Fergus's baby.'

'I would not have dreamed of suggesting otherwise, Becky,' admonished Fanny. 'The great tragedy is that he isn't here to see her, and hold her. He won't even be aware that he's a father.'

'You haven't heard from him, then?' There was a note of pathos in Becky's question.

Instead of replying immediately, Fanny introduced Catherine to her, adding, 'Catherine can probably tell you more than I, but I am very much afraid that Fergus is not in the country. He's probably in India by now.'

'India! What's he doing there?'

India meant no more to Becky than did Africa, China . . . or the moon! Wherever India was, it meant that the hope she had nursed all the time she was bearing the baby – Fergus's baby – had crumbled away into nothingness.

She had always believed Fergus would return to her when he learned she had given birth to his child.

It was a hope she had not openly admitted to herself, until now.

It was rarely that Becky had faced up to anything in life with complete honesty. She tried to do so now – and it hurt. She had always believed, deep down inside, that Fergus would one day come back. Becky had carefully rehearsed what would happen when he did. She would apologise for the way she had behaved. There would be an emotional reunion, then everything would be all right between them once more. He would return to Lewin's Mead to paint and they would enjoy a comfortable and happy life together – with Lucy.

Life had shattered many of Becky's dreams, but it seemed to her that nothing had ever mattered more than this. As her face contorted in anguish, she fought to hold back her tears and it was some moments before she realised that Catherine was talking.

'. . . he's accompanying Captain Cunningham, my

employer, on his ship, the *Venus*. He'll be sketching the action if they go to war against the Indians.'

'War!' Becky forgot her own misery for a moment. 'Is Fergus going to be in danger?'

'I doubt it. Everyone will do their best to ensure he is safe. He's with them as an artist, not as a fighting man.'

Fanny hoped she sounded convincing. In truth, she believed it had been irresponsible of Sir James Stott to suggest that Fergus should make such a voyage. He had been invalided from the navy with a serious leg injury that had left him with a bad limp. It was even more foolish of Fergus to accept. But, of course, he did not know then that he was to become a father. The thought brought Fanny back to the here-and-now.

'What are we going to do with you, Becky? It is quite out of the question for you to bring up the baby here, in these surroundings.'

'Lewin's Mead is where *I* grew up. It's my home – and Lucy is *my* baby. I'll decide what's right for her.'

Fanny had realised her mistake as soon as it was made. 'Of course you will, and you'll want the best for her. You'll want Lucy to have more of a chance than you had. To grow up aware that there is more to life than . . . than the hard times you have had.'

'I didn't have a mother to help me. She has.'

'She also has a father, Becky. Fergus would want the very best for her too. Why don't you and Lucy come to Clifton? To my home.'

'Me and Lucy are staying here. Everything would be all right if Fergus was here. If he cared so much he wouldn't have left.'

Fanny knew it was futile to point out to Becky that Fergus had not even been aware she was pregnant when he went away – or that Becky herself was probably largely to blame for his abrupt departure.

'I'm tired now. I want you to go.' Becky turned her head towards the baby that lay beside her.

'Of course. But I have some money here for you. Before he left for India, Fergus made arrangements for Catherine to bring me money and pass it on to you, as it's needed.'

Fanny did not think it necessary to inform Becky that the 'arrangement' was to ensure Becky did not spend all the money at once. Such a control was more important now than before. It meant that Fanny would be able to check on Lucy's welfare at regular intervals.

The baby was a novelty to Becky at the moment. Unique, even. Becky had never before possessed anything that she could claim to be completely her very own. But Becky was not the most dependable person in the world.

Fanny would try to do what she felt Fergus would want for the daughter he was not aware he had.

Chapter 4

'How can anyone *want* to live in a place like this?' Catherine posed the question to Fanny as they walked through Lewin's Mead on their way from Back Lane to the ragged school.

'It's a question I would often ask myself when the ragged school first opened. The children would scurry back here the moment school ended each day and I never understood why,' replied Fanny. 'But there is no simple answer. Most who live here have known nothing else. They feel as threatened by the thought of life outside Lewin's Mead as would someone from outside, forced to live here.'

'Yet Fergus *chose* to live here.'

Fanny would rather that Catherine had not brought Fergus into the conversation. She needed to come to terms with the knowledge that he and Becky now had a child.

'Fergus was waging a crusade. With the paintings he did here, he brought the attention of much of the country to bear on the problems of Lewin's Mead, and places like it. He said the only way he could achieve this was by living among the people he painted. Many of his friends disagreed with him. I was one of them.'

'I think it's marvellous that someone with his talent should use it in such a way,' declared Catherine. 'But that is so like him.' She went on to tell Fanny of Fergus's involvement with the escaped naval prisoner and of his visit to the prison hulk at Plymouth.

'Yes, that *is* typical of Fergus,' agreed Fanny. 'I sometimes wished . . .'

What it was that Fanny wished was never told. They were

within sight of the ragged school now and a tall, uniformed figure was waiting for them close to the entrance.

'You are about to meet another friend of Fergus's,' said Fanny. 'Constable Ivor Primrose. A man with more sympathy and understanding than most in his profession. He too tried to persuade Fergus to leave Lewin's Mead before this latest problem arose.'

Ivor was sporting brand new sergeant's stripes on the sleeves of his tunic. Fanny offered her congratulations on his promotion. She had learned of it from her father, but it was the first time she had seen Ivor since then.

After introducing Catherine, Fanny told Ivor of Becky's baby and of Fergus's whereabouts.

'I'm very sorry to hear that he has left Bristol,' said Ivor, sincerely. 'But I can't say that I'm very surprised. He has far too much talent to give to the world beyond Lewin's Mead. Mind you, he wouldn't have gone had he known about the baby. As soon as he finds out, he'll be back – but who's to tell him?'

'I would write to him,' declared Fanny. 'But I am not quite sure where I should send the letter. What do you suggest, Catherine?'

'Send it to *HMS Venus*, care of the Admiralty, in London,' suggested Catherine. 'It will reach him eventually, I don't doubt, although it has sometimes been as long as a year before Captain Cunningham has replied to the letters Sarah and I send to him.'

Fanny told Ivor of the part Catherine had played in Fergus's latest adventure. The newly promoted sergeant asked Catherine a number of polite questions and, as they spoke, Fanny thought of Fergus, of Becky, and of their baby.

She felt suddenly old. Her father was fond of telling her that life was passing her by as a result of her interest in the ragged school and the children who went there. She thought he was probably right.

'Would you like to come inside and have a good look around the ragged school, Catherine?' asked Fanny.

'I would love to, but I really must be catching a train back to Bridgwater. I would like to be there in time to put Sarah to bed. Perhaps I might come again, soon?'

'Of course! If you really must be leaving us then I'll have a cab called for you.'

'I'd rather walk. I rarely have the opportunity to visit Bristol. I would like to savour the bustling atmosphere of the city.'

'That's all very well, but it's not always the safest of places. Perhaps Ivor will walk with you to the station?'

Fanny knew that because he had been promoted only recently, Ivor might be reluctant to go so far from the police station, so she added, 'My request comes not from a ragged school teacher, Ivor, but from the daughter of the Chairman of the Watch Committee.'

The Watch Committee was the council-appointed body which controlled the Bristol constabulary. Ivor said, 'My wife is shopping in the arcades at the moment. We'll walk through there and find her. She'll be happy to see Miss Bell safely on to the train.'

As Fanny watched the tall policeman and the governess walk off together, she began to think of Fergus once more. A sense of loneliness came over her as it had disturbingly often of late.

Determined to shake off the feeling, she turned and entered the ragged school. There was no place in her life for self-pity. She had important issues to face. Not least among them the question of the future of Becky's baby – Fergus's baby.

Fanny was determined that, whether or not Fergus was around to help her, Lucy Vincent was not going to grow up in the slums of Lewin's Mead. She would use every means at her disposal to bring the baby out and ensure she had a reasonable start in life.

Opportunities such as Fanny would have desired for her own baby.

Chapter 5

'You don't want to let that old ragged school teacher tell you what you ought to be doing, Becky. It's your life, and Lucy's your baby. That Fanny Tennant's just a frustrated old maid who wants to spend her life telling other people what they ought to do. When she's got no kids to boss about at school she comes to Lewin's Mead and has a go at people like us. Tell her to bugger off and mind her own business. That's what I'd do.'

Having delivered this advice, Maude Garrett downed the remainder of the gin in her cup and reached out for the half-empty bottle that stood on the table between them in the attic room of the Back Lane house.

'You wouldn't do anything of the sort, Maude, any more than I will. If it wasn't for the money she brought we wouldn't be sitting here now, drinking Blue Ruin.'

'She's not doing you any favours, you can be sure of that,' said Maude, indignantly. 'Anyway, it's your money, ain't it? Left for you by that husband of yours. And how d'you know she's giving you all of it, eh? Just 'cos she's got no need to go out dolly-mopping, it don't mean she's *honest*. You ought to make her give you *all* the money she's keeping for you. She's got no right to keep it.'

'She says she's "following Fergus's instructions". At least, that's what she told me.'

'What "instructions"?' Maude had consumed a sufficient quantity of gin to find difficulty with the word. It did not prevent her from repeating it. 'Have you seen any . . . instructions saying you can't have what's rightfully yours?

No, of course you haven't – and d'you know why you haven't?'

Pouring herself another generous drink from the bottle, she fixed Becky with a belligerent stare. Not bothering to await a reply, she nodded approval of her own disjointed and drunken logic. 'When's she coming here again?'

'She's not. At least, not for a while. She says that when I need more money I'm to go and see her at the ragged school – and I'm to bring Lucy along with me.'

'She says . . .? She says? Just who does she think she is, bleedin' Queen Victoria?'

Maude spoke indignantly, apparently in full sympathy with Becky. But her mind was racing ahead of this conversation. She had consumed a great deal of the gin that had been bought with Becky's money, but she was by no means drunk. Maude was used to drinking heavily.

'You know what you ought to do, Becky? You ought to go out and enjoy yourself tonight. Have a few drinks and bring a man back here with you.'

The idea appealed to Becky. She had not shared her bed with a man for many months. But there were obstacles that would need to be overcome first. 'That's all very well, Maude, but what would I do with Lucy?'

'You don't have to worry about her. She can come down to my room with me and Alfie.'

'Aren't *you* going out?'

Maude was a very popular prostitute in the taverns frequented by seamen from the ships that berthed in the city's docks.

'I think I'd better wait until that Italian boat's sailed. One of the sailors lost all his money out of his pocket when he was drinking with me at the Hatchet. He's a bit hot-headed and accused me of pinching it from him. I'll stay away from there until his ship's sailed.'

Becky bit back the obvious question. Maude was a known thief and would not give her a truthful reply. Anyway, she did not need to know the answer.

'Are you quite certain you wouldn't mind looking after Lucy for me?'

83

'Of course I wouldn't mind. Off you go and enjoy yourself – but leave that gin bottle here for me.'

'All right. If you take Lucy, I'll get tidied up – that's if you *really* don't mind?'

'I've already said I don't, haven't I? Go on, get yourself ready before I change my mind. We're going to be fine here without her, aren't we, Lucy?'

Becky went to the Cabot Arms tavern where she had been a regular customer in the months before Lucy was born. Her arrival in the crowded bar room was greeted with noisy enthusiasm by the other girls there. Many of the rowdy customers joined in too, although few of them understood why they were cheering.

Most of the male customers in the tavern were seamen from ships berthed in the city's harbours. They did not know Becky, but she was young and attractive. It was not long before she was being bought drinks by two young Spanish seamen, both of whom wanted to secure the right to take her home afterwards.

Suddenly Becky's attention was attracted to a crowd occupying a corner of the crowded bar room. When someone pushed through them carrying drinks she glimpsed an artist making rapid portraits of the tavern's patrons.

She could not see the artist's face, but she leaped to her feet immediately. Deserting the two protesting Spanish sailors, she hurried across the room. In spite of what Fanny and Catherine Bell had told her, Becky believed for a moment that the artist might be Fergus. He had once earned his living this way.

Pushing her way through the crowd, she reached the artist. Aware of her sudden arrival, he looked up and smiled at her.

The artist was not Fergus. He was a man at least twice her own age. A quick glance at the portrait on which he was working was sufficient to show her that he lacked Fergus's skills.

Momentarily, the disappointment she suffered caused

her whole body to sag, but the artist seemed not to notice. Winking at her, he said, 'Well, here's a pretty girl come to admire my work. Invite me back to your place and I'll paint a portrait of you that will drive men wild . . .'

Suddenly, Becky realised she no longer wanted to be here among these men, the prostitutes, and this sadly untalented artist. She floundered in thoughts of all she had thrown away as the memories washed over her like a giant wave.

Pushing her way back through the crowd, she crossed the room and stumbled out through the doorway. She fled from the noisy tavern, impervious to the protests of the two Spanish seamen who had been buying drinks for her.

Even had Becky heard them it would have made no difference. Something had snapped in her mind. All she wanted now was to get home to the room in Back Lane where she had left Lucy.

The confrontation with the artist in the Cabot Arms had shattered the thin shell she had built around herself since Fergus had left. She might be able to fool others, but she could no longer delude herself. Becky longed for Fergus. She missed him dreadfully. If only he would return to her now she would give up once and for all the way of life that had driven him away.

In the meantime, she wanted only to get home and hold Lucy, her baby. Fergus's baby.

By the time Becky reached the house in Back Lane she was in a state akin to shock, but she was brought up suddenly when she entered the doorway and became aware of the sound of crying babies.

As she climbed the first flight of stairs, the door of Ida Stokes's room opened and the landlady's voice called; 'Is that you, Maude Garrett?'

'No. It's Becky.'

'You'll do. I've been listening to those babies crying for this past fifteen minutes. If you don't shut them up then both you and that Garrett girl can go. I've had enough of it. I should never have let either of you stay here with babies in the first place.'

'I'm very sorry, Ida. I left Lucy with Maude and she promised to look after her. It's the first evening since she was born that I've been out of the house.'

'If you go out again, you'd better leave her with someone a bit more responsible. Maude was out of the house almost before you had time to turn the corner.'

'Maude's out? Where's she gone?' Becky paused on the stairs once more to ask the question.

'I'd have thought you'd know more about that than me. I don't go asking anyone's business in this house. Now, just get upstairs and stop all that racket. I can't hear myself think down here.'

Becky hardly heard the landlady's last words as she hurried up the second flight of stairs to Maude's room.

A lamp was burning low in here. By its light Becky saw both babies lying together on Maude's bed. Only a sparsely filled feather pillow had been placed on the mattress to prevent them from rolling over and falling to the wooden floor.

Becky snatched up Lucy and held her close, murmuring, 'Hush, now. Hush! It's all right, Mummy's home.'

When Lucy continued to cry, Becky unbuttoned the front of her dress and put the baby to her breast.

Lucy began sucking immediately, although her feeding was interspersed with body-wracking sobs. Meanwhile, Alfie's cry was unabated and he threw himself about on the bed in sheer temper. Words would not quieten him and soon he too was feeding from Becky.

Alfie attacked her breast with a ferocity that was painful and quite unlike the much gentler demands of Lucy. Becky realised that he was ravenously hungry.

Becky remained in Maude's room feeding both babies for perhaps twenty minutes. By this time Lucy, exhausted from her crying, was half-asleep.

Not so Alfie. When Becky tried to prise him from her breast, he came back at her like a terrier pup. When she finally succeeded in pulling him from her and laid him on the bed, he began screaming in temper. She watched in fascination as his arms and legs flailed about in an impressive display of infantile rage.

'You have your father's temper, young man,' she declared. 'It'll get you into serious trouble one day, just as it did him.'

It had been Alfie's father who had died in a fall from the attic window of this very house, after the police siege on the night Fergus had left. Becky had not mourned his death. He had been one of the most loathsome men she had ever known.

As it did not appear that Maude was likely to return to the house in the immediate future, Becky decided to take both babies upstairs to her own room. She wondered where the other girl could have gone. Most likely it was to another of the town's public houses.

Two hours later Becky was still waiting for her friend and trying to control her anger. Maude was supposed to have been taking care of both babies. To have abandoned them in such a manner was unforgivable.

Fortunately, the babies were asleep now. Alfie's hunger had been finally appeased by a thick broth Becky had concocted. It was made up of milk mixed with some mashed potatoes left over from her evening meal.

When Becky heard someone climbing the stairs to the rooms below, accompanied by the sound of only half-stifled whispering, she called down, 'Is that you Maude?'

'No, it's Iris,' came the reply. Iris was the prostitute who rented the room next to Maude's. Now in her early-thirties, she did not always bring her men back to Lewin's Mead. Popular with the senior crew members of merchant ships, she spent most nights on board their vessels in the city's port.

'Have you got Maude's baby up there?' Iris put the question to Becky.

'Yes.'

'Good. Then it's not likely to disturb us tonight, even though Maude won't be here with it.'

'What do you mean, she won't be here?'

'She's been arrested. One of the girls saw her being carted off by a constable in St James's Square. I don't know what it was she'd done. Whatever it was, they certainly won't release her before morning.'

Chapter 6

The idea of breaking into the ragged school had occurred to Maude while she was talking to Becky and drinking gin bought with the money delivered by Fanny Tennant. Somewhere in the ragged school there had to be a great deal of money if the teacher was able to dole some of it out to Becky whenever she called. There might be hundreds of pounds. Enough to enable Maude to live comfortably for years!

Once the decision to break into the school had been made, she wasted no time in putting it into practice. It was a simple matter to persuade Becky to go off to the Cabot Arms. That would provide her with a perfect alibi. Should anything go wrong and she be suspected, Becky would confirm that Maude was in Back Lane taking care of both babies.

Hopefully, nothing *would* go wrong. She should be able to return to Back Lane without anyone even knowing she had left the house.

However, Maude needed help to carry out her plan. It had to be someone she could trust. As soon as she was certain Becky had left the house, she put both babies on her bed. Positioning a pillow to prevent them falling to the floor, she set off for Broadmead, only a few streets away.

Maude's brothers and sisters lived with their drunken father above an ironmonger's shop in Broadmead. It was here she found Albert, her thirteen-year-old brother. Small and agile, he would serve her purposes admirably.

Maude's visit was not greeted with delight by her young brother. Threading half of a broken leather lace through the eyes of one of his dilapidated boots, he looked up only long enough to identify her as she came through the door.

'What d'you want? If it's money, you're out of luck. The old man's been on another of his binges and spent every penny we had in the house.'

'I'm not here to cadge money but to help you get some. You had lessons at the ragged school once, didn't you?'

Albert looked startled. 'Not for long. They're too bossy there, always telling you what you can do and what you can't. What's that got to do with making some money?'

'I want you to help me break in the ragged school and show me where Fanny Tennant's office is.'

'You won't find much there, except perhaps a few old pencils and things.'

'That's where you're wrong. She's got money in there. Lots of it. Help me find it and you'll have more guineas jangling in your pocket than you've ever seen before.'

Albert looked at his sister suspiciously. 'You having me on? Why should there be money there? Anyway, how d'you know?'

'Never you mind about that. Are you going to help me, or shall I find someone else?'

Albert slipped his foot into the dilapidated boot and tied a knot in the shortened lace with some difficulty. 'I might as well help you, I'm not doing anything else – but I'll want half.'

'You'll have what I give you,' retorted Maude. 'But there'll be plenty enough for both of us.'

'How we going to get in?'

'You're the one who's been there. You tell me.'

'There's a small window in the porch, by the door. I can break a pane of glass and open it. I'm skinny enough to squeeze in. You're too big. They keep a spare set of keys in the office. I'll get them and let you in through the door.'

'You make sure you do. No searching the office until I get there. You hear me?'

Entry to the ragged school was as simple as Albert had promised it to be, although climbing through the narrow window was a squeeze, even for the slightly built boy.

He seemed to be inside for a very long time before the door was finally opened to Maude.

'Have you already searched the office?' she hissed at him.

'Shut up and get inside before someone comes along.' Albert sounded nervous.

'Well, have you?' Maude repeated her question when she was inside the building.

'It took me all my time to find the key,' he retorted indignantly. 'Come on, hurry up and find what you want before a constable comes along and sees that window broken.'

It was dark in the corridor where they were and Maude clung to the back of Albert's shirt as he led the way to the office.

It was easier to see in here. Lamplight from nearby houses shone through the two office windows, giving enough light for them to see around the room.

'Where's this money?' demanded Albert.

'Which is Fanny Tennant's desk?' Maude countered. There were two desks in the office.

'This one.' Albert pointed to the larger of the two. Only a brass and porcelain inkstand stood on the polished top.

Maude began a systematic search of the desk while Albert rifled through the drawers of the second.

There was nothing of any value in eight of the nine drawers searched by Maude. The ninth was locked.

'This must be the one,' she said to Albert. 'It's locked. Can you open it?'

'Let me have a look.' Albert tried the drawer, then slipped a small, curved piece of flat iron from his pocket. 'It's a good job I came prepared.'

Two attempts to lever the drawer open were all that were needed to force it without even splitting the wood around the lock. There was a metal cash box inside the drawer – and it was unlocked. Maude opened the lid eagerly. After peering inside, she tipped the contents into the palm of her hand. It consisted of two shillings and a couple of pennies.

'Is that the "fortune" you had me break in to find?' Albert

had been in close attendance upon his sister and now he spoke scornfully.

'Of course not. There's a lot of money in here somewhere. Hundreds of pounds.'

'I suppose it wouldn't be in here?'

Maude turned to find Albert leaning against a large safe standing in a corner of the office.

She looked at the safe in dismay. 'Have you known all along that was here?'

'No, I only just noticed it,' he admitted. 'But that's where this money will be, I've no doubt.'

'Is there a key in here anywhere?' They were both aware that Maude was clutching at straws.

'Don't be daft. Fanny Tennant might be far too fond of telling everyone else what to do, but she's not stupid. The only key in here was the spare key to the door. She'll have the safe key with her.'

'Isn't there some way we can force the safe door open? That iron bar you used on the door . . .'

Albert gave his sister a scornful look. 'It wouldn't even put a scratch on this safe. There's no one in Lewin's Mead who could open it either, not even if the Crown jewels was hidden inside it.'

'Let's have another look around the office. The money might not be inside the safe.'

'You know very well it *is* – and those couple of shillings you found in the box are mine, for all the trouble I've gone to for you. Come on, let's get out of here, before a constable finds that broken window.'

Maude knew her brother was right. After only a moment's hesitation, she followed him from the office.

At the front door of the ragged school, Albert let her out of the building then closed and locked the door behind him. Pocketing the key, he said, 'It might come in handy again, some time.'

Before leaving, he peered around the edge of the porch – and started back immediately. 'It's a copper – quick run!'

Before Maude could gather her thoughts, Albert had gone. Dashing from the entrance porch of the ragged school he sprinted around the line of iron railings fencing off the graveyard that occupied the centre of the square.

A moment later, Maude followed him – but she was too late. Seeing Albert running from the school entrance, the constable had set off in pursuit when suddenly Maude ran out in front of him. He grabbed her before she had gone half-a-dozen paces.

'No you don't, my girl. I may have lost him, but you're coming with me.'

Maude struggled desperately to break free, but less than a minute later she was securely handcuffed to her captor.

The constable took her back to the school porch and saw the window with the broken pane of glass.

'Right, young lady. I don't know what else has been going on, but you'll be charged with breaking that window, that's certain. It's no good you telling me you didn't do it because I checked it myself not an hour since. It was all right then.'

Maude's heart sank, but she was thinking rapidly. She and Albert had returned everything to its rightful place inside the office. He had even levered the drawer shut once more. There was the key he had pocketed, of course, and the money he had stolen from the box, but she might just get away with it . . .

'I haven't done nothing, Constable, honest. Breaking the window was an accident. Me and me boyfriend was just standing in the porch . . . having a cuddle. His elbow broke it . . . It was an accident, that's all. I'll pay for the damage.'

'I've no doubt you will, but it'll be by order of a magistrate. What's your name?'

Maude had never seen the constable before. He was probably a new recruit to the force and would not know her.

'It's Becky. Becky Vincent.'

Chapter 7

Reporting for duty the next morning, Ivor Primrose
checked the charge sheet for the night and saw Becky's
name entered there. Beside it was the information that she
had been arrested for 'causing wilful damage to a window
at the ragged school in St James's Square'.

The constable who had made the arrest was still in the
police station, laboriously preparing a report to place before
the Clerk of the Magistrates' Court that morning. At Ivor's
request he took him down the stairs to the cell which Maude
was sharing with two older women, both of whom had been
arrested for being drunk and disorderly during the night.

One was sitting on the edge of a wooden cot, holding her
head in her hands. The other was lying on the floor of the
cell, snoring.

'This isn't Becky Vincent!' said Ivor, immediately he saw
Maude. 'You've arrested Maude Garrett, as busy a young
dollymop as you'll find anywhere in Bristol. Tell me about
last night.'

The constable told his story, ignoring the occasional
interjection from Maude. When he'd ended his explanation, Ivor said to the young prisoner, 'What were you up
to, Maude? What were you trying to do at the ragged
school?'

'I wasn't doing nothing. Me and my young man was just
standing in the doorway, that's all.'

'Then why give Becky's name to the constable, instead of
your own?'

Maude appeared only mildly embarrassed. 'I wasn't
thinking right. When the window was broken – entirely by

94

accident, mind – I knew I'd get the blame. I was all mixed up, what with worrying about my baby. I'd left Becky looking after him and her name was the first thing that came into my head. Anyway, he didn't mean to break the window, honest.'

Ivor knew from experience that 'honesty' was not a quality that might even loosely be associated with Maude Garrett. 'This young man of yours . . . no doubt he'll verify your story. Who is he?'

When Maude fell silent, he continued patiently, 'You have just heard what the constable has said. He didn't have a good view of this young man, but his impression is that he was no more than a lad. Someone about the size of your young brother Albert, perhaps?'

'He's bigger than Albert!'

Maude's retort was scornful, but Ivor's acumen concerned her. She did not want him questioning Albert. Her young brother was not clever enough to fool the tall sergeant for very long. 'Whether a bloke's big or small don't matter very much to me, but he's got to be bigger than *Albert!*'

'Why didn't you take this man of yours back to your room – as you do all the other men you pick up?'

'This one's not like the others. He doesn't want me just for *that*. He . . . I think he wants to marry me.'

Maude was blatantly playing on the sympathy of both policemen now.

'He wants to marry you, even though you've got another man's baby?' Ivor asked the question though he did not believe a word of her story.

'He doesn't know about the baby. Not yet, anyway. That's why I wouldn't take him back to my place.'

'It's going to come as a nasty shock to him, Maude. It could make him take to his heels again, same as he seems to do whenever he sees a constable. He must be easily frightened, this young man of yours.'

Instead of replying to Ivor's sarcastic remark, Maude asked, 'What's going to happen to me now?'

'A lot depends on the chat I'll have this morning at the ragged school with Miss Tennant. I want to be certain that no one's been inside the school during the night. If they have then you'll be sent to a higher court for trial and no doubt go to prison for a few years. On the other hand, if the only damage is to the window, you'll appear before the magistrate later this morning, charged with wilful damage.'

'What will I get for that?'

Ivor shrugged. 'It depends on the magistrate's mood this morning. Probably a couple of months in prison. No more.'

'But . . . my baby! What's going to happen to him? He's still being breast fed. No one else can take care of him. He'll . . . he'll starve to death and it'll be all your fault. Yours and the magistrate's.'

Ivor thought Maude's distress had more to do with the thought of spending two months in prison, than from concern for her baby. However, he knew she *did* have a baby and arrangements would need to be made to care for him.

'When I speak to Miss Tennant this morning I'll ask her to go to Back Lane and find out what's going on there. If she thinks it necessary, we'll have the baby brought to you here, or in prison.'

'I don't want my baby brought up in no prison! Look . . . can't we forget about this old window? I'll pay Miss Tennant whatever it costs to mend it, but don't let me go to prison. Think of my baby . . . Please!'

'You'll have to save that sort of plea for the magistrate, Maude. In the meantime I'll see what Miss Tennant can do about the baby.'

In a sudden mood swing, Maude said angrily, '*She* won't do anything to help me. Not when I'm coming up in court because it's *her* old window that's been broken, she won't.'

'Fortunately for you, Fanny Tennant wouldn't allow a broken window to stand in the way of doing whatever's best for a young child. If she thinks there's a need for it to be with you then she'll probably bring it here herself.'

'That's what *you* say. You and everyone else around here seem to think she's got a bleedin' halo. I don't. You tell her I want my baby here – and I want him here quick.'

Chapter 8

At nine o'clock in the morning Lewin's Mead was at its quietest. Those residents who were in employment had long since left. Others, with no work, or who enjoyed a more nefarious life-style, tended to keep late hours and saw no reason to rise early.

Fanny Tennant, making her way towards Back Lane, picked her way through the filth that littered the narrow alleyways. She wondered whether she would bother to leave her bed at all if she lived in such surroundings.

She dismissed the thought immediately. If she were forced to live in such squalor she would want to do something to bring about a change in her surroundings.

When she reached the house in Back Lane, she found it as quiet as the rest of Lewin's Mead. Climbing the stairs to Becky's room, the only sounds came from the room occupied by Mrs O'Ryan and her bewilderingly large family. Even this was strangely subdued. The O'Ryans had learned over the years that making any form of noise before their mother awoke was likely to prove a painful experience.

Fanny went first to Maude's room. As she had anticipated, it was empty. She expected to find Alfie being cared for by Becky, in her attic room.

Somewhat to Fanny's surprise, Becky was out of bed – but only just. Still in her nightdress, she had Lucy feeding at her breast. Last night's dirty plates were on the table and three dirty napkins were lying in the fireplace.

'What do you want?' Becky gave her visitor a less than gracious welcome. She had shared her bed with both babies the previous night. Alfie was much larger than Lucy and had been very restless. Eventually she had emptied the contents of a clothes drawer on the floor and used the drawer to house him.

Maude's abandoned son had not cared for his makeshift bed. He complained vociferously for much of the night.

'I've been asked to come here and check on Maude Garrett's baby. You know she was arrested yesterday evening?'

'Someone said she'd been copped for something last night. What's she done?'

'She broke a window in the ragged school. The police thought she might have got inside. She was accompanied by a young man who was seen running away just before Maude was arrested.'

'Why would she have wanted to break into the ragged school?' asked Becky, scornfully.

Even as she asked the question, she realised she already knew the answer. Maude had taken a great deal of interest in the whereabouts of the money Fanny was doling out to her on Fergus's behalf.

'I thought you might know the answer to that, Becky?'

'Me? All I know is that Maude said she'd look after Lucy for me if I wanted to go out for the evening. I decided to come home early – and it's a good job I did. Lucy and Alfie were in her room screaming their heads off and there was no sign of Maude. Then Iris came in and said someone saw her being arrested in St James's Square. Was anything taken from the school?'

'No. A window was broken, but I don't think anyone could have got inside.'

This was a blatant lie. Fanny had discovered the broken drawer and seen that the spare door key was missing even before Ivor had called at the ragged school to speak to her. However, she would not be instrumental in having Maude sentenced to a long period of imprisonment for the sake of a couple of shillings and a key. She would have the locks changed and bars put up at the window to prevent any future attempts.

'What will happen to Alfie if Maude is sent to prison?'

'That's what I'm here to find out. Can you look after him for her?'

'No, I can't! I've got quite enough to do with my own baby. Alfie's quite a few months older than Lucy – and he's a right handful!'

'That's what I thought you would say. Well, I shall just have to take him to the police station. If Maude goes to prison, she'll take him with her.'

Walking across the attic room to where Alfie lay in the drawer, sucking on a soggy crust of bread, Fanny said, 'I presume this is Alfie?'

'That's him, all right. The sooner you take him out of here, the happier I'll be – and so will everyone else in the house. Anyway, he might just as well get used to prison while he's young. He'll probably spend most of his life inside one when he's older.'

'I don't know about that, but prison life will be easier for Maude if she has a baby to care for. I expect she is aware of that.'

'There might even be someone there who'll teach her how to do it properly,' said Becky, unfeelingly. 'She hasn't made a very good job of it so far.'

Baby Alfie proved useful to Maude even before she went to prison. When she appeared before the magistrate later that morning, he was left in the cells beneath the court, in the care of a wardress.

During the hearing his cries could be clearly heard in the courtroom. Eventually the irate magistrate demanded to know the reason for such a disturbance.

When he learned the baby belonged to Maude, he erred on the side of leniency. He found her guilty of the offence of breaking a window in the ragged school. However, instead of being sentenced to two months imprisonment, as recommended by the clerk of the court, the magistrate gave her only six weeks.

Fanny was in court to hear the sentence passed. Afterwards, in the cells, she gave Maude a couple of pounds to buy some extras for the baby while she served her sentence.

As she left the court building, Fanny saw Maude depart in a prison van that contained three other women. One was the older of the two with whom Maude had shared a cell during the night. Another was a young girl of no more than twelve years of age who had been found in possession of a single forged coin. She was sent to prison to await trial for her offence. The third occupant of the prison van was a woman who was palpably insane. She had violently assaulted a neighbour for no reason that anyone could comprehend.

Watching Maude climb into the prison van holding Alfie, Fanny was more determined than ever that Lucy should not follow the same path as the baby with whom she had shared the Back Lane attic room the previous night.

Chapter 9

Baby Alfie proved to be a useful asset to Maude during her six weeks' imprisonment. Having a baby living within the grim walls provided other prisoners and the gaolers with a welcome break in the harsh and monotonous prison routine. They all vied for an opportunity to hold him. The prisoners, in particular, were prepared to pay for the privilege by taking on many of Maude's prison chores.

Unfortunately, the attention given to Alfie inside the women's wing of Bristol's gaol was to have tragic consequences.

Maude returned to the Back Lane house of Ida Stokes fully expecting her room to have been let to someone else. She was surprised and relieved to be told she could have it back. However, the avaricious old landlady told her she would need to pay half-rent for the time she had spent in prison. It would be an acknowledgement of Ida's 'big-heartedness' in keeping the room for her.

In fact, Ida Stokes had tried very hard to let the room. Fortunately for Maude, Back Lane was one of the least salubrious parts of Lewin's Mead. As a result, Ida had been unable to find a new tenant.

Maude was telling Becky of the landlady's demand as she sipped tea in the attic room. When Becky made no comment, Maude took her to task for not paying a visit to the gaol during her incarceration there.

'Visit you?' retorted Becky. 'You're lucky I never told Fanny Tennant what you'd gone looking for in the ragged school.'

'What d'you mean? I hadn't gone looking for anything. I just happened to break a window, that's all.'

'Don't give me that, Maude Garrett. You were there because you were hoping to find the money Fergus gave her for me. If you'd found it you'd have left me with nothing, but I don't suppose that would have troubled you at all.'

'I wouldn't have seen you go without, Becky, you know that. Besides, if that Tennant woman lost your money she'd have had to replace it. That wouldn't have been any hardship to her.'

'That's what *you* say. No doubt she'd see things differently. Anyway, you're out now – and back in your own room too. You're lucky Ida wasn't able to let it. She's been telling everyone how nice it is not to have Alfie screaming his head off day and night.'

'Oh, she's let me have the room back all right, but I'll be out on the streets if I haven't paid her something off the rent by the weekend.' Maude hesitated. 'I suppose you wouldn't look after Alfie for me tonight, so I can go out and earn some money? Quite apart from the rent, the only man I've seen for the past six weeks was the old grandfather who did odd-jobs around the prison.'

'You've got a cheek, Maude. If it hadn't been for Fanny Tennant I'd have been landed with Alfie for all the time you were in prison. As it is, *I've* had to stay in because I had no one to look after Lucy. You find someone else to take care of him. If you can't, then you'll just have to take care of him yourself – or take Alfie out with you.'

'You know I can't do that, Becky. Look, why don't we try to find someone who'll look after both of them? Then you and me can go out and have a good time. We both deserve it.'

'The last time we both went out I came home because I wasn't enjoying myself and you ended up in prison.'

'Then we *ought* to go out together, to put things right between us.'

'Even if I did say I'd go out with you, who could we get to take care of two young babies? There's no one in this house I'd trust Lucy with.'

102

'I know just the woman. Annie Stapleton. She lives in one of the houses down by the river. She was in prison with me but came out a couple of days ago. While we were in there together she'd look after Alfie every chance she got.'

'What was she in there for?' Becky was suspicious of Maude's 'friends'.

'All she did was pinch a couple of turnips from a field out Bedminster way, so her kids could have a bit of taste in their stew. They gave her a month for that.'

It was a common enough occurrence, but Becky was still sceptical. Nevertheless, she agreed she might allow the woman to take care of Lucy for a while – but only if she approved of her.

The door to the small house by the side of the river was opened by a girl of about thirteen or fourteen years of age. Although wearing a threadbare dress that was far too small for her, she was clean and seemed to be reasonably intelligent.

When Maude asked for Annie Stapleton, the girl said, 'Ma's upstairs in bed. She hasn't been well since she came home. I'm Maggie, can I help you?'

'I'm Maude Garrett. Your ma and me were in prison together. While we were there she often used to look after Alfie. She might have mentioned it?'

'Not that I can remember, but that's Ma. No matter where she is she always manages to find a baby to take care of.'

'I know. That's why we're here, really. I was hoping she'd take care of Alfie and my friend's baby for a few hours tonight. We wanted to celebrate my coming out.'

Maude spoke hopefully. Perhaps Annie wasn't too ill to care for the babies. If only for a short while . . .

'Mum couldn't cope with them but I can, 'though it'll cost you a shilling.'

'That's far too much,' protested Maude. 'I'll give you a sixpence.'

'It's a shilling or nothing,' declared Maggie, firmly.

'What's wrong with your ma?' asked Becky.

'She seems to have some sort of fever and can't keep food

103

inside her. Something to do with being in prison, I expect. That's what she says it must be.'

'I expect she's right,' agreed Maude. 'The food in there didn't agree with me.'

'Well, do I get my shilling, or shall I wish you "good day" and thank you for calling?'

'Do you know anything about looking after babies?' Becky was still undecided.

'Lor' love us! I've had five younger brothers and sisters. I've spent more time looking after babies than Ma has!'

Maggie thought it inadvisable to add that only two of the five had survived infancy. Not that the deaths could be blamed upon her. Two of them had been carried away by a raging torrent when the River Frome burst its banks and seriously flooded all the homes in the vicinity.

'What do you think, Becky?' Maude asked her friend, hopefully.

Becky had been studying the young girl closely. She was clean, for all that she was shabbily dressed. She also had a pleasant and open smile. Maggie reminded Becky a little of herself when she was that age.

'I'm willing to let her look after Lucy.'

Maude was delighted. She had expected Becky to raise objections to such an arrangement, but Maggie's next words took the smile from her face.

'I'll want cash in advance, mind.'

'I've just come out of prison,' Maude protested. 'There's no way I can find any money until I've had a chance to earn some.'

'That's all right.' Becky produced a shilling and gave it to the young girl, saying to Maude, 'You can give me your half when you get some money.'

'I will, I promise.'

Becky was aware just how hollow were Maude's promises, but she made no comment. Handing over Lucy, she was relieved to see the assurance with which Maggie took the baby. As she held it, she displayed an affection that would have been difficult to feign. Becky was confident the young girl would take care of her.

Chapter 10

As they walked away from the small, riverside house, Maude said gleefully to Becky, 'That's the first time for weeks I've been able to really turn my back on Alfie and walk away from the little brat. I feel as though I've just shed years off my life. Where shall we go?'

'Well, I've no intention of going to the Cabot Arms. Let's take a walk through the Arcade and look at the shops for a while. While we're looking we can decide where we want to go.'

Despite her earlier reluctance, Becky found herself suddenly enthusiastic at the thought of an evening free from the responsibility of taking care of Lucy.

Maude pouted. She had been eagerly anticipating the moment when she would sit in a crowded, noisy public house, with a gin in her hand. While she drank she would eye up the customers, seeking a prospective client. However, she said nothing. Maude had no money of her own and would need to rely upon Becky, for her initial drink at least.

The already flexible plan of the two girls was hastily modified when they were no more than a quarter of the length of the first of Bristol's two shopping arcades.

They were looking in the window of a shop that sold ladies' gowns of all descriptions. The fashions were of a type that neither would ever possess or wear, and they were giggling at the wide-skirted crinolines and various extravagances of the dresses when an elderly man stopped beside them.

He was as fashionably dressed as any of the dummies

in the windows of the Arcade shops. Sporting long, full sideburns, he wore a polished beaver top hat, black frock coat and tight, light grey trousers. In his hand he carried a silver-topped walking stick.

Becky gave the man no more than a passing glance, but Maude flashed him a smile which was instantly returned.

Raising his hat an inch or two from his head, the man said, 'Good evening, ladies. Are you out enjoying the evening air, or are you hoping to find something a little more exciting?'

'We're admiring the dresses,' replied Maude, immediately. 'They're like the ones we make.'

'Ah! So you're seamstresses?' The elegant man appeared to be disappointed with the false explanation. 'I seem to have made a mistake. I thought you might be available for something a little more rewarding than needlework.'

'Well now, I didn't say I *wasn't*,' said Maude, coyly. 'It depends what the *something* is – and just how rewarding it's likely to be. If it's enough, I might just be tempted.'

'I think I can offer you enough to overcome any scruples you may have, young lady.'

'Hark at his long words!' Maude teased as she nudged Becky and played to the full the part of a simple seamstress. 'How long was you thinking of helping me to enjoy myself? All night?'

'Dear me, no!' replied the man. 'I need to be home at a reasonable hour. I trust you have a room not too far away?'

'Just around the corner,' said Maude, promptly, 'though I hope my pa ain't home.'

This at least was the truth. She intended making use of the family home above the ironmonger's shop in Broadmead. She had used it frequently in the past and knew from experience there was little chance of being confronted by her father. He spent the hours between work and bedtime in the beer-houses of the dock area.

Maude could see that the elderly prospective client was in a state of eager anticipation at the thought of what lay in store for him. Because of this, she decided to push her luck even farther. 'I can't leave my friend out here on her own while we're away. How about giving her some money to buy a cup of coffee while she's waiting?'

The man was slightly taken aback by Maude's audacity, but he reached into a pocket and pulled out some coins, peering at them in the yellow light from the lamp above the shop window. Picking out two coins, he proffered them to Becky, saying, 'Here you are, girl, here's two shillings for you. Buy yourself a drink while you're waiting for your friend. Perhaps another night you and I might meet and have a little fun together, eh?'

Becky took the money without comment. Maude linked arms with her new-found friend and began walking along the Arcade in the direction of Broadmead.

She had not gone far when she broke away and hurried back to Becky. In a low voice, she said, 'That two shillings will take care of the sixpence I owe you. I'll meet you in the White Hart. I shouldn't be long. This old codger's likely to suffer a stroke if I let him go on for longer than half-an-hour.'

A few moments later Maude had caught up with the waiting man and they set off along the Arcade together. As they walked along she clung to his arm and looked up at him as though she thought he must be the most wonderful man in the whole of Bristol.

Chapter 11

When Maude and her friend had passed from sight, Becky turned and made her way to the White Hart. When she reached the door, she paused. It sounded noisy inside. As on her most recent visit to a public house, Becky found she needed to pluck up courage to step inside.

She did so eventually and when she paused inside the door hesitantly, somebody called, 'Becky! What are you doing here? Come and have a drink with us.'

It was Iris who was drinking with a group of women, some of whom Becky recognised. All were older than Becky, and each was an experienced prostitute. Most were more usually to be found in the taverns and ale-houses around the city's docks.

As Iris called for another gin to be brought to the table, the women moved along the bench seat to make room for Becky. She sat down gratefully, relieved to find someone she knew in here.

After introducing her to the others, Iris asked, 'What are you doing here? I thought you were settling down to enjoy motherhood?'

Iris's own story was one of the tragedies of Lewin's Mead. A prostitute for as long as anyone could remember, Iris had married a Dutch sea captain only a couple of years earlier. After a wedding party attended by many of the women at the table with her now, her new husband had taken Iris to his home in Holland to begin a new life. They had been married for only a few months when the captain and his ship were lost at sea.

Left alone in a strange land, unable to speak the language, Iris had eventually abandoned their home and returned to the familiar surroundings of Lewin's Mead. There she had no alternative but to resume her former way of life.

'Someone's looking after Lucy for me. They're taking care of Alfie too. Maude and I came out together, but the chance came along for her to earn a bit of money, and she took it. She only came out of prison today and she's a bit hard up.'

'She's lucky to have found a customer,' commented Iris. 'There's no business to be had around the docks. The weather's been so bad out in the Channel there's not been a ship come in for a week. Those that are already here are stormbound and their crews have spent all their money. That's why we're in here.'

Becky looked around the crowded taproom. 'This place is full enough.'

'True, but they're all locals. Most have wives to go home to. They're more interested in drinking than giving business to us.'

As they were talking together a man who had been playing a fiddle softly in a corner of the room began singing, his voice almost drowned by the sounds around him. It was a Scots ballad that Becky remembered Fergus singing on occasions.

She looked across the room and saw a young, good-looking man with long blond hair tinged with red.

'Who's the singer?' Becky asked Iris.

'I don't know,' replied Iris. 'I don't often come in here – but whoever he is, he's not going to be with us for very much longer.'

Becky returned her glance to the singer in time to see the landlord grasp him by the shoulder of his coat and propel him to the door. Pushing him out into the street, he said, 'I don't mind you in here as long as you keep the customers happy. But when they complain and you don't spend so much as a farthing, then you're taking up good drinking space.'

The landlord swaggered back towards his counter, to

the accompaniment of cheers from some of the rowdier customers.

Becky was disappointed. It had not been possible to hear the songs properly above the noise of the taproom, but she had enjoyed the brief snatches she had been able to hear.

The fate of the young musician was forgotten when, a few minutes later, Maude came into the public house.

As she made her way to the table a group of younger customers called to her, some making crude remarks, another whistling loudly.

No one in the taproom took offence at their actions. Only women of a certain type frequented such places. The deference shown to 'decent' women was not extended to such as these.

Their calls and whistles did not bother Maude. Rather, they made her swing her hips in deliberate provocation as she walked across the room.

'How was your well-dressed gentleman?' asked Becky, as she moved up to allow Maude to sit down.

'All puff and no wind,' she replied dismissively. 'But he was generous enough, I'll give him that. If I had one like him every night I wouldn't need to worry about where my rent was coming from.'

It was to prove a profitable night for Maude. Fifteen minutes later she left the White Hart in the company of one of the men who had called to her as she came in.

One of the man's friends was interested in Becky, but she tried to ignore him. He was grossly overweight, loud and belligerent. She was not yet ready to take on someone with such unprepossessing characteristics.

The man was persistent. So much so that eventually Becky said to the others, 'I've had enough. I've enjoyed drinking with you, but I'm off home now.'

'Don't let him drive you away,' protested Iris, glaring at the man who was pestering Becky. 'I'll speak to the landlord and have *him* put out.'

'I can't see the landlord putting out someone who spends as much as he must, on the say-so of the likes of us. It's all right, I don't mind. I'll pick up Lucy and get her home to bed.'

Becky left the White Hart and almost immediately heard footsteps behind her. When she turned into a dark alleyway which led to the River Frome, the unseen follower came too.

When Becky stopped, the footsteps slowed and then they too ceased.

'Who's that? Why are you following me?'

'Oh, come on now, why do you *think* I'm following you? Just name your price. I'll pay it.'

Becky recognised the voice as belonging to the man who had been pestering her in the White Hart. She retorted, 'I told you just now that I wasn't interested in you, or your money. Nothing's changed.'

'Oh yes it has, luvvie. Back there you were surrounded by all your friends. Out here it's just you and me.'

'That's not quite true.' A soft voice came from the deeper shadows of a nearby doorway. 'And I'm inclined to side with the lady.'

The large man who had followed Becky was startled by the unexpected interruption, but he said, belligerently, 'Keep out of this, whoever you are. She's just playing hard to get in the hope that I'll agree to pay more for her, that's all.'

'I wouldn't want you if you were to offer me ten pounds,' retorted Becky.

'You've not got ten *shillings* worth of meat on your bones, girl, but I'll have you, just the same.'

'No, you won't.' The unknown man had stepped from the doorway now, although it was far too dark to see his face.

'I've told you to keep out of this . . .' The large man took a pace towards the other man and there was the sound of a blow being struck.

It was impossible to see who had thrown the punch, but one of the men staggered back across the narrow alleyway. Then he retreated towards the road.

'I won't forget this. I'll get you one day. Both of you.'

111

It was the big man from the White Hart and he spoke as though he was unable to breathe properly through his nose. Moments later the sound of his footsteps had gone from the cobbled alleyway.

'Thank you, sir,' said Becky, gratefully, to her rescuer. 'You saved me from a great deal of unpleasantness, at the very least.'

'That's all right. The man is a bully. Like most bullies, he's also a coward. Now he's gone, will you be so kind as to guide me to the doorway where I was when you came along? My belongings are there and I seem to have lost my bearings.'

The request puzzled Becky for a moment, but his next words supplied the answer. 'Unfortunately, I'm blind and my fiddle is with my things. I need it to earn a living.'

Suddenly she realised who he was. 'You're the man who was singing in the White Hart.'

'You were there? I'm surprised anyone could hear me above the din.'

'But you just fought with that man! How . . .'

'How was I able to hit him so accurately? It's night-time, is it not? In the dark I'm the equal of my fellow men. Indeed, my hearing has developed to such an extent, I probably possess the advantage. Anyway, I only needed to strike a single blow.'

'All the same, it was very brave of you.' Becky meant it. She was greatly impressed by the courage shown by the blind man.

She led him to the doorway. Groping inside he located his fiddle and said, 'Ah! Here it is, safe and sound.'

'Can I guide you on your way before I leave?'

'I'm not going anywhere. This doorway will do as well as any other.'

'But . . . you can't stay here.' Becky had passed this way in daylight. The doorway belonged to a shop that had been derelict for many months. Rumour had it the buildings in this alleyway would soon be pulled down to make way for a factory. In the meantime it was occupied by hundreds of rats.

'It's all right. One place is the same as another to a blind man.'

There was more than a hint of rain in the air and the doorway was not deep enough to provide adequate shelter for a sleeping man. Becky arrived at a sudden decision.

'Come back to my room for the night. You'd be sleeping on the floor and I have to collect my baby first, but it will be better than staying here.'

'There's no need. You owe me nothing.'

'Yes, I do,' Becky contradicted him. 'You'll come with me.'

'Well . . . since you're so insistent, I have to admit that your offer is rather more tempting than this doorway.'

As he gathered his bundle of belongings and tucked the fiddle beneath his arm, he said, 'You spoke of a baby. Is there a husband too?'

'There is, but he left me before the baby was born.'

Her reply filled in much of the picture that he had formed of her in his mind. A young girl alone with a baby who lived in Lewin's Mead and frequented inns . . .'

'Since I'm to be your lodger, however temporary it may be, you should know my name. Simon McAllister, minstrel and wanderer, at your service.'

'You *are* a Scot! I thought you sounded like my husband. He's from Edinburgh.'

'I'm from Oban, but you are?'

'Becky. Becky Vincent.'

'I'm delighted to make your acquaintance, Becky. It will be a great luxury to sleep beneath a roof for a night. May I take your arm? Thank you, now I am relying upon your guidance. I manage very well, as a rule, but I have never been to Bristol before.'

113

Chapter 12

At the house by the river, Maggie Stapleton gave up Lucy with obvious reluctance. She offered to take care of her whenever Becky cared to bring her to the house.

While Lucy was being handed over, Alfie could be heard screaming in another room in a noisy tantrum. 'You wouldn't care to take him with you as well, I suppose?' Maggie jerked a thumb in the general direction of the sound.

'I couldn't manage the pair of them,' said Becky candidly. 'I might if they were both like Lucy, but Alfie's beyond me.'

'He'll be lucky if someone doesn't strangle him before he's much older,' the young girl declared in exasperation. 'I'd better go in and shut him up now. He'll be disturbing Ma. But don't forget, I'll happily take care of Lucy for you, anytime.'

As Becky carried Lucy through the narrow streets of Lewin's Mead, with Simon maintaining a loose grip on her arm, Lucy made contented noises.

'That sound reminds me of my sister's baby,' said Simon at length.

'Does she live in Scotland?'

'Yes.'

'Why did you leave there?' Becky welcomed the opportunity to ask the question. If the blind singer was coming to live in her room for a while, she felt she ought to know as much about him as possible.

'Oh, it was all right letting her take care of me when I could see. I wasn't there very often, anyway. But once my sight went I felt it was too much for her, having me and a

114

family to care for. One day I just walked out – and here I am.'

'So you haven't always been blind?' Becky was surprised by his disclosure. He seemed so self-assured in spite of his disability.

'I lost my sight as a result of an illness. It took me a long while to accept. I always believed that one day I would wake and find I was able to see again.' He shrugged. 'Now I realise that's just not going to happen.'

'Didn't you have any parents to turn to?'

'No. My father was killed in a riding accident. My mother died just before my sight went.'

'What sort of work did you do before you went blind?'

Becky had already realised that Simon McAllister came from a very different background to her own. It might even be on a par with that of Fanny Tennant. Her view was confirmed by his reply.

'I was at University in Edinburgh, studying medicine. That's how I picked up the illness that cost me my sight.'

Becky looked at him in awed deference. She thought of the room she had offered to share with him in Back Lane and began to apologise in advance. He cut her short.

'If you're regretting inviting me to stay with you, then say so. I'll understand.'

'It's not that. I don't want you thinking it's going to be better than it is, that's all.'

'Becky, you've offered to put a roof over my head for the night. Whatever it is, it will be an improvement upon a doorway – and it will be dry.'

It had begun raining as they walked from the house by the river and Simon added, 'Who knows, I might even get a decent cup of tea! Something I don't seem to have had for longer than I care to remember.'

'I can certainly make you a cup of tea. I might even find something stronger for you.'

'It gets better and better! I really am very grateful to you for your offer, Becky. I don't enjoy sleeping out. When I arrive in a strange town I usually seek two things right away. A room that's not too expensive and an inn where a landlord will allow me to entertain his customers. I don't seem to have done very well on either count today. At least, I hadn't until you offered to let me lodge with you for the night.'

When they arrived at the attic room in Back Lane, Becky managed to breathe new life into the embers of the fire. While a kettle was boiling she fed Lucy and put her in the bed they shared. Then she heated up some soup, leftover from the midday meal. She put it on the table with some bread, fresh that morning.

As Simon ate, Becky studied the man she had invited to Back Lane. He was taller than Fergus. Good-looking too. He also had a gentle way with him. It was a trait that had always endeared Fergus to her.

There was a brief period of embarrassment when he finished soup and tea and she made him up a bed on the floor. She thought he might have been expecting to sleep with her – and admitted to herself she had not decided whether she would disillusion him, or go along with the idea.

When he made no move to take advantage of the situation, she went to bed feeling vaguely disappointed.

She had been lying in bed for some minutes when he asked, 'What does your husband do for a living, Becky?'

It was not the type of question she had been expecting, but she replied, 'He's an artist.'

'A good one?'

'Very good.'

'I won't be offended if you tell me to mind my own business, Becky, but why did he leave you?'

She was about to make up a story that would make it seem the parting was entirely Fergus's fault, but she stopped short. For some inexplicable reason she found it difficult to lie to this man.

'I messed around with other men while he was away exhibiting his pictures in London. I think he must have found out.'

'You *think*? Didn't he confront you with it? I would have thought something important enough to break up a marriage would have erupted in a blazing row, at the very least.'

'It wasn't the first time,' admitted Becky, unhappily. 'I came home and found he'd just gathered up his things and left. I have no one to blame but myself. I could have found excuses for what I did the other times, but not when he went for good.'

In the darkness, she felt hot tears well up in her eyes and tried unsuccessfully to blink them away.

'Do you think he's ever likely to come back to you – and Lucy?'

'He doesn't know about Lucy – and before you ask, she *is* his. Anyway, I don't think it would make any difference. He's gone off as an artist to India somewhere.'

Simon was silent for a few minutes, then he said quietly, 'I'm sorry for asking about him and upsetting you, Becky.'

She realised that although Simon had no sight, his perception was acute. 'I'm not upset. I'm just not used to talking about Fergus to anyone, that's all.'

'That's all right then. Good night, Becky.'

'Good night.'

Once again, she wished he was sleeping beside her, instead of on the floor.

Becky dropped off in a deep sleep. She must have been asleep for a couple of hours when she clawed her way back to reluctant wakefulness. Something had disturbed her, but it was a moment or two before she realised it was Simon singing softly. At the same time she became aware that Lucy was not in the bed beside her.

Sitting up, she called out in alarm, 'What are you doing? Where's Lucy?'

'Shh!' Simon's voice came to her from the darkness. 'I think she's asleep now. She woke up – but you didn't. I thought I'd try to sing her to sleep without waking you. It worked for Lucy, but not for you. I'm sorry.'

As he spoke he moved across the room to the bed. Reaching across her, he was about to place Lucy between Becky and the wall when she reached up and touched his arm.

'What is it, Becky?'

'Put Lucy in your bed, on the floor. You can come here and hold me for a while, if you'd like to?'

'No, Becky. For one thing, you'd wake in the morning and regret it and then we wouldn't be friends any more.'

He placed Lucy gently on the bed, between the wall and Becky.

'I don't think so, Simon. There have been many mornings when I've woken up with lots to regret, but not this time.'

'It's still no. I'm a Scot, like Fergus. I like to get to know someone well before becoming involved in that way.'

Becky was both hurt and bewildered. She had never before been refused by a man to whom she had offered herself.

'Goodnight, Becky.' Bending over her he kissed her with remarkable accuracy at the corner of her mouth.

Becky listened as Simon settled down in his bed on the floor, then she lay awake in the darkness. She recalled that when she had first met Fergus, he too had slept in this room with her without making love.

It was as though Simon had been sent to Lewin's Mead to remind her of the past . . .

Chapter 13

It was mid-morning before Maude made her way to the attic room. Bleary-eyed and scantily dressed, she came in without knocking. Becky was seated on her bed, taking in the seams of a dress she had worn when expecting Lucy. Simon sat on the floor in a corner of the room, skilfully replacing a string on his violin.

Not at all embarrassed at finding Simon in the room or because she was not fully dressed, Maude said, 'Hello, I came up here to see if you'd brought Alfie home with you when you collected Lucy. Now I can see you probably had other things on your mind.'

Ignoring her pointed remark, Becky said, 'Do you mean to say that Alfie's been with Maggie since last night? What will have happened if she had to go to work this morning?'

'From what her mother told me in prison I'd say there are enough people in the house to keep an eye on Alfie. After all, she was paid a shilling to look after him.'

'Well, he's *your* baby.'

'That's right. I suppose you haven't got a drop of Blue Ruin tucked away somewhere? Just to pick me up a bit and give me the strength to dress and go off to fetch Alfie.'

'We drank it all last night,' replied Becky. It was a lie. Simon was not a heavy drinker and there was almost half a bottle of gin left in a cupboard, but Becky knew that if she brought it out for Maude she would not leave the attic room until the bottle was empty.

'Then I suppose I'd better go and get Alfie,' she said, disappointed.

'You better had,' agreed Becky, unsympathetically.

119

When Maude had gone, Simon asked, 'Does your friend often leave her baby with someone overnight?'

'Yes. Usually it's with me.' After only a moment's hesitation, Becky added, 'Maude was sent to prison for breaking a window at the ragged school. She only came out yesterday and wanted me to go out with her last night, to celebrate her release. We left the babies with the daughter of one of the women she met inside. I wasn't keen to leave Lucy with a stranger, but Maggie seems a very nice girl. I'm sure she won't be too put out at being left with Alfie for the night.'

'Was Maude in the Bridewell prison?'

'That's right. She wasn't very far from home, although I never went to see her. Why do you ask?'

'No particular reason, really. I heard two people talking in the White Hart last night. I think one of them was a warder in the Bridewell.'

'It's not a very nice place,' said Becky. 'I've heard they're thinking of pulling it down soon. It certainly won't be before time.'

The repair to his violin completed, Simon rose to his feet. 'Well, I suppose it's time I made a move. I really must thank you for letting me stay here last night, Becky, and for . . . everything.'

'You're not leaving already?'

'I must. I have a living to earn and I'd like to find a room before I look for work.'

'You don't need to do that. You can stay here, if you like. I have money.'

'I have no intention of living off a woman,' said Simon, sharply. '*Any* woman.'

'I don't earn my living the way you think,' retorted Becky. 'Fergus left money for me. I have enough never to need to work any more if I don't want to.'

'That doesn't make any difference. I won't be kept by a woman's money, or that of another man.'

'All right, but that doesn't mean you can't stay here. What if you go to work and earn your money and I collect you at the end of each evening – at least, until you've found somewhere? You can pay me for your food and lodging if it'll make you feel better.'

Simon thought over the offer before saying, 'You really want me to stay here?'

'Yes.' Once again Becky felt the need to be honest with this man who had been in her life for no more than twelve hours. 'I never realised just how lonely I'd become – until now. You'd be doing me a favour, Simon, and it would give me another reason to stay in at night.'

'I get lonely at times too, Becky. Very lonely. It's not easy to find someone willing to give their time to a blind man. Even for a little while. Because of this, and because of your generosity, I'm really in no position to impose any conditions on your offer – but I'm going to anyway. I'll happily accept but only if you promise not to go out and find other men while I'm staying here.'

Becky was taken aback. Not because she felt Simon had no right to impose such a condition, but because she was fully aware that it was her inability to keep such a promise that had been the reason she had lost Fergus.

Before she could reply, Simon said, 'My condition has nothing to do with morality or jealousy. But I have enough problems to cope with in my life. I'm not going to sit outside on the landing, or on the stairs, waiting for a man to satisfy his needs and leave your bed.'

'You're a great one for making speeches and using long words, Simon McAllister. What *I* ought to do is tell you I'm making you a good offer by letting you stay here. That what I choose to do in my own room is none of your business. But I won't. Since you're being honest with me, I'll be the same. I'll do as you ask – but only for as long as it suits me. All right?'

'You're being very generous, Becky – and now I'll use more words to tell you what I feel. I'm already fond of you and I'll be very happy to stay with you – but only until I find a room of my own. Now we've got all that out of the way, where do you suggest I can go to earn a few shillings to contribute to my keep?'

'You really don't have to . . .' Observing his expression

change abruptly, Becky added hastily, 'But if you really want somewhere then you'll need to try the city taverns. For the moment, anyway. You'll make more money down at the docks when the weather improves and ships start coming in again, but it's not worth your while right now. There's no sense in going out just yet. No one starts spending money until the evening.'

It was a way of life with which Becky was well acquainted and Simon did not argue with her.

They were discussing the merits of various inns and taverns when they both heard someone hurrying up the stairs to the attic.

Becky and Simon stopped talking as the door was thrown open and Maude stumbled into the room clutching Alfie. Her face was the colour of chalk.

As she struggled to regain her breath, Becky asked, 'What's happened, Maude? You look as though you've seen a ghost!'

'I've just had a dreadful shock! I went to pick up Alfie and found the Stapleton house in turmoil. Annie died during the night – and with my Alfie in the house too!'

Becky was almost as shocked as Maude. 'Maggie said her ma was ill but I didn't realise she was *that* ill.'

'What was wrong with her?' The question came from Simon.

'Maggie said she had a fever and could keep nothing inside her, but no one knows for certain. They couldn't afford to call a doctor.'

Maude shook her head sadly. 'It just doesn't seem possible. The day she was released from prison she was as happy and healthy as anyone else.'

'Are you aware they have an outbreak of cholera in the Bridewell?'

Maude's expression registered both horror and disbelief. Cholera had raged through Lewin's Mead on more than one occasion. Those who had not experienced it for themselves had been regaled with horrific stories told by those who had.

'That can't be true. I only came out of there myself

yesterday. I never heard a whisper about cholera.'

'I don't suppose you would. It's something the authorities try to keep quiet for as long as possible, to avoid a panic.'

Maude looked at Simon suspiciously, not wanting to believe him. 'How is it you know about it then?'

'I heard two people talking quietly in the White Hart last night. One man, I think he was a gaoler, was telling it to the other, in strict confidence.' Simon shrugged. 'I often overhear conversations that I shouldn't. It's some form of compensation for the loss of my sight, I suppose.'

When Maude still looked sceptical, Becky said, 'Simon's blind, but I know how good his hearing is. If it hadn't been, then I'd have had serious trouble last night.'

Becky would have told Maude how Simon had saved her from the persistent 'suitor', but she could see the other girl was far too concerned about the cholera to listen. Instead, she added, 'Simon was also learning to be a doctor before he went blind.'

'But . . . surely they'd *have* to do something if they had cholera in a prison?'

'They have. There's been no one admitted to the Bridewell for a week. If it gets any worse they'll stop releasing prisoners too.'

Maude thought about what Simon had said and suddenly she nodded. 'You're right. No one was brought to the Bridewell last week. We joked about it, saying the world outside must have turned honest. We wondered how we'd get on when we were released.'

Even more agitated than before, she asked, 'Is there anything that can be done for me and Alfie?'

'You can drink lots of water. It's said to help, but I can't remember whether that's after you've got it or not. The only other thing is to try praying. I think your baby is probably more at risk than you. He spent last night in the house where this woman died. Do you know if he went anywhere near her?'

Looking scared, Maude nodded, 'I believe he was taken in for her to see. Knowing Annie's love of babies, she probably wanted to hold him. I don't know . . .'

Simon tried hard not to allow the concern he felt to show. 'Keep Alfie in your room and don't allow anyone else near him. If he hasn't shown any symptoms in a couple of days' time he's probably going to be all right, but it's as well not to take any chances.'

Her bloodless face showing the fear she felt, Maude left the room. When the door had closed behind her, Becky said to Simon, 'You've put the fear of God into Maude. I've never seen her so scared. Do you really think it's so serious?'

'Yes, and I hope she stays scared. Cholera's a killer, Becky. Some adults survive – but if cholera breaks out in this house, Lucy wouldn't stand a chance.'

Chapter 14

Baby Alfie Garrett died from cholera only two days after Annie Stapleton. He died during the night hours far more silently than he had lived.

Not until long after dawn, when Maude thought to check her strangely silent baby son, did she discover his body, stiff and cold in the drawer that served as his cot.

Her screams echoed through the Back Lane house, bringing Becky from the attic and the other residents from their rooms. Even the ageing Ida Stokes wheezed her way to the source of the noise, brandishing an iron poker and demanding to know what was happening.

'It's my Alfie,' wailed Maude. 'He's died of the cholera. I knew this would happen. As soon as I learned that Annie Stapleton had died, I knew my Alfie would be next.'

'Cholera!' For a moment Becky thought Ida Stokes was about to strike Maude with the poker she brandished before her face. 'You've brought the cholera here, into my house?'

'Who says it's cholera?' The question came from Iris.

'Becky's bloke does. He says they've got it in the Bridewell. He heard someone talking.' Maude's grief was tempered by fear of the poker in Ida Stokes's hand.

Ida rounded upon Becky. 'How does he know? Does he claim to be a doctor, or something?'

'He would have been one if he hadn't been struck blind,' replied Becky.

Simon, feeling his way downstairs from the attic room, heard the exchange and said, 'I don't think there's any doubt about its being cholera, but a doctor will confirm it — and I think you should call one right away.'

125

'I'm having no doctor coming here!' declared Ida Stokes. 'And don't you tell me what I ought to do in my own house, young man.'

'I'm trying to help you,' said Simon, placatingly. 'I think you're obliged to notify the City Corporation if there's a case of cholera in the house. Even without that, it makes sense to do so. If something isn't done to check it cholera could kill off everyone in this house.'

There was a gasp of horror from Simon's listeners. He had the manner and speech of an educated man and this impressed them as much as his words.

Struggling to come to terms with all that was happening, Ida Stokes said eventually, 'What can I do? Who do I tell?'

For Ida, as for almost everyone else in Lewin's Mead, reporting something to the authorities – any authority – was unthinkable. Lewin's Mead was a refuge for all who had something to fear from the law, or the regulations that were applied to *others*. It was the boast of those who lived here that the police dared not walk its narrow alleyways. Similarly, decisions arrived at in the chambers of the City Corporation had little effect on those who made their homes here.

Actually to *invite* anyone in authority in and act upon their instructions was unheard of! However, this was clearly a matter of life and death. 'Well, seeing as it was you who brought this in here, it had better be you who goes and reports it, Maude Garrett.'

Word that there was an outbreak of cholera in Back Lane went round Lewin's Mead – and beyond – in a matter of hours.

A doctor and his assistant came to the house later that same morning and the body of baby Alfie was taken to the mortuary. The doctor agreed with Simon. There was little doubt it was cholera. He suggested the house should be scrubbed from attic to hallway and the whole of the interior limewashed.

Ida Stokes complained bitterly that a poor widow-woman should not be expected to meet the cost of such a course of action. However, when the doctor warned her of the consequences should others in the house contract the disease, she agreed to supply the materials for her tenants to limewash their own rooms.

Later that afternoon, another visitor came to the house and hurriedly made her way to the attic. Becky had Lucy at her breast when Fanny Tennant knocked at the door and entered without waiting for an invitation.

Her glance took in the scene of Becky sitting on her bed, feeding the baby, and Simon seated on a chair at the table nearby.

Fanny frowned disapprovingly, but came straight to the point of her visit. 'I've been told there's cholera in the house, Becky. What are you doing about it?'

Becky began telling her of the limewashing and scrubbing of floors, some of which had already taken place, but Fanny interrupted, impatiently.

'That's not what I'm talking about. What do you intend doing to remove Lucy from danger altogether?'

At that moment Becky's nipple slipped from the baby's mouth. Seemingly almost asleep only a moment before, Lucy came suddenly and furiously awake, making loud sucking sounds as her tiny mouth sought the displaced source of comfort and nourishment.

Fanny's disapproving glance moved from the baby to Simon and back to Becky. 'Do you have to feed Lucy in front of your man friend? Could you not at least turn your back on him?'

'It wouldn't make any difference to anyone. Lucy doesn't mind and Simon's blind.'

'Oh! Well, what's he doing here? Couldn't you have managed without going back to your old ways – for Lucy's sake?'

Fanny realised she was being unreasonably narrow-minded, and Becky's morals were not the most important issue at the moment. But she felt angry on Fergus's behalf to see another man ensconced in this room with his wife and daughter.

Before Becky could reply to her, Simon said, 'I may be

blind, but I am not an imbecile. I can answer for myself. We've not met before, but I think I can identify you from a very accurate description Becky has given to me.'

Without amplifying this contentious statement, he continued, 'I'm Simon McAllister. Becky was compassionate enough to take pity on me and allow me to stay here for a while. Thanks to her I exchanged a draughty doorway for a warm fire and a blanket on the floor – I do *not* share her bed. Would you have done the same for a blind musician?'

Fanny was immediately aware from his reply that Becky's lodger was an educated man. She wondered, not for the first time, what it was about Becky that attracted such men as Fergus and Simon McAllister to her.

But she had not come to Back Lane to discuss Becky's inexplicable appeal to men. 'I have never doubted Becky's compassion, Mr McAllister. All I'm asking is that she extends it to Lucy. You can't remain here, Becky. Not with the threat of cholera hanging over you. Bring Lucy to stay in my house, in Clifton. I've suggested it to you before. Now I am begging you. For the sake of your daughter, remove her from Lewin's Mead while there's a chance of saving her.'

Once again it was Simon who replied to Fanny's plea. 'That would not be wise, Miss Tennant. It would also be contrary to the advice of the doctor who came here this morning on behalf of the City Corporation. He has ordered us all to remain in the house, allowing only one person – I believe her name is Iris – to go shopping on behalf of everyone else. The plan is to minimise our contact with the outside. He'll also have done something similar at the home of Maude's friend, where poor Alfie caught cholera.'

'I know that everything is being done to prevent an epidemic. I've been ordered to close the ragged school for a while, for the same reason. But I doubt if it would defeat the aims of the City Corporation if Becky and Lucy were isolated in Clifton instead of Lewin's Mead.'

'Do you mind if I have something to say about this?' Becky spoke belligerently. 'I don't *want* to leave Lewin's Mead. I'll take my chance here, the same as everyone else.'

'Becky, I'm giving you the opportunity to reduce the chances of catching cholera. It's a killer disease. At least two people have died already – probably more. One of them was a baby in this very house. We're not talking of something trivial. It's quite literally a matter of life and death.'

'I don't care. I'm staying here.'

Fanny was angry at Becky's intransigence, but she knew better than to allow it to show. Stubbornness was a part of Becky's nature. Fanny tried a new line of argument.

'I know you don't feel happy outside Lewin's Mead, Becky, you've shown that very often in the past – but think of what could happen to Lucy. She's too tiny to put up any resistance against the disease. She wouldn't have a chance. If she's taken ill she'll die within twenty-four hours, just as Alfie Garrett did. Let *her* come with me. At least until the danger of catching cholera is past.'

Becky was about to protest that Lucy and she would both remain in Lewin's Mead, when Simon said quietly, 'Miss Tennant's right, Becky, even though it's against Corporation advice. Not every cholera victim will die – but a baby stands no chance of survival. None at all.'

In the few days she had known Simon, Becky had come to respect his views, but she was dismayed by his words.

'I can't! I can't give up Lucy!'

'No one's asking you to give her up, Becky. What I *really* want is for both you and Lucy to leave this house. To come and live with me, in Clifton. It's a very large house. You could have your own rooms and need never be disturbed by anyone.'

'I . . . I just can't!'

'Then you must allow Lucy to have a chance to live. You owe it to her – and you owe it to Fergus. What would he tell you to do?'

Becky knew very well what Fergus would tell her. He would say the same as Fanny Tennant. The same as Simon . . . She struggled to find an argument against parting with Lucy, even though it was likely to be for only a few days. She did not believe it could be for any longer.

'It's the only responsible thing to do, Becky.' Simon's

quiet voice broke the long silence.

'I know, but . . .' Becky felt as though she were offering up her daughter for sacrificial slaughter. 'I will have her back, when I want her? You won't try to take her from me?'

'She's *your* baby, Becky.' Fanny could hardly contain the elation she felt. 'It will only be until the danger of cholera has passed.'

'When . . . when would you want to take her?'

'Immediately. The longer she remains here, the greater the danger she's in.'

After a long and poignant silence, the words escaped from her. 'All right!'

Becky felt as though someone else had spoken. 'But I don't want you making any fuss when I ask to have her back again.'

'Of course not.' Fanny held out her arms for the baby. 'You're being very sensible, Becky. I'll get in a nanny for her and I promise you she'll have the very best of attention.'

Becky looked around for a small piece of blanket and wrapped it around Lucy. She kissed her and then handed her to Fanny, hardly able to see through the tears that blinded her.

'Goodbye, Becky – and thank you, Mr McAllister. I believe you have probably saved Lucy's life.'

Chapter 15

Standing beside his daughter, Alderman Tennant looked down uncertainly at the baby sleeping in its brand-new swing-cot. 'She's a lovely child, Fanny – but then, all babies are. How do you see the future for her?'

'For the moment I intend allowing the future to take care of itself. I'm just happy to have been able to remove Lucy from Lewin's Mead. I feel certain Fergus would have approved.'

'You can't run your life doing things "because Fergus would approve", Fanny. He chose to marry Becky. Then he left her and set off for India without saying a word to you.'

'Fergus is a friend, Father. A very dear friend. You don't ask friends to explain their every action. You accept them for what they are.'

'You fool yourself if you must, Fanny. You certainly don't fool *me*. For better, or for worse, Fergus Vincent has been the only man in your life. You've spent all the years since he came to Bristol doing things you think would please him. You know my thoughts on the matter. All I'll say now is, don't get too fond of this baby. Winsome though she may be, she belongs to someone else.'

Fanny was reluctant to admit that her father was right, but it did not matter for the moment. She had possession of Fergus's baby. A great deal could happen between now and the time when she might be required to give her up.

Whatever Fanny's reasons for insisting that Lucy be removed from Lewin's Mead, it proved a wise decision.

Cholera struck the house in Back Lane again, even while the inside of the building was being scrubbed and limewashed. Two of the younger children of the ever-expanding family of Mary O'Ryan fell ill. Both were dead within the space of twenty-four hours.

The O'Ryans' room was on the first floor in the room beneath Maude, but the children enjoyed the run of the house. Their deaths provoked as much concern as sympathy for the family. It was probable both children had been into every room in the house while they were carrying the seeds of the disease.

After the latest tragic deaths, the remaining residents of the Back Lane house held their breath, awaiting cholera to claim its next victim.

It was not long in pursuing its inexplicable course. The night after the second of the O'Ryan children died, Becky became ill. By morning she was too weak to leave her bed.

Simon went downstairs to inform Maude, but she refused to put herself at risk by coming up to the attic room to help. It was Iris who volunteered to help him nurse Becky.

For much of that first day Simon battled to keep her comfortable. He forced her to drink copiously, while Iris tended to her more personal needs.

By evening it was apparent to both of them that they were fighting a losing battle. Becky lapsed in and out of a coma, noticeably weaker.

Simon had not left her bedside and he was sensitive to every change in her condition. When she slipped into unconsciousness yet again, he rose to his feet, his expression showing the agitation he felt.

'We've got to do something drastic, Iris. If we don't, we're going to lose her.'

Iris shared his concern, but felt there was nothing more they could do to help, and said so.

'There *is*, Iris. There *has* to be.' He began pacing the room, each time passing so close to a jug of water balanced on the edge of the table that Iris expected it to be knocked off by his sightless agitation at any minute.

Suddenly, Simon stopped in front of Iris. 'When I was studying medicine in Edinburgh we were given a lecture by a man named Snow . . . John Snow, yes, that was his name. He'd spent his life investigating the causes and treatment of cholera. Much of the work he did was dismissed by our own doctors, but I remember thinking that the results he achieved were very impressive. I felt more research should have been carried out on his theories. I believe we should try the methods he recommended. We *must* try something – and very quickly. Is there a pharmacist in the city?'

'There's one not far from the docks. He mixes up a good potion for the seamen who catch the pox.'

'I want you to go to him and fetch some things for me, Iris. You'll find money in the second drawer down over there. I hope there's enough. Can you write?'

'Yes . . . but I'm not very good at spelling.'

'That doesn't matter. Write what I say the way it sounds. I'm sure the chemist will understand. Can you find something to write on? There should be something here. Fergus used a lot of pads.'

Iris found paper and pencil and Simon dictated to her. There was a syringe, and sodium . . . the list seemed endless to Iris as she struggled with the unaccustomed words.

'That's it, I think,' said Simon, eventually. 'Oh, before you go, will you fill as many kettles and pots as will go on the fire. I want lots of hot water, to ensure that the salts will dissolve. It will probably need to be boiled to make sure, as I won't be able to see it.'

When Iris had hurried away, Simon returned his attentions to Becky. In the main his ministrations were restricted to wiping her face and keeping her lips moist.

At one stage she returned to a delirious consciousness. Reaching up, she grasped Simon's arm and held it tightly.

'Fergus . . . Fergus. I'm sorry . . .'

'Shh! It's all right.'

'I do love you, Fergus. You know that, don't you?'

'Yes. Yes, I know that, Becky.'

Gradually the grip on his arm relaxed and then slid away as Becky slipped into unconsciousness once more.

When Iris returned to the attic room she had everything for which Simon had asked. She was also impressed that the pharmacist had thought the items must have been ordered by a doctor.

'We've got to be better than doctors, Iris – both of us. Now, I need to rely upon you to do a lot of the work. To be my eyes. Can you do that?'

Iris assured him that she could. She was less certain when Simon instructed her to make a tiny incision in a vein on Becky's arm. However, she succeeded in her task, although she had to turn her head away when he inserted the nozzle of the syringe in the vein and injected the solution he had prepared into it.

When he repeated the process and announced that he would continue to do so until there was a change in Becky's condition, Iris was horrified.

'But . . . you'll kill her!'

'I hope not, Iris. What *is* certain is that if I do nothing she'll die. You know that as well as I do.'

Iris conceded he was undoubtedly right. The deaths that had already occurred in Back Lane laid a tragic emphasis on his words.

Simon continued his unorthodox treatment of Becky during the whole of what seemed to be a very long night. When morning came there was no noticeable improvement, but at least she was no worse.

The treatment continued throughout the day. By that evening Iris was excitedly declaring to everyone in the house that Simon was curing Becky of her cholera.

He was less certain. During that second night Becky lapsed into a coma once more, but Simon continued his intravenous injections. He also tried to force water down her throat. This proved to be more difficult.

By now, Simon himself was close to exhaustion. For two days and two nights he had ministered to Becky without total conviction that the treatment would be successful.

Early on the third morning, despite his efforts to remain alert, Simon dropped off in a deep sleep from which only sheer will-power brought him to wakefulness once more.

He was still not properly awake when Becky's voice came to him.

'You should have stayed asleep for a while longer, Simon. You look absolutely exhausted.'

'Becky! How do you feel?' His hand went out to explore her face, emaciated from the ravages wrought by the cholera.

Her own hand came up and gripped his. 'I'm fine, Simon. Tired, yes. *Very* tired, but I'm going to be all right, I know I am – and I think I have you to thank.'

'Shh! Save your strength. I must go and tell Iris. She's worked as hard as I have to help you recover. She'll be absolutely thrilled.'

Feeling as though he wanted to shout the news to the world that Becky was going to be all right, Simon made his way to the door of the attic room. He was opening it when Becky's voice came to him once again.

'Simon? When can I have Lucy back with me again? I want her . . .'

'It will be a while yet, Becky. Not until there has been no cholera in Lewin's Mead for a couple of weeks. We can't risk having anything happen to her. Not if there's to be any hope of bringing you and Fergus together again – and I know that's what you so desperately want.'

Chapter 16

The Lewin's Mead cholera epidemic raged for almost two months. When it was at the peak of its ravages, the situation became so frightening that the residents of the Bristol slum fled in their hundreds. It was a phenomenon that no one had ever expected to witness.

For as long as anyone could remember the residents of Lewin's Mead had felt secure in their narrow alleyways, close-packed houses and overcrowded rooms.

During the weeks of the epidemic it seemed for a while as though the whole world had turned topsy-turvy.

The members of the City Corporation would previously have been delighted to witness a large-scale exodus from the city slum. Now they posted officials at the various narrow passageways. Their duties were to prevent the escape of the slum-dwellers. By keeping them within the confines of the crowded alleyways they hoped to prevent cholera from spreading to other parts of the city.

Despite these precautions, many did leave. Packing their meagre belongings, they took their families and slipped away in the dead of night.

Fortunately for the health of the citizens of Bristol, almost all those who fled deserted not only Lewin's Mead, but the city itself. Many of those who carried disease with them died by the wayside. Here they were left, without proper burial, by friends or family.

Others reached unfamiliar open countryside before pausing to consider their futures. While they pondered, they drew water for their needs from unpolluted streams. By so doing they unwittingly laid the foundation stones of their survival. The disease from which they fled was contained in the heavily polluted waters of the River Frome. It was this river which supplied water for the Bridewell *and* for Lewin's Mead.

Among those who managed to escape were Mary O'Ryan and her surviving children. Mary left Back Lane owing Ida Stokes nine weeks' rent. This was probably as pressing a reason for her clandestine departure as the dread of cholera.

Ida was furious as she searched through the scant belongings of the prolific Irishwoman.

'Look at this,' she said in disgust, throwing out a blanket that had covered a torn and stained mattress. 'It wouldn't even make a decent rag to clean the floor with. To think that after all the years I've put up with her, her men and her children, she'd go off owing me more than two months' rent. That's what comes of being soft-hearted with someone and not demanding what was due to me. I felt sorry for the woman, having just lost two children and all.'

Angrily, she threw a handleless tea-pot out of the room to the landing, 'After living in my house all these years, she's just slipped away like a thief in the night, without a word. No doubt there's a man involved. There always has been with her. There's not two of her kids who share the same father. Not that I've ever said anything about it to her, or to anyone else. I mind my own business, even if it is going on in my own house.'

She was talking to Iris who had just got out of bed and come down from the second floor to find out who was making so much noise. Also on the first-floor landing was Simon, who was returning to the house with a few groceries, for Becky.

Looking around the hurriedly vacated room, Iris said, 'This room's a lot bigger than mine.'

'True, dearie,' agreed Ida. 'It's the best room in the whole house. Almost twice the size of yours, I'd say. You'd think Mary O'Ryan would have appreciated it, wouldn't you? Me having paid for it to be limewashed, an' all. I don't know where she's gone, but if it's back to Ireland she'll not find a room like it anywhere there.'

'Can I change my room for this one, Ida?' asked Iris, as she looked around.

The request took Ida by surprise, but she recovered quickly. 'Well . . . I don't know, dearie. Like you say, it *is* a lot bigger than the one you've got now.'

'How much extra would you want, Ida?'

'Two shillings.' The reply was immediate. Mary O'Ryan had paid no more for the room than Iris was paying for hers, but Ida had no scruples about asking more.

'I know what Mary was paying you, Ida. I'll give you a shilling extra. No more.'

An extra shilling was what Ida had intended asking in the first place, but she said, 'Make it one and sixpence and the room is yours.'

'One and threepence – and I'll move in right away and clean it up for you.'

'If Iris moves in here I'll take her old room – at the same rent she's been paying.' Simon's amusement at the exchange between the two women had suddenly become interest. 'But I won't be able to move in until the week-end. I'll need to earn some money first. Besides, I don't think Becky is ready to be left alone for too long just yet.'

'You can have the room for an extra one and threepence,' said Ida to Iris. 'As for you, young man, Iris was on a low rent only because she's been here so long. I was saying to someone only the other day that if ever she left I'd need to put the rent up.'

'In that case, I'm sorry, Mrs Stokes. I couldn't commit myself to paying more. If you think you can get more for it then you'll need to look elsewhere, but people aren't exactly falling over themselves to move into Lewin's Mead at the moment. In fact, I believe there are a great many rooms available in this very lane. I'll just have to find one of those.'

'Well, seeing as how you've been so good to that poor young Becky, I'll let you have the room for what Iris has been paying. But I'll have the rent a week in advance – and don't you go around spreading the word that Ida Stokes has gone soft. I'll have every rogue in Lewin's Mead rushing around here to take advantage of a poor widow-woman who

138

has no one to take care of her interests.'

'I won't breathe a word to a soul,' promised Simon. 'But thank you anyway.'

'Well, seeing as there's no more work for me to do up here, I'll go downstairs and enjoy a well-earned rest.'

When the door to Ida Stokes's room closed behind her, Iris said, 'She's no doubt reaching down the gin bottle now, to celebrate the extra money she'll be getting from me. But I don't care. A room on the first floor will be better for business. Some of the men I'm bringing home these days can barely manage *two* flights of stairs and still do what they've paid me for.' Suddenly serious, she said, 'Does Becky know you'll be moving out of her room?'

'Not yet, but my staying there was only a temporary arrangement. Besides, I've only been sharing her room, Not her bed.'

'All the same, she'll be upset. You've done a lot for her while she's been ill.'

'She won't miss me too much. Not really. She's still very much in love with Fergus. While she was delirious she'd sometimes imagine I was him. Whose fault is it that they've broken up?'

'It was the fault of both of them – yet I doubt if either of 'em could help it. Perhaps Lewin's Mead is to blame. Becky has never known anywhere else. Fergus could see it for what it is and he realised it has to change. I think he made the mistake of thinking he could change Becky too.'

'People *can* change, Iris.'

Her sad smile was lost on the blind young man. 'I don't think you can tell me anything about people that I don't already know, Simon. Yes, they can change, but the sort of change Fergus was looking for from Becky needs to come from within. It can't be forced upon her. He needed to be patient – very patient – and understanding too. If only he'd stayed around until Lucy was born I think he would have won. She's the one who's going to make all the difference. She already has. So, if *you* care anything for Becky, then you carry on taking care of her – and don't allow Fanny to come between her and the baby.'

Chapter 17

While Becky was recuperating in the attic room in Back Lane, Sergeant Ivor Primrose paid an off-duty call on Fanny, at the Clifton home of her father.

The news Ivor brought was of some importance, otherwise he would not have chosen to visit the daughter of the Watch Committee chairman this evening. Alderman Tennant was hosting a small dinner party at which one of the guests was the city's Chief Constable.

Fanny was listening to the rather boring chatter of one of the other women at the table, when a servant girl entered the room nervously. The girl spoke first to Alderman Tennant.

'Excuse me, sir. There's someone in the hall who is asking to speak to Miss Fanny.'

Frowning, the Alderman said, 'Well, tell whoever it is to come back some other time.'

'I did say I thought that would be best, sir, but he sent his apologies and said I was to say it's urgent.'

'Oh, does he? Who is this man?'

'Ivor Primrose. He's a policeman, sir, although he's not in uniform at the moment.'

'It's all right, Father. I'll go and see him. Ivor wouldn't have come here if it wasn't something serious.' In truth, Fanny was grateful for an excuse to escape from the attentions of the guest seated beside her. She was a bore who seemed to have no original thoughts of her own and had spent the whole of the evening repeating the gossip of others.

'I'll come too, young lady,' said Bristol's Chief Constable, removing the napkin tucked in the front of his shirt. 'I'd

140

like to know what one of my sergeants considers to be of sufficient importance to interrupt your father's dinner party.'

'That won't be necessary, John,' said a now placated host, soothingly. 'I know Sergeant Primrose. He's a very good policeman. One of the best on the force, I'd say. He's only newly promoted to sergeant, but when you're next looking for an inspector you needn't look any farther than Primrose. He's helped Fanny many times in the past at the ragged school. If he says he has an urgent message for Fanny it will be something she should know, you can count on that.'

In fact, as Fanny discovered when she met Ivor in the hallway, there was no immediate action she was expected to take. He handed a letter to her, saying, 'I was shown this when I went home this evening, Miss Fanny. It was sent to my wife from Catherine Bell, the governess who visited you a few months back.'

In response to the surprised lift of Fanny's eyebrows, the policeman said, 'My wife took her to the railway station after her visit to the ragged school, when she came up to tell you about Fergus, if you remember. They've written to each other regularly since then. In fact, we've been worried because we hadn't heard from her for a couple of weeks. Now we know why – although she hasn't explained herself very well.'

As Fanny read the letter her face paled. After apologising for not replying to the last letter from Ivor's wife, Catherine informed her that 'due to tragic circumstances', her life had changed dramatically. She was no longer in employment as governess to Sarah Cunningham. She regretted that she also had upsetting news for Ivor and Fanny too – news concerning Fergus. She did not explain what this was, but said she intended paying a visit to Fanny at the ragged school, when she would explain all to them.

'But . . . what does this mean, Ivor?' Fanny was alarmed. 'What could be the upsetting news about Fergus?'

'I don't know any more than is in the letter, Miss Fanny. But you'll notice the date when she says she intends coming to Bristol. It's tomorrow – and of course she'll find the ragged school closed because of the cholera. You won't be there, I'll be on duty, and my wife has to go to take care of her mother . . .'

'I'll go down and open the school, Ivor. It needs cleaning up ready to take pupils again. If you can't get to the school during the day, I'll keep Catherine there until you can.'

'Thank you.' Ivor's relief was evident. 'My wife's almost as worried about what might have happened to Catherine as you must be about Fergus.'

'Well, we should both know tomorrow.'

'I just hope it's not too serious, that's all. But how is Becky's baby? Do you still have her here?'

'She's coming on wonderfully! Would you like to see her, as you're here?'

'I've taken up enough of your time – and you have guests.'

'They are Father's friends, not mine, Ivor. Come along. You must see the nursery I've had decorated for her – and the cot. It was made especially and is a delightful piece of carpentry.'

Ivor threw her a concerned look. Fanny saw it and made a quick gesture of resignation. 'I know, Ivor. Becky will want her back one day. When that day comes it will upset the servants – yes, and Father too – almost as much as it will me. But I don't think about that. I'll enjoy her for as long as I possibly can and allow the future to take care of itself.'

Catherine arrived at the ragged school late the following morning. In the meantime, Ivor had contrived his duties so that he was in St James's Square when the hackney carriage that had brought Catherine from the station drew up.

Watching from a window, Fanny saw her arrive, but gave her a few minutes to talk to Ivor. Then her attention was distracted by the surprising amount of luggage that was off-loaded in the square with Catherine.

She was in the hall to greet the governess, who entered the building with Ivor in her wake. One look at her face told Fanny that something was very seriously wrong indeed.

'Come and sit down in my office, Catherine. I have a woman in cleaning, I'll get her to make us a cup of tea. You

142

look as though you are in need of one – and you have so much luggage with you! Are you moving to Bristol?'

'I really don't know yet where I'm going. I haven't had time to make any sensible decisions. I have an aunt who lives near Oxford. I may end up there. Just at the moment I feel that my whole life has collapsed around me – as indeed it has.'

Catherine fought back her tears as she said, 'Sarah's been taken from me and sent to a boarding school. Just at a time when the poor child is in need of someone to love and comfort her.'

'But why? What's happened? The last time we met we spoke of this happening one day, but you thought it would be at some time in the future. Not now. Isn't this all rather sudden?'

'The whole thing is tragic . . .' Although she was trying very hard to maintain control of herself, a tear escaped and trickled down Catherine's cheek. 'Poor Sarah's been made an orphan. Her dear father was lost at sea. His ship was wrecked off the coast of India. Sarah's become a ward of her grandfather.'

Fanny was no longer listening. Fergus had been on Captain Cunningham's ship! Was he dead too?

Catherine saw Fanny's horrified expression and was aware of its cause. 'I'm sorry . . . I know you're concerned for Mr Vincent, but I know very little more. I can tell you there were *some* survivors, only very few, apparently, but I don't know if he was among them.'

'Tell us all you know of what happened,' Ivor spoke for Fanny.

'I heard so very little. It seems nobody knows anything very much. The ship was sunk off the Indian coast on its way to Calcutta. There was an explosion as a result of which most of the men were lost . . . That's about all I know.'

'How many is "most"?' asked Fanny. 'Do you know exactly how many were *saved*?'

'No. Even the Admiralty doesn't know. Sarah's grandfather has been to London to see them. It seems that all is in a state of confusion in India. Much of the native army there had mutinied. Ships are on their way from all over the world. A Naval Brigade is marching inland and it's thought the *Venus* survivors have gone with it. The Admiralty says it is awaiting further details but has no idea when they might be received.'

Fanny tried to hide the deep distress she felt. 'I wrote to Fergus, telling him about Lucy.' She tried to control her voice as she added, 'I might never know if the letter reached him. If he was aware he had a daughter . . .'

At that moment a woman entered the office. In her hands she carefully balanced a tray, carrying a pot of tea and some cups.

Her arrival helped to break the drama of the moment. Suddenly briskly efficient, Fanny said, 'Let's have some tea, shall we? You must be ready for something after your journey and all the anguish you've been through, Catherine. Now, while we're having this, let's discuss your future. Do you have any money?'

'Yes. Captain Cunningham has kindly left me a small annuity in his will, but I would still like to work at something.'

'Well, for the time being you'll stay with me, at Clifton. I could do with someone responsible there to look after Lucy. When she returns to her mother I would appreciate some intelligent help here in the school. But you and I can talk about that later.'

'What will you tell Becky, Miss Fanny?' The question came from Ivor.

'What is there to tell? We know nothing certain of Fergus – and for now that's exactly what we will tell her. Nothing. But talking of Becky reminds me . . . I must go and see her again soon, to give her some more of the money Fergus left for her.'

Fanny seemed to have regained full control of herself once more.

'I think you'd better leave going into Lewin's Mead for a while,' said Ivor. 'The cholera epidemic is on the wane, but I heard the other day that two more girls died in the house next to where Becky lives. They were friends of the O'Ryan children.'

144

'Thank you for the warning, Ivor. Do you think you could learn more of the situation there for me? If you do, come to the house this evening and let me know exactly what it is. By then I hope Catherine will have settled in a little and we can all have a chat about things.'

Fanny was trying very hard to push thoughts of what might have happened to Fergus to the back of her mind. At the same time she was formulating plans for her future course of action.

She would write to the Admiralty in London, asking for news of Fergus. Someone must have details of what had happened to him. That night too, she would spend a couple of hours praying for him.

Two days after the arrival of Catherine in Bristol, Simon McAllister found his way to the ragged school. Fanny came into the hall as he was explaining to a member of her staff that he had come to the school to speak to her.

'What is it you want, Mr McAllister?' she asked, briskly. 'We are preparing the school for its re-opening and are extremely busy.'

'I've come on behalf of Becky. She's in need of more of her money.'

'Nonsense! The money I gave her should last for another week, at least.'

Fanny hid her guilt in belligerence. She had intended taking money to Becky before today. However, she viewed the blind man suspiciously. 'Is it Becky who wants the money – or is it you?'

Simon would have been entitled to take offence at her question. Instead, he said patiently, 'I had to use some of Becky's money to buy things from the pharmacist for her when she had cholera.'

'Becky has had cholera?' Fanny was taken aback. 'I'm sorry, I didn't know.'

'You *do* surprise me, Miss Tennant. I had assumed you knew all there was to know about the people who live in Lewin's Mead.'

Fanny flushed angrily. 'Thank you for informing me of

Becky's illness and of her needs, Mr McAllister. Is she cured now? If so, she is probably quite capable of coming here and collecting the money for herself.'

'She has had a very severe bout of cholera. I didn't think she would survive. I believe it's a miracle that she did. She certainly won't be fit enough to leave the house for some time to come. She's still very weak.'

'Very well, I'll come to the house and bring money for her.'

'Thank you. Perhaps you'll be kind enough to bring some food too. I find shopping in unfamiliar shops rather difficult and she is in need of all the extra nourishment she can get.'

It was obvious to Simon that Fanny Tennant did not trust him with Becky's money and he added, 'Please come as soon as possible. There are a number of things she needs as a matter of urgency.'

He paused. There was something he felt he should say, but he could not make up his mind how it should be put.

When Simon reached a decision, he said, 'Becky is talking of taking Lucy back because she misses her so much. I've persuaded her it would be advisable to wait until there hasn't been a case of cholera in Lewin's Mead for a week or two. Unfortunately, she's very lonely. Sitting in her room thinking about things isn't good for her.'

'I'll visit her just as soon as I am able. In the meantime . . . is it too much to expect you to contribute something towards the household bills?'

'No. Friends should always help each other in times of need. I've paid Becky's rent for the past three weeks. Unfortunately, I also have to pay for the upkeep of my own room and my funds are not unlimited. Bristol innkeepers are reluctant to employ a troubador who lives in Lewin's Mead while the spectre of cholera still hovers over the place.'

It was not until Simon had made his way from the ragged school, hand outstretched to feel his way, that the full import of what he had said registered with Fanny.

The blind Scotsman had said he was *not* living with Becky, as she had assumed.

But of more immediate importance to her was the information that Becky was contemplating having Lucy returned to her in the Back Lane attic room.

Fanny had grown ever fonder of Lucy while the baby had been living in Clifton and was determined that she should not be brought up in the Lewin's Mead slum. With such uncertainty over whether Fergus was still alive she believed there was no one but herself who cared where Lucy lived.

Furthermore, there was no doubt that if Lucy was brought up by a mother who earned a living by taking men back to her bed, she would end up doing the same.

It was a prospect that was unthinkable to Fanny. For Fergus's sake, she would not allow it to happen.

Chapter 18

Fanny visited Becky the day after speaking to Simon. She was shocked by her appearance. She had believed the blind musician to be exaggerating Becky's condition in a bid to ensure the money for her was forthcoming. Now she realised Becky must have been very ill indeed.

She was seated in a chair close to the window. There was nothing outside for her to see except the damp grey rooftops but she seemed too listless to care.

When Becky spoke, it was to ask her visitor about Lucy.

'She's well. A lovely, happy, healthy child. She has a splendid nanny too. Do you remember Catherine Bell? She was with me when I last came to visit you? She's staying with me at Clifton and has taken over caring for Lucy.'

'I want to look after her myself.'

'Of course you do,' said Fanny soothingly. 'But you certainly aren't capable of caring for a child at the moment.'

'I'm a lot better now, thanks to Simon. If it hadn't been for him, I'd be dead. I may have more water than blood in my veins now, but at least I'm alive.'

'I'm sorry, I don't understand . . .'

Becky explained as best she could the treatment given to her by Simon. It made Fanny realise once again that he had told her the truth about spending money at the pharmacist's. It also alarmed her.

'What qualifications does Mr McAllister have to do such a thing? There can be no precedent for a *doctor* carrying out such treatment for cholera, let alone a layman. Had you died he could have been charged with your murder – and undoubtedly convicted. I've never heard of anything like it!'

'I didn't die – and he's the one who saved me,' declared Becky defensively. 'Anyway, Simon was training to be a doctor when he went blind. He knew what he was doing.'

The claim that Simon McAllister had some medical training took Fanny by surprise. She had already realised he was an educated man and had not always sung and played in taverns to earn a living. But a doctor! Fanny had grave doubts about him.

'Who told you . . . Simon?'

'Yes, and I believe him. So would you too if he'd cured you of cholera.'

Fanny conceded to herself that Becky had a very valid point, but she would admit it to no one else. 'I'm glad you're on the mend, Becky. If there is anything I can do for you, please get word to me.'

'When can I have Lucy back?'

'As soon as you are fully well I would like to talk to you about it.'

Becky bridled immediately and Fanny said, hurriedly, 'She is your baby, Becky, but she deserves more than a future in Lewin's Mead – and so do you. Think of what Fergus would have wanted for you and your baby.'

'If Fergus had wanted anything for me and Lucy, he would have stayed here and made sure we got it, instead of going off and leaving me on my own.'

Had it not been for the news Catherine had brought to Bristol with her, Fanny might have argued with Becky. Instead, she said, 'We'll talk about that when you are fully recovered. There's a place for both you and Lucy in Clifton, in my house.'

'I don't want to live in Clifton. I *like* it here in Lewin's Mead.'

Fanny might have argued that no one in their right mind would choose to live in Lewin's Mead in preference to Clifton. As it was, she kept quiet. She could not break the news about Fergus to Becky. She was far too sick to take such a blow. If she needed to be told at all, it was best kept until she had more strength. Time to argue about Lucy's future then, too.

On her way out of the house, Fanny met Simon McAllister. He was making his way up the stairs between the hall and the first floor.

'Good morning, Mr McAllister. I've just been to see Becky and listened to her singing your praises. Your somewhat unorthodox medical methods seem to have worked – in this instance. However, as you are *not* a qualified doctor may I suggest you practise no more quackery. You may not have such fortunate results next time.'

'Thank you for your concern, Miss Tennant, but I practised no *quackery*. The treatment I carried out was tried and found remarkably successful by a Doctor Snow. He dedicated his life to the study of cholera and the means of curing it. He impressed all the medical students at Edinburgh University who heard him speak.'

'Are you saying you *were* a medical student?'

'Yes, indeed. When blindness struck I was in my final year. Within months of qualification.' Simon shrugged. 'But have you ever heard of a blind doctor?'

'Oh! I am sorry for doubting your ability, Mr McAllister. I thought it might have been something you said in order to impress Becky.'

'Why should I want to impress Becky . . . or anyone else, Miss Tennant? I was taught certain medical skills. If it means I am able to help anyone, then I will. If not . . . well, I am told I am not unmusical.'

Fanny was looking at Simon speculatively as he spoke. Now she said, 'Have you ever taught in a school, Mr McAllister – any school?'

'Never. What would I teach?'

'Music, perhaps? I feel it is something that might well enrich the lives of the children who attend the ragged school. Few will have had an opportunity either to enjoy or understand music.'

'I agree it might well bring something into their lives that they have never before experienced, but I am blind, Miss Tennant. Your children are from Lewin's Mead. They are taught from infancy to exploit the slightest weakness in anyone. How could I possibly teach them anything?'

'Yours is the mistake that so many people make who have not taught these children, Mr McAllister. They are bright. Very bright, many of them. Show them something new and they are eager to learn all they can about it. I believe you accompany yourself on the fiddle when you are singing. Do you play any other musical instruments?'

'Yes, the flute, penny whistle and the harmonica.'

'The penny whistle would be a wonderful instrument for the children to learn to play. If any of them showed talent I would be happy to purchase instruments for them. Will you come to the school to teach them? Say, twice a week, on Tuesdays and Thursdays? There will be a fee paid, of course. It will not be over-generous, but I have no doubt you will be able to make use of it.'

Simon was silent for a few moments and Fanny thought he was about to refuse. Then he said, 'You are a strange woman, Miss Tennant. Each time we meet I am forced to change my opinion of you. All right, I will come to the ragged school and introduce your pupils to music. If only one or two of them enjoy it then it will have been worthwhile.'

He began to make his way up the stairs once more, pausing at the first-floor landing to say, 'No doubt Becky mentioned having Lucy back with her again. I would like to think you were able to come up with an argument for bringing Lucy up outside Lewin's Mead. For taking Becky away too. If you haven't, then I suggest you go home and think very seriously about it. Becky is determined to bring Lucy up herself – and I would support that aim. However, I may be blind, but I don't need eyes to know about Lewin's Mead. If Lucy were mine I would fight tooth and nail to have her brought up somewhere else. Work on it, Miss Tennant. You'll find I am on your side in this.'

As she walked away from Back Lane, Fanny thought that if Becky needed to have a new man in her life, Fergus would have approved of Simon McAllister. She found she was thinking about him in a more sympathetic light too.

Chapter 19

It was another three weeks before Becky was fit enough to make the journey to Clifton in company with Simon. The ragged school had re-opened a few days earlier and she had been there twice to ask Fanny to bring Lucy from Clifton. Fanny had flatly refused.

A number of reasons had been given for the refusal. The main one was that although there had been no more cholera cases in the area, there was a high incidence of measles among children attending the school. It would be foolish to expose Lucy to such dangers unnecessarily.

At least, this was Fanny's reasoning – and she had possession of the baby.

Despite Becky's protests that she was well enough to walk to Clifton, Simon insisted they take a hackney carriage. Fanny had told him there were a number of steep hills to climb on the way to her home. Becky was not sufficiently recovered to make such a journey on foot.

When they reached the house, Fanny was in the hallway, about to take Lucy for a walk. With her was Catherine.

Her eyes filled with tears, Becky held out her arms. Reluctantly, Lucy was handed over to her. Becky cuddled her close, rocking back and forth. When she could trust her voice, she said, 'She's grown! She's grown so much.'

Lucy was five months old now and Becky had been parted from her for more than half this time.

'She's an absolutely lovely baby, Becky,' said Catherine, gently. 'I shall miss her so much when she's gone.'

'I'm hoping we might not need to lose her altogether,' said Fanny.

Becky looked up at her sharply. 'I'm not leaving her here! She's coming home with me.'

'I'm not suggesting you should leave her, but that you too should come and stay here with her. Get away from the smells and diseases of Lewin's Mead. It's the best start in life you could possibly give to Lucy.'

'There's nothing wrong with the place we have in Lewin's Mead. It's a good room and as snug and dry as anywhere else you might name.'

'I'm not saying anything about your *room*, Becky. You keep that well. It's Lewin's Mead itself about which I'm concerned. It's no place to bring up a child. Especially a girl. Surely you must see that for yourself?'

'*I* was brought up there.'

Fanny bit back an obvious retort and said patiently, 'You had a tragic childhood, Becky. Surely you want something better for Lucy? I know Fergus would.'

'You've heard from him?' Becky's eagerness was so evident, it hurt.

'No, Becky. But you know what I mean.' Becky would have to know the truth about Fergus some time, but this was not the moment to break such news to her. 'Besides, there's another reason.'

Catherine looked at her apprehensively, fearing she was about to disclose the news they had received about the fate of the ship on which Fergus had been taking passage to India.

'The City Corporation have had a meeting about Lewin's Mead. Because of the latest cholera epidemic and the general state of the place, they are going to make a start on knocking down some of the worst parts of it.'

'Can they do that? What about all the people living there?'

'The Corporation will need to make some arrangements for them, Becky, so it's not going to happen immediately – but it *will* happen. Isn't it much better to leave now, while you have a choice of where to go and what to do? Begin a new life, you and Lucy.'

'What if Fergus comes back looking for me there and finds Back Lane has been pulled down?'

153

The lie was harder this time, but it came nevertheless. 'If you weren't there I don't doubt he'd come to the ragged school to ask for news of you. If I could tell him you were living here, in Clifton with his baby, he would be overjoyed.'

Fanny was encouraged by the fact that Becky had not rejected her suggestion out of hand. 'You would have the freedom to come and go as and when you liked, Becky.'

'You want me to live here? In this house? I wouldn't like that. It's too big. Too grand.'

'Can I make a suggestion?' The question came from Catherine and she did not wait for a reply. Talking to Fanny, she said, 'The other day you showed me over the place where Fergus lived and painted when he was in Clifton. The studio in Lady Hammond's garden. That would be ideal, surely? It would be like Becky's own little house – that's if Lady Hammond would allow her to use it, of course.'

'I'm sure she would,' said Fanny. 'It's been empty since Fergus left.'

'But . . . Lucy and I would be all alone there. I'd have no one to talk to. It would drive me mad!'

'I think I have the answer to that problem too,' said Catherine. 'I'm very happy in your house, Fanny, but I do feel I'm imposing upon you and your father by remaining here. If Becky could put up with me it would be far more satisfactory were I to share the studio with her. I could also help with Lucy sometimes – and I would dearly love that.'

Fanny had a suspicion that Catherine was making the offer because she knew how desperately keen Fanny herself was to keep Lucy from returning to Lewin's Mead. She seized on the idea immediately.

'It sounds a wonderful idea, Catherine. What do you think, Becky?'

'I . . . I don't know. I've never lived outside Lewin's Mead. I'm not sure I could.'

'May I say something?' For the first time, Simon entered the discussion. 'Why don't you give it a try, Becky? You can keep the room in Lewin's Mead for a month or two, just in case things don't work. I'm living in the house, so I could

154

take care of it for you. I'm sure Iris would help too, if necessary.'

'There!' said Fanny, triumphantly. 'Even Simon thinks it's a good idea.'

'Give it a try, Becky . . . please!' The plea came from Catherine. 'I've grown to love Lucy very much in the short time I've known her. I would like to get to know you better too. I . . . I only knew Fergus during the week before he went away, but I respected him immensely. If I could help you and his baby to enjoy a new and better way of life, I would feel I'd done something really worthwhile. Truly I would.'

Catherine's voice seemed in danger of breaking at this point. Knowing the tragic secret they shared, Fanny feared Becky would suspect something.

She was wrong. Catherine's plea and Simon's offer won her round.

'All right then. I'll come and live in Clifton – just to give it a try, mind. If I don't like it then I'm going back to Lewin's Mead – and I don't want you to try and stop me.'

'No one will try to stop you from doing anything you really want to do, Becky. You've made the right decision. Fergus would be proud of you, I'm quite certain of that.'

Chapter 20

'I don't know how you put up with *her* without losing your temper. She's so *bossy*!'

Becky made the comment to Catherine. Earlier that day, Fanny had made her third visit in two days to the small Clifton cottage in the garden of Lady Hammond's home. She had left after 'suggesting' to Catherine and Becky they should consider re-arranging some of the furniture in the large room that had once been Fergus's studio.

'True,' agreed Catherine. 'It's something to do with her being a teacher, I suppose. Mind you, she'd be very hurt if you told her you thought she was bossy. Fanny's a very kind person at heart. She absolutely adores Lucy – and she'd give her life for any one of the children who attend her ragged school.'

'Yes, I suppose so.' Becky carefully placed the flat-iron she was using on its stand and tried to smooth out the baby dress she was ironing. It was one of the many dresses Fanny had bought for Lucy.

Eventually she dropped the dress on the table in exasperation. 'Just look at this. There are so many frills and flounces . . . She'd never have bought it if she'd had to iron it herself.'

Catherine smiled sympathetically. 'Well, she did suggest that one of her servants should come here and help out . . . But let me try. I'm probably more used to ironing baby clothes than you.'

Becky's lips tightened in immediate resentment, and Catherine added, hurriedly. 'What I mean is . . . I've spent my whole life looking after children and their clothes. It's not great accomplishment, but it's *all* I'm good at.'

Her appeasement worked and Becky stepped aside to watch the ex-governess deal quickly and efficiently with the small dress.

'Can you imagine me telling a servant what to do?' asked Becky. 'She'd know far more than me of what goes on in a proper house. She'd know I didn't belong here.'

'Don't put yourself down, Becky. Fanny's told me how quick you were to learn when you had some schooling. She thinks you're a very able girl.'

'No, she doesn't. She puts up with me because of Fergus, that's all. She's always fancied him. Mind you, *I* only learnt things because I knew that's what he wanted me to do.'

Catherine had no wish to bring Fergus into the conversation. She tried to change the subject by saying how pretty was the dress she was ironing. But Becky would not be sidetracked.

'Tell me again about meeting up with Fergus. Did he show you any sketches of me? He took some of them with him, I know.'

'Yes, I saw them.' Catherine wished she could end this conversation.

'He's a very good artist, isn't he?'

'Yes, Becky, he's a wonderful artist. Now . . .'

'I wonder what he's doing now? What do *you* think he's doing?'

'Painting, I expect. That's obviously what he enjoys doing best.'

'Do you think he'll come back to me when he hears about Lucy? Fanny Tennant's written to tell him. She told me she was going to, anyway.'

'Then I'm quite sure she has. She's very good at keeping her word.'

'I think he'll come back. When he does, I shall spend the rest of my life making up to him for all the trouble I've caused. It was my fault he went away, I think. It wasn't as though I didn't love him enough – or that he didn't love me. It was . . . It was a mistake, that's all. He'd left me enough money to live on while he was in London, but he was away

157

longer than I expected. I spent it all. It wasn't on myself. I bought him a present. A watch. I even had his name put on it.'

Catherine desperately wanted to stop Becky talking about Fergus. Knowing what she did about him, it hurt.

'That was a foolish thing to do, Becky. A very generous thing, of course. But quite foolish.'

'I suppose it was. It's like what I said to Miss Fanny in the first place – I don't belong here, in Clifton, among people who always think before doing things. I expect you always think about what you're going to do, don't you?'

'Usually, Becky, but I'm not so certain I always *do* the sensible thing.'

Suddenly changing the subject, Becky asked, 'Are you soft on Sergeant Primrose?'

'Of course not!' Catherine was genuinely shocked. 'He's a married man. As a matter of fact, his wife is a friend of mine.'

'It's funny, really. You don't think of people falling for coppers. At least, you don't when you live in Lewin's Mead.' Aware that she was being less than sensitive, Becky said hurriedly, 'Mind you, Ivor Primrose isn't an ordinary sort of copper. He's helped me once or twice, and him and Fergus were friends.'

'So I believe and, as you say, Ivor isn't an ordinary sort of "copper". Miss Fanny thinks very highly of him.'

As they were talking, Becky had taken the flat-iron back from Catherine and was working on a less frilly dress.

'Would you marry a copper?'

'I would no doubt need to think about it. I'm not certain it would be easy to live with a man who did such demanding work.'

Becky was quiet for a few minutes. Then she asked, 'Why did you leave the place where you worked before coming here? When you came visiting me with Fanny I thought you were happy there.'

Once again, Catherine felt she was on dangerous ground. 'Sarah . . . that's the girl I cared for, was sent off to boarding school.'

Catherine told herself this was not a lie. She was merely concealing the *whole* truth. To her relief, Becky accepted the explanation without question.

'I suppose that's the trouble with working for rich people. I'd never send Lucy away. I want to be the sort of mum to her that I never had.'

After a few more moments of silence, she added, wistfully, 'I'd like her to have a dad too. Then we'd be a proper family, wouldn't we?'

Close to tears, Catherine put her arms about Becky and hugged her.

'Yes, Becky. Then you'd all be a proper family.'

That afternoon Becky was seated in the living room of the small house with Lucy on her lap when there came a knock at the door.

Catherine went to see who was there. When she returned she tried hard to hide her disapproval. 'You have a visitor, Becky.'

Walking behind her, smiling at Becky, was Maude.

Before Becky could greet her, Maude blurted out, 'I just had to come and see you. To see how you're keeping, and to say how sorry I am.'

Puzzled, Becky said, 'Sorry for what?'

'Sorry to hear about what happened to Fergus's ship. The *Venus*. Isn't that the one you told me he'd left England on?'

'That's right, but what about it?'

'It's been blown up. Somewhere off the coast of India. Surely you know about it? I took a sailor home last night. He was off a ship that's just come back from there. He told me about it.'

Becky seemed unable to take in Maude's statement and a distressed Catherine said, 'Look, let's talk about it later. Not now.'

Becky looked from Maude to Catherine and said, 'You've known about this all the time, haven't you? You've known all along. You must have done because you worked for the captain of the *Venus*. *That's* why you left and came to Bristol.'

159

'Nothing's known for certain at the moment, Becky. Fanny's father's written to the Admiralty to try to find out more details . . .'

'So she knows too? Maude, tell me what else this sailor told you.'

Maude had always possessed a malicious streak, especially where Becky was concerned. She was eager to tell all she knew, although she pretended reluctance. 'I feel awful that I've been the one to break the news to you, Becky, but you have a right to know. Fergus's ship was blown up off the Indian coast. Some gunpowder blew up, or something. The captain died and so did almost all the other men on the ship.'

Becky looked to Catherine once more, white-faced and shaking now. 'Was Fergus one of those who died?'

'We don't know yet, Becky. That's why we haven't said anything to you. We didn't want you upset until something was known for certain.'

'The seaman who told me said he'd sailed that coast. He said there's so many sharks about, and storms come up so sudden, that shipwrecked sailors haven't got a chance.'

'That's a cruel and unnecessary thing to say, Maude,' said Catherine, rounding on her angrily. 'We know there are survivors from the *Venus*. We just don't know how many, or who they are at the moment.'

Suddenly, Becky shook her head. 'No! You must think Fergus is dead or you'd have told me what had happened. Instead, you've been lying to me.'

'Only because you've been too ill to hear anything about it, Becky. That's the only reason, I swear it is.'

'I'm not ill now, yet you were lying to me only an hour or two ago.'

'Not lies, Becky, I promise you . . .'

'Your promises mean nothing. You've lied to me all along, you and Fanny. Why? Why did you let me go on talking about my hopes that Fergus would come back one day? It was cruel.'

Suddenly, Becky's voice broke and she could not say any more. She was devastated by Maude's revelation. She felt she wanted to take herself off to a dark corner somewhere and crouch there by herself until all she had heard had sunk in properly.

But she could never again go off anywhere by herself. She had Lucy to consider – and she was more important than ever now.

'Becky, listen to me. There's still a chance that Fergus *will* come back to you. A number of men *were* saved from the *Venus*. Honestly. Hopefully, Fergus is among them. *I* believe he's alive. You've been very ill and there was no sense in worrying you unnecessarily.'

'Well, you can tell Fanny Tennant that she need never bother about me again. She's never been interested in *me*, not really, she hasn't. It was always Fergus – and she tried hard to get him away from me. She never stopped trying, right up to the time he went. Now he's gone it's Lucy she wants. Well, she's not having her. Lucy's mine and I'm not giving her up for anyone. We're both going back where we belong. To Lewin's Mead.'

'That's right, Becky. It's high time you told that bossy Fanny Tennant where to get off,' Maude urged. 'But it doesn't mean you've got to give up anything that's rightfully yours. She's keeping money of yours, remember? You make sure she sends it to you, regular. Blind Simon can bring it. He's working at the ragged school now.'

Becky said nothing, she was choking on a sob and fighting a losing battle to blink back tears as she picked up things in the room that belonged to her and Lucy. She would take nothing given to Lucy by Fanny Tennant. Such things would be unsuitable for Lewin's Mead.

For these few days she had tried to settle in to an alien way of life, but it had not worked. Had Fergus been with her it might have been different. She choked up again. She would have to learn not to think about Fergus now.

She was on her own and returning to where she belonged. She was taking Lucy back to the place where she had been born.

Lewin's Mead.

BOOK THREE

BOOK THREE.

Chapter 1

Fergus very soon discovered that a civilian artist on board a man-o'-war enjoyed a vastly superior standard of comfort to that he had once experienced as a sailor on the lower deck. He was given a cabin of his own and shared the wardroom facilities enjoyed by the ship's officers. The majority came from wealthy families and strove to maintain the standard of living to which they were accustomed ashore.

The *Venus* was a happy ship. When the weather was fair, and the vessel making good progress, there was a relaxed atmosphere on board. This in spite of the fact that more than six hundred men were accommodated on the ship.

Three days out of Plymouth, as they were slowly overhauling a heavily laden merchantman, Fergus brought a canvas up to the quarterdeck and began painting the scene.

The merchantman under full sail was a fascinating subject. It rode low in the water with a considerable swell rising and falling about it.

Fergus had plenty of time for his composition. *Venus* was under full sail, but it took more than two hours to pass the other ship.

The officer on duty on the upper deck was Lieutenant Lewis Callington – the *Honourable* Lewis Callington, heir to a Cornish Viscountcy.

The lieutenant was extremely friendly, and had been since Fergus first came on board at Plymouth. It was Lewis who had allocated him a cabin. Now he came across to watch Fergus at work.

After studying the painting for some minutes in silence,

165

he said, 'Your painting reminds me of some of my reasons for joining the Royal Navy. You've captured both the magic of a ship under sail, and the sheer beauty of the sea.'

Without looking up from his painting, Fergus said, conversationally, 'I know what you mean. Every ship has an individual beauty. No doubt the *Venus* looks even more impressive to the men on the merchantman.'

'In my opinion, a man-o'-war under full sail is one of the most memorable sights that anyone could wish to view. It's an unforgettable experience.'

Looking critically at Fergus's painting, Lewis Callington said, 'That's very good, Fergus. Very good indeed. Is it part of the portfolio you're putting together for Sir James Stott?'

The officers on board were well aware that he was there at the express wish of the Admiral of the Fleet. Because of this they treated him with a great deal of respect.

'No. I doubt if there is a shortage of paintings of merchantmen in any gallery in London. I'm painting this purely for pleasure.'

'Good! I would like to buy it from you when it's completed.'

Fergus hesitated. Lieutenant Callington had been very good to him since he had come aboard. He did not like charging him for the painting.

The naval officer correctly guessed the reason for Fergus's hesitation, 'I really would like the painting, but I insist upon paying. After all, it will be an investment. If you agree, I will send it home from the next port of call.'

Fergus gave in gracefully. 'All right – it's yours.' The price he suggested was considerably lower than he would have charged anyone else and Lieutenant Callington was delighted.

'When I leave the navy it will hang in the study of Pendower House, in Cornwall, to remind me of more carefree days. I hope you might visit me and see it there, when you return from India.'

Fergus looked at Lewis Callington in surprise. 'But you will be in the navy for many more years, surely? Are you not a career officer?'

166

Callington was well liked by the crew and his fellow officers. He was also a very efficient seaman. Fergus was convinced he would reach flag officer rank at some time in the future.

Lewis Callington shook his head. 'One day – probably sooner than I would wish – I will succeed to my father's Viscountcy. I am an only son. When that day arrives I must return home and settle down to manage the family estates. In the meantime, I intend enjoying whatever adventures come my way.'

'Do you think we are likely to find any real excitement on this mission? Everyone seems to think the talk of mutiny in India is very much exaggerated. That we'll find things quiet when we arrive there.'

'That is also the opinion of one of my uncles. He is a general with the Company's army in India and is adamant that he would trust his own life, and that of his family, to the sepoys of his regiment. I hope such faith in his men is justified. I sometimes feel we have pushed things too far, too quickly, in India. Deposed too many of its rajahs and taken their lands under our "protection". When I was there some three years ago I sensed a deep resentment among educated Indians. My uncle dismissed such views out of hand, but since then they have had to put down more than one serious outbreak of trouble. We've trained a native army of almost half a million men and trained them well. Most have gained battle experience on the border with Afghanistan. It would be a tough army to defeat should it be turned against us.'

'Then let's hope things have cooled down by the time we reach India and it isn't necessary for us to fight anyone.'

Even as he spoke, Fergus's thoughts had already strayed from the subject of what might happen when *Venus* reached India. The man-o'-war had drawn level with the merchantman now and he was busily filling in details he had not been able to see properly before.

An hour later, the cargo-carrying ship had fallen well astern. Fergus had achieved what he had intended. He gathered up his painting materials. The picture would be

167

completed in his cabin, in due course.

As he passed Lieutenant Callington, Fergus looked up at the sky and said, 'It looks as though we might have some bad weather.'

The high clouds formed a herringbone pattern against a pale sky and the wind was increasing in strength.

Lewis Callington nodded his agreement. 'It certainly looks like it. But there's no need to worry. *Venus* behaves like the lady she is, whatever the weather.'

Lewis Callington's claim for the *Venus* was put to a severe test during the next twenty-four hours. The ship encountered weather that would test its Chatham-built hull to the full.

The storm increased in intensity during the night and woke Fergus in the early hours. His cot was slung hammock-style in his cabin, but its design lessened only the effects of the ship's lateral movement. Butting through the crest of each giant wave, the man-o'-war would slide headlong down the next watery slope into the trough beyond. As it did so, Fergus felt as though he was being tossed in the air and caught again. It was part of some cruel game being played out by the elements.

Things were far more uncomfortable on the decks occupied by the seamen. Each hammock was allowed only a twenty-eight inch width. As the ship pitched and tossed, the men would bump together alarmingly. In addition, they were subject to draughts and leaks as the wind howled around the ship and waves broke over the bow and raced along the wooden deck.

Seamen trying to sleep between their duty watches became irritable with each other and with the ship. They cursed the unfortunate helmsman who could do nothing to lessen the ship's frenzied movements – but most of all they cursed the sea that was at the root of all their troubles.

In the gunroom, Harry Downton, a young midshipman who had also befriended Fergus early in the voyage, was violently ill. It was a condition that affected him whenever the vessel encountered rough weather and it made him the butt of the jibes of his fellow midshipmen.

He consoled himself with the thought that the navy's greatest admiral, Lord Nelson, had also suffered in the same way whenever he put to sea.

Towards dawn the storm lessened in ferocity, but by now Fergus was beyond sleep. He lay in his cot listening to the constant creaking and groaning of the ship's timbers and his thoughts wandered to Lewin's Mead. He remembered a storm he had once experienced there.

He had lain in bed with Becky in his arms as the wind rattled windows and moaned down the chimney of their room. Outside, there was the occasional sound of a slate sliding from the roof and, once, the crash of a falling chimney-pot.

Fergus remembered he had felt warm and safe on that occasion. Happy. His paintings had begun to sell well and all was right with the world he shared with Becky.

As he lay in his cot now, he tried to pinpoint exactly when they had begun to go wrong. Who was to blame? He for having ambition, or Becky for being unable to throw off the restrictive ties of the only life she had ever known?

He wondered if there was something more he should have done to keep them together? There must have been something . . . Fergus knew that he still missed her desperately, despite his attempts to forget all he had lost.

Yet, no matter how long he thought about it, he could find no answers. Only more questions. Perhaps he never would find an answer. He could not change himself, or his way of life. Perhaps he could have changed Becky . . .

He dismissed this thought immediately. Only Becky herself could change the way she was. He was no longer certain he wanted to change her. Certainly not *everything* about her.

Chapter 2

The *Venus* encountered many more storms during the long voyage to India. None was as ferocious as the first, but Harry Downton never mastered his sea-sickness. However, there were many interesting places to see, to help the unfortunate midshipman and the crew to forget the perils and discomfort of bad weather.

The first port of call was Lisbon, reached only a few days after the ship had been battered by the sea in the Bay of Biscay. Here the officers were given the hospitality of the many British residents and the officials of the city.

The sailors were not allowed to go ashore, but they did not lack 'entertainment'. Boatloads of women were rowed out to the ship's anchorage and brought with them a plentiful supply of cheap wine.

The scenes were repeated at the next port of call, Tenerife in the Canary Islands – also known as the 'Fortunate Islands'. This brief interlude was followed by a long haul down the coast of West Africa to the Cape of Good Hope and the naval base at Simon's Bay.

The *Venus* was delayed here while some damaged spars and rigging were replaced and the crew given the rare luxury of going ashore. When repairs were completed to the satisfaction of Captain Cunningham, the ship headed northwards once again, but now they were hugging Africa's east coast.

Eventually, the ship turned away from Africa. Striking out across the wide Indian Ocean, it headed for the vast sub-continent of India.

For the new sailors on board *Venus*, this was one of the

most exciting legs of the long voyage. There were frequent sightings of whales and porpoises. Sharks too. The triangular fins of the ocean predators followed the ship for miles. A bucket of rubbish thrown over the stern provoked a frenzy of activity among the streamlined killers and it became a daily entertainment for the sailors.

There were also 'flying' fish here. Their elongated pectoral fins enabled them to glide for long distances clear of the water when being pursued by larger fish. A number of them landed on the deck of *Venus* and were promptly seized by the seamen.

During their off-duty hours the men who had captured these unusual fish would patiently gut and clean their prizes before embalming them. One day they would be shown to disbelieving relatives in England. A few of the seamen were more mercenary. Their work would be offered for sale in the ports of the world.

Fergus made many drawings of these unique creatures. The sketches sometimes included the proud owners who wanted a record of one of the wonders they were seeing, whilst in the service of the Queen.

It was late-June when *Venus* edged towards a jetty at the Trincomalee naval base in Ceylon. The ship's arrival aroused a great deal of interest. By the time it berthed a government official was impatiently waiting on shore to come aboard.

Minutes later Captain Cunningham left the ship in the company of the official. Behind him, on board, officers and men speculated on the reason for such an interest in the ship's arrival.

They did not have long to wait. Even before Captain Cunningham's return, bullock-drawn wagons were lining up on the quay with victuals to be loaded on board. *Venus* would not remain at Trincomalee for very long.

Fergus was standing with Lieutenant Callington, watching the Ceylonese labourers trotting up the ship's gangway, bent double beneath enormous sacks of flour, when Captain Cunningham returned to his ship.

One look at his face as he hurried up the gangway, cursing one of the Ceylonese who was slow to get out of his way, told both watchers that something serious was afoot.

Lewis Callington saluted his commanding officer when he reached the top of the gangway. Making a cursory return of the salute, Captain Cunningham said, 'Muster all the officers on the quarterdeck, Lieutenant. I have something of importance to say to them.'

Fergus and his companion exchanged glances before the lieutenant hurried away to carry out his commanding officer's instructions. The ship's captain was given neither to hurrying, nor to curtness.

The captain did not consider it necessary to muster the crew to inform them of what was happening. Those sailors on duty nearby would be listening carefully to what he said. Within the hour, every man on board *Venus* would know as much as the ship's officers.

Ten minutes later, the assembled officers, Fergus among them, learned what had happened to cause such concern. It was as serious as Fergus had feared it might be.

The troubles in India had not faded away, as had been expected. On the contrary, the country was in a state of turmoil. When the sepoys of the East India Company's army had been issued with a new type of cartridge, word went around that it was greased with the fat of cattle and pigs.

Because of religious taboos, handling such a product was anathema to both Hindus and Moslems. It was to prove the catalyst for all the grievances the sepoys had nursed against their European overlords with increasing intensity in recent years.

Opposition to the use of the new cartridges grew until, on 10 May 1857, there was an uprising of the sepoys in the northern garrison town of Meerut. The Indian soldiers rounded on their English officers and killed them. Then they turned their attentions to the wives and families, the European officials, and their homes. The Indian 'mutiny' was under way.

Once it began, there was no turning back for the sepoys.

172

They marched upon Delhi, joined along the way by others. When Delhi fell to them, trouble erupted throughout most of northern India. Regiment after Indian regiment turned upon their officers, killing them, or putting them to flight. Next they looted treasuries and committed atrocities against British officials and their families.

There was utter panic among the Europeans, many of whom had spent a lifetime in the country, and had expected to remain here until they retired – and beyond. Now they believed that India was lost to Britain and the East India Company forever.

All this was told to the silent naval officers assembled on the quarterdeck of the *Venus*. Behind them was the background of the busy dockyard with the lush vegetation of the island of Ceylon beyond its fences.

Captain Cunningham informed his officers that word of the uprising had been sent to England, to Hong Kong, and to other British outposts. Troops and ships were on their way to restore law and order to India. The Ceylonese administrator had already sent most of the island's army to Calcutta.

However, it would be some time before soldiers from Britain reached India in any strength. The *Venus* had orders to proceed to Calcutta immediately. Once there, the ship would be moored in such a position that her guns would command the Calcutta fort. Hopefully, this would prevent any attempted mutiny by its garrison.

When this had been achieved, the marines of the *Venus*, together with volunteers from the crew, were to form a Naval Brigade. They would make their way inland to join up with European soldiers of the East India Company's army. Together they would bid to rescue the surviving men, women and children reported to be besieged in the Residency at Lucknow, and in great danger of being overrun.

Looking at the officers gathered before him, Captain Cunningham said, 'I have no need to tell you we have been asked to attempt a very difficult task. The Indian mutineers are numerous, well-armed and highly trained. We, and the soldiers we will support, are few in number. However, women and children are depending upon us to save them. They know what their fate will be if they submit to their besiegers. I know you would give the same answer to them as I gave to the Ceylonese governor, less than an hour ago. I told him the officers and men of *Venus* would do everything humanly possible to save our countrymen and women. Stores are already arriving on board. Victualling will continue day and night for as long as need be. When we are fully stored we will sail for Calcutta.

'Thank you, gentlemen. I have no need to tell you how important it is that we leave as soon as is possible. Admiral Lord Nelson once signalled to his fleet that England expected every man to do his duty. Our country expects no less from the officers and men of *Venus* in these difficult days.'

Chapter 3

'This damned weather! I can't remember it being as hot as this when I was last here.'

Lieutenant Lewis Callington slumped into a seat in the *Venus*'s wardroom and gratefully accepted a drink from the steward.

'I expect it's because there's no wind,' commented Harry Downton.

The gunroom had been filled with stores and the midshipmen were forced to share the more staid atmosphere of the wardroom with the senior ship's officers.

'If only we were underway there would at least be *some* breeze getting into the ship. The men are feeling it far more than we are. Even the simplest task is exhausting and leaves them bathed in sweat,' said Fergus, sympathetically.

Since leaving Trincomalee *Venus* had made frustratingly slow progress northwards to Calcutta. Today, as on many other days, there was no wind to fill the man-o'-war's canvas sails. They hung disconsolately from the yardarm, limp as the seamen who perspired and cursed while performing their daily, routine tasks as slowly as the watching petty officers would allow.

On the gun-decks men were engaged in repetitious gun drill. Insert an imitation cartridge in the barrel of the gun, follow it with a wad and ram it home. Then a shot was put in, followed by another wad to prevent the shot from falling out with the movement of the ship. Run out the gun, stand clear of the recoil, and pull the lanyard which activated the gunlock.

Each day only two guns were allowed to be fired using a

live charge. Extra gunpowder and shot had been loaded at Trincomalee, but it was not intended that it should be wasted on training.

In fact, so much extra gunpowder had been loaded that the gunnery officer expressed deep concern to Captain Cunningham. It had been impossible to store the powder in the safe conditions usually considered essential for such a dangerous cargo.

The captain acknowledged that facilities for securing the extra gunpowder were far from satisfactory. However, as he pointed out, these were exceptional times. Gunpowder would be sorely needed by the men of the Naval Brigade. He urged the gunnery officer to make it as secure as was possible in the present circumstances.

The gunnery officer would do his best, but he would remain a worried man until the volatile cargo was removed from the ship. A major cause for his concern was an assistant gunner who was prone to carelessness when he had been drinking heavily – and this occurred all too frequently. Strong drink and gunpowder were a dangerous combination on board a man-o'-war.

The seamen too were making far more mistakes than was usual under normal sailing conditions. When one man's hand was crushed by the recoil of a gun, Captain Cunningham called his crew together. He told them he would not tolerate anything less than absolute efficiency on board his ship, no matter what pressures they were facing. The lives of countless British women and children depended upon them. He called upon his crew to dwell upon the fate of these innocent victims of the mutiny, should *Venus* not arrive in Calcutta ready for whatever may be required of its crew.

To emphasise his determination, the following day the crew were assembled to witness the flogging of two seamen who had fought each other after a minor disagreement.

Things improved for a while when a light breeze sprang up and enabled the becalmed ship to get underway once more. However, when still a hundred miles short of its destination, the wind failed them once more.

'I feel sorry for the crew. This heat is killing.'

Fergus spoke to Lewis without looking up from his sketch pad. He was working on the latest of a series of drawings showing men stripped to the waist, carrying out their chores in the relentless heat.

Lewis Callington and Harry Downton had been standing on the deck for some time, watching him at work.

It was the second sketch pad Fergus had used since leaving Plymouth. The first, together with many of his completed paintings, had been sent from Trincomalee, to the Admiralty in London.

Fergus was later to be thankful for this forethought.

'It's going to get worse,' replied Lewis. 'Captain Cunningham feels we've wasted far too much time already. He's going to have the boats lowered tonight. *Venus* will be taken in tow. In his present mood he'll have the men pull the ship all the way to Calcutta, if necessary.'

While Harry protested as strongly as any junior officer dared, Fergus winced. If the men had to man the oars in this heat, some would die, even if they only toiled during the night hours.

Nevertheless, he appreciated Captain Cunningham's dilemma. Without a Naval Brigade and the guns to support them, women and children would die at the hands of the rebellious sepoys. Whatever he did, Captain Cunningham would be criticised.

Talking with his friend about boats being lowered gave Fergus an idea. 'Will the men be carrying out gunnery practice today?'

'Yes. They're mustering on the gun-decks right now.'

'I know the seamen have quite enough to do already, but do you think I could take a boat out and sketch them running out the guns? It will be the closest thing to a sketch of a sea action I'm likely to get. If you could arrange for the two live shots to be fired on the side where I'm working it would be even more realistic.'

After thinking about Fergus's request for a few moments, the lieutenant nodded his head. 'I'll speak to Captain

Cunningham, but he won't object. After all, you're Sir James Stott's man. Anything you want is yours – and it will provide some extra interest for the men. The captain's gig is already in the water. We'll use that. I'll have an awning rigged up to protect you while you make your sketches.'

'Can I take the gig out?' asked Harry, eagerly. Junior officers were sometimes allowed to command a small boat.

'You haven't had sufficient experience,' said Lewis. 'I'll take it myself – but you can come if you like?' he added in response to the midshipman's undisguised disappointment.

'Are you sure you don't mind?' Fergus was aware that Lewis had performed watchkeeping duties during the previous night.

'I've said so, haven't I?' A sudden grin wiped any hint of irritability from his words. 'Isn't that what friends are for?'

The gig was manned by a dozen oarsmen in addition to the lieutenant and midshipman. The crew seemed happy to be escaping from the sweltering confines of the *Venus*. It was hardly cooler out here, but merely leaving behind the low deckheads and crowded messdecks of the man-o'-war was a relief.

'How far from the ship do you need to be?'

Lewis Callington asked the question and Fergus looked over his shoulder. *Venus* rocked gently on the unruffled sea about a hundred and fifty yards away.

'Just a little further. I want to have the whole of the ship in my sketch and still leave room at the sides to fill in some sort of background later.'

He had been sketching for about half-an-hour when the *Venus* fired off her two guns. He hurried to catch the billowing clouds of gunpowder smoke on paper, when suddenly there was another explosion. Louder than the firing of the cannons, it caused him to look up and the crew of the gig to stare back at the *Venus*. A huge pall of smoke rose in the air from the centre of the ship. As the men looked on in horror, sparks and flames rose to colour the smoke.

'That's coming from the temporary powder room, close

178

to the magazine. That damned fool of an assistant gunner . . .'

Before Lewis Callington had completed his sentence there was a devastating explosion from the heart of the *Venus* that hurt Fergus's eardrums. Suddenly the whole ship erupted before the eyes of the horrified men in the gig. Masts, sails, timbers, guns, water – and men too – were flung in the air in all directions.

The gig was two hundred yards from the ship, yet debris rained around them only moments after they were struck by a blast of searing air.

Then they were hit by a wave that tumbled the men about the boat. For a moment it threatened to overturn the gig.

The turbulence ceased as suddenly as it had begun, although the gig still agitated, as though disturbed by what had occurred.

When Fergus looked again, the once magnificent man-o'-war had disappeared. All that remained were pieces of timber and other debris covering a wide area.

There were men too, pitifully few. Even as they screamed for help, the sharks that had trailed the *Venus* for many ocean miles, moved in to reap the reward of their patience.

'Quick! Get over there. Pull for the ship . . .'

Lewis Callington bellowed his orders at the numbed gig crew. Still stunned by the sheer scale of the catastrophe, they obeyed him automatically.

The largest number of live men in the water were in the area where the ship's bow had been – but here too were the greatest number of sharks.

Eleven survivors were pulled on board the gig. Eleven men from more than six hundred who had been on *Venus* when the ship exploded.

Of the eleven, six were so badly injured by the explosion and the sharks that they were dead within the hour. Three more would succumb to their injuries during the next few hours.

For more than an hour the numbed crew of the gig manoeuvred their boat among the debris. Ostensibly searching for survivors, they were reluctant to leave the remains of the ship that had provided them with security for so long.

Not until the debris had been distributed over an ever-widening area by the sea did Lieutenant Lewis Callington reluctantly bring the bow of the small vessel around to the west. He gave the order for the seamen to row for the shore that no one could see. Somewhere beyond the horizon.

Chapter 4

'Lieutenant Callington, sir . . . wake up!' Midshipman Harry Downton shook the lieutenant who was curled up in the bottom of the boat.

'What is it?' Lewis had difficulty waking from a deep and exhausted sleep.

'One of the men heard something, sir, then I heard it too.'

It was still dark, although to the east there was a lightening of the night sky. Only Fergus, Harry and two other men in the boat were fully awake. During the night hours the oarsmen had worked in watches of two, plying the oars in an endeavour to keep the boat's head pointing in the direction of the Indian coast.

'What did you hear?'

'I'm not sure. It sounded like voices. That might just have been my imagination, but it was definitely something unusual.'

'Could it have been sea birds? That would mean we are coming close to land . . .'

'Shh! There it is again, sir.'

This time there could be no mistake. Fergus and the lieutenant both heard the sound. It *was* voices. Men's voices, calling to each other, some distance away.

'Wake up!' Lewis Callington went among the sleeping men, shaking them into wakefulness. 'We're close to land. Ship your oars – quickly now! We need to hold the boat here until it's light enough to see what's ahead.'

Dawn came swiftly in this part of the world. Only minutes after the seamen had been awakened, one of them said suddenly, 'I can see trees. Palm trees.'

At first, Fergus thought the sailor was imagining things. Then he realised he could see them too. He had actually been looking at them for some moments without recognising them for what they were.

The boat was much closer to land than anyone had expected. Less than a mile away. To westward, for as far as could be seen, was a long, low, sandy shore-line fringed with trees. In shadow when the sky lightened in the east, the low-lying land had appeared to be no more than an extension of the shadowed sea.

Daylight advanced quickly. Within minutes Fergus had identified the source of the voices that had first alerted the seamen on the gig. They originated from a small fishing village about a mile or so distant, along the shore.

The fishermen saw them at about the same moment. As Fergus watched, they pointed in the direction of the gig, and their shrill, excited cries reached the ears of the seamen.

Women, children and old men spilled from flimsy, ramshackle houses located in a clearing behind the sand of the beach. Boats, almost as flimsy as the houses, were lined up on the sand. The fishermen had been dragging them towards the water when the gig came into view.

'What do we do now, sir?'

Harry put the question that was in the minds of the other sailors.

'We have very little alternative but to land at the village,' replied Lewis Callington. 'If we stay in the boat we'll all shrivel up when the sun is high.'

'What if they're hostile?' This time the question came from Fergus. 'For all we know the whole country might have risen against us.'

'It's possible,' admitted the naval officer. 'But if that's the case we'll stand more chance here than we would elsewhere. It's a small fishing village. There are probably no more than twenty-five or thirty men there. I doubt very much if they'll possess arms. What weapons can we muster between us?'

'There's an axe in the locker – and most men are carrying knives.' The young midshipman did his best to sound cheerful.

Lewis grimaced, then managed a weak smile. 'We're practically a fully armed fighting force. All right, let's get under way and head for the shore. We'll soon see what sort of a welcome they're going to give us.'

As the gig from the ill-fated *Venus* drew near to the shore and it was obvious the crew intended landing the excitement of the villagers subsided to an uneasy silence. However, Lewis Callington could see no weapons among the small crowd.

'Go straight in,' he said to the coxswain. 'The moment we touch the sand the bowmen will jump ashore and hold the boat steady. The others will ship oars and go over the side. We'll draw the boat up on the beach – but not too high. We might feel we need to leave again in a hurry.'

The angle of the beach was fairly steep and the boat was heavy. Pulling it clear of the water was hard work, yet none of the villagers came forward to help them. This in itself was unusual. Then one of the villagers who appeared to be the headman issued a command. Instantly the seamen were surrounded by eager fishermen. They slid the gig up on the sand until it straddled the highwater mark of dried seaweed and sun-bleached shells.

The headman next spoke to Lieutenant Callington, but the British naval officer shook his head. The man was speaking Bengali.

The headman began walking towards the village. Turning around as he went, he beckoned for the sailors to follow him.

Lewis hesitated uncertainly. 'I don't want to offend him unnecessarily and there are too few of us as it is, without splitting the party, but I must leave men here to guard the boat.'

'You go to the village and leave me here with two men,' said Fergus immediately. 'They can be tidying the boat while I sketch the village and the people. If we have any problems, I'll come and find you.'

The headman now returned to Lewis. Pointing first to the gig, he held his hands close together. Then, indicating the British sailors, he held his arms wide.

'He's asking where our ship is,' suggested Fergus.

'I don't think it's a good idea to let him know there's no more of us,' murmured the naval lieutenant. Pointing out to sea, he made signs that he hoped would lead the headman to believe a large man-o'-war was just over the horizon.

The senior villager seemed satisfied with the answer and smiled for the first time. Calling once more for Lewis Callington and the sailors to follow him, he headed for the village. After a few moments, the small naval party followed him, surrounded by most of the curious villagers.

Those remaining on the beach were mainly children. They crowded uncomfortably close about Fergus as he took out his pad and began to record the scene before him. This was a welcome escape for him. A way of pushing the traumatic experiences of the past twenty-four hours to the back of his mind.

He was eventually able to persuade the children to leave him by pointing out that they could be included in his sketch only by standing at least twenty paces away.

They went off quite happily, posing for the drawing. Every few minutes one would run back to him, to check that *he* was part of the sketch.

Fergus was pleased with the composition. Houses, fishing boats, a background of trees, and the children in the foreground. To one side of the village were cultivated fields with healthy crops and a small cart being pulled by a water buffalo and he managed to include much of this.

He had been working for perhaps half an hour when a young woman walked towards him along the path from the village, one hand raised to support a wicker basket, carried on her head. Tall, slim and graceful, she was dressed in a pale blue sari made from a chiffon type of material. Wrapped close about her body, the clothing accentuated her figure and height.

So striking was the woman, the seamen in the boat stopped work to watch her as she approached. Fergus hastily turned a page of his sketch pad and attempted to capture her on paper as she walked towards the beach.

184

Much to his surprise, she came straight to him. She glanced only briefly at the two men in the boat who were staring at her in open admiration.

Lowering the basket to the ground, she knelt on the sand before Fergus. Placing both her hands together in a salute, she bowed her head low before him.

'I have brought you some food.'

Fergus stopped sketching and gazed at her in astonishment. 'You speak English?!'

There was no trace of modesty in the bold gaze she gave him in return. 'You will please eat.'

'Thank you, but . . . where did you learn to speak such excellent English?'

'I studied while I worked in a temple. Afterwards I was an *ayah*, a servant, to a *memsahib* at Janithran. But this is not important for now.'

The girl gave a quick look behind her to where the boys posed for Fergus's sketch. 'I have been forbidden to speak with you. Please keep working while I set out your food – but listen very carefully.'

Bewildered, Fergus resumed sketching, wondering what it could be that she had to say that was so important – and why she wished to speak to him at all.

Head down, the woman set out a number of dishes, mixed with rice, but her words made Fergus forget that he was ravenously hungry.

'You must leave this village as quickly as you can.'

'Why?' he countered. There was no reason why this woman was to be trusted any more than the other villagers.

'The headman of the village is not friendly towards you. Three of his brothers were sepoys. One was hung for helping to kill his officers. Another is with the army of the *Nana Sahib*. The third is hiding in the jungle, near here. Between them they have killed many English *sahibs* and *memsahibs*.'

'The headman intends us harm?' Fergus was still not convinced this girl was telling the truth.

'Only the fear that your ship might call here for you soon is preventing him from killing you immediately. Many of

185

the sepoys who caused trouble in Barrackpore are hiding in the jungle near here. Word has been sent to them that you are here. You must leave as quickly as you can . . . I must go now.'

Fergus would have liked to question the woman further, but two of the small boys were coming towards them. The woman bowed once more then rose to leave.

'Wait . . . what is your name?'

'Shashi. Keep the name in your head, but do not let it reach your tongue.'

Chapter 5

While Fergus and the two seamen ate the food brought to them by the mysterious young Indian woman, he thought of what Shashi had said to him. He was still not convinced she was telling the truth, but decided he needed to discuss her warning with Lewis Callington.

Climbing to his feet, he said, 'I'm going to the village to find the lieutenant.'

'It's more likely to be that Indian girl you're hoping to see there!' replied one of the seamen. Neither of the sailors had overheard her warning, but both had been very taken with her looks.

Fergus did not confide in them now. 'When you've finished the food stay with the boat. I'll make certain someone comes to relieve you before too long.'

Carrying his sketching materials and accompanied by a dozen or so young boys, he made his way to the village. The children chattered to him incessantly along the way. It made no difference that he could understand nothing of what they said.

Guided by the boys, Fergus had no difficulty locating the shelter occupied by the other survivors from *Venus*. They had been given two large huts on the far side of the small village.

The caste system of the Hindu villagers meant they were acutely aware of the importance of rank. Lieutenant Callington and Midshipman Downton had been given one hut; the seamen occupied the other.

The boys led Fergus unhesitatingly to the hut occupied by the officers, but he soon discovered there was little privacy here. Villagers were in and out of the hut the whole time, fetching or carrying food, or simply remaining to stare in open curiosity at their European guests.

The two officers squatted on rugs, spread on the earth floor. Before them was a large quantity of food and drink.

Grinning up at Fergus as he entered, Harry Downton said, 'Hello, Fergus. Have you come to help clear some of this feast they've laid out for us? If this is a sample of life in India I think I'm going to enjoy it.'

'Make the most of it while you can,' replied Fergus, ominously. 'I don't think it's likely to last. Not here, anyway.'

To Lewis, he said, 'Do you think we could take a walk? I'll pretend to be sketching you along the way. We need to have a talk.'

Lewis Callington was clearly puzzled, but he did not question Fergus there and then. Rising to his feet, he followed him from the hut.

The two men walked away from the houses to where a team of water buffalo were being brought in from the nearby fields. They had been followed by a small knot of curious bystanders, but Fergus persuaded them to go to where the buffalo had halted, so they might be included in his sketch. It was unlikely any of them spoke English, but he was taking no chances.

When the villagers were out of hearing, Fergus began his sketch. As he worked he repeated to his companion what Shashi had told him.

'Do you believe the woman?' Lewis Callington asked the question with less scepticism than Fergus had anticipated.

'I wasn't certain at first, but I can't think of any reason why she should lie.'

'I wouldn't argue with you. Ever since we were first met by the headman and his villagers I've had a feeling that everything here isn't quite the way it should be. I haven't been able to put my finger on anything that doesn't sound vaguely foolish. But getting away from here won't be easy if the headman doesn't want us to go. We have no weapons

188

with which to back up our decision. How far away are these mutineers?'

'She didn't say, but I gained the impression they weren't too far from here.'

'We can't afford to take a chance. We'll leave this afternoon. Let's go back and tell Harry to have the crew make ready.'

Midshipman Downton returned to the officers' hut to report that the men were not happy with the lieutenant's decision.

'They're saying we'll be getting underway just before the hottest part of the day – and it's unbearably hot already. They will be collapsing with heat exhaustion.'

Harry Downton had not yet been told of the reason for the sudden order to make ready to leave. In common with the seamen, he could see no valid reason to depart when the villagers were going out of their way to make them welcome.

'I wouldn't be doing it if I didn't think it was necessary,' retorted Lewis Callington. 'Go across to their hut and tell them they're to take what food and drink they can with them to the boat. I don't know how long it will take us to reach Calcutta.'

The movement among the sailors brought the headman hurrying to the huts. Hobbling along behind him was an old man who spoke halting, unpractised English at the prompting of the village leader.

'Where are you going?' queried the old man in a thin high voice.

'To our boat,' replied Lewis Callington. He was uncomfortably aware that village men were spilling from their huts and gathering on the path that led to the beach. It was even more ominous that all the women and children seemed to have disappeared from view. 'My captain will be awaiting our return.'

'Surely not so quickly?' The old man was openly sceptical. After exchanging words with the headman, he added, 'You cannot leave in the heat of the day. Also, messengers have been sent to tell our rajah of your visit. He will wish to come here and welcome you to his lands.'

'If we do not return to the ship then our captain will come seeking us.' Lewis Callington managed a false smile. 'It would not go well with any of us if the ship had to come here to find me.'

'Think how much worse it will be if the rajah arrives and learns you have gone! He would believe you had not been made welcome. It would bring great shame upon us. No, you must stay – for tonight, at least. Let your ship come here. It will be a great honour for our humble village. A fine feast will be prepared for the captain-*sahib*.'

There was more talk between the two Indians before the old man said, 'Please, you will return inside your huts. More food will be brought. Then you must rest, away from the heat of the day. Tonight there will be much feasting with girls to dance for you.'

Both the headman and his ancient companion bowed to Lieutenant Callington before walking away, as though all had been settled. However, the village men still blocked the path the seamen would need to take. For the first time, Fergus observed that every one of them was carrying a heavy stick.

Lewis Callington saw it too. It was evident the sailors from *Venus* could not depart without a fight. He doubted whether it was one they could win.

Admitting at least a temporary defeat, he waved the delighted sailors back inside their hut.

'What's happening, sir?' The question came from Harry Downton. During the conversation between the lieutenant and the old man, the midshipman had become increasingly aware that all was not as it should be. 'Are we being held prisoner?'

The headman and his companion had passed from view now and there were no villagers within hearing.

'The village headman would protest that it was "hospitality" but, yes, I'd say we were prisoners.'

'What are we going to do about it?'

'The best thing we can do for the moment is to return to the hut and convince the villagers that we're enjoying ourselves. Then, as soon after dark as is possible, we'll get to the boat and put out to sea.'

'What will we do if they try to stop us then?' asked the young midshipman, nervously.

'We'll fight!' declared Lewis Callington, firmly. 'If we do go down, we'll take a whole lot of the villagers with us.'

Chapter 6

The uneasy state of truce between hosts and reluctant guests finally collapsed when the searing heat of the day was at its height.

In the hut he shared with Lewis Callington and the young midshipman, Fergus lay on a cotton-covered cot watching a dark green lizard. Spread-eagled against the dried-grass wall of the hut, the heat was such that the reptile was too lethargic to take a plump blue-green fly, gyrating on an invisible axis, only inches from its nose.

Perspiration oozed from every pore of Fergus's body, but he was unable to call up the sleep that would give him temporary relief from the heat. The past twenty-four hours had been so eventful his mind would not be still. Brushing a persistent fly from his eye, he switched his gaze to the roof above him. Here two shield-shaped beetles trundled, one behind the other, along a wooden roof support, each carrying a fragment of leaf.

Suddenly there was a faint sound at the doorway. He turned his head in that direction to see Shashi entering the hut.

Fergus had already reached the conclusion that there was far more in the young Indian woman's background than she had disclosed to him. He also felt that she preferred Englishmen to her own people. However, she could not possibly have any romantic notions in this heat.

Sitting up, he called to her, 'What are you doing here, Shashi?'

'Please . . . you must all leave now. You are in very great danger.'

192

'What sort of danger?' Also unable to sleep, the naval lieutenant swung himself from his own makeshift bed, his skin glistening with perspiration.

'The brother of our headman is in the jungle near the village. With him are many sepoys who rose against their officers. They have guns. Soon they will come to kill you, thinking to find you sleeping.'

Midshipman Harry Downton had listened to the exchange with some alarm. Lewis turned to him now.

'We need to rouse the men. This time we'll tell them exactly what's happening.'

'You will not be allowed to reach your boat. Men have been posted to stop you.'

'We'll see about that. Where's the headman now?' Lewis was thinking fast as he put the question to her.

'In his hut, but . . .'

'Harry, I want the men brought here at the double – be sure each of them is carrying a knife.'

The seamen from the *Venus* had found it no easier to sleep than their officers. They entered the hut grumpily, but their irritability disappeared when the lieutenant outlined what was happening.

'You all have knives, take them out now – and don't be afraid to use them if you need to.'

Turning to Shashi, he said, 'Take us to the headman's hut. We need to get there before the rest of the village is roused.'

She looked suddenly scared. 'When they know I have warned you, I will be killed.'

'If we don't reach the headman before his brother does, we'll all be killed. When we get to the boat we'll take you with us.'

'You promise?' Shashi spoke uncertainly.

'I've said so. Now, take us to his hut – quickly! If anything goes wrong each man must try to reach the boat. It's our only way out.'

'I'll take my sketch pad and get to the boat before the trouble starts here,' said Fergus. 'I'll have the two men who are guarding it get it as ready as possible before you arrive.'

'Good!' Grim-faced, the lieutenant said, 'Let's go. Everyone stay together – and be ready to do whatever I tell you.'

The villagers were following their usual routine of sleeping away the hottest hours of the day. Most were inside their flimsy huts, others lay sprawled in the shade of the many trees growing among the houses.

Only once did Fergus encounter anyone awake. A village woman, breast-feeding a tiny naked baby just inside the doorway of her hut, looked up at him as he passed. She was startled to see him. For one fearful moment Fergus thought she would scream, despite his reassuring smile. To his great relief, she cradled her baby's head in one hand and gave Fergus a shy smile in return.

Afterwards, he wished he had been able to capture the moment on paper, but on this occasion there were more important matters than his art.

The two seamen were dozing in the shade of the boat. The nearest Indians were beneath some trees at the edge of the sand, fast asleep. Fergus woke the sailors and gave them a whispered explanation of the situation.

'We need to prepare the boat for sea. I saw some large poles a little way along the beach. Get them and lay them behind the boat. We may be able to roll it down to the water – but go about it quietly. We don't want to waken the guards.'

There were only half a dozen round, wooden poles, but they proved to be enough. Placing them on the sand, they managed to heave the heavy boat on them with a strength born of desperation and use them as makeshift rollers.

The gig was not quite at the water's edge when a babble of sound erupted in the village. Brushing away the perspiration which blinded him, Fergus saw the sailors heading towards the boat. In their midst were the headman and Shashi.

The villagers, waving their arms furiously, surrounded them, but were keeping a respectful distance.

As the men drew nearer, Fergus could see that one of the

sailors had the headman firmly in his grip, a knife held conspicuously against his throat. Another of the seamen had acquired a musket, probably taken from the headman's hut. He was swinging this from side-to-side, menacingly, keeping the crowd at bay.

By the time the men reached the beach the stern of the boat was actually in the water, but it was beyond the strength of Fergus and his companions to move it any farther.

The seamen and their hostage crossed the beach at a run and Lewis Callington called urgently, 'Get the boat in the water. Quickly now!'

There was a very good reason for his increased concern. Uniformed men carrying muskets could be seen running towards the village from the nearby jungle.

The villagers had seen them too. They surged towards the sailors with a new enthusiasm. However, when the headman's captor gave his prisoner a sharp jab with his knife that caused him to scream in pain and terror, the villagers came to a hesitant halt.

The boat was afloat now and Fergus scrambled in. Beside him, Shashi was pulled on board by the young midshipman. The headman too was bundled on board. As the last of the seamen clambered over the side, their colleagues were already manning the oars.

The villagers set up a howl of anger and surged forward once more, but a shot from the musket made them hold back just long enough.

Lewis Callington was the last man to come on board and it was a desperately close call. He was dragged inboard as the boat was being edged away from the shore.

Some of the mutinous sepoys were within musket range now. Aware that their quarry was escaping, they paused to take aim and fire. Fortunately, they were hurried shots. Only one musket ball came close and it struck harmlessly against the stout wooden planking of the gig.

It took a few minutes for the sepoys to gather at the water's edge and take a more leisurely aim, but the distance between the boat and the shore was being increased with every desperate stroke of the oars and their shots fell short.

Eventually, when the sailors realised they were well beyond range, they paused to rest their heavily perspiring bodies over the oars. Nevertheless, they possessed strength enough to set up a cheer that could be heard by the frustrated Indians on the shore.

There was still one problem to be solved and it was voiced by young Harry Downton. Greatly relieved to have come out of his first action with his life, he asked, 'What do we do with the village headman?'

The lieutenant looked at the headman thoughtfully for a moment or two before replying. 'We'll give him more of a chance then he gave us. Throw him over the side. We have no further use for him.'

'But . . . there are sharks here!'

'I didn't say it was a *great* chance,' replied Lewis, callously. 'But it's more than he intended we should have. Over the side with him, men.'

A moment later the headman, who had been a reluctant prisoner, was pleading to be allowed to remain on board the gig.

His pleading was in vain. Thrown unceremoniously over the side, he immediately struck out for the shore. He swam with the desperation of a man aware that his life was at stake. It rested upon the speed at which he could swim – and the dubious mercy of the gods he worshipped.

It seemed the gods were looking in another direction this day. Fergus watched the man for some time as he swam frantically towards the shore. He turned away for only a moment, but when he looked back again the headman had disappeared.

There was no sign of a disturbance in the water and no fin to mark the presence of a shark, but it was the end of the headman – and the beginning of many gruelling hours for the crew of the gig.

Chapter 7

Thoroughly exhausted and suffering from the effects of heat and dehydration, the survivors from the *Venus* and their Indian passenger were rescued the day after their escape from the fishing village, plucked from the sea by the crew of the Calcutta-bound East India Company merchantman, *Brilliant*.

It was a fortuitous rescue for those in the gig. Out of sight of the low-lying land, they were making very little progress against the currents in the Bay of Bengal and had been swept miles off course.

Had they not been found they might never have made landfall and would undoubtedly have perished.

Helped on board the merchantman, the sun-scorched and weak sailors gave brief explanations to their marvelling rescuers.

There was a momentary hitch when Shashi was helped over the side of the *Brilliant*.

'What's she doing in the boat with you?' demanded Captain Ezra Sims, the master of the East Indiaman. 'I'll have no women aboard my ship – especially not Indian women. They are sinful, bring bad luck, and a whole lot of trouble follows in their wake.'

'Without her there would have been no survivors from the *Venus* alive today,' declared Lewis Callington. 'She comes with us. If I have my way she'll be given a heroine's welcome when we reach Calcutta.'

Captain Sims appeared inclined to argue, but Fergus was already leading Shashi in the wake of the seamen being taken below decks.

'The woman will be your responsibility,' declared the merchantman's captain, aggressively. 'I run a Christian ship, with a God-fearing crew. If she causes any trouble a report will go to your Commander-in-Chief when we reach Calcutta.'

Other members of the crew did not share their captain's views. The seaman guiding Fergus said, quietly, 'Cap'n Sims is the greatest hypocrite sailing these seas. He's Christian enough – when it suits him – but if the Indian girl means anything to you, you'd best keep him away from her, especially when he's got drink inside him.'

The same seaman gave Shashi the use of a passenger cabin. Fergus, Lewis Callington and Harry Downton were also allocated cabins to themselves. The *Brilliant* had accommodation for a number of passengers, but was not carrying any on this voyage.

Despite his misgivings about having Shashi on board, Captain Sims was unstinting in his hospitality towards the Royal Navy men. While Shashi ate in her cabin and the seamen took their meals with his own crew, Sims entertained the two officers and Fergus in his own large cabin that evening. He listened to their story sympathetically.

'The loss of your ship will be sorely felt by the authorities in Calcutta,' he said as they ate. 'We exchanged news with one of the Company's outbound ships only yesterday. A Naval Brigade has been sent upriver to Lucknow to relieve the garrison and the families there. Another is being formed. Men from the merchant ships now at Calcutta are being recruited to join it. Upcountry, the mutineers have been massacring European women and children wherever they've found them. The whole of the interior is said to be in their hands – or it very soon will be. This mutiny has been brewing for a long time. It will take the whole of the British army to put it down – at least, that's my belief. I blame the Company. They should have brought missionaries in and made India a Christian country by now.'

Choosing not to comment on the evangelistic views

expressed by the merchantman's captain, Lewis said, 'It sounds as though we're likely to see some action while we're in India.'

'More than you would wish, I suspect,' replied Captain Sims. 'The chances are I'll lose half my crew to this latest Naval Brigade when we reach Calcutta. The Governor-General is desperate to gather fighting men from every available source.'

'Then the sooner we are able to offer our services the better,' declared Lewis. 'When can we expect to reach the mouth of the Hugli River?'

'Tomorrow afternoon.'

'Splendid! It means we should be in Calcutta two days after that.'

'Three,' corrected Captain Sims. 'The day after tomorrow is a Sunday. We will anchor in the river and celebrate the Lord's day in a proper fashion. I trust you and your men will attend the services I hold on the upper deck. It wouldn't do that young woman any harm were she to do the same.'

'Surely you can forego your Sunday routine on this occasion?' protested Lewis. 'India is on a war footing and I have fourteen fighting men with me. Besides, I must inform the Admiralty of the loss of my ship and its crew as quickly as possible.'

'One day will not influence the outcome of the war,' retorted Captain Sims. 'And a report, early or late, will not bring your ship back.'

'I still think . . .'

'You are at liberty to think as much as you wish, Lieutenant Callington, but you are on a merchantman now, not a man-o'-war. We do not possess the same eagerness to kill our fellow men.'

'My eagerness is rather to *save* lives,' said Lewis, trying very hard to contain his anger at the other's smug complacency. 'The women and children besieged at Lucknow. Christian men and women.'

'No doubt the Lord will take care of His own. Now, shall we pass the port once more?'

Brilliant reached the wide mouth of the Hugli River early the following afternoon. The merchant ship anchored in the shipping lane, with lush green jungle no more than a couple of miles away on either bank.

Lewis had appealed once more to Captain Sims to change his mind and proceed upriver to Calcutta immediately. The merchantman's captain remained adamant. God had decreed the Sabbath to be a day of rest. So be it. The naval lieutenant was forced to watch as two other ships entered the Hugli behind *Brilliant*. Both were taken in tow by steam-tugs and quickly disappeared from view upstream.

The Sunday morning service was attended by every man in the merchantman's crew and also the survivors of the *Venus*. At the heart of the service was a sermon by Captain Sims which rambled on for more than half-an-hour. By the time it ended, Fergus had the impression that the captain had been drinking heavily, despite the early hour.

After the service, before the heat became too unbearable, Fergus gathered up his sketch pad and crayons and made his way to the cabin occupied by Shashi. He would have liked to sketch her on the upper deck, but felt Captain Sims might not approve of such a Sunday activity.

Shashi was happy to have someone to talk to. She readily agreed that Fergus might sketch her and made an excellent model, her features and dress appealing greatly to his artistic sense.

As he worked, they talked. Among the subjects upon which they touched was the loss of *Venus*. Like the villagers, Shashi had believed the sailors in the gig to have a man-o'-war waiting for them over the horizon. The truth had come as a shock to her.

Fergus had not been sketching for very many minutes when there was a gentle knock on the door. When Shashi called out, 'Come in, please,' the door opened and a rather self-conscious Harry Downton stood in the doorway.

Taken aback to see Fergus in the cabin, the young midshipman would have backed out hurriedly had not both Shashi and Fergus insisted that he come inside.

'I . . . I'm sorry, to interrupt,' stammered the young officer. 'I thought Shashi would be here on her own . . . probably lonely with no one to talk to. I didn't know . . .'

'That's all right,' said Fergus, smiling at Harry's embarrassment. It had been apparent to him from the first time Shashi had appeared on the scene that Harry was smitten by her. 'We're doing nothing to which anyone – except Captain Sims – could possibly object. I think she makes a lovely subject for a portrait, don't you?'

'I . . . yes. Beautiful.'

'I think you too are beautiful. May I call you "Harry"?'

'Yes, of course.' The midshipman's face was scarlet, and he could not hide his pleasure at her words.

'Please . . . can you make a picture of Harry and me together?'

'Certainly!' Fergus had already completed a brief sketch of Shashi. Now he turned a page and persuaded the young midshipman to sit on the bunk, beside the Indian girl.

Fergus made a number of sketches of both Harry and Shashi. Some were of them together, others of each individual.

Eventually, and with obvious reluctance, Harry Downton said, 'I'm sorry, I must go now. Lieutenant Callington said he wished to speak to me at eleven o'clock. It's almost that now.'

When the midshipman had left them, Shashi said, 'Harry is very nice.'

'He's also very young, Shashi.' Fergus spoke without thinking, intent on capturing her expression – both gentle and worldly.

It suddenly came to him that he had sketched such an expression before. It was some minutes before he realised when it had been. It came as a shock to remember. It had been on the face of Becky.

'You think I am so much older than Harry?'

Fergus looked up in surprise. 'No . . . No, of course not.'

It was perfectly true. Despite Shashi's air of worldliness, he had realised while he was sketching her that she was probably no more than eighteen or nineteen. Perhaps a year

201

older than Midshipman Harry Downton.

Yet again there was this disturbing similarity between Becky and Shashi. When she was no more than a child Becky had given those who met her for the first time the impression of self-confidence. The feeling that she knew about everything that went on in the sordid world of Lewin's Mead. Had experienced much of it for herself.

It had taken Fergus some time to realise much of this was a front. A deception practised by so many of her fellow slum-dwellers. A need to appear to be as tough as the toughest. He wondered how much of Shashi's air of self-assurance sprang from the same source.

'You told me you learned to speak English when you were an *ayah* – that's a servant, isn't it? I understand there are servants for every aspect of life in India. What were your duties?'

Shashi looked uncomfortable. 'I did not tell you the truth. I was a *deva dasi*. A servant of the Gods, in the temple of Janithran.'

'Oh?' Fergus looked at her quickly. 'What were your duties there?'

'I would sing and dance for the gods. With the other servants of the temple, it was my duty to see they wanted for nothing.'

Something in her voice prompted Fergus to ask, 'Were you there only to attend to the needs of the gods, Shashi?'

'No.' Suddenly the worldliness had been replaced by a childlike unhappiness and Fergus was about to apologise for asking the question when she amplified her reply. 'I was a servant of the temple – and all who belonged to the family of the temple. I did all that was asked of me. It was my duty.'

Her distress was so evident now that Fergus said, 'You don't have to explain your life to me, Shashi.'

'Please . . . I would like to tell you. May I?'

He nodded, working on yet another rapid sketch. He felt there was a need in her to talk. Almost an eagerness now to share her story with someone.

It was a tragic tale. Shashi had been given to the temple by her parents when she was only ten years old. She found many other young girls there. Learned men too. She was taught to dance, to sing, to write, and was encouraged to study English.

The temple tutors told her this was the language of the men who had taken away the powers of the rightful rulers of many Indian states and overrun the country. The only chance the Indian people had of one day defeating them was to learn their ways. They would then prove themselves better at doing all those things the English did.

Shashi also learned that even holy men shared the carnal desires of lesser mortals – and with similar consequences. At the age of fifteen, heavily pregnant, she was cast out of the temple.

Her baby, a girl, died within a week of its birth. Shashi had no one . . . nowhere . . . Just when it seemed she had no alternative but to become a prostitute in the bazaar, her path crossed that of a British army officer.

More than twice her age, the officer's wife had returned to England with a sick child. Shashi became his mistress and remained with him for more than two years.

Then the officer's wife returned to India and Shashi was alone once more. It was then she went to the fishing village where she had met up with the survivors from *Venus*. Here she lived in the house of the widowed mother of a servant girl who had befriended her while she was the British officer's mistress.

For the future . . .? Shashi shrugged, resigned. She doubted whether even those holy men who specialised in such matters could tell what it held for her.

While she was speaking, her expressions changed so rapidly Fergus had been hard pressed to capture even a fraction of them. Now she said, anxiously, 'You will tell Harry about me? Of the things I have done?'

Glancing up at her, he realised that his reply was important to her. 'Is there a particular reason why he should know? If there is I am sure you'll tell him yourself.'

'But . . . he is your friend.'

'Yes, he's a friend, but as we've already said, he's still young. He knows little of life. I think he should make up his mind how he feels about you as today's person before he learns about the woman you were before.'

Putting down his pencil, Fergus gave her a sympathetic smile. 'It's becoming too hot to work, Shashi. We'll call it a day.'

She crossed the cabin and knelt beside him to look at the sketches he had made of her. There were a surprising number. Looking at one which showed her in a thoughtful mood, she smiled up at him. 'I like this one.'

'Then you shall have it. I'll make a proper painting of it if we have time at Calcutta.'

'That would make me very happy.' She broke off as she came to a sketch he had made while she was telling him the story of her life.

She looked at it so long that he asked, 'Don't you like that one?'

'I am not certain. You seem to show what I am thinking. As though you can read what is in my mind.'

'Perhaps I can, Shashi.'

It was meant to be a joke, but she suddenly looked scared. 'I would not like you to be able to know what is in my mind. My thoughts are not always good.' Looking up at him, she asked, 'Do you have a wife?'

The question caught him off guard and now she saw a number of expressions pass across his face in quick succession. 'Yes, Shashi. I have a wife ... At least, I *had* a wife. Now ... I don't know any more.'

'I am sorry. It makes you unhappy to think of her. I should not have asked.'

'You've made me think of her since I first spoke to you, Shashi. You and she are very alike in many ways.'

'Oh? She makes you unhappy too?'

'Sometimes, yes. Yet very happy too, at times.'

Shashi said nothing for some moments then she looked up at him and said almost meekly, 'It is a woman's duty to make a man happy. I am sorry if I have made you unhappy.'

Had the statement come from any other woman it might have been interpreted as an invitation. Coming from

Shashi, he believed she was genuinely sorry that she might have upset him.

'You haven't made me unhappy. I think about my wife a lot. It's good to be able to talk to someone about her.'

There was a knock at the door and in answer to Shashi's call, Harry entered the cabin once more.

He was disconcerted at the sight of her kneeling beside Fergus, but she pointed to the pad and said, 'Look, Harry. There are lots of drawings of me. Come and see.'

Rising to his feet, Fergus said, 'I'll leave the pad here with you. Choose a couple of sketches you would like and Harry can bring the pad to my cabin later.'

In his cabin, Fergus lay on his bunk, staring up at the deckhead and thinking. Shashi *was* like Becky. Dangerously so. Was he right to say nothing of her past to Harry? Would Harry *want* him to say anything?

He tried to imagine what his reaction might have been had someone tried to tell him stories of Becky's past when he first met her.

In truth, Shashi's past had been dictated by the life she had been forced to lead. It was not of her own choosing.

The same was true of Becky. She had known only Lewin's Mead. It was the Bristol slum that had shaped her life. Perhaps he had expected too much of her? Had hoped for too much, too quickly. There had been many things in their married life that were unacceptable to him. He wondered whether, by talking about them to her, it might have been possible to put them right, once and for all. He told himself he *had* tried. There had been occasions when he had forgiven her for a great many things for which other men would have thrown a wife out of the house. But, then, he had believed his love to be stronger than that of most other men.

It was certainly true that Becky was not like most other women. There was the same basic honesty in her that he believed was in Shashi. It was the reason she had been compelled to tell her story to him. Even though she believed he would repeat it to Harry Downton and spoil what little chance of happiness she might be hoping for with him.

Fergus believed he understood Shashi. Could sympathise with her and offer her the help he felt she so desperately needed.

Could he not have been as understanding towards Becky, the woman he loved more than anyone else?

In the heat of the cabin on board the merchantman, thousands of miles from Lewin's Mead, Fergus went over all the things he might have done to prevent the break up of his marriage to Becky.

He thought about it until his head ached and he could think no more. Then, he fell asleep.

Chapter 8

Fergus awoke with a start, aware of a commotion somewhere close at hand. There were a number of excited voices. Among the loudest he was able to identify that of Captain Sims. Of the many words uttered in anger by the merchantman's captain, 'strumpet', 'slattern' and 'whore' were the most often repeated.

He opened the door to find a number of men milling about the passageway. Many were *Brilliant*'s officers, but there were seamen present too. As Fergus stood in the doorway of his cabin, Lewis clattered down the gangway from the upper deck.

'Take her away and put her under lock and key until we reach Calcutta. If I have my way she'll be whipped through the streets . . .' Captain Sims's voice carried above all the other sounds.

Then Fergus saw Shashi.

The young Indian woman was struggling in the grip of two of the merchant seamen.

'Just a minute, where are you taking her – and why?' Fergus stepped out into the narrow passageway, forcing the men to come to a halt with their struggling captive.

'This is a disciplinary matter. I'm dealing with it in my way, artist. It has nothing to do with you.'

Captain Sims pushed his way roughly through the men crowding the corridor. He was red-faced and hot, but Fergus was of the opinion that the perspiration running down his face owed as much to alcohol as to the heat.

'She came on board with my party and I take full responsibility for her, Captain Sims.' Lewis reached Fergus's side and spoke to the merchantman's commanding officer. 'She is not subject to your discipline, whatever you believe her to have done.'

'Believe? I *know*! And don't tell me what I can or can't do on board my ship. The woman's a whore. She tried to compromise me. *Me*, a Christian, married man. As for being your responsibility . . . If you'd kept your officers in order this wouldn't have happened.'

The slurring of the captain's voice was not lost upon Lewis. 'Perhaps you'll tell me exactly what *has* happened?'

'I heard noises as I passed this woman's cabin. I went in and found her and your young midshipman in there. They were behaving in a disgusting manner. They were about to get into the bunk together . . .'

'That is a lie!' Shashi pulled herself free from the men who were holding her and turned to face Captain Sims angrily.

'She's right. It *is* a lie. A deliberate lie.' Fergus had not noticed Harry, but he was among the crowd of men in the passageway. He was every bit as angry as Shashi.

'Don't you dare to argue with me, young man! I don't know what your parents would think of your behaviour on my ship. No doubt they gave you a Christian upbringing?'

Turning back to Lewis Callington, the merchantman's captain put out a hand to steady himself against the bulk-head. 'I've told you what happened. What you do with the midshipman is your business, but I'll not have the Indian woman loose on my ship to corrupt the crew. I run a Christian ship. Always have, and always will.'

'I think you have jumped to the wrong conclusion, Captain Sims.' Lewis had also realised the other man was drunk, but he remained icily polite. 'Midshipman Downton and I were talking about the sketches made of Shashi by Fergus, and left by him in her cabin. I expressed an interest and Harry came down here to fetch them. He was away for a matter of minutes only. When I heard the hubbub I came down from the upper deck to investigate. There was no time for him to get up to any mischief. No time at all.'

Captain Sims glared at the naval lieutenant belligerently

as he gathered his befuddled thoughts. 'Your loyalty is mis-
guided, Lieutenant . . . but that doesn't matter. I'm not
placing the midshipman under arrest, only this hussy. She
followed me to my cabin after I'd sent him away. Offered
herself to me if I'd take no action on what I'd seen. I've
never heard of anything so outrageous. I won't have her
loose, corrupting my seamen . . .'

Shashi exploded in anger, but before she could speak,
Harry cried, 'That's another lie! It's *you* who ought to be
locked up.'

Pushing one of his seamen aside, Captain Sims advanced
upon the young man, but Harry stood his ground. 'I saw
what happened after you ordered me from Shashi's cabin. I
stayed back here in the shadows because I was afraid of
what you might do to her. She didn't follow you to your
cabin. You led her there by the arm and she was struggling
to get away from you. You went in and closed the door.
While I was wondering what to do, I heard her shout. It was
only then that *you* began crying out.'

'He tried to push me on to his bed and was pulling at my
sari. See? It is torn. I called for him to stop.'

'Shut up! No one wants to hear your lies. As for you,
young man . . .' Captain Sims raised his fist as though to
strike Harry, but Fergus stepped between the two men.

Lowering his fist, Captain Sims said, 'I'll not be spied on
in my own ship.'

'But you don't argue with what he said he saw?' Lewis
Callington asked the question quietly. 'It does put an
entirely different light on this disturbance.'

'I . . . I remember now. I took the woman to my cabin to
fetch my Bible. I intended reading a part of it to her, telling
her that those who sow wickedness will reap iniquity. I
wanted to tell her something of our Christian principles.'

Captain Sims gave an exaggerated gesture of despair, 'I
should have known better than to try. I should have locked
her up the moment she set foot on my ship. I knew she
would cause trouble. I knew it . . .'

'No one's going to be locked up, Captain Sims. Shortly
before I sent Midshipman Downton down here, he and I

were watching a naval brig come upriver. It has just anchored and run up a signal for a tug. I intend taking the gig and transferring my men – and Shashi – to the brig immediately. My duty is to put my men at the disposal of the Commander-in-Chief at the earliest opportunity. The brig will reach Calcutta a day earlier than your ship.'

'You can do whatever you like, Lieutenant, but you can be quite certain I'll write a report on this affair. No doubt you'll be hearing from this Commander-in-Chief of yours.'

'That would be a great pity, Captain Sims. It was my intention to express my gratitude to the Honourable East India Company for the services you have rendered me and the other survivors from *Venus*. I would have delivered my message personally to Sir George Pershing. As you will be aware, he is on the board of the Company. He is also my uncle. I could still do this. However, should you file a report along the lines you have suggested, I will, of course, respond. I will express certain opinions I hold to Sir George. Again, in person. I leave the matter to your discretion, Captain Sims. Now, on behalf of my crew, I thank you for your hospitality while we have been your guests. If you will be so kind as to instruct your seamen to release their hold on Shashi, we will embark in our gig.'

The seamen holding the girl had released her while Lewis Callington was speaking. All that remained was for the lieutenant to muster his crew and have the gig brought alongside the ship's gangway.

Twenty minutes later, they were heading for the Royal Naval brig. In another hour, despite its being the sabbath, the sloop was taken in tow by a steam-tug and was beginning the two-day journey to Calcutta.

Chapter 9

The commanding officer of Her Majesty's brig *Pincher* was a young lieutenant, some years junior to Callington. He listened with horror-filled disbelief to the story of the loss of *Venus*. The subsequent adventures of the survivors left him bubbling with angry indignation. He declared that, had it been his ship that had rescued the crew of the gig, he would have stood his brig off the village and shelled it out of existence.

Unlike the captain of the *Brilliant*, Shashi's part in the escape of Lewis Callington and the others was fully appreciated by the brig's commanding officer and crew. The second-in-command readily gave up his cabin to her, a respect that was as novel as it was genuine.

For the two days she was on board the small fighting vessel, Shashi was given as much deference as might have been accorded the wife of a naval officer.

In return, she delighted the crew by taking a close interest in all their duties on board.

It also quickly became apparent to every man that Harry Downton had fallen very heavily for her. He missed no opportunity to spend time in her company and dealt with her every wish as though it were a holy quest.

Although her own emotions were less openly displayed, Shashi was just as devoted to the young midshipman. On board the *Brilliant* he had taken her part against Captain Sims, even though it might have had serious consequences for him. It was a unique experience for anyone to consider her important enough to take such a risk for her.

On the second and last night of the journey upriver to

Calcutta, the tugboat anchored early with the brig tied alongside.

By the light of lanterns slung around the upper deck of the brig, the British sailors put on an impromptu concert, the music supplied by a penny whistle.

The surprise highlight of the evening was provided by Shashi. After speaking to the Bengali crew of the tugboat, a drum and drummer were produced. She then said she would like to dance for the Royal Naval seamen. It would be her way of saying 'thank you' to the men of the brig and to the survivors of the *Venus* for their many acts of kindness.

The dance was performed against the backdrop of a starlit sky and yellow lantern lights with the occasional visit from a firefly. In the rare pauses of the drumbeat an elephant might be heard trumpeting somewhere close at hand on the shadowed shore.

It was a memorable evening, but most of all the seamen would remember Shashi's dance. Her body swayed in erotic time to the beat of the drums while her hands and arms told a story that had been passed down through generations of temple dancers.

Eventually, her dark skin glistening with perspiration, the drumbeats came to an abrupt halt and Shashi sank gracefully to the deck of the brig in an attitude of submission.

The crew erupted in enthusiastic applause. Harry stepped forward to help Shashi to her feet and congratulate her on the breathtaking performance she had just given.

The sun rose swiftly in India but Fergus beat it to the deck of the brig the following morning. He felt he should record the work of the tugboat for Admiralty records in London.

He squatted down beneath a small, temporary shelter erected by a sailmaker to protect him from the sun as he worked during the heat of the day. From here, Fergus saw Harry emerge from the hatch which led to the second-in-command's cabin, currently occupied by Shashi.

As the midshipman walked by, treading softly, Fergus

called quietly, 'Good morning, Harry. You're up and about early.'

Even in the dim light he observed the young man's start of surprise. 'Oh! Good morning, Fergus . . . You saw me . . .?'

'I saw where you came from. I'm happy it was you and nobody else. Should I be congratulating you, or offering my blessing or something?' Fergus was sharper than he needed to be with the midshipman. He could not understand why.

'Neither. I . . . I've never met anyone like Shashi before, Fergus.'

'You probably never will again.' He was remembering what Shashi had told him in the cabin on board *Brilliant*. 'All the same, don't get *too* attached to her, Harry. For both your sakes.'

Even as he said it, Fergus realised it was the sort of well-meaning remark that might have been made to him about his relationship with Becky. It disturbed him that he should think of her whenever he spoke to Harry about Shashi.

'You'd better get ready to face the day, Harry. Dawn's almost here. We'll be getting underway very soon.' He could hear movement on the tug as steam was raised in readiness for the voyage upriver.

The midshipman began to walk away, but he suddenly turned back to Fergus again. 'In case you're wondering, the *Brilliant*'s captain *was* lying. This is the first time anything's happened between Shashi and me.'

'I've never doubted you, Harry – or Shashi, either. But I repeat what I just said. Don't allow yourself to grow too fond of her.'

As the young midshipman walked away once more, Fergus thought he might as well have kept such advice to himself. Where Shashi was concerned, Harry Downton would take no more notice of his words than Fergus ever had about Becky.

There it was again. The association between Becky and Shashi . . .

Fergus stood up and tucked the sketch pad beneath his arm. The sun was showing its fiery red arc above the trees to the east of the river. Closer, on the west bank, a long line of elephants was trundling along the river bank, heading for work in a timber-cutting area passed by the brig the previous evening.

The whole scene would have made a wonderful painting, but it would not be captured on paper or canvas this morning. Fergus had momentarily lost all taste for his art.

Chapter 10

'Who is this?'

Towed by the noisy, heavily smoking tug, the brig was no more than two hours' steaming time from Calcutta. Recovered from his earlier temporary aversion, Fergus was squatting on the upper deck, sketching the increasingly busy river scenes about him.

Beside him, Shashi sat rummaging through the canvas satchel in which he kept his artist's materials. The thought had not even crossed her mind that Fergus might not approve of her examining the only belongings that had not gone down with the *Venus*.

She had located a sketch pad that was half full of work he had done whilst living in Lewin's Mead.

Looking up from the sketch he was making, he found himself looking at a drawing of a young girl. Trying hard to conceal his feelings, he said, 'Her name's Becky.'

'There are some more sketches of her in here?'

'Yes.'

Something in the tone of his reply made Shashi look up from the pad she held.

'Is she your wife?'

'Yes.'

'She looks very young.'

'About the same age as you, I would think.'

'When we were on the other ship and spoke about her, you said you did not know if you were still married. How can that be?'

'I left her. She might have decided I'm dead and found someone else. Most probably she has.'

215

Shashi looked at him, her thoughts troubled. 'You say she and I are very like each other. Has she too known many men? Is this why you left her?'

Fergus found her direct and unsophisticated mode of questioning, disconcerting. 'I don't think I want to talk about her to anyone, Shashi.'

The silence that followed his words lasted for a couple of minutes before she asked, 'Is this why it makes you unhappy to see that Harry is very fond of me?'

'Has he said . . .' Fergus was indignant.

Shashi shook her head. 'He has no need to say anything to me. It is not hard to know what you are thinking. Others are thinking the same, I know.'

'He has been in the navy since he was a boy, Shashi. He has had very little experience with women. Especially women as attractive as you.'

'You speak the truth. He has known no other woman before me,' she declared in her forthright manner. 'But you need not fear I will do anything to hurt Harry. He means a great deal to me. More than any other man I have known.'

'I believe you,' said Fergus. 'But I think he's quite capable of hurting himself – *because* of you.'

'Are you saying this because you believe it to be true, or because you have been hurt?'

'For both reasons.' Matching honesty with honesty, he added, 'For your sake too, Shashi. You've had a very hard life. You deserve some happiness. I'd like to think you and Harry might find it together. You probably will – for a very brief time – but it can't last. You'll both end up being very badly hurt.'

'Perhaps, but in the temple I had no happiness at all. I do not seek more than I have now.'

Their conversation was interrupted for a few moments when a fishing boat bumped alongside and the occupant tried to sell some of his catch to the crew of the brig. He failed to make a sale. Very soon the brig would be moored in Calcutta. All the food required by the cooks would be purchased on shore.

As the fisherman propelled his boat away from the brig,

heading for another incoming vessel, Shashi said quietly, 'You still love your Becky very much.'

'Yes, but it's too late now to put things right between us.'

'What has time to do with it? You either love or you do not. If you do then it will be the same tomorrow as it was yesterday and is today.'

'Did they teach you dancing *and* wisdom in the temple, Shashi?' Fergus attempted to lighten the conversation between them. It had become too serious and he did not want to discuss Becky with anyone. He had not realised how much the parting from her still hurt him.

'I learned many things in the temple. Most I wish I could forget, but I cannot. You have told me very little about your "Becky", so I cannot say whether she too might have learned things she did not want to know. Only one thing more I would say to you. In the temple my body belonged to others. They took what was theirs, but they could not take my heart or my mind. They belong to me. It was the same when I lived with the English officer. I used my body because it was the only way I could survive.'

'Where does Harry fit into this life of yours that's able to separate body and mind?'

'Ah!' Shashi's expression changed perceptibly, becoming altogether more gentle. She smiled at him. 'Harry is not like the others. He is gentle. Kind. He does not use me. Oh, yes, I have given a large part of my heart to Harry already. One day I think he will have it all.'

'Harry's a sailor, Shashi. He serves our queen. Once we arrive in Calcutta we'll probably be going inland with a Naval Brigade. It's quite likely that you'll never see him again once that happens.'

'We will see,' she said, defiantly. 'This is India. My country. I will find a way of being with Harry for as long as he wants me – and I think he will want me for a very long time.'

Shashi rose to her feet, then suddenly stooped to pick up the sketch pad once again. Turning to the page on which was the sketch of Becky, she held it up before him.

'Look at her again, artist-*sahib*. Look at her and

remember the thoughts you had on the day when you first knew you loved her. Remember all the things about her that made you love her.'

Shashi dropped the sketch pad to the deck in front of him. 'I think if you want her enough you will find her again. She already has your heart. Perhaps when you meet her again you will know that you have hers too.'

Chapter 11

When the brig reached Calcutta it was discovered that two men-o'-war, the *Shannon* and the *Pearl*, were already moored there. *Shannon* was the larger of the two vessels and the commander of the brig and Lewis Callington made their way to the ship immediately. The one would report his arrival. To the other fell the sad duty of informing a senior naval officer of the fate of the *Venus*.

When they went on board, the two men learned that all the senior officers were on their way inland, together with most of the seamen from the men-o'-war. There was a critical shortage of European troops in the mutinous country. Reports of horrific atrocities against British women and children were constantly reaching Calcutta. The Royal Naval men had adapted many of their guns for land use and were now headed for the besieged Residency at Lucknow.

Even as they spoke a naval officer from *Shannon* was ashore giving small-arms training to seamen drawn from the merchant ships at Calcutta.

The acting commanding officer of the man-o'-war suggested that news of the loss of *Venus* should be communicated to the Admiralty in London immediately. The quickest method was by telegraph, but this could only be sanctioned by the office of the Governor General, Viscount Canning.

Lewis Callington made his way to Government House and Fergus went with him.

They were taken to a senior official of the governor's staff. Shocked at the loss of the *Venus*, he agreed to send a report to London immediately. He also felt that news of the calamity should be passed on to the Governor General without delay. He personally took them to the man who represented Queen Victoria in India.

Viscount Charles Canning was a handsome man in his mid-forties who carried an enormous responsibility in such troubled times. A vigorous, hardworking man, he wore an air of brisk efficiency, but was able to produce a warm smile for his visitors.

The son of an outstanding politician who had died whilst holding office as Prime Minister of his country, Charles Canning probably worked harder than any of the men on his staff. It was something quite exceptional in this country where so many daily tasks were dealt with by servants.

He was shocked by Lewis Callington's report of the fate of the *Venus* and deeply solicitous of the welfare of the survivors.

'You can billet your men in the army barracks at Dum Dum,' he said. 'They will be made comfortable there and have plenty of room to relax. Most of the soldiers are away, seeking the mutineers. You and your officers must stay in Government House. I am also very interested in this Indian girl who has been so helpful to you. Where is she now?'

'I've allowed her to remain on board my ship until some provision is made for her,' replied the commanding lieutenant of the brig. 'After all she's done for Lieutenant Callington and his men, it seemed ungrateful simply to put her ashore to fend for herself as best she can, here in Calcutta.'

'Quite!' agreed Canning. 'Actually, I think I may be able to put her in the way of some rather interesting employment. She will be rewarded on behalf of the British government, of course, but it will not be sufficient for her to live a life of idle luxury. Besides, she may well be able to solve one of my own rather ticklish problems.

'We have an American lady staying here at Government House. She is closely related to President Buchanan of the United States of America. A most interesting woman, but I don't think I am being unduly unkind when I describe her

220

as "formidable". She is fully aware of the situation in India, yet insists upon travelling to Patna to visit her brother who has some business interest there. If I had not promised her an escort I swear she would have set off alone. She is seeking an Indian girl as an *ayah* – a companion. This girl of yours sounds as though she might fit the bill admirably.'

Exchanging glances with Fergus, Lewis said, 'I feel certain they'll suit each other very well, Your Excellency. May I also request your permission to take my men upcountry with the American lady's escort? I would like to offer our services to the Naval Brigade which I understand is operating against the mutineers.'

'Of course. There's a desperate need for fighting men in the force trying to relieve Lucknow. The defenders there are a hairsbreadth away from defeat and annihilation. The fact that they have held out until now is little short of a miracle. Give details of your men to my secretary. The East India Company is paying a war allowance to all combatants. It should double the pay of your men and provide a useful incentive for them.'

The interview came to an end and the two men were about to leave when Fergus said, 'I presume I will be allowed to go with the men from the *Venus*, Your Excellency?'

'Ah, yes! You're an artist, I believe. Tell me how you came to be on the *Venus*?'

Fergus told him of the brief given to him by Admiral of the Fleet Sir James Stott.

'Fascinating! Fascinating! You must show me the sketches you have with you. We are having a banquet in Government House sometime next week. Come early and bring your sketches with you. As for going with the men . . . I can see no reason why not. After all, you have Sir James's blessing. When you return I would also like to see the sketches you will have made of the actions involving the Naval Brigade. I will probably buy some of them from you. In the meantime you'll stay in Government House too, of course. The accommodation isn't all it could be, but the service can't be faulted – and bring the Indian girl along tonight for Miss Buchanan to meet.'

Lewis Callington and Harry were kept busy that evening settling their crew into the large army barracks at nearby Dum Dum. As a result, it was left to Fergus to take Shashi to Government House to meet her prospective employer.

Shashi was not too keen on becoming an *ayah* until Fergus pointed out that she would be embarking on a journey lasting some weeks – and Harry would be one of the escort party.

It was impossible to forecast what might happen when she reached Patna, but Shashi would leave that to take care of itself. It was enough that she would be close to Harry for the foreseeable future at least.

Shirley Buchanan was a strong, loud, no-nonsense woman who was probably in her late-thirties. Fergus discovered that she had a disconcerting habit of fixing the person to whom she was speaking with a fierce glance, calculated to make them quake.

Nevertheless, the American woman and Shashi took an instant liking to each other. Shashi's intelligence and lack of total subservience appealed to Shirley Buchanan.

The American woman had herself consistently refused to allow her sex to stand in the way of anything she wanted. What she wanted to do now – what she fully intended doing – was to journey more than three hundred miles to the interior of India and find the brother she had travelled so far to visit.

Told that such a journey would be impossible in the present circumstances because her safety could not be guaranteed, Shirley Buchanan had fixed the apologetic official with her 'look'.

As he squirmed uncomfortably in the face of her fury, she informed him she was not asking for any guarantees. If she were allowed to travel in the company of some of the soldiers being sent from Calcutta to the areas beyond Patna, she would be delighted. Were this to be refused, she would make her own arrangements – but she was certainly going to Patna.

Shirley Buchanan was persuasive as well as determined. Passed from official to harassed official until she eventually confronted the Governor himself, she was able to persuade him to allow her to travel with the next large party of reinforcements that would pass through Patna.

The survivors of *Venus* would form part of this escort. They hoped to join up with the Naval Brigade at Allahabad, a couple of hundred miles higher up the great Ganges River.

Fergus would have liked to learn more about Shirley Buchanan, but once she had decided that Shashi was going to be a suitable companion for her travels in India, he was dismissed from her presence in a typical fashion.

'You may leave us now, young man. I'm sure you have far more to do than listen to two women chatting. Besides, I wish to get to know Shashi. I'll not do that with you hanging on to every word we say. Run along now. You don't need to worry about her, I'll arrange for her to be given a room here, close to me.'

223

Chapter 12

Fergus's next meeting with Shirley Buchanan was at the banquet given at Government House, a few evenings after he had delivered Shashi to her. He had been invited together with Lewis Callington and Harry Downton.

There was little in the magnificent banqueting hall to prepare the three men for the hardships they would suffer on their long journey inland. Some sixty guests sat at a single long table. The magnificent silver plate and cutlery with which it was laid was so highly polished it threw back the light from the chandeliers sparkling overhead.

Behind each chair stood a servant armed with a horse-tail whisk to keep flies from the table and from the guest they were attending. Meanwhile, a whole army of other servants was serving, fetching and carrying food and drink.

The guests were, in the main, officials of the Company, or of the British Government. Normally, there would have been a number of senior officers from the army here too, but they were with their regiments, on active service.

Fergus found himself seated beside the redoubtable Miss Buchanan and it was not long before she crossed swords with her fellow guests.

Seated across the table from her was a middle-aged senior clerk of the East India Company, and his wife. This woman was in the habit of calling on her husband to confirm every statement she made, ending each pronouncement with, 'Isn't that right, dear?'

Eventually, Shirley Buchanan lost patience with her when the woman replied to one of her questions. 'It doesn't matter whether or not your husband agrees, is it what *you* think?'

The Company wife was taken aback. 'But of course, Charles and I never disagree about anything, do we, dear?'

The American woman stared at the Company wife for some moments before remarking, 'How terribly boring.'

Turning to Fergus she said, 'I hope you have found many *interesting* subjects to sketch while you have been in Calcutta, Mr Vincent?'

'A great many. I must show some of my work to you.'

'I look forward to that very much. Now, tell me how you met up with Shashi? I've heard her version, of course, but she is a very modest girl. I would like to hear it from you.'

'Whatever she has or hasn't told you, there's no doubt at all that the *Venus* survivors owe their lives to her,' said Fergus. He told Miss Buchanan how Shashi had warned him and the others of the village headman's treachery, adding, 'There's not one of us who wouldn't give his life for Shashi.'

'The young midshipman feels that way too, no doubt?' She nodded in the direction of Harry who was farther down the table, surrounded by matronly figures.

'Of course.' Fergus hesitated. 'You've met Harry?'

'Is that his name? No, but I've seen him walking with Shashi in the garden during the evening.'

Shirley Buchanan showed more discretion than others would have credited her with. Checking that the Company wife and her husband were engaged in conversation with their neighbours, she added, quietly, 'They make a most appealing young couple. However, I've been led to believe that such liaisons are frowned upon by your people here.'

'You're probably right, but they are both young and attractive. Given the circumstances in which they met it would be surprising if they weren't taken with each other.'

Shirley Buchanan smiled at Fergus unexpectedly. 'You a romantic, Mr Vincent, but then, you're an artist.'

'I wouldn't dream of arguing with you, Miss Bu but it's your opinion that's important to them,

225

After all, Shashi is your companion. How do *you* feel about it?'

'They'll find no censure from me. Unfortunately, it won't be *my* opinion that counts in the end. We live in a world which has double standards, Mr Vincent. In my own country half the States in the Union still practise slavery. If a baby is born with a black skin that child is a chattel, to be bought and sold by someone fortunate enough to be born white. Your own country has made slavery illegal, yet leads the world in asserting the superiority of the British over all other races. It's sheer hypocrisy, Mr Vincent.'

Fergus realised he had touched upon a subject about which Shirley Buchanan held extremely strong views. Her voice had grown louder as she warmed to the subject. Those around her at the table ceased their own conversations and looked in her direction.

Aware she had become the centre of attention, the American woman looked about her disdainfully before returning her gaze to Fergus. 'Most people, especially men, find a woman who has positive ideas about anything embarrassing, Mr Vincent. I hope I am not embarrassing *you*?'

Fergus smiled enigmatically at her. 'My only thought is that I would like to paint a portrait of you when you are talking of something that really matters to you. I wonder if we could arrange a few sittings before we leave Calcutta? It's been a very long time since I was on land for long enough to produce a really good painting.'

The suggestion successfully diverted Shirley from airing more opinions that would have been controversial, at the very least. They would certainly not have been popular among the present company, whose soldiers had turned ~~on~~ their overlords in a vicious and bloody uprising.

~~Her v~~iews would have been particularly ill-received ~~with news~~ reaching Calcutta of events that had ~~taken place~~ bore some weeks before. In this riverside ~~town~~ of about four hundred, together with ~~a number of~~ women and children and a couple of ~~civilian~~s, had been besieged by a large army

226

Led by *Nana Sahib*, the adopted son of a deposed Indian monarch, the mutineers had surrounded the Europeans who held a weak defensive position in a barracks near the town.

Desperately short of food, water and medical supplies, a quarter of those within the barracks were killed by the enemy's guns which pounded them day and night. Many more were wounded. It soon became apparent there was no hope of a relief force reaching them.

Eventually, against the advice of some of his officers and his own inclinations, the general commanding the defenders accepted an offer of safe conduct made to him by *Nana Sahib*.

The Europeans, many of them wounded and having to be carried, filed out of the battle-torn barracks with few regrets. Their departure was watched by the residents of Cawnpore City who had gathered *en masse* to see the sorry party make its way to the river.

Boats awaited the Europeans at the river bank – but so too did the treachery of *Nana Sahib*. As the men waded into the water to help the women and children on board, a well-planned trap was sprung. Disguised cannons opened fire and armed sepoys sprang from their hiding places.

It was a bloody massacre. When the shooting stopped the surviving European men were taken away and killed. A hundred and twenty-five women and children, many suffering from wounds, were taken prisoner.

They were crammed into a single house where they were joined from time to time by other women and children, captured in surrounding areas. Soon there were more than two hundred of them incarcerated in what became known as the 'House of the Ladies'.

Bullied, reviled and degraded, the only consolation the women had was that they were at least alive. Little more than two weeks later, information was received by *Nana Sahib* that British troops were approaching Cawnpore. It was suggested that if the women were released, it would divert the attention of the troops.

Other advisers pleaded it would be better to kill the

women and children out of hand, then there would be no incentive for the British troops to attempt to rescue them.

Nana Sahib decided upon the latter course. He issued his orders accordingly. While he and his court feasted and were being entertained by dancing girls, the European women and children were murdered. They died in the most savage and brutal manner imaginable.

This single incident would unleash reprisals of a ferocity unequalled among the forces of any civilised nation. It would ultimately result in the deaths of tens of thousands of *Nana Sahib*'s countrymen.

This was no time for Shirley Buchanan to voice her opinions on the equality of men and women of all races.

Chapter 13

While Fergus painted her portrait, he and Shirley spoke of the latest developments in the bitter war that was raging in India. It was a topic guaranteed to provoke the expression he wanted.

She was indeed a formidable woman. Possessed of a keen brain, she truly believed in all she advocated. Despite this, Shashi thought she was probably one of the kindest women she had ever met.

She spoke to Fergus about her when the American woman brought the sitting to a halt and left the room to go for a walk. She had sat for Fergus for perhaps forty minutes and declared she could sit still no longer.

He continued to work on the incomplete portrait and Shashi came and stood at his shoulder studying the painting. When she had not spoken for some minutes, Fergus asked, 'Do you approve of the portrait?'

'Yes, I do. You have captured the *real Memsahib* Buchanan. She speaks like a very fierce lady for much of the time and makes people believe she is always angry with them. But when you look at her more closely you find there is much kindness in her face. You have seen it and it is here, in the picture. Her face is alive, yes, but it is not unkind.'

'You are very perceptive, Shashi. I'm impressed.'

'Perceptive?' She said it slowly and carefully. 'This is not a word I have heard before. What does it mean?'

'It means you can see things that others might not notice. It usually means that you care enough about people to understand what they are really like. Talking of which, have you discussed Harry with her?'

'We have talked of him. Yesterday he spent the evening here. *Memsahib* Buchanan says I am very good for him.'

'Oh? Have you told her about your life in the temple, Shashi?'

'Yes. She has written much of it in her diary. She says she will use it in a book she will write one day.'

'I've painted your portrait, now Miss Buchanan is going to mention you in a book. You'll be famous one day.'

'I don't want to be famous, Fergus *Sahib*. But I would like to be happy.'

'With Harry?'

Instead of replying, Shashi nodded. When he made no comment, she asked, 'Do you think Harry cannot be happy with me?'

'It certainly won't be easy, Shashi – but nothing is impossible. You have me and Miss Buchanan on your side, at least. That's a very good start.'

'Thank you. I know you are a good man too. *Memsahib* Buchanan says so. She says you have much understanding of people.'

Walking through the garden en route to his own room, Fergus thought despondently that his own life would have been a whole lot happier had he been able to extend to Becky the understanding with which he was credited.

He had found himself thinking a great deal about her recently. Before he left Calcutta he would perhaps write to Fanny and ask about her. Somehow, his reasons for leaving her – reasons which had assumed such magnitude in Bristol – seemed less important now he was here, in India.

Fergus believed that, had he stayed to face things out with Becky, their marriage might have been saved.

However, he realised he would have needed to prise her from the grip of Lewin's Mead if they were to make a new start together. Becky had always strongly resisted any attempt to take her away from the only place where she felt she belonged. But had he tried hard enough? Was it something she might eventually have contemplated had he provided enough incentive?

* * *

Fergus never wrote his letter. The very next day urgent orders were sent from the Governor General to the officer training the combined force of Merchant and Royal Navy sailors. They were to set off immediately to join the forces converging upon Lucknow. The siege there was to be broken – whatever the cost.

Confirmation of the slaughter of British women and children at Cawnpore had been received in Calcutta. Lord Canning was determined it would not be repeated at Lucknow.

Within twenty-four hours a force of a hundred and twenty-six men set off from Calcutta.

The men took passage in a 'flat', a large, flat-bottomed, shallow barge. It would prove to be exceptionally unwieldy when towed by an under-powered steamer.

The 'flat' also contained the arms, ammunition and baggage, plus as many stores as could be gathered and loaded in the short time given to the party to make ready and depart.

The officers, together with Shashi and Shirley Buchanan, were accommodated in a river steamer. This fussy little vessel would tow the 'flat' first up the Hugli River, and then inland on the waterway that was the highway to the Indian interior: the mighty Ganges. Their destination was Allahabad, about two hundred and fifty miles upriver from Patna. Here they expected to join up with the main body of the Naval Brigade.

The small party was given a rousing send off. A band played on the quay and the Governor General and a great many of the Calcutta residents came to cheer them on their way. Theirs was a noble quest, to bring succour to their desperate countrymen and women trapped in the Lucknow Residency.

For the survivors of the *Venus* – and in particular Shashi – the occasion was not as auspicious as it might have been. They had learned that Captain Sims of the *Brilliant* was to accompany them as baggage master.

His ship was one of three that had been laid up at Calcutta

231

by the East India Company. The men so released would swell the ranks of the small Naval Brigade.

The dismay of the *Venus* survivors was echoed by Captain Sims when he discovered that he was attached to a party commanded by Lieutenant Lewis Callington.

He occupied his post of baggage master for only four days. Three days after setting out, he was warned by Lewis for being drunk on duty. Passing from the steamer to the 'flat' when it was drawn alongside for the night, the Merchant Navy captain overbalanced and fell in the river. Only the prompt action of Harry averted a tragedy.

A small boat was tied behind the 'flat'. With four seamen, the young midshipman leaped into the boat and set off after the wildly yelling sea captain. It was a remarkable rescue, carried out in a sudden rainstorm that reduced visibility to almost nil.

Captain Sims was recovered half-a-mile downriver and returned safely to the steamer. However, the dressing-down he received from Lewis Callington was more than he could swallow. The following day he developed severe stomach pains and was transferred to a steamer heading downriver to Calcutta.

It was to be the last the men of the Naval Brigade would see of the hard-drinking, Bible-quoting sea captain. There were few who regretted the loss.

Chapter 14

The journey upriver from Calcutta was not unpleasant – when the weather was fine. Even when it rained, as it did frequently, it was not so bad for those on the steamboat. However, it was extremely uncomfortable for the sailors who were taking passage on the 'flat'.

The ungainly barge had a raffia and bamboo canopy which effectively protected the men from the sun, but it was useless in a torrential downpour.

After each such storm, Lewis Callington would order the steamboat's captain to take his boat alongside the bank. Here the men would disembark and take part in rifle drill. Half-an-hour of this was usually sufficient to dry the men's uniforms and give them some much needed exercise.

Among those who most enjoyed the river voyage were Shashi and Harry. Despite the difficult conditions they managed to spend a great deal of time in each other's company.

They were often to be seen seated on the deck, chatting, usually with Fergus, Shirley Buchanan and Lewis Callington in attendance.

Fergus spent much of his time on the voyage sketching. There were many fascinating new scenes to record in his sketch pad – villages, towns, people. On at least three occasions shots were fired at them from the river bank, but always at such a range that they were not even of nuisance value.

Far more often there would be waves from the women and children who were either bathing, or washing clothes at the water's edge.

Each week-end, or sooner if they had suffered a spell of especially atrocious weather, Lewis would stop the boat at a particularly picturesque spot. Here the men would be allowed to camp on shore for twenty-four hours.

They would put up tents, play games or listen to music provided for them by the half-dozen bandsmen travelling with the party.

Further diversions were provided by local villagers. No matter how remote the spot where they made camp, within an hour it had attracted dozens of Indians of all ages and sexes. Goat-girls brought their charges to provide fresh milk for the sailors, there was fresh fruit in abundance, and the men could purchase Indian food and have it cooked for them on the spot.

The men enjoyed these camping breaks, but trouble erupted when the party was no more than a week away from Patna. They camped overnight near a large village which was unusually well stocked with arrack, the fiery alcohol produced by the villagers.

Two men who had drunk enough arrack to cloud their judgement, decided to pay Shashi a nocturnal visit and force themselves upon her. Both had been crew members on *Brilliant*, the ship that had picked up Shashi and the *Venus* survivors.

Creeping among the tents, they successfully evaded the armed guards set by Lewis Callington to patrol the camp and guard the perimeter.

Unfortunately, at the moment of their 'triumph', they chose the wrong tent. Instead of the slightly built Indian girl they were expecting, they found themselves up against the formidable Shirley Buchanan.

The guards were alerted not by *her* cries, but by those of the two would-be amorous sailors.

When the guards threw back the flaps of the American woman's tent they found one man lying unconscious. The other was so dazed he was incapable of coherent speech, or thought – and Shirley Buchanan was still banging their heads together.

The next morning, both men were given thirty-six lashes

each. The punishment was witnessed by their shipmates and by hordes of Indian villagers who watched with great interest from a distance.

After the flogging, Lieutenant Callington received a deputation of merchant seamen. They claimed that he had exceeded his authority in ordering such punishment for men of the merchant service.

Sternly, he pointed out to them that they were part of the Naval Brigade and were on a war footing, receiving an active service allowance. Because of this they were subject to service discipline. He would have been quite within his rights to have both men shot.

The delegation went back to their shipmates in a sober mood which was reflected throughout the camp.

Standing with Fergus, Lewis admitted, 'It had been my hope that I would never have to order a man to be flogged. It's thoroughly degrading.'

'It was necessary,' said Fergus. 'Without it you would have found it impossible to maintain discipline among the merchant seamen.'

'I don't think the men who just came to see me would agree with you,' declared Lewis. 'Their complaint was that there is one law for the officers – especially Royal Naval officers – and another for the men. They were no doubt hinting at the affair being carried on between Harry and Shashi.'

'There's a whole lot of difference between that and attempted rape,' said Fergus, heatedly.

'I agree. All the same, I'm going to have to talk to him. I can't afford to build up resentment between us and the merchant seamen. We need to operate as a single fighting force.'

'Don't say anything for the time being,' said Fergus. 'We'll be at Patna in a few days. Shashi and Miss Buchanan will be leaving us there. In the meantime, let me speak to both of them.'

Fergus spoke to Harry and Shashi that evening, when the three of them were seated on the upper deck of the steamer.

The sun had only just disappeared over the horizon and a light breeze from the river was dissipating the fiery heat of the day.

As tactfully as he could, he mentioned that the affair between the midshipman and the Indian girl was now an open secret. He also hinted that it was resented by some of the merchant seamen.

Harry's immediate reaction was one of anger. 'What Shashi and I do is hurting no one. What the *Brilliant*'s men are trying to do is get back at Lieutenant Callington through me, because he had two of their men flogged – and they brought that on themselves. They were lucky it was only thirty-six lashes. I'd have given them far more.'

'It's not just that, Harry. They resent the fact that you and Shashi have each other at a time when they have no one and are on their way to a war they didn't expect to be involved in. Anyway, no one's saying you should stop seeing each other. I'm speaking to you as a friend. Just try to be discreet, that's all.'

Harry was still angry. 'I don't feel like being discreet. If you want the truth, I love Shashi. I believe she feels the same way about me. Far from being discreet, I feel I want to stand up and shout the news to the world – and why shouldn't I?'

His anger had become defiance now. 'If they don't like it then I'll resign the service. Find work here in India. With the East India Company, perhaps. Lots of the Company's officials have married Indian women. Some of their sons are senior officials – generals, even. I'd find work easily enough . . .'

'No, Harry.' Seated beside him, Shashi reached out a hand and laid a long, slim finger across his lips. 'You will not leave the navy. You are an officer, an important man. Your mother and father must be very proud of you. If you left the navy because of me they would hate me. I would not like that. One day you too might grow to hate me. When you saw your friends become very important officers in the navy, you would think, "If it were not for Shashi, I too would be important now." That would make me very unhappy.'

'I would never think like that!' Once more the finger applied gentle pressure on his lips.

'Hush! You must speak no more of leaving the navy.'

Removing her finger and resting the hand on his arm, she smiled at him in the half-light.

'I'm *not* going to stop seeing you, Shashi.'

'I am pleased.' She squeezed his arm affectionately. 'We will spend time together – but others will not know. It will be all right. You will see.'

Chapter 15

Fate stepped in to take the minds of the seamen off the affair between Harry and Shashi. The next morning two men were taken ill, including one of those who had been flogged. Both showed symptoms of cholera.

Brought on board the steamer and placed in a cabin, the men were nursed by Shashi and Shirley Buchanan. Despite all their efforts, the man who had been flogged died during the night. His body was immediately consigned to the Ganges.

His place in the cabin was taken within hours by another of the merchant seamen, struck down with the same killer disease.

All that day the two women tended the men who fought very hard for their lives. Nevertheless, they showed very little improvement.

When the boat and the 'flat' moored alongside the river bank that evening, Shashi said she would go to a nearby village to buy herbs with which to treat the sick men. Cholera was endemic among her people. They had developed methods of treating it which were still unknown to western physicians.

Harry suggested that he should accompany her with an escort, but Shashi refused his offer. The attitude of the local people to the present troubles was unknown. It would probably be far safer for everyone if she went alone.

Lewis agreed with her, but when two hours had passed without her return, he began to think he might have been wrong. He was actually discussing sending out a party to look for her when she returned on board.

More serious than Fergus had recently seen her, she entered the cabin where he and the two naval officers were discussing her long absence. She had brought more than herbs with her from the Indian village.

Looking fearful, she told them there were mutineers in the village from the 40th Regiment. With them they had brought some captured 'big guns' with which they had impressed the villagers. It was their plan to lie in wait for the steamboat and the 'flat' some miles up the river. The chosen spot was where an island divided it. Here the steamboat would be forced into a narrow channel between island and bank. The attack was intended to cause such confusion that the steamboat would run aground, putting its occupants at their mercy.

'How did you learn all this, Shashi?' Lewis was justifiably concerned, but also somewhat incredulous.

'There was a *Moulvi* – a holy man – in the marketplace. He was telling all the people of the village that they must help the sepoys. Give them food and shelter, and loan their elephants to pull the guns. He said that the fight of the sepoys is the people's fight too. This I heard with my own ears.'

'They said all this in your hearing? Was no one suspicious of you?'

'Yes. One of the sepoys asked who I was. He said I was too well dressed to be a villager. I told him I was a servant of the gods in the great temple of Darjeeling. That I was on my way to collect the daughters of a widow who were being given to the temple.'

'Do you think he believed you?'

'I *know* he did. He gave me money to buy food along my journey.'

'Good girl! We'd better go and speak to the captain and the pilot. We'll find this island on the map and see if we can't arrange a surprise for these mutineers.'

The Scots captain of the steamer was enthusiastic about turning the tables on the would-be ambushers. The Indian pilot was not. He protested that he was not paid to involve himself in such matters. When he suggested he should leave the ship and they should find themselves another pilot, Lewis ordered him to be confined to his cabin and set two of the seamen to guard him.

Before the man was taken away, Lewis told him he would act under orders the following morning – or be shot.

When the pilot had been taken away, still protesting, the naval officer said, 'Now he's gone, let's discuss what we're going to do. I'll give you my ideas, but I'm open to suggestions . . .'

There was no sleep for either officers or men that night. At an hour when they would normally have been sleeping, about a hundred men were put ashore. They were all well-armed. In addition, they took with them two howitzers.

The party was marching on a course that would curve around the spot where they believed the mutineers to be hiding in strength. Ahead of the party, Lewis sent out scouts. Their duty was to prevent the main body being detected by any of the sepoys who might be travelling between the river and the village where Shashi had heard of the plot.

Meanwhile, Harry set off upriver in command of two boats, in which were some thirty armed seamen. They were to land on the island where it was believed many of the mutineers were hiding.

They approached the island from the wider, shallower channel and found a number of native boats tied to the bank. A quick examination convinced Harry there were probably no more than fifty or sixty men in the enemy's party. There might be more if they had made more than one trip in the boats – but he did not dwell upon this thought. With surprise on his side, such odds were not daunting, even though the mutineers were highly trained soldiers.

Deploying the sailors in a defensive position guarding the boats, Harry settled down to wait out the hour until dawn.

This was the hardest part of the action and it proved to be a very long hour. The slightest sound made by the cautious men seemed amplified out of all proportion. The soft sound of water against the muddy bank of the island would at one moment sound like a footstep; at another it resembled the approach of yet another boat bringing reinforcements to the unseen mutineers.

The most tense moments arrived with the dawn. As the light increased Harry wondered whether he and his small party would be discovered by the ambushing party. As the sun rose, he breathed a deep sigh of relief. The island was a wooded hill, rising out of the river. The sepoys would have positioned themselves on the far side, waiting for the steamer to approach.

It seemed another age before the waiting men heard the throbbing note of the steamer's engine. Not until now did Harry lead his men forward, warning them once again about maintaining absolute silence.

When they gained the crest of the low hill, the seamen could hear the excited voices of the sepoys. Signalling for his men to remain where they were, he went on alone to reconnoitre.

He did not have to go far. When the trees thinned, he found himself looking down on the mutineers' position. They had cut down branches and laid them out to form a low screen between them and their intended target. There were fifty of them. Although well-armed, they would have nothing to protect them from the fire of the seamen who would be above and behind them.

Returning to his party, Harry told them in a low but excited voice what he had seen. It was agreed they would take no action until the sepoys began firing upon the steamboat and the empty 'flat'.

The steamer approached the channel slowly. Then, when it was almost within range, increased speed to the maximum that its underpowered engine would allow.

This unexpected tactic caught the ambushers off guard and they opened fire prematurely, fearing the steamboat would escape.

At the same time, from the far bank of the river, there was the boom of the two howitzers of Lieutenant Callington's party. He had located the sepoys on that side of the river and opened fire before they could bring their own cannon to bear on the steamer.

Suddenly, all was confusion. Harry and his men moved quietly into position and at his signal poured a deadly volley into the backs of the sepoys.

It took the mutineers completely by surprise. At first they seemed unable to comprehend that the shots had come from behind them. By the time realisation dawned, the seamen had re-loaded and fired another volley.

A few of the surviving sepoys recovered sufficiently to return the fire of the seamen, others threw up their arms in a vain gesture of surrender. All fell in the third and fourth volleys.

The defeat of the mutineers on the island had taken no more than five minutes. Fighting was still taking place on the far bank, but both actions had been completely successful. On the mainland the howitzers, loaded with canister-shot, had wreaked havoc in the sepoy ranks. The sailors had followed up the bombardment with small arms fire and the bayonet.

Thanks to Shashi, a potential disaster had been turned into a crushing defeat for the sepoys. It had provided the reinforcements for the Naval Brigade with a victory of which they could be proud.

Chapter 16

When the steamboat reached Patna, Shirley Buchanan went ashore to find her brother. She would arrange through him for her luggage to be collected. Back on board Lewis Callington turned a blind eye to the fact that his midshipman was saying farewell to Shashi in her cabin.

The young couple were now held in high esteem by everyone on board: Shashi for her part in discovering the plot against the steamer, and her unstinting nursing of the sick and wounded on board; Harry for wiping out the sepoys on the island without sustaining a single casualty among his own men.

Shirley Buchanan returned to the steamboat after only half-an-hour ashore – and posed yet another problem for Lewis. Her brother was not in Patna. He had been transferred to Allahabad by the East India Company. Now she wanted to stay with the steamer for the three-week journey there.

The naval officer was doubtful about acceding to her request. The sick and wounded had been landed and the presence of the women could no longer be justified. There were reports of a serious uprising of mutineers at Allahabad which had been put down with extreme severity. Although the city was said to be under control now, it was at the heart of the most troubled area. He did not like the idea of taking women there.

Shirley solved the matter in her own forthright manner. As she had at Calcutta, she threatened to make her own arrangements to travel to Allahabad. When this failed to win Lewis over, she stormed ashore to visit the Patna Commissioner.

The East India official had been congratulated by the Company for the forceful manner with which he had dealt with an attempted uprising in Patna. He was far from forceful when he came on board the steamer an hour later, almost begging the naval officer to take the American woman on to Allahabad and out of Patna.

Lewis protested that Allahabad was too close to the fighting. It was no place for a woman. The official assured him that the town was the gathering point for the huge army that had marched inland to relieve Lucknow. When the women and children were rescued they would be brought back to Allahabad. As a result, it would be strongly garrisoned. Shirley Buchanan would be in no danger.

Despite his misgivings, Lewis eventually gave in to the commissioner's pleas. He would take the American woman and her Indian companion on to Allahabad – but no farther.

The steamer with the 'flat' in tow never reached Allahabad. The pilot taken on at Patna proved to be less knowledgeable of the river than he should have been. When no more than four or five steaming days from their destination, he ran the steamer so firmly aground on a mud bank that it could not be refloated.

After twenty-four hours of futile effort, Lewis Callington decided to abandon the boat. By landing the men and using their combined strength, the 'flat' was pulled alongside the river bank. Here work began on unloading the vast quantity of stores, guns and ammunition carried by the unwieldy vessel.

A camp was set up on the shore. When everything had been landed, Harry was sent off with twenty men to march to Allahabad. His mission was to notify the military authorities of their misadventure and arrange for animals and men to come to their aid with transport for the baggage and stores.

Harry and his men had not travelled more than five miles along a narrow path when they reached a major road. Here they discovered a huge army on the move. In addition to the soldiers, there were elephants, horses, ox carts, flocks of goats and a vast number of servants, men and women.

They appeared to be Indian troops. Not certain whether or not they belonged to the army of the mutineers, Harry and his men settled down in a clump of trees. It would take some time for the long column to pass by.

Then a troop of horsemen moved along the road, over-taking the infantry. Their uniforms were the most colourful Harry had ever seen – but the men wearing them were European.

Hurrying from the shelter of the trees, the sailors shouted to attract the attention of the cavalrymen. Their leader saw them and turned his horse off the road to meet them. Four of his companions rode with him.

The man who appeared to be the cavalry leader wore no recognisable badges of rank, but Harry saluted him anyway. 'Midshipman Harry Downton, sir. I'm with a naval party of a hundred and twenty-six men. We're making our way upriver to Allahabad to join the Naval Brigade, but the pilot has put our boat fast on a mud bank. We've unloaded everything from the "flat", but have no transport. My commanding officer would be grateful for any assistance you might be able to offer.'

Returning the salute in a distinctly unmilitary manner, the horseman said, 'Damned pilots! One did the same to us when we came upriver. Matter of fact he ran us aground on just about every bend we came to. Well, you might be in luck. We're travelling with a battalion of Gurkhas. They're commanded by a Nepalese prince. He and his entourage have enough elephants and bullock carts with them to move the whole Indian nation. I think we'll be able to find enough to do the job. I'll send one of my men to let the others know what's happening, then come with you to see what's needed.'

The accent of the man was American – and there was

something vaguely familiar about him. Harry asked, 'Excuse me, sir, but your name wouldn't be Buchanan by any chance?'

'That's right. I'm sorry, in my surprise at meeting you and your men out here in the middle of nowhere, I've forgotten to introduce myself. Colonel Sam Buchanan – that's a United States rank, not one of yours. These are my men, Buchanan's Horse. I raised 'em myself, right after we heard of the massacre at Cawnpore. We probably wouldn't win any praise on a parade ground, but we can sure as hell fight.'

Harry smiled. He was unused to such informality and the man seemed extremely young to be a colonel in command of his own cavalry unit.

'You can smile, sir, but I'm speaking the truth. I picked up my rank fighting Mexicans. There wasn't any fight in them worth writing home about, but a bullet's a bullet, no matter who's behind the gun.'

'I wouldn't argue with that, sir – but that wasn't the reason I was smiling. You see, we've brought your sister upriver with us. She came up to Patna with us to visit you. When she heard you'd moved to Allahabad she insisted upon travelling on with us. I don't think she was expecting you to be in command of your own cavalry. I don't know what she's going to do now.'

'You've got Shirley with you?' The young American colonel looked flabbergasted. His mouth opened and closed a couple of times but the words failed to escape. Then he shook his head. 'She's my *elder* sister, Harry, and unless she's changed a hell of a lot since I last met her I'm going to be hard pressed to stop her taking over my men from me. She's a pretty formidable woman.'

Chapter 17

Leaving the sailors to be fed by the servants accompanying the Gurkhas, Harry accepted the loan of a horse from the cavalrymen. With Sam Buchanan and a quarter of the mounted soldiers, he made his way back to where he had left Lewis, Fergus and the others.

The new arrivals were given a rousing welcome by the sailors, but the reunion of brother and sister was as matter-of-fact as though they had met on a New York street. Sam Buchanan expressed no surprise that they should meet here, in the heart of India, many thousands of miles from their home.

After receiving satisfactory replies to his questions about the health of family and friends in America, he went off with Lewis to discuss the needs of the naval party.

Meanwhile, Fergus was hurriedly sketching the irregular cavalrymen, anxious to capture something of their flamboyance and colourful dress. As he worked, Harry told him he would have a busy time over the next few days, sketching the Gurkhas and all the followers of their small army.

Fergus was still busy when he was called to a meeting with Sam Buchanan and Harry. It seemed the Gurkhas and cavalrymen were not making for Allahabad after all. They were heading for a rendezvous with General Sir Colin Campbell, Commander-in-Chief of the army in India. He was on the road to Lucknow. The Naval Brigade from the *Shannon* was with him.

Fergus found it gratifying to be given details of what was happening. At the same time, he was puzzled. He felt this was not the reason he had been called to the meeting.

247

'That's quite true,' agreed Lewis. 'But there's a very strong sepoy force investing the Residency in Lucknow. There's bound to be some fierce fighting. You're a non-combatant. We felt you should be given the opportunity to go to Allahabad instead. You'd be given an escort of Gurkhas. I'm afraid we need to keep all the cavalry with us.'

This still did not ring true to Fergus. 'Would I be the only one being escorted to Allahabad?'

Lewis appeared suddenly ill-at-ease and Fergus felt he was about to hear the true reason for the suggestion he should leave the expeditionary force.

'No. Miss Buchanan would go with you. I . . . we, were rather hoping you would have words with her. Try to persuade her this is the best course. She seems to listen to you rather more than she does anyone else. Convince her she would be placing her life – and that of Shashi – in danger by remaining with us. Unfortunately, we cannot spare soldiers in sufficient strength to provide her with a satisfactory escort.'

Fergus grinned. 'What you're really saying is that no one wants to tell Shirley Buchanan that she can't go with you to Lucknow and you'd like me to do the dirty work! Sorry, you can count me out. I'm coming with you to Lucknow. Admiral Sir James Stott sent me out here to record the Naval Brigade at war. I can't do that in Allahabad.'

Lewis sighed. 'That's what I thought you would say.' Switching his glance to the American cavalry leader, he said, 'I'm sorry, Sam. It looks as though you're going to have to carry out your brotherly duty.'

'I think I'd rather take on a full regiment of mutineering sepoys,' moaned Sam Buchanan. 'But, as you so rightly say, she's *my* sister.'

For perhaps the seventh time that evening, and with increasing weariness, Sam Buchanan said, 'It's quite out of the question, Shirley. I can't take you with me to Lucknow. There's going to be one hell of a fight there and men just can't be spared to guard you. I'll detail some of my own troops to escort you to Allahabad if you don't like the idea

248

of travelling with a Gurkha escort. You can leave first thing in the morning. It will be a hard ride, but you'll be there before dark.'

'I have no intention of going to Allahabad. I never intended going there in the first place. All I wanted to do was to find you. Well, I have. I'll stay with you now.'

Sam Buchanan spread his hands wide in a gesture of exasperation. 'I've told you . . .'

'I know very well what you've told me, Sam, but you don't need to worry about taking care of me. You never have. Besides, that Nepalese prince has a whole harem travelling with him, as well as more women servants than you've got cavalrymen. If there's trouble along the way Shashi and I will stay with them. The prince won't allow anything to harm his women. Then, if you or your men get hurt, you'll have Shashi and I here to take care of you.'

Sam Buchanan threw up his hands in despair and appealed to Fergus who was an interested bystander with Harry and Lewis. 'You tell her. You're neutral. Tell her it's impossible for her to come along with us.'

Fergus smiled wryly. 'I think she'd treat such a statement from me, you, or anyone else, as a challenge. You might as well give in with good grace. Ask the prince if he'll let Shirley and Shashi stay with his women if we meet up with any trouble along the way.'

'Thank you, friend. I hoped I might be able to depend upon you to back me up.'

Fergus shrugged, secretly amused at the cavalry leader's inability to influence his sister. 'As you said, I'm neutral – and I intend staying that way. Besides, if someone's going to be annoyed with me, I'd rather it was you than your sister.'

Chapter 18

The army of Gurkhas travelling with Sam Buchanan's irregular cavalry made painfully slow progress on the road to Lucknow. But so too did General Campbell whose route took him via Cawnpore. After a brief stay there he resumed his ponderous advance, leaving some of his men behind to guard an important bridge over the river.

It was an avenging army, incensed by the recent massacre of women and children. The stories of atrocities were enhanced with each telling. As a result, villages on either side of the advance were razed to the ground. Natives who *might* have had anything to do with the fighting, or were believed to support the sepoys, were hung from the nearest tree without any pretence of a trial.

Sam Buchanan's irregular cavalry, eager to do battle with the mutineering sepoys, fumed impatiently at the rate of progress. Many of the sailors too were anxious to bring the war against the sepoys to a close so they might return to the more familiar sea once more.

It seemed that only Harry and Shashi were content with the pace of the column which extended for more than a mile along the dusty roads in the wake of the cavalry vanguard.

For Fergus, travelling with Prince Narayan, there was so much to sketch that he was kept busy for most of the time. The prince's entourage provided with him enough subjects to fill more artists' pads than he carried with him.

'Buchanan's Horse' too was full of characters, most as colourful as the gaudy uniforms they sported.

There were a couple of minor skirmishes along the way

to remind the party of the purpose of their long and uncomfortable journey. These broke the monotony of the daily routine, but posed no real threat to anyone and Fergus was able to sketch without interruption.

Word of his skills eventually reached the ears of Prince Narayan. One evening, when the column had made camp, Fergus was invited to dine with the prince in his huge and luxurious tent. He was instructed to bring his sketch pad with him.

The prince was a well-educated man who spoke excellent English. As they ate, he glanced through Fergus's sketches. Occasionally something in the book would delight him and he would point it out to a courtier seated beside him before beaming in Fergus's direction.

Eventually the sketch pad was handed to a servant and returned to Fergus and the prince said, 'I would like you to sketch me now.'

It was the moment Fergus had been waiting for all evening. The prince was dressed in colourful silks, heavily decorated with gold braid and adorned with a wealth of precious stones. He also had a fine face with carefully trimmed beard and moustache. Using pastel crayons, Fergus set about reproducing the Nepalese prince on his sketch pad.

With a speed born of the experience he had gained in dockside taverns, he produced not one but two sketches. One would be kept in the pad for himself, the other he cut out carefully and handed to a servant to be taken to his host.

Prince Narayan looked at the sketch for a long time and his entourage studied his expression anxiously. The sketch would be passed to them in due course. Their opinion of it would need to be in line with that of their ruler.

Eventually, the prince handed the sketch to the courtier nearest to him and nodded benignly in Fergus's direction. It was the signal for which the others had been waiting. The first courtier went into raptures about the sketch. As it was passed from hand to hand, the others did their best to outdo his enthusiasm.

Moments later entertainment was provided by a group of musicians armed with drums and a variety of string instruments. Fergus found the sound unpleasing to his ears, but the dancing girls who performed with them delighted him. His sketch pad was brought into use once more and he tried to capture the grace of their movements.

When the dancers ended their performance, each of them dropped to her knees in front of the prince and bowed her head to the ground at his feet. Then they stood back in a line and appeared to be waiting for something.

Fergus looked up from his sketching to see the prince's glance upon him. Pointing to the girls, Narayan said, 'You will choose one, artist?'

Startled, Fergus shook his head. 'I am honoured, your Highness – but, no.'

The prince shrugged and signalled for the girls to leave. A servant now stepped forward with a container the size of a cigar box. Kneeling before Fergus, he lifted the lid and the lights illuminating the tent struck fire from its contents.

'You will choose one – as a gift from me, artist. It is in recognition of your talent. May I suggest you make your choice from the rubies? They are among the finest in the world.'

Fergus was speechless. Some of the stones were larger in diameter than his thumbnail. He had heard rumours of the generosity of Indian princes. Now he was sampling it at first hand.

He chose a beautifully cut ruby, and knew he was holding a considerable fortune in his hand. He was still stammering his thanks when an official said to him, 'You will go now. Tomorrow night you will return to make a picture of the Prince's favourite wife.'

'It will be a pleasure.' Fergus was still bemused by the generosity of Prince Narayan, but doubted whether he would be able to please him as much with his wife's portrait. The Prince was a man of about fifty and Fergus thought his favourite wife would probably be about the same age. It would be difficult to make a sketch that was both truthful and flattering. However, he would do his best.

Later that evening, Fergus showed Harry the gift given to him by the Nepalese prince.

After turning it over in his hand a number of times, Harry held it up to the lamp and watched the light strike sparks from it. 'It's magnificent, Fergus. If I had the money I'd buy it from you. It would make a wonderful engagement ring for Shashi.'

His words startled Fergus. 'Engagement ring? You're surely not serious, Harry?'

Handing back the ruby, he said stiffly, 'And why shouldn't I be? I want to marry her. I thought that you of all people would understand. You've always been far more sympathetic towards her than anyone else.'

'I think she's a wonderful girl, Harry.' Fergus knew he needed to be extremely careful if he were not to offend the sensitive young man beyond all redemption. 'But you're still a young man and there's a great future ahead of you. Tie yourself to Shashi now and, rightly or wrongly, your career will come to an abrupt halt.'

'So? The navy's not the only thing in life.'

'It was before you met Shashi. I'm not saying you should give her up, but just be happy with what you have right now. Don't think too much about the future. I think that's the way Shashi sees it too. These are uncertain times, Harry.'

Later that same night, in the darkness of Harry's tent, as she lay in the arms of her young lover, Shashi echoed Fergus's words.

The young midshipman always managed to have his tent pitched in as secluded a spot as was possible in a camp of such a size. Tonight it was in the shadow of the wall of a ruined house, on a bank close to a small river.

'You must not talk of marriage, Harry. It is not possible.'

'Of course it's possible. There are many Europeans here who have married Indian girls. Men in high places. One is a general.'

'They are living in India, Harry. You are a sailor. Your life is spent on the sea. You will visit many countries. Meet many people.'

'I don't *have* to be in the navy. I can find work with the Company and stay here in India.'

Lying with Harry, Shashi was happier than she had ever been before. But she knew that what he was saying was impossible. She had been given to the temple to be a *deva dasi*, a servant of the gods. She still belonged to them. One day, if Harry remained in India, he would learn what she had been. What she had done. He would be ashamed of her. Shashi knew this would hurt her more than anything else he could do. She would do anything for him – but marriage was out of the question.

'We will talk of it later, Harry. When all the fighting is done. For now, all I want is to be with you. To have you love me. Please, no more talking. Just love me . . .'

Chapter 19

The meeting between the small army of Gurkhas and the greater one led by General Sir Colin Campbell took place well short of their destination. As a result there was an immediate change of plan.

General Campbell sent the Gurkha army off to guard the road between Lucknow and Cawnpore. Their orders were to secure a number of strategic positions and hold them. This was the route Campbell intended taking when he evacuated the women and the wounded from the Lucknow Residency.

Prince Narayan was not at all pleased with his orders. He had brought his army from Nepal to put down the mutineers. The Gurkhas were fighting men, not garrison guards.

The British general was able to convince the prince that the role of his troops would be a vital one. As for fighting . . . Campbell did not believe the mutineer sepoy army would allow the Gurkhas to take and hold such important positions without putting up a stiff resistance. The prince would experience enough fighting to satisfy the most warlike of his warriors.

The fiery little general had far less success in his dealings with Shirley Buchanan.

When told there was a white woman travelling with Buchanan's Horse, he suggested the Gurkhas should provide her with an escort to Allahabad. He could not have a woman travelling with his army.

His decision was passed down through a series of increasingly junior officers, until it reached a young subaltern, newly arrived in India. He was detailed to inform Shirley Buchanan.

The American woman's reply was less than ladylike. 'You can tell your general that if he wants me to go to Allahabad he'll need to carry me there himself – and I won't go quietly. I came here to be with my brother and I intend staying with him. That means I'll be coming to Lucknow.'

The message was relayed back along the line of command until it arrived in the tent of Lieutenant General Sir Colin Campbell, KGCB, and was passed on to him by a nervous aide-de-camp.

Bristling with annoyance, the general demanded, 'Damn the woman! Who is she, anyway?'

'She's an American,' said the aide, as though this explained everything, adding, 'Actually, I believe she's related to the President of the United States.'

'That's all I need,' declared General Campbell, angrily thumping the table in front of him with his fist. 'An awkward woman with influential relatives. Very well, send her *and* her brother to Allahabad.'

'We could do that, of course,' agreed the increasingly agitated aide. 'Unfortunately, he is Colonel Buchanan of Buchanan's Horse. They're irregulars. If he goes they will no doubt go with him. As you know, we're desperately short of good cavalrymen.'

'Damn and blast! Do I have to deal personally with every trifling little matter that occurs in my army? Very well, bring the woman here. I'll talk some sense into her. She may be American, but she can't be *totally* stupid. Go and fetch her yourself, Andrew. I'll sort this out quickly then get on with the business of conducting a war.'

Captain Andrew Mackinnon's mission was no more successful than had been that of the junior subaltern. After a lengthy and frustrating search for Shirley Buchanan, he eventually located her in the Gurkha camp. She had made a number of friends among the women of Prince Narayan's household and was bidding farewell to them before they set off in a different direction to the main force.

By this time, the aide-de-camp was somewhat fraught

and Shirley Buchanan did nothing to make him less so. When told the general wished to speak to her about going to Allahabad, she informed Andrew Mackinnon there was nothing to talk about. She was *not* going to Allahabad. Perhaps the general would care to discuss the matter when they arrived in Lucknow?

The aide protested that in addition to leading an army in wartime, General Campbell had considerable responsibility for all those travelling with him. If she had any consideration at all, she would make his onerous task easier by understanding his concern for her and doing as she was asked.

'I'll do better than that,' replied Shirley Buchanan. 'I'll remove myself from the general's responsibility and travel unescorted to Lucknow. After all, the sepoys are in dispute with Britain and not with the United States of America.'

Having delivered her own solution to the matter, she said, 'Now, I'll be obliged if you'll go off and attend to your own duties. I have a few more friends to find before I return to my own tent and prepare for my departure.'

Andrew Mackinnon hurried back to the Headquarters tent to report the failure of his errand and to suffer the inevitable fury of his Commander-in-Chief.

All went much as the harassed aide-de-camp had predicted. When General Campbell's anger subsided, he said, 'Take me to this damned woman, Captain Mackinnon. I'll tell her myself what she's to do.'

The general's temper was not improved when they reached Shirley Buchanan's tent only to learn that she had not yet returned. The general was on his way back to his headquarters, berating the unfortunate aide, when Andrew Mackinnon suddenly said, 'I believe this is Miss Buchanan coming our way now, sir.'

Shirley was returning from the Gurkha camp with Shashi when she was confronted by the diminutive figure of Sir Colin Campbell. She had not met the general before, but knew immediately who he was.

Before he had time to vent his anger upon her, she said,

'General! How kind of you to come to speak to me in person.'

Fighting to keep a tight rein on his notorious temper, General Campbell said, 'Andrew, you may leave us. I will walk Miss Buchanan to her tent.'

Turning to Shashi, he was less polite. 'You! Leave us.'

'Her name is Shashi, General Campbell. She's my companion. *I* will give her any instructions that need to be obeyed. By the way, Captain Peel of the Naval Brigade sent for her today. He is recommending that her bravery in saving the survivors of *HMS Venus* be officially recognised by your government.'

General Sir Colin Campbell's temper was well-known but so too was his normally chivalrous attitude to women. Inclining his head to Shashi, he said, 'My apologies if my manner seemed rather brusque, young lady. I fear I have a great deal on my mind at the moment. Perhaps you would be kind enough to leave me alone with Miss Buchanan for a few minutes. There is a small matter I wish to discuss with her.'

'That was very gallant of you, General. Thank you, Shashi, you may leave us now.'

'Yes, Miss Buchanan – and thank you, General Campbell. There was really no need to apologise.'

Controlling his anger at having Shashi speak to him as an equal, as though she were a European woman, he said, 'The girl speaks excellent English.' The observation was made as she walked away.

'Yes, General. She's an intelligent human being – despite the fact that she's both Indian and a woman.'

General Campbell looked at Shirley sharply, but she gave him an enigmatic smile and said, 'I believe you have something you wish to discuss with me. Shall we walk along the river bank?'

When General Campbell returned to the headquarters tent, he found his aide-de-camp waiting nervously. As the general entered, the young captain jumped to his feet.

'You've spoken to her, sir? When . . .?'

'Bring Dr Browne to me, if you please, Andrew.'

Dr Browne, employed by the Honourable East India Company, was accompanying the army to Lucknow as the Superintending Surgeon.

'The surgeon, sir? Has there been an accident?'

'Dammit, man! Shall I need to go and find *him* for myself too!'

A few minutes later Andrew Mackinnon returned to the tent in the wake of a tall, distinguished man dressed in the casual manner of those who had lived in India for a long time.

Waving him to a seat, General Campbell said, 'Thank you for coming, Browne. I have something to say that I hope you will find pleasing. You will know, of course, how helpful that woman Nightingale proved to be at the hospitals we had in the Crimea? Well, I think I've found someone of similar character with a first-class knowledge of nursing, and a great deal of administrative experience. She is travelling with another extremely able young woman – an Indian girl – who should be of help too. You're going to need all the assistance you can get when we reach Lucknow. Not only will there be our own casualties, but there will be the women and children who have been trapped in the Residency for all these months. It will be extremely helpful to have a competent woman around . . .'

General Campbell continued to sing the praises of Shirley Buchanan and Shashi to the Superintending Surgeon. While he was speaking he was careful to avoid meeting the smug gaze levelled at him by his young aide-de-camp.

Andrew Mackinnon said nothing, but he was enjoying his rare moment of silent vindication.

Chapter 20

On the outskirts of Lucknow was the palace of Dilkoosha. Although it was held by a strong force of rebel sepoys, they retreated from it without putting up a fight. It was here that Dr Browne set up his hospital. It would prove to be sorely needed by the attacking troops.

It was a very pleasant setting, with a superb garden and a deer park. Sir Colin Campbell put his army into camp here for two nights. It would give them a well-deserved respite before he threw them into battle to relieve the Lucknow Residency.

For two evenings, Harry and Shashi were able to walk together in the gardens of the palace and imagine that the war was far away. It was something of which they never spoke.

Both were apprehensive about the forthcoming battle. Shashi was concerned for Harry's safety. In his turn, he feared that the sepoys, who greatly outnumbered Sir Colin's army, would try an encircling movement. If they did so they might attack the makeshift hospital.

The lovers spent as much of the last night together as was possible, but it seemed all too brief. Harry was on watchkeeping duties with the Naval Brigade at midnight. Shashi shared a room in the hospital with Shirley Buchanan and could not be too late returning.

When they parted Shashi was in tears, although Harry tried to comfort her by insisting that the Naval Brigade was basically an artillery unit. He lied that it would not be involved in actual close combat.

The British army set off at an early hour the following

morning. They took a roundabout route to the Residency. This had been suggested by one of the men formerly beleaguered in the building. He had succeeded in making a daring escape and reaching the British army to give General Campbell invaluable information.

Despite this, their circuitous advance was slow and strongly contested. The main opposition was coming from a very large building that was in their line of advance. General Campbell decided it must be taken before they could progress any further.

The approach to the building was by way of a narrow roadway between houses. So fierce was the fighting that it was not long before the troops were pinned down, unable to move forward, or back.

At this point, the British general called upon the Naval Brigade. Raked by the musket fire of the sepoys, they brought their heavy guns to bear on the building.

For an hour the naval guns pounded the stout walls of the building and eventually had the desired effect. The wall was breached. True, it was only a small opening, but the Highlanders of the 93rd Regiment declared it was enough to enable them to climb through and take the building.

They made it into the building – but not until a great many of their number had died in the attempt. Once inside they continued to encounter stiff resistance and the battle developed into a hard-fought contest for room after bloody room in the huge building.

Suddenly, it was all over. The gunfire ceased. Now the only sound was the groaning of the wounded, many of them lying buried beneath the bodies of their comrades. The last of the rebels to be killed was shot out of the branches of a tree in the garden. It turned out not to be a sepoy, but a young woman. Her slim body joined those of almost two thousand mutineers killed in the house and gardens. Seasoned soldiers agreed it was one of the hardest battles they had ever fought.

The cost of the battle for the British soldiers was also high. Many of Fergus's sketches depicted the wounded being carried or helped back to the hospital.

He had been ordered by Sir Colin Campbell to remain behind at the hospital, but Fergus protested that this was not why he had come to India. He reminded the general that he had been sent out from England by Admiral of the Fleet Sir James Stott.

His words provoked one of the general's wrathful outbursts. 'I don't take my orders from admirals, young man – and while you are with my army, neither will you. You will remain here, with the hospital staff.'

Fergus made no further argument, but when the Naval Brigade left the palace grounds, he went with them. As the Brigade manhandled their guns into position under withering fire at the end of the narrow street, he was there to record the scene.

Beyond the building for which the Highlanders had fought so fiercely was a high-walled, domed building which housed the tomb of an ancient Indian ruler. This too needed to be taken before Sir Colin Campbell would rest easy that night. Once again the guns of the Naval Brigade were called in to breach the walls – and here too Fergus was at hand to record the action.

It was while he was busily sketching that he saw Harry fall wounded as the guns were being dragged to a more advanced position.

Stuffing his sketch pad in the satchel he carried over one shoulder, Fergus ran forward as musket balls whined around him.

Harry lay in the middle of a street, exposed to the fire of the mutineers. The first thing Fergus needed to do was drag him to a less open spot. He chose the shaded side of a partly demolished house wall. Minutes later other wounded men were dragged to the same place and an army surgeon and his assistant arrived on the scene.

Harry lay gasping in pain. A musket ball had struck him in the thigh and he was bleeding profusely. A pad was placed on the wound by the surgeon's assistant, but little more could be done immediately. There were others more seriously wounded than the young midshipman. Fergus was told to hold the pad firmly in place until the surgeon could see him.

For more than an hour he remained with Harry while around him the surgeon operated on an ever-growing number of casualties, a number of whom had lost limbs, or who required immediate amputations.

Meanwhile, the battle raged on about them. The sepoys were also using artillery now. With bullets, cannonballs and masonry crashing about him, the surgeon carried out his grisly task.

Eventually, he found time to attend to Harry.

'There's a musket ball still inside there,' he said to Fergus. 'It will need to come out but he'll have a better chance of recovery if the operation is carried out in the hospital. I'll have him taken there.'

It was another hour before two native bearers arrived with a *doolie*, a covered stretcher which they would use to carry Harry away.

Fergus went with him. On the way he constantly cursed the bearers when they stumbled, causing Harry to writhe in pain. Even while he was berating them, Fergus admired the bravery of the two Indians who were under fire for much of the way. They might have been forgiven at one point had they abandoned the stretcher altogether and run for safety.

They had covered only half the distance to the hospital when a slim figure came running along the street towards them. It was Shashi.

When she saw Fergus and the *doolie* bearers, her face showed her fear as she gasped, 'Harry . . .?'

He nodded towards the *doolie* which had been placed on the ground by the bearers while they took a brief breather. 'He's here – and he's alive.'

Shashi dropped to her knees and drew back the piece of dirty muslin which hung down from the ragged canopy to keep off flies.

In considerable pain, Harry's delight at seeing her was apparent to Fergus. Shashi was distressed when she saw the blood-soaked bandage about his leg, but Harry reached up and took her hand. 'It's all right, Shashi. I'm going to be all right.'

A musket ball glanced off a stone wall nearby and sang out as it headed in a new direction. 'We need to move on,' declared Fergus, signalling for the bearers to take up the *doolie*. 'You shouldn't be out here, Shashi. It's not safe – either from the sepoys or our own troops. They're far too excited to be reasoned with.'

'It does not matter now. I have found Harry. A wounded sailor was brought to the hospital – one of those who came with us from Calcutta. I asked him about Harry. The sailor said he saw him shot down. I believed he was dead and could think of nothing else. I . . . I just ran until I found you.'

'Fergus is right, Shashi. You shouldn't be out here . . .' Harry winced as the two bearers lifted the *doolie*. He squeezed Shashi's hand reassuringly as she berated her two countrymen. 'I'm all right. Everything will be all right now. You'll see . . .'

Chapter 21

The wounded men at the palace hospital were numbered in their hundreds, and more were being carried in all the time. It was not until late in the evening that a surgeon operated to remove the musket ball from Harry's leg.

Afterwards, the surgeon told Fergus that the ball had come to rest against Harry's thigh bone. Fortunately, there appeared to be nothing broken. Nevertheless, he had lost a great deal of blood and would be in considerable pain for some time. But he had Shashi to nurse him.

Shirley Buchanan also visited him whenever she had a spare few moments. She was proving to be a tower of strength to both surgeons and wounded. The Superintending Surgeon was heard to say during the long evening that she was a woman 'cast from the same mould as the redoubtable Miss Nightingale'.

Wounded men continued to be brought to the hospital even after darkness had fallen. The rebels were not relinquishing their stranglehold on the Lucknow Residency easily.

Fergus remained at the hospital for the whole of that night, but he was not wanted at the beside of Harry. Shashi worked for others too, but was never far away from the young midshipman.

Fergus made many sketches of the harrowing scenes within the hospital and then, next morning, went back to the King's tomb. He made his way there with a party of stretcher bearers, who were going out in preparation for the new day's grim harvest.

Fergus found the Naval Brigade awaiting the order to

sally forth with their guns once more. They and the artillery had suffered many casualties, but Lewis Callington asked anxiously after Harry. So too did Captain Peel, the commanding officer of the Brigade. He informed Fergus that he had forwarded Harry's name for promotion to the rank of lieutenant for his part in foiling the ambush on the steamboat and 'flat' on their way up the Ganges.

Two well-defended palaces stood between Sir Colin Campbell's army and the besieged Residency. Minutes later the Naval Brigade were ordered to bring their guns to bear on the first of these. It was not long before a breach was made in the high wall and the troops poured through to find the enemy in full flight.

There was no stopping General Campbell's men now and they rushed on to storm the second palace. The battle was still raging when an explosion blew in part of the wall on the far side from the attacking men. When the smoke and dust cleared, a party of men from the Residency stepped through the rubble and greeted their comrades.

The Lucknow Residency had been finally relieved, after a siege that had lasted for four and a half months.

The cost of relieving Lucknow had been high. Sir Colin Campbell now found he had a thousand sick and wounded men on his hands, as well as five hundred or so women and children.

To add to his problems, the rebels in and around Lucknow far outnumbered the army he commanded.

The survivors from inside the Residency were in a particularly bad way. The clothes of everyone, including the soldiers, were in tatters. Many were wearing clothing that was both ill-fitting and unmilitary. The women and children too were suffering the results of so many weeks under constant bombardment. For all this time they had lived with the ever-present fear that the enemy sepoys might break in at any time.

Most of the children had lost one, or both, parents. Many wives had lost both husbands and children. They needed to be removed to safety as soon as possible.

With such a responsibility, the general could not afford to stay to do further battle with the mutineers. The fifteen hundred non-combatants needed to be evacuated as swiftly and efficiently as was possible. He decided that Lucknow and the Residency that had been defended so stubbornly should be abandoned.

While the army and the Naval Brigade fought to keep the sepoys at a distance, the women and children, the sick and wounded, were led from the battered Residency. The pathetic column first made its way to the grounds of the palace hospital where Harry and the other wounded men lay.

Leaving more than half of his troops behind in a strongly fortified position to keep the sepoys occupied, General Campbell set off to take his charges to safety, the straggling convoy extending for almost ten miles. Every possible form of conveyance was put to use, including a number of camels.

Their initial destination was Cawnpore where Campbell hoped to take the huge party across the river. Once on the far side the risk of attack from mutinous sepoys would be far less likely.

This part of the arduous journey took six days. When they were still two days away from the river, Harry caught a fever. He had been carefully nursed by Shashi every mile of the way, but she had not been able to prevent his being put in a building with some sick soldiers from the Residency for the whole of a wet and stormy night.

Her close attention to Harry did not pass unnoticed. After visiting Harry and Shashi when they camped for the night, Shirley Buchanan stopped to talk to some of the women from the Residency who were washing their shabby clothes in a small river.

One of the women, the wife of a sergeant in the Cornwall Regiment, looked up from the clothes she was pounding with considerable gusto on a flat rock.

'That Indian girl and the young navy lad . . . Sweet on each other, are they?'

'I'd say that's a fair description of the way they feel, yes.'

'No good'll come of it, you know. If he's not careful he'll

spoil his chances of promotion for the whole of his service. I've seen it happen more than once, here in India.' She sniffed disparagingly. 'I don't know what the men see in these girls, I'm sure. I mean, look at her! She's no more than skin and bone. Can you imagine *her* having eleven kids? That's what I've had since I came out here. Mind you, only three of 'em are alive now, but that's India.'

She turned over the mess of laundry she was pounding on the stone and attacked it with renewed vigour before speaking again. 'I've had three husbands, too. Jim, Sergeant Moyle, is me third, and the best of the bunch. Every one of 'em was army. I've been in India now for twenty-seven years. There's nothing you can tell me about Indian girls and soldiers – and I doubt if sailors are any different. She'll lead him on to believe he's some kind of god to her, then one day he'll be sent somewhere else and the next night she'll be in bed with someone else.'

'I don't think I entirely agree with you, Mrs Moyle,' said Shirley Buchanan. 'But that doesn't matter. Harry's a very sick young man. He's got a fever *and* a serious wound. I'm almost as worried about him as Shashi is.'

'If you like, I'll have a look at him when I've finished this washing. I had an *ayah* to do this sort of thing for me, but she got her head blown off in Lucknow.'

The sergeant's wife nodded her head in the general direction of Harry. 'I've seen a few of 'em pull through who've been worse than him. I've seen a lot more who've died, too, but that's India, ain't it? What he could really do with is some good food inside him, but there's precious little of that around. The only ones I've seen with enough to spare is them there gherkins who joined up with us yesterday. They've got food enough to feed us and the Pandies as well, but they won't share it with anyone.'

A 'pandy' was the British troops' name for a mutinous sepoy. Pande was the name of a sepoy who was executed for running amok when the mutiny was simmering, earlier in the year. Shirley Buchanan presumed the 'gherkins' were Prince Narayan's Gurkha troops who had joined up with General Campbell's army the day before.

One thing said by the sergeant's wife was certainly true. The lack of sufficient good quality food was a feature of the long trek from Lucknow to Cawnpore. Shashi had voiced her concern about this to Fergus on more than one occasion. He was therefore very surprised when he came to visit Harry a couple of hours after the next day's march had ended, to see Shashi feeding him with fresh fruit and holding a mug of milk to his lips.

After greeting Harry, he asked Shashi where she had obtained such delicacies, adding that some of the mothers from Lucknow would murder for such food.

'It was given to me by the women of Prince Narayan's household,' replied Shashi. Unusually, she did not look at him while she was speaking and he felt she was not telling him the truth.

All this came to mind the following day when the long column once again came to a halt and tents were pitched. There was the possibility of a storm and Harry was settled in a huge hospital tent with other wounded officers.

Fergus was on his way to visit the young midshipman when he saw Shashi. She was hurrying towards the camp being set up by the Gurkhas.

Acting upon impulse and ignoring the thought that he was spying on her, Fergus followed at a discreet distance.

When Shashi reached the Gurkha camp she went straight up to an elderly man who appeared to have been waiting for her. Together they made their way to a huge covered wagon and climbed inside.

Fergus remained at a distance for some minutes before moving closer. Eventually, he stood beside the wagon. Inside he could hear grunts and a rhythmic creaking. It was a sound that told its own story. He realised that Shashi had reverted to the way of life she had led before meeting up with the *Venus* survivors.

The thought of it pained him greatly. Why now, when Harry was lying desperately ill? Was this perhaps a man she had known before?

Fergus did not have long to wait before the man climbed from the wagon adjusting his clothing. Moments later

269

Shashi emerged, fastening her sari. On her arm was a soft basket. Inside it Fergus was able to see fruit as she sprang to the ground.

Now he thought he knew *why* she had been with the man, but he could not believe it had been necessary for her to pay the price she had.

The man went off without saying anything to Shashi and suddenly Fergus saw her looking at him. She appeared momentarily startled, then began walking, her glance to the ground. She would have walked past him without acknowledging his presence had he not fallen in beside her.

'Why, Shashi? Why when Harry thinks so much of you did you do that?'

'Because I love him more than I love myself.' Thrusting the basket towards him, she added, 'To get him this. Fruit and food that will help him get well.'

'But you didn't have to get it the way you have. I'd have given you money. So too would Lieutenant Callington. What you've done could destroy everything that you and Harry have.'

'The man you saw me with is responsible for all the food and stores for Prince Narayan. He would not have parted with anything for money. Only for me. Is my body more precious than Harry's life? I may lose him because of what I have done, but in my heart I will be happy, knowing I have helped him to live. His life is of more importance than my happiness. Besides, unless it is with Harry, it means nothing to me . . . honestly.'

It means nothing to me . . . honestly . . .

Suddenly, Fergus felt as though an unseen hand had reached inside his body and squeezed his heart until he could not breathe. They were words he had heard before. When Becky had once pleaded with him when he had been unable to work because he had seriously burned his hands. He looked at them now, still scarred, and thought of that occasion, in far off Lewin's Mead.

Suddenly he realised Shashi was talking to him.

'. . . you will tell Harry?'

Trying to control his own emotions, Fergus shook his

head. 'No, I won't tell him. He's a lucky man. Lucky to have someone who loves him as much as you do, Shashi. I wouldn't take that away from him. I wouldn't take it away from either of you.'

She took his arm and hugged it to her in a warm and spontaneous gesture of affection. As they walked together towards the hospital tent, Fergus was very aware of the fact that he had not been so understanding of Becky and he wondered why.

Suddenly, realisation came to him that he already knew the answer to his self-imposed question. It was because it had mattered so much to him. Because Becky mattered so much.

Harry would never know the price paid by Shashi for the luxuries she brought to him. When she and Fergus returned to the large hospital tent she found his bed space empty.

Totally confused, she looked about her, wondering why he could have been moved.

Suddenly, Shirley was hurrying towards them. There were tears in her eyes and reaching out both arms, she cried, 'I'm sorry, Shashi. So very, very sorry.'

An anguished wail escaped from the girl. She dropped the basket she was carrying and as the fruit rolled across the ground it was pounced on by eager patients. She turned to run from the tent but Fergus caught her and held her.

She struggled like a wild animal for a while, then her struggles ceased. As Fergus held her to him, she began to cry.

He held her for a long time before Shirley took her from him and led her away to the tent they both shared.

Fergus returned to the Naval Brigade feeling extremely depressed. He found Lewis waiting for him in his tent and the lieutenant said, 'I don't think I need ask if you've heard the sad news of Harry.'

Fergus shook his head. 'No, but it's come as a dreadful shock to Shashi. I knew he had a fever, but he was talking perfectly normally when I spoke to him earlier today. I thought he was improving . . .'

'We all did – and I include the surgeon in that. He suddenly went into a spasm and died. The surgeon said the fever must have weakened his heart. How has Shashi taken it?'

'You've known all along just how close they were?'

Lewis gave Fergus a sad smile. 'It was probably the worst kept secret ever. It was all rather touching – although I must admit I was concerned about how it was going to end. Even so, I would have preferred any other way to this.'

'It would have ended in whatever way was best for Harry, had he lived. Shashi would have made certain of that.'

'I think perhaps you're right. I'll go and see her later. She can have the pick of his things. I believe a collection is being taken among the Brigade for her too. That's how much of a secret it was.'

Midshipman Harry Downton was buried in a shallow grave by the side of the road to Cawnpore. No marker was left at the spot for fear the grave would be desecrated by the rebel sepoys. Harry's memorial would be in the hearts of those who knew and loved him.

The next day, the head of the long column came within view of the bridge across the Ganges. On the other side was the road to Calcutta and comparative safety – but there was still a vast army of mutineers between the Lucknow survivors and the river.

The rescue of the besieged women and children from the Residency in Lucknow had been a severe blow to the prestige of the leader of the mutineers. He was determined they would not escape across the river.

The rebel soldiers following in Campbell's wake numbered some twenty-five thousand. They had already defeated the small force the British general had left behind when he passed through Cawnpore on his way to Lucknow.

Nevertheless, the survivors still held a large, fortified position in the spot from where the European men and women had been taken to their deaths, earlier in the year. The defenders had also succeeded in preventing the bridge from being destroyed by the rebels.

Realising that the bridge was the key to their destiny, the mutineers now began a heavy bombardment intended to destroy it.

General Campbell immediately ordered the Naval

Brigade to return the fire and put the enemy guns out of action.

So successful were the sailors that the rebel leader sent out a force of cavalry to wipe out the gun crews.

As the rebel cavalry swept towards them, the naval gunners prepared to withdraw temporarily to a more protected position. As they did so, a shell exploded among the gun crew led by Lewis Callington, wounding him and some of his men.

Now the rebels had found the range, more shells rained down, scattering shrapnel and dust over the sailors. As the guns were hitched up and trundled away to safety, men of the Naval Brigade recovered their wounded and carried them off after the guns.

During the confusion, the wounded lieutenant was overlooked. Fergus had packed his sketch pad away in his satchel and was preparing to run after the guns, when some of the dust cleared and he saw Lewis's prostrate body lying in a small gully beside the road.

Shouting to attract the attention of the sailors, Fergus snatched up the rifle he had been given to protect himself and ran across the road to where Lewis lay.

The rebel cavalry was almost upon them, but three sailors leaped down into the gully with him and fired at the nearest horsemen bearing down upon them.

The volley unseated three of the horsemen. As men and horses crashed to the ground, other cavalrymen swerved around them, giving the men in the gully a brief respite.

One of the fallen cavalrymen was uninjured. He leaped to his feet and rushed upon the sailors, sword raised menacingly.

His attack ended on the bayonet of one of the sailors as the others frantically reloaded their rifles. Suddenly, the rebel cavalrymen returned, but now they were in full flight, not even pausing to finish off the practically defenceless sailors.

A whole mass of British cavalry, led by Buchanan's Horse, had seen the danger the Naval Brigade was in and galloped out to the rescue.

Much to Fergus's relief, Lewis Callington was sitting up now. Although he clutched a bloody elbow and was in considerable pain, he was very much alive.

The Naval Brigade had also returned to its former position, wheeling about and following the cavalry as they routed the rebel horsemen.

There were many willing hands to help Lewis back to the British lines and Fergus went with him. Only a few men had been wounded in the incident and Lewis was given immediate attention.

The wound was not life-threatening, but an army surgeon informed Lewis that shrapnel had taken away a small piece of the bone from his elbow. The arm would never be fully functional again.

Binding up the arm, the surgeon said, 'You'll no doubt be able to continue your career, but you'll play no further part in this war, Lieutenant Callington. You'll go back to Calcutta with the other wounded men. What happens to you then will be up to your Commander-in-Chief.'

Lieutenant the Honourable Lewis Callington's future was decided for him long before he reached Calcutta and the jurisdiction of the navy's Commander-in-Chief.

When all the wounded and the women and children were safely over the river bridge, Sir Colin Campbell's army was reinforced by almost six thousand infantry and cavalry. With them were a great many more guns. The army commander was now in a strong position to mount an offensive calculated to end the mutiny in this part of India.

The reinforcements had arrived from England, via Calcutta. With them they brought mail for the men fighting in the interior. Somewhat to his surprise, there was a letter for Lewis Callington, addressed to *HMS Venus*.

He was reading it in his tent when Fergus came in with a bottle of whisky. It had been donated by Captain Peel, commander of the Naval Brigade, as a farewell gift.

Fergus was about to make a cheerful remark about having a bottle of whisky, when he saw the expression on Lewis's face as he read his letter. Putting the bottle on a small table,

Fergus asked, 'Is something wrong? Have you had bad news?'

Lewis nodded, gazing out of the tent to where elephants, bullocks, carts and their handlers milled about against a background of lush green jungle. It was a scene that was entirely Indian, but the lieutenant's mind was far away. In England.

'My father is dead.'

'Oh! I'm very, very sorry, Lewis.' Fergus hurriedly poured out a large glass of whisky and pushed it in the lieutenant's direction. 'Is . . . is there anything I can do?' It was a hollow and foolish offer, but Fergus could think of nothing else to say.

Lewis said nothing for a few minutes, then reaching out for the glass, he drank the contents in one draught and Fergus quickly poured another for him.

'It will at least relieve their Lordships at the Admiralty of having to find a post for a partly disabled officer,' he said, treating his second glass of whisky with more respect than the last.

'Why?'

'Because I shall retire from the navy now. Return home, manage the family estate and find myself a wife by whom I can beget a son and heir. The carefree days of Lieutenant Callington, RN, are over, Fergus. You see before you the seventh Viscount Callington.'

Lewis gazed down at his drink for some time before he said, 'Poor old Father. He took the title when he was little more than a boy. He's had the responsibility all his life. Was never able to enjoy the freedom I've had in the navy.'

Standing up suddenly, he put his drink down on the small folding table beside him. 'If you'll excuse me, Fergus, I think I'd like to take a walk on my own for a while. Oh, by the way, a letter came for you too. It's on your bed. It looks as though it might have been chasing you for quite a while.'

Hurrying to his own tent, Fergus picked up the letter. It was addressed to 'Fergus Vincent, Esq., *HMS Venus*, c/o The Admiralty, London'.

He did not recognise the writing and viewed it with some

puzzlement before tearing open the envelope.

He glanced at the signature first. It was signed, 'Your sincere friend, Fanny Tennant'.

Fergus's immediate thought was that the letter contained bad news of Becky. As he began to read, it seemed to confirm his fears. The letter informed him that there had been cholera in Lewin's Mead – but added that all was well now.

Then came the news that made him sit down abruptly, gasping in disbelief. Fanny told him that Becky had given birth to a baby daughter – his daughter. Fanny stated that the little girl looked so like him that it was uncanny.

Reading on in a daze he learned Fanny had looked after the baby while cholera was raging in Lewin's Mead, but had now returned her – and was missing her dreadfully.

It seemed Fanny wanted Becky to leave Lewin's Mead, but she would not, even though Fanny felt it would be in the child's best interests. She believed that only Fergus could persuade Becky to change her mind.

Fanny added that she knew Becky was missing him and hoped he would write to her. In the meantime, Fanny would keep Becky and the baby supplied with money, even when the amount he had sent to her ran out. He could pay her back upon his return.

The letter ended, 'By the way, the baby's name is Lucy, and she really is the sweetest child'.

Fergus felt he wanted to go out and shout the news that he was a father – but who was there to tell? Lewis had just learned that he had lost his father. Shashi had lost Harry.

Fergus decided he would keep the news to himself and savour it. One thing was certain: he would return to England as quickly as he could. He would travel home with Lewis – and return to Becky.

Chapter 23

It proved to be a long journey to Calcutta with the survivors from Lucknow and the many wounded men. Fergus hugged the thought of his daughter to him whenever the going became particularly hard, as it often did. The number of attacks lessened as they moved farther away from the troubled areas, but the long column possessed very few luxuries to ease the discomfort.

Sam Buchanan and his disgruntled cavalrymen travelled with the column, detailed off by General Campbell for escort duties. The Commander-in-Chief had regular cavalry serving with his army now, men used to discipline who would obey orders to the letter. Neither of these qualities had been particularly apparent among the irregulars of 'Buchanan's Horse'.

With most of the dangers behind them, life in the column became increasingly relaxed. Despite this, there was much to do. Shirley Buchanan still worked as enthusiastically as ever, nursing the wounded and sick. She ensured that they were given precedence when camp was made for the night. If there were any substantial buildings available, they went to the wounded. Any unexpected luxuries were shared among the children. The American woman was invaluable at organising such matters.

The senior surgeon travelling with the party left her to it and the other women never made any complaint about the arrangement. At least, no complaint was ever made within the hearing of Shirley.

Shashi also gave unstintingly of her time. She worked harder than anyone, but was seldom seen to smile. As the long journey progressed she became increasingly withdrawn.

Shirley viewed her unhappiness with a great deal of concern. So too did Lewis. He commented upon it one evening when the convoy had made camp on the outskirts of a small town.

The palace of a minor rajah, deposed during the uprising, had been turned over to the party. Shashi was tending to the needs of a young invalid at one end of the palace's great hall while Shirley was dressing wounds at the other.

Lewis was well enough to be quartered with the other officers now, but his wound was proving reluctant to heal. It needed to be dressed daily.

Fergus was with him while he was being tended by Shirley, and all three had been watching Shashi.

'She still shows no sign of recovering from the loss of Harry,' commented Lewis. 'I had hoped the grief would have worn off a little by now.'

'I've been giving her more work to do than anyone else in the hope it might take her mind off him,' said Shirley. 'She does everything I ask without complaint, but I haven't seen a single smile on her face since that day – and it seems to be getting no better.'

'She's had a very hard life,' said Fergus. 'Harry was the only really good thing that ever happened to her. She was just getting used to being happy when he died. It was a great tragedy.'

'Why don't you try to have a heart-to-heart chat with her?' suggested Shirley. 'She and I are close, but she's always been able to talk to you more freely than anyone else – except for Harry, of course.'

'All right,' agreed Fergus. 'But let me think about it first. Saying the wrong thing will be worse than saying nothing at all.'

'Don't leave it too long,' warned Lewis. 'We'll be in Calcutta within a week.'

'I'll need to choose my time – but it will be before we reach Calcutta,' promised Fergus.

But Fergus had left it too late to chose his time to speak to Shashi. She had already made up her own mind about the future.

Early the next morning he was awakened by Shirley. The American woman was in an uncharacteristic state of agitation. 'Quick, Fergus. Get up and dressed. Shashi's gone.'

'Gone where?' He tried to shake off his sleepiness and gather his wits.

'If I knew that I'd have gone after her, instead of coming to you. I thought *you* might know. You were talking to her last night.'

This was true. Fergus had waited near the hospital until Shashi completed her duties and had walked with her to the tent she shared with Shirley. He had hoped she might give him an opening to broach the subject of her unhappiness.

She had proved even more uncommunicative than she had been in recent days, even when he suggested that he realised how much she was missing Harry. Eventually, being particularly persistent, he had suggested she take a walk with him along the river bank, away from the camp.

With what he believed to be deliberate misunder-standing, she asked, 'Why do you want me to walk with you? Do you think I miss Harry so much I would want to make love with you? All right, if that is what you want, I will come to your tent. You have always been kind to me. I will show you my gratitude.'

'That isn't what I want, Shashi. I just want to talk to you. I'm worried about the way you've been since Harry died. All your friends are concerned for you.'

'I do not want to talk of Harry. If you do not want me to come to your bed then I will go to my own. I am very tired. Goodnight, Fergus.'

With this, she had gone to her tent, leaving Fergus feeling he had somehow failed her.

'Do you have any idea where she might have gone?' Shirley persisted.

'I'm not certain,' he said, hesitantly. 'Leave me to get dressed and I'll see what I can find out.'

Dressing as quickly as he could, Fergus hurried off to find the Bengali servant who had been taking care of Lewis's needs since they had set off from Cawnpore. He spoke good English and Fergus was aware he was familiar with the country through which they were passing.

It was early, but the servant was already heating water for Lewis's morning ablutions. He was able to answer all the questions put to him and Fergus felt he now had a very good idea of where to look for Shashi.

He went in search of Sam Buchanan. Without going into a detailed explanation, he succeeded in borrowing one of the spare cavalry horses. Not wanting to meet up with the cavalry leader's sister again just yet, he asked Sam Buchanan to tell her and Lewis that he would catch up with the slow-moving convoy later in the day.

Fergus was not the most experienced of horsemen, but fortunately he had been supplied with a well-behaved horse. Even so, after riding for perphaps eight miles, following the directions given to him by Lewis's servant, he began to fear he had been mistaken in thinking he would find Shashi.

Then, some distance ahead, he espied a lone figure walking along the road, a small bundle balanced on her head. He recognised her immediately. It was Shashi.

As he drew nearer, she moved to one side of the road to allow him to pass. He was level with her before she looked up and saw who it was.

'Hello, Shashi. Were you going to leave without a single word of goodbye to all your friends?'

'Why have you come after me? I am not going back. There is nothing for me any more. I do not belong with your people.'

'Oh? I don't think Harry would have agreed with you.'

'Harry is dead.'

'Sadly, that's true. But he would have died a very unhappy man had he known how many people would be affected by his death.'

'I am the only one whose life must change. No one else.'

'That isn't so, Shashi . . . but we can't talk like this. Can we go and sit down somewhere for a while?'

It seemed for a few moments that she would refuse. Instead, she shrugged. 'If you wish.'

Fergus dismounted. Leading the horse, he walked beside her as she left the path and went to a clearing beside the river.

They attracted considerable attention from a number of women who were washing clothes at the water's edge some distance away. However, there was nothing hostile in their attitude.

Tying the horse to a tree, Fergus sat down beside Shashi.

'You must have left early,' she said, unwrapping her bundle. 'I have some food here.' She handed him a piece of Indian bread.

'Why are you going back to the Janithran temple, Shashi? Do you think you will find happiness there this time? Or are you determined to suffer for something you think you've done wrong?'

Shashi did not quite conceal her astonishment that Fergus should know where she was going.

'I should never have left the temple. I was given to be a servant of the gods.'

'I doubt if your parents knew everything about the life you would lead there, Shashi. You were used.'

'It is the way of our people.'

'It's the wrong way for any people. Harry would have been the first to tell you so, had he known.'

'Why do you keep talking of Harry?' Shashi showed the first emotion she had displayed for some days. 'If I am making anyone unhappy it is only me. No one else.'

'That's where you're wrong, Shashi. What you're doing is affecting many more people than you realise. Let me tell you about it.'

He had her attention now and spoke with all the intensity he felt. 'You once asked me about my wife. About Becky. I didn't tell you all then. I think it's time I did. She started life rather like you, without having a chance to choose what she

282

come back with you. I will go to America with *Memsahib* Shirley – but it is not only for me. Neither is it because you were Harry's friend and, like him, you are a good man. I do this to show that it *is* possible to begin a new life. A good life. I do it for Becky.'

Chapter 24

'There it is, Lewis, the mouth of the River Avon. Gateway to the greatest port in the British Isles.'

Fergus and Lewis were standing on the deck of the merchant steamer which had carried them from Calcutta. It had been a long journey, but Fergus could hardly contain his excitement at being home after an absence of more than a year.

'So I've heard it said,' replied Lewis. 'Mind you, it can't match the Carrick Roads for beauty, and I'd hate to try to take a ship upriver here on a falling tide.'

'It's tricky,' admitted Fergus. 'Becky and I were once on a pleasure steamer that ran aground and broke its back on the Horseshoe Bend.' He smiled at the memory. 'It was quite an experience.'

The frightening, yet exhilarating grounding had occurred when he first went to live in Bristol. He had been a struggling artist and Becky little more than a child – or so he had thought at the time. He, Becky and the other passengers had been forced to crawl to safety across ladders laid upon the Avon mud.

'You must be very excited at the thought of being reunited with her – and meeting your daughter for the first time.'

'Yes.' Fergus felt very emotional at the thought of being so close to his family without Becky's being aware he was here. Apprehensive too. After all, although he could claim a great deal of provocation, he *had* abandoned Becky. 'It seems a lifetime since I was here last. A lot has happened during that time.'

On the slow journey from India, Fergus and Lewis had

become close friends. Fergus had told him the outline of his life with Becky and the other man had been able to guess much of what had been left out.

The new Lord Callington was not without problems of his own. His wounded elbow had stubbornly refused to heal properly and was a cause of great concern to him.

Surgeons in Calcutta had told him it would improve once the unhealthy climate of India had been left behind, but they had been proven wrong.

As the two men watched, a pilot came on board the merchantman, ferried to the ship by a steam launch. Half-an-hour later the ship from India entered the River Avon.

The steamship *Nile* had been the first passenger-carrying vessel available from Calcutta to England. As luck would have it, the ship was bound for the port of Bristol.

Fergus and Lewis remained on deck for the whole of the passage upriver, marvelling as they passed between the high cliffs of the gorge. High above them the suspension bridge was taking shape, brainchild of the brilliant engineer Isambard Kingdom Brunel.

They also negotiated the difficult Horseshoe Bend, scene of the disaster experienced by Fergus and Becky when he had last made the voyage upriver in a ship.

Eventually, in mid-afternoon, the ship entered the city's floating dock and was secured. The dockside immediately erupted in furious activity. Amidst swinging derricks, clanking railway wagons and lumbering carts, the few passengers and their piles of luggage were unloaded on the quayside.

It was all familiar to Fergus. The docks, the nearby inns and taverns. Even the smell was unaltered. It was the smell of home.

But, first of all, he needed to know what was happening in Lewin's Mead. What the situation was with Becky and baby Lucy. He thought he should call upon Fanny at the ragged school before he decided upon a course of action. There was always the possibility that she had persuaded Becky to leave Lewin's Mead now she had Lucy's future to consider.

Lewis would remain with Fergus until he knew what was happening. They would find a Bristol hotel for him and he could travel onward the next day. His estate was awaiting him in Cornwall, but there were no close relatives there to hurry home to. His mother had died many years before, and now his father too was dead.

As they waited on the quayside, Fergus looked about him. Little seemed to have changed here while he was in India. There were the same shops, even the same street-sellers.

Suddenly, a carriage pulled up not far away and a voice called excitedly, 'Fergus! Fergus, it *is* you!'

Turning in the direction of the voice, Fergus could hardly believe his eyes. Fanny was running towards him.

When she reached him, Fanny flung her arms about him, and gave him a hug. Then, standing back, she held him at arm's-length and tears sprang to her eyes.

'Fergus . . . You don't know how wonderful it is to see you. We haven't known whether you were alive or dead.'

Then she hugged him once more – and Fergus began to shake.

He had gone through the months in India without knowing real, deep-down fear, even in the hard fighting at Lucknow and afterwards, when his life was threatened by rebel cavalry.

Yet, suddenly, meeting up with Fanny had brought home to him that he was within hours of a meeting with Becky. He feared what the outcome might be.

He knew now, if he had never been fully certain before, that making a life together with Becky and their baby, mattered more to him than anything ever had, or ever would.

He was frightened that Becky would not have him back.

BOOK FOUR

BOOK FOUR

Chapter 1

When Becky took Lucy back to Lewin's Mead from Lady Hammond's studio at Clifton, her sense of relief was mixed with a certain apprehension. She was back in familiar surroundings, it was true. The people she met every day were known to her and the pattern of life was one to which she reacted instinctively.

Yet, despite all this, things were not the same. They never would be quite the same again. She had Lucy to think of now. *Her* daughter. Becky now had more responsibilities than she had ever known before – but she was facing up to them in a manner that surprised those who had known her through the years.

Her new role as mother did not please everyone. Maude, in particular, found it difficult to understand. She frequently asked Becky to accompany her to one or other of the dockside taverns. 'You ought to be out enjoying yourself,' she declared more than once. 'There's no sense wasting your life looking after someone who's going to grow up and leave you anyway, one day.'

The first few weeks were the most difficult of all for Becky. Only Simon showed any sympathy and understanding, but he was not always in the house.

He had made a niche for himself in Bristol. During the week he taught singing and music in the ragged school. At weekends he sang and played in the taverns around the city, where he was fast becoming popular with both customers and landlords.

Fanny had purchased a number of cheap, simple wooden flutes for the ragged school and Simon had formed a

291

number of the more musical pupils into a 'band'.

It was he who brought Becky her first glimmer of hope about Fergus, some three weeks after she had left Clifton.

Fanny Tennant had received news that a number of Fergus's sketches and paintings had been received at the Admiralty, in London. Accompanying the paintings had been a sum of money. It was the salary paid to him as an official naval artist, and with it was a request from Fergus that it be passed on to Becky, via Fanny.

Unfortunately, the sender at the Admiralty had been uncertain whether the money and pictures had been despatched *before* or *after* the date on which the *Venus* had been lost.

'But it gives us cause for optimism,' declared Simon. 'It means you certainly shouldn't give up hope for him.'

'I hope, for Fergus's sake, that he's alive and well,' Becky said. 'But I doubt if it will make very much difference to me. Even if he *is* alive there's no reason to think I'll ever see him again. He went away of his own accord.'

'We established long ago exactly *why* he went away,' said Simon, firmly. 'He came back from London when you were out drinking at the Cabot Arms with some men. The chances are that he went there looking for you. You've said yourself that someone thought they saw him looking in at the doorway. You've also told me you almost parted a couple of times before for similar reasons.'

He did not add that there was a great deal Becky had *not* told him about her behaviour with other men.

She shrugged. 'There you are, then. Why *should* he come back to me?'

'Because Fanny has written to tell him about Lucy. From what everyone has said about Fergus, I'd guess he's a decent sort of man. He'll want to come and see his daughter.'

'That doesn't mean he'll come back to me,' replied Becky, seemingly determined not to be optimistic about anything.

'What happens when he comes back will depend a great deal upon you. So far I can vouch for the fact that you've done nothing while I've known you that you need be ashamed of. But I still believe you'd find it a whole lot easier to keep things that way if you were to leave Lewin's Mead.'

'You too! Everyone's beginning to sound like Fanny Tennant.'

'If we do then it's because it's what we all believe. But no one can force you to do something you don't want to, Becky. It's your life.'

Simon hoped he might have sown a seed for the future and decided to change the subject. 'The children are giving a concert at the ragged school tomorrow night. My flute band will be playing, there's a small choir, and a young lady who I hope will one day be able to use her voice to break free from her background. Why don't you come along and enjoy an evening out?'

'How can I come?' asked Becky, scornfully. 'I've got Lucy to look after.'

'Bring her with you,' was the surprising reply. 'She'll come to no harm and no one will mind having her there.'

'I've never been to a concert,' said Becky doubtfully.

'Then it will be a new experience for you. You'll come?'

'I don't know.' She hesitated. 'Who else is going to be there?'

'Fanny won't be coming, she's had to go to London, but Catherine has promised to come and give me her support. She'd like you to be there too, I know. She's always asking after you and Lucy.'

Becky reached a sudden decision. 'All right. I'll come.'

In fact, she welcomed the idea of going out somewhere. She felt desperately lonely, much more than anyone would ever know, even though she had Lucy. Going to a concert was not like going out with Maude, but it would be something different in her life.

In order to go anywhere with Maude she would have had to find someone to look after Lucy. Then the evening would have been spent in the company of men Becky did not know and whom she would probably never see again after one of them had gone to bed with her.

Such an arrangement would make her feel that she was relegating Lucy to second place for the sake of a complete stranger. It did not feel right to her. She could not do it.

Becky loved Lucy with a fierce, possessive love, in the same way she had, and still did, love Fergus. Somehow, now he had gone, she realised to the full something of how he had felt about what she had done in the past.

If only she were given the opportunity to tell him so, she would not let him slip from her grasp again.

Chapter 2

The concert in the ragged school was a unique experience for Becky. Music was provided by a half-dozen boys playing their flutes. It was not of a particularly high standard, even to Becky's untrained ear. Nevertheless, the applause from an audience of twenty or so parents and relatives, who had attended with about the same number of pupils, turned the faces of the amateur musicians pink with pleasure.

A choir made a more enjoyable sound and a young girl, Simon's protégée, sang really beautifully, accompanied by his violin. The song was an old North Country folksong and when it came to an end Becky was close to tears.

The enthusiastic clapping woke Lucy who had slept peacefully throughout the performance and she began to cry. She was promptly whisked out of the classroom by Catherine, who took her to the office.

When the concert came to an end, the small audience filed out, all chattering happily about an event which was declared a great success for Simon's ragged school pupils.

Among the audience was Francis Gilbert, minister of the Unitarian Church at the edge of Lewin's Mead. A friend of Fanny Tennant, he had done much to support the ragged school.

Afterwards, the minister was one of those who gathered in the office. He had met Fergus on a number of occasions in the past, and Becky too. However, when he asked after Fergus he had only to look at Becky's strained expression to know he had made a mistake.

Simon stepped in quickly. He told the minister that everyone was worried about Fergus. Without mentioning the circumstances of his leaving, he explained about Fergus's commission from the Admiralty and of the tragic sinking of the *Venus*.

'We believe he is among the survivors landed in India,' explained Simon. 'But it's a great worry to Becky and to his many friends here.'

The minister expressed his sympathy and said he would ask his congregation to pray for Fergus. He also suggested that Becky should bring baby Lucy along to his chapel and have her christened.

When Becky prevaricated, the understanding minister assured her there was plenty of time for her to think about it, then turned his attention to Simon.

'I am very impressed by all I have seen and heard here tonight. Do you think that young girl might sing for the congregation in my little chapel?'

'She would be happy to sing anywhere. If you felt able to offer a small monetary incentive, I have no doubt at all that her parents would view that arrangement as more satisfactory than helping their daughter to find salvation.'

'I realised long ago that St Peter would need a well-filled purse in order to attract many of the residents of Lewin's Mead. I have no doubt we could afford a small fee for her. By the way, I don't suppose you are an organist?'

'As a matter of fact, I am. I used to play in my parish church, at home in Scotland. Why do you ask?'

'I am in need of an organist and choirmaster. I would also welcome any of your boys in our choir. For you there would be a small salary and the boys would be paid at the end of each attendance.'

'That sounds a wonderful idea – especially for the boys.' Catherine broke in on the conversation and Becky was startled by the way she looked at Simon. It was a great pity he could not see it for himself.

Becky felt a momentary pang of jealousy, but it passed very quickly. If ever there was a man who deserved to find some happiness, it was he.

When everyone else had gone, Catherine locked up the

ragged school, delighted that the concert had proved to be such a success. After seeing her safely into a hackney carriage that would take her to Clifton, Becky and Simon walked to their Back Lane home.

Simon carried Lucy who was once more sleeping. As they walked through the narrow streets, he asked, 'Did you enjoy the concert, Becky?'

'Yes, very much. You've worked miracles with the children at the school.'

'Do you think Catherine enjoyed it too?'

'I *know* she did, Simon.' Becky looked at him as he walked along with Lucy held in one arm, his other linked through hers for guidance. 'Is it important to you?'

'Yes – but I'm telling you as a friend. It's not to be passed on to her.'

'Why on earth not?'

'Because I'm quite certain she's a lovely girl. She also has independent means and I can offer her nothing in return.'

In fact, Catherine was a somewhat plain girl, for all that she had a very loving and caring nature. Becky thought she would make a wonderful wife for Simon.

'You have a great deal to offer her, Simon. You're from a good family. You have had medical training and now you're capable of earning a good and respectable living with your music. Why, Minister Gilbert offered you work only today. Besides, Catherine is head-over-heels in love with you. You wouldn't want to break her heart.'

'How can you possibly know of her feelings for me, Becky? If you tell me she's said anything to you about me, I won't believe you.'

'She doesn't have to. I was watching her tonight, when you were around. I felt guilty being in the way.'

Simon went quiet for a long time before he said, 'Do you really believe what you've just told me, Becky? Do you think she sees me in that way?'

'There's no doubt about it at all. She was looking at you in the way I used to look at Fergus. She's not only in love with you, she admires you too.'

Becky could sense the uncertainty in him as he asked, 'Do you think I dare say anything to her about the way I feel?'

'I honestly believe she'll be very disappointed if you don't.'

'Becky, you're an angel. If Fergus doesn't hurry up and come back for you, I'll become a Mormon and take you as my second wife.'

Becky smiled, but there was sadness too. She had come to rely heavily upon Simon for advice and support. If he married Catherine she could not be expected to come to live here, in Lewin's Mead. It was not where he belonged, either. She sometimes wondered whether he remained because of her and Lucy, but dismissed the thought as preposterous. She believed he would only live here until he sorted out his life. Then he would leave.

When they reached the house in Back Lane, Simon carried Lucy as far as the second floor where his room was situated and handed her over to Becky.

'Thank you for a very nice evening, Simon. I thoroughly enjoyed it.'

'Thank you for saying what you have about Catherine. I shall go to bed now and try to work out what I'm going to say to her – and when.'

'Just tell her how you feel about her, that's all she wants to hear. But don't leave it too long. I made that mistake with Fergus and I've bitterly regretted it ever since. Lewin's Mead has a nasty habit of coming between those who love each other.'

It was not until she reached her room that Becky wondered what had prompted her to make such a comment about Lewin's Mead. Whatever it was, it was certainly true. She could think of a great many men and women she had known who had lost all they held dear because of the slum where they lived.

Someone had once said to her that the poor had no rights. Not even the right to be happy. She had not thought too much about it then. Now she did. As a result she arrived at a sobering conclusion.

She could think of no one, no one at all, who had found lasting happiness here, in Lewin's Mead.

Chapter 3

Becky had just put Lucy down to sleep for the night when she heard footsteps on the stairs. Moments later the door opened and Simon entered with a puzzled expression on his face.

'Becky, I wonder if you would come to my room for a moment, please. I seem to have mislaid some money I had there. I've probably been careless and put it down somewhere, but it's not the sort of thing I usually do.'

'That's funny. I thought I left a few coppers on the table but they're not there now. I told myself I must have imagined it. But if you've lost money too . . .'

Tucking the bedclothes about Lucy, Becky followed Simon down the stairs to his room. It was incredibly tidy in here and she marvelled, as she had on other occasions, that he could achieve such a standard without sight.

'Where do you usually keep your money?' she asked, looking about the room.

'In a small leather bag, in here.' Simon ran his hand along the mantelshelf until it reached a small vase. Lifting it, he handed it to her. It was empty. 'I took some money out today, but I'm quite certain I put the bag back. There was probably about seven pounds there.'

Becky winced in sympathy with him. 'That's a lot of money to lose. I'll have a look around in case you put it down somewhere else.'

Becky made a thorough search of the room, even checking the floor in case Simon had dropped it some-where. By the time she finished she was satisfied there was no money in the room. Simon had been robbed.

'We've never had anything like this happen before in the house,' she said. 'I'll go downstairs and ask Ida if she saw anything suspicious while we were out. Then I'll come back and make a cup of tea for you.'

Becky felt very upset for Simon. She also knew it was fortunate she had not left any large amount of money in the room when she went out. She always carried it with her in a bag hung around her neck, inside her dress.

Ida was adamant there had been no strangers in the house while Becky and Simon were out. 'The only ones to come in were Maude and that brother of hers. They weren't in the house no more than ten minutes before they was off out again.'

Maude was not the most honest of people, neither was her young brother, but it was unthinkable that they should rob those with whom Maude shared a house.

'Are you quite sure that no one else could have come in? When you popped out to the privy, perhaps?'

'I don't go out there to the privy, lovey. Not when I've got a perfectly good chamber-pot in here and a gutter outside to empty it in. No, if you've lost something you won't have far to look for it, will you? You speak to Maude. I've always said it was a bad day when I let that one into my house.'

Becky was upstairs in Simon's room, talking about the theft with him, when they heard Iris coming upstairs to the room across the landing. She had a man with her.

They were still discussing whether they should say anything to her, when they heard her voice raised in anger. A few moments later a man's voice with a heavy accent was bellowing of what the voice's owner would do if he caught 'The dirty thief who would rob a poor working girl of her money!'

Becky went outside with Simon. She soon confirmed that Iris too had been robbed. Her loss was considerably more than that of the other two.

Becky told Iris what Ida Stokes had said. In spite of her distress at losing a large sum of money, Iris also refused to believe that Maude would rob her friends.

They had not been talking for very long when the loud-voiced sailor tired of the debate taking place between Iris and her fellow victims. Now he began complaining because she was not providing the service for which he was paying her.

Eventually, Iris pushed the seaman into the room ahead of her with the comment that those who made the most noise were always the most easily satisfied. She called back that she would be up and about early in the morning to tackle Maude.

Maude failed to return to Back Lane the next morning. To those who had suffered losses it seemed their suspicions were fully justified. They believed she had stolen the money and gone away from Lewin's Mead.

Ida thought the same. Later in the day she searched Maude's room, bundling up the few possessions she had left there. They would be sold to the rag-and-bone man, for whatever they would fetch. Ida grumbled that the money so raised would probably not be enough to pay for her 'valuable time'.

It was fortunate that the house's owner did not get rid of the clothes immediately. The following morning Maude took everyone by surprise by returning to the house.

It was too early in the morning for Ida to be keeping watch at her window. The first intimation anyone had that Maude was back was when she came out of her room demanding to know who had been in there, interfering with her things.

She and Ida met on the stairs. The resulting row brought Becky and a bleary-eyed Iris from their rooms. Simon had already gone to the ragged school.

Maude was berating Ida when Iris joined in the argument, saying, 'You've got a nerve coming back here, Maude Garrett. What have you done with my money?'

'What money? I don't know what the bleedin' hell you're talking about. I've just spent two nights and a day keeping the whole crew of an American ship happy. I come back here, hardly able to walk and looking forward to going to bed for at least twenty-four hours. And what do I find?

My landlady's gone through my room and bundled all me clothes up, and now I'm being accused of pinching someone's money! I reckon everyone's gone mad!'

'Are you saying you haven't pinched my money?' Iris's disbelief was plain to see.

'I'm saying I don't know nothing about any money. Yours, or anyone else's. *I've* got money – but I've earned every penny of it.'

'We were all robbed the night before last,' explained Becky, uncertain whether or not to believe Maude. 'You were the only one to come in the house while we were all out. You and Albert, that brother of yours.'

'Who says so – her?' Angrily, Maude jabbed a finger in the direction of Ida Stokes. 'She don't know what she does or doesn't see, come the end of the day. By then she's poured so much gin down her throat you could march an army through the house without her seeing it.'

'That's enough of such talk from you,' snapped Ida. 'Your stuff's all bundled up and ready. You'll be out on the street if I have any more of your lip. It's where you belong, anyway.'

'My rent's paid up until the end of the week,' retorted Maude. 'You'll not put me out before then.'

'Let's get this other business sorted out instead of everyone arguing with everyone else,' said Becky, doggedly. 'Are you telling us you didn't come back here when we were out?'

'Oh, I came back here all right. The American sailors had asked me to spend a couple of nights on board their ship and I came back here to get a few things to take with me. They'd have taken me to America with 'em if I'd wanted to go, I've no doubt. I might have gone too if I thought they'd let me get any sleep on the way.'

'Well, if you didn't take the money, then who did? That brother of yours?'

'Not while he was with me, he didn't.' Maude sniffed derisively. 'Perhaps you ought to go and report it to the police? Now, if you've finished accusing me of all sorts of things that I haven't done, I'm going up to bed. If another burglar comes calling, tell him he can take what he likes, just so long as he don't wake me up.'

Pushing past the others, she made her way upstairs, followed by their resentful gazes. Becky thought she seemed far too cocksure.

'Well, we didn't get very far with *her*, did we?' said Iris, despondently. 'I reckon I can kiss goodbye to my money. It's a good thing you weren't out too, Ida. You'd have lost far more than the rest of us put together.'

'In or out, anyone would have a job finding my money,' boasted Ida, surprisingly loudly. 'They'd need to pull the whole of my fireplace down before they found so much as a penny piece.'

Glancing up the stairs, Becky saw that Maude had paused on the landing outside her room. She would have heard every word spoken by Ida Stokes.

It was unlike the house's owner to be so loose-tongued. Becky decided that age must be catching up with her.

Chapter 4

Exactly two weeks after the thefts from the rooms of the Back Lane house, Ida Stokes proved that the passing years had not affected her as much as Becky had feared. She still possessed the guile and acumen that had gained for her ownership of the Lewin's Mead house.

Carrying Lucy in her arms, Becky was leaving the house accompanied by Maude when she met the landlady in the hallway.

'I'm just going down to the market, Ida. Is there anything I can bring back for you?'

'No, thank you, lovie. I'll be off to the shops myself in a minute or two. I've burned a hole in the bottom of my old kettle, I'll need to buy a new one. It's not the sort of thing anyone can get for me. I need to choose my own. No doubt they'll make a poor old woman pay through the nose for it.'

'Poor old woman, indeed!' said Maude, scornfully. 'She must have hundreds – no, *thousands* – of pounds hidden away somewhere. More than enough for someone not so mean to go off and make a new life for themselves somewhere nice.'

'I thought you wouldn't want to live anywhere except Lewin's Mead? That's what you told me when you came to see me at Clifton.'

'Oh, well, I wouldn't want to live at *Clifton*,' said Maude, hastily. 'No one would want to live *there*. But I wouldn't mind going to America, or somewhere like that.'

'Then why didn't you go when you had the chance a couple of weeks ago?' Becky had still not made up her mind whether she believed Maude's story of her absence from

Lewin's Mead after the money had been stolen.

'I wouldn't go unless I had enough money to live on when I got there. I'd travel in style, too, in a cabin on me own, not sharing a bunk with anyone who fancied me. With that randy lot I was with on the boat I'd have needed to be carried ashore when I got there. I certainly wouldn't have been able to walk. No, when I leave Lewin's Mead I'll leave as a lady, not as a whore.'

'Then you're going to be here for a very long time,' said Becky, unkindly.

'Don't you be too sure,' declared Maude, indignantly. 'I don't intend staying all my life. I'll find a way out. When I do, you'll never see me here again. I won't waste my chances the way you have.'

Becky was flabbergasted. 'But . . . you were the one who came to Clifton and told me I ought to be back here because it's where I belong!'

'And so it is,' retorted Maude, spitefully. 'Anyone who's messed up the number of chances to get out that you've had, belongs in Lewin's Mead. I wasn't born here, like you. I certainly don't intend dying here. Now, you go on and get your six penn'orth of shopping. I've got other, more important things to attend to.'

Maude hurried away in the direction of Broadmead, leaving Becky gazing after her with mixed emotions. She had never realised that Maude disliked her so much. Envied her too. Perhaps she should have known. There had been many incidents in the past where Maude had demonstrated that she was no real friend.

Simon was in his room fitting a new string to his violin when he heard screams from one of the lower floors of the house. He had been at the ragged school practising for a lesson when the string had broken. Hurrying home, he worked to repair the instrument before his practice with the children's choir.

Hurrying down the stairs as quickly as he could, he heard someone on the stairs ahead of him.

'Is that you, Becky?'

'No, it's me,' Iris replied. 'Did you hear that screaming?'

'Yes. It sounded as though it came from downstairs. Ida's room.'

'It wasn't her who was screaming. It was a boy's voice.'

They had reached the ground floor now and Simon asked, 'What can you see?'

'Ida's door's open – and there's a trail of blood! It leads from her room and out through the passage to the lane.'

'Is there anyone in her room?'

'I don't know . . . I'm scared to look!'

'We must go in, Iris. We're not doing any good standing out here wondering.'

'All right . . . but you come with me.' She took hold of his hand, gripping it very tightly. They went into Ida's room together. Very cautiously.

'I can't see anything,' said Iris, with obvious relief. 'There's nobody here.'

'Ida couldn't have fallen behind a chair, or another piece of furniture?'

'There's nowhere big enough to hide her – but someone's been in here doing something. There's a brick out of the hearth and that's where most of the blood seems to be . . .'

Just then someone entered the house. Standing in the doorway to the room, they obstructed most of the light. It was Ida.

'What are you two doing in my room?'

'We heard screaming and came down to see what it was. When we got here we saw a trail of blood from your room to the lane. We thought something might have happened in here.'

'Oh, something's happened, all right, lovie – but it's nothing I wasn't expecting. Oh, no, I set my trap and by the looks of it it's been sprung good and proper. Maude's screams you heard, was it?'

'No, it sounded like a boy,' said Iris.

'Ah! then it'll be young Albert, that brother of hers. Him as is named after our Queen's husband – not that she'd be any too pleased if she was to hear of it. He's as much a young thief as Maude is herself.'

Suddenly, the elderly landlady chuckled throatily. 'Well, he won't be doing very much thieving for a while, you can be certain of that!'

She chuckled once again and this unusual expression of pleasure brought on a fit of coughing.

'You set a trap?' queried Simon. 'What sort of a trap?'

'A real one. That lad got no less than he deserved. When I knew Maude was listening, I made a comment about keeping money hidden in my fireplace – and that's where I set the trap. Hidden behind a loose brick. I used to keep money there once. But all he found this time was a gin trap. I bought it 'specially after the money was pinched from your rooms.'

'You set a gin trap to catch a young thief?' Simon was appalled. 'It's likely to have taken his fingers off.'

'It wouldn't have if his fingers hadn't been where they had no right to be,' declared Ida, unfeelingly. 'Anyway, if young Albert is seen running around with a finger or two missing then we'll know for certain it was him who stole your money, won't we? Now you can get out of my room. By the looks of it I've got a bit of cleaning up to do.'

Outside, on the stairs, Iris asked Simon uncertainly, 'Do you believe she really did set a gin trap to catch the thief who stole our money?'

'You saw the amount of blood that was in the room. I didn't. What do *you* think?'

As they walked together up the stairs, Iris was silent for a while before she said, 'Yes, I believe that's what she did, all right. Poor little scrap. I don't know whether he's still got all the fingers that God gave him, but he's certainly lost a whole lot of blood.'

Chapter 5

Early that same evening, Becky was cooking a meal for Simon before he returned to teach at the ragged school.

It was busier than it had ever been. As a result, the teaching day had been divided into three. In the mornings about a hundred children attended lessons. During the afternoons, the younger ones had games and Simon led them in songs and stories. Meanwhile, the older pupils would be making clothes and shoes from materials donated to the school.

The largest attendance was in the evenings when close to a hundred and fifty pupils would fill the school. Their ages ranged from six to fifteen and their lessons covered many subjects.

In recent months the school had made significant progress. Those who had first come to it out of curiosity, or to mock the teachers – or even just to have free soup – had stayed to learn. Everyone involved with the school was now working very hard.

As Simon ate, he told Becky all that had happened that day on the ground floor of the house in Back Lane. He was still appalled at the thought that Ida Stokes had used a gin trap to maim the thief.

Becky's feelings lay somewhere between those of Simon and Ida. If Albert had not tried to steal he would not have been hurt. Nevertheless, she agreed that Ida's idea of justice was particularly harsh.

They were still talking about it when there was a soft knock on the door and Maude entered the attic room. Looking somewhat embarrassed, she said to Becky, 'I'd like 'to talk to Simon, if you don't mind, Becky.'

It was a broad hint for her to leave the room, but she ignored it. 'He's eating, but go on and speak to him.'

'What is it you want?' asked Simon.

'It's my young brother. He's ... he's had a nasty accident.'

'What you mean is that his fingers have been caught in the gin trap set by Ida to catch a thief?'

'Oh! You've heard.' Maude seemed genuinely dejected. 'Then there's not a lot more I can do for him.'

'I didn't say that. How badly is he hurt?'

'I've managed to stop most of the bleeding, but he's still crying with the pain.'

'Where is he now?' asked Simon.

'I've left him sitting in a doorway along the lane.'

'Bring him up here and I'll do what I can for him.'

'But ... Ida?'

'She's done what she set out to do. Bring him up here to see me.'

Maude left the room hurriedly. A short while later she returned to the house once more. This time she was accompanied by Albert.

Their arrival did not pass unnoticed. Simon and Becky could hear Ida's voice pursuing them upstairs, interrupted by Maude's shrill responses.

Albert was whimpering in pain when he entered the room and Simon felt his fingers through the rags wrapped about them.

'Will you take these off for me, Becky, please?'

She unwound the bloody rags and drew in her breath sharply when she saw the injuries the gin trap had inflicted.

'Is it very bad?' Simon asked. 'Can you see bone?'

'I think I can. It's difficult to say. His fingers are a dreadful mess.'

Simon felt the fingers carefully, murmuring his sympathy but not pausing when the young boy cried out in pain.

His sightless examination ended, he said, 'At least one of your fingers is broken, young man. Possibly two. It's going to be difficult to do anything with them because they are

310

badly gashed – and so is a third finger. I'm going to try to use a flat piece of wood as a splint. There's some in my room, among the kindling – can you fetch it please, Becky? I'll secure the splint to the top part of the three fingers and to your hand, Albert. I'll then have to dress the wounds separately and they'll need to be re-dressed every day – not here, but at the ragged school. They have more dressings there and Catherine is a very competent nurse.'

'I don't want to go to that old ragged school. I went there once but all they do is boss you around.'

'You'll need to put up with the bossing around if you want to save your fingers. If you neglect them you're likely to lose your hand as well. Do you understand?'

'He'll be there,' promised Maude. 'Thank you, Simon.'

'Oh, I'm not doing it for nothing,' declared Simon, unexpectedly. 'I'm charging you for doing all this. The price is seven pounds. The exact amount I had stolen from my room.'

Albert began to protest, but Maude cut him short. 'Shut up, you. Think yourself lucky he's helping you. All right, Simon. I'll give you the money.'

'I'll have it now, if you don't mind. Gratitude and promises are easily forgotten when a patient begins to heal.'

'I wouldn't forget,' said Maude, indignantly. 'But don't worry. I'll pay you. I'll go down to my room now and get the money.'

Becky returned to the room with the wood Simon had asked for. In the meantime a heated argument could be heard downstairs between Maude and Ida.

When Maude returned to the room, she thrust some coins into Simon's hand. As he placed them in his pocket, she said, 'I've just met that old cow downstairs and told her what I think of someone who'd set a trap like that to catch a young boy.'

'Oh! What did she say?' Simon thought Maude was probably given short shrift by the crusty old landlady.

'She said it was my hand she was hoping to catch in it, not his – although she wasn't too fussed, she said. "Them as puts their finger in the pot can expect to get scalded",

311

those were her words. She said if I wasn't happy with it then I should go and make a complaint to the police.'

Wryly, Becky remembered that similar words had been spoken by Maude when Iris was questioning her about the thefts in the house that had caused Ida to set her trap in the first place.

'That wasn't all she said, either,' complained Maude. 'The old cow has told me to get out of my room. Wants me out of the house by tonight.'

'That's all right, our Maude,' said Albert, forgetting his suffering for a moment. 'You can come back and live at home. In Broadmead.'

'What! Put up with a beating every other night from our Pa. Oh, no, Albert. You won't catch me coming home there again.'

'It's all right, Maude. He won't beat you any more. He's not there. When I . . . when I hurt my fingers today and ran home, a copper had just been to the house. He said that Pa's been arrested for breaking into the office at his work and pinching some money. The copper said he'll probably go down for five years this time. So, you see, you can come home. You can bring your blokes there at night and look after us for the rest of the time. It'll be just like it was when Ma was alive. We'll be a family again without him.'

Chapter 6

The trouble in the Back Lane house of Ida Stokes was merely a microcosm of what was happening throughout the Lewin's Mead slum during the hot summer of 1857. It was as though the latest cholera epidemic had released a poison into the air that eroded the traditional camaraderie of the slum-dwellers.

There had always been fights in the beer-houses and gin-parlours, and domestic violence was commonplace. Yet there had also been a mutual respect for the property of those who dwelled in the slum. They did not steal from each other.

Without such self-imposed standards, the narrow alley-ways and crowded houses of Lewin's Mead would have been in a permanent state of anarchy. By the autumn of that year, this appeared to be the case.

It was no longer safe to leave a door unlocked and elderly residents who had always been able to walk the alleyways in safety were being knocked down and robbed. There were three murders in the course of robbery during the last week of August alone.

The police were powerless to intervene, even had they wanted to. In fact, most of the senior officers were quite content for those who inhabited Lewin's Mead to do what they liked in their man-made warren.

However, in September, the violence and mayhem spilled over into the surrounding Bristol streets. Passers-by were caught up in the fighting, and windows of shops and houses were broken. In the wake of numerous complaints, a meeting was held between the Chief Constable and members of the Watch Committee, chaired by Alderman Tennant, father of Fanny.

The Chief Constable was reluctant to commit his men to entering Lewin's Mead. In his opinion it would only stir up more serious trouble. His suggestion was to increase the police presence in the streets around the perimeter of the Bristol slum in a bid to contain the problem.

Members of the Watch Committee would have preferred a more positive approach to the problem, but they reluctantly agreed to give the Chief Constable's solution a trial.

Within a matter of weeks, two events occurred which alarmed the Bristol public – Alderman Tennant in particular – and forced the city's Chief Constable to change his views.

The first was the brutal murder of two policemen on the dockside on a busy Saturday evening. They had stopped to question a man who was leaving the dock area, carrying a small sea trunk beneath his arm.

What was said between them was never known and no witnesses came forward who had seen what happened from start to tragic finish. What was not in doubt was that no more than minutes after stopping the man, both constables lay dying on the dockside, fatally stabbed. The man they were questioning made good his escape in the narrow alleyways of Lewin's Mead.

The incident provoked a flood of letters to the Corporation and the local newspapers. The furore had not died down when a second incident occurred, one that was far more personal to the Chairman of the Watch Committee.

Becky was bathing Lucy, late one evening, prior to putting her to bed, when she heard the sound of someone climbing the stairs to the attic room.

After only a cursory knock, the door opened and Fanny entered the room.

Whatever she was going to say was momentarily forgotten as the baby gurgled happily at her and she beamed in return.

'Becky, you are *so* lucky to have her. She is a truly adorable little girl.'

'Yes, she's beautiful and she loves everybody. But you haven't come all this way so late in the evening to tell me that. Are you here for anything special?'

Becky was still resentful of this woman, in spite of all she had done in the past to help her.

'As a matter of fact, I am – and it's very, very encouraging news indeed concerning Fergus.'

'He's alive? You've heard from him?'

'I have not heard from him personally but, yes, I would say it's almost certain that he's alive. I have just received a letter from the Admiralty. They are being very cautious about saying *positively* that he is alive, but a wounded naval officer has just returned from India. He says there is an artist with the Naval Brigade in the Lucknow area. This officer did not know his name, but says he came upriver from Calcutta with a Lieutenant Callington – and Callington is one of the survivors from the *Venus*. It would be too much of a coincidence for the artist to be anyone but Fergus. He must have survived the sinking and is now in India. Isn't that wonderful news?'

Becky hardly knew what to say. If the news were true . . . If Fergus really was alive . . . Lucy slipped from her grasp and almost disappeared beneath the water in the bowl before Becky caught her again.

'If Fergus really is alive, it *is* wonderful news. Do you believe it to be true?'

'Yes, I do. I've always been convinced he survived the sinking of the *Venus*. I've told you so before.'

'Thank you for coming to tell me. I . . . I don't know what to say.'

'You don't need to say anything, Becky. I'm very happy for you – and for Lucy. Please bring her to visit me sometime. Either at home or at the ragged school. I do miss seeing her.'

Fanny left Back Lane knowing she had given Becky's hopes for the future a huge boost. Fergus would come back to see

Lucy, Fanny was certain of it. So too, she believed, was Becky.

What would happen then would depend entirely upon Becky herself. Having seen how well she was looking after her baby, Fanny had hopes that she and Fergus might settle their differences. She sincerely hoped so, for Lucy's sake. Fanny believed that having a baby had matured Becky. It might be all that was needed in the marriage.

Making her way along a narrow, evil-smelling alleyway, she suddenly became aware that someone was walking along behind her and had been for some time.

She began to walk faster. So too did whoever was behind her. Fanny slowed, in the hope that the other person would walk past.

It seemed to work and a man with hands thrust deep in his pockets overtook her. However, when he was no more than a couple of paces ahead, he suddenly swung around to confront her.

'What was you hurrying for, back there? You wasn't scared of who was following you, surely? You wouldn't be walking around here on your own if you was.'

'I was neither hurrying, nor dawdling. Merely going on my way.'

'Cor! Listen to you! It's easy to tell you don't belong in Lewin's Mead. What you here for then? Come in search of a little excitement, have you? Well, I'm happy to oblige you.'

'I suggest you go back to your gin-parlour, or wherever it is you've spent the last few hours. You're more likely to find what you want there.'

Fanny had smelled gin on the man's breath, even though he was standing some distance away from her.

'Now why should I go back there when I like what I have right here? You're the sort of woman I used to dream about while I was in prison.'

'If you don't leave me alone and go on your way, you'll be back in prison very quickly.'

'Oh, no, missie! Neither you nor anyone else is going to put me back in there. I'll swing first – and if I'm going to hang then it'll be for something worthwhile. What's more, you won't be in court to give evidence against me, you can be certain of that.'

Belatedly, Fanny realised that this was a situation she was not going to be able to talk herself out of. She looked about her for a means of escape, but there was none.

She was in an alleyway flanked by houses that were too dilapidated for even the Lewin's Mead residents to live in. The last people to live here had been the homeless, jobless Irish, fleeing from starvation in their own country. The man facing her had chosen his spot well before accosting her.

'Where would you like it to be? I can't offer you anywhere very grand, but that won't make any difference, will it? Whatever you say, you're here looking for a bit of fun and you'll have that, I promise you.'

As he spoke, Fanny had been deciding what she should do. Suddenly, she turned and ran back the way she had come – but she was hampered by her long skirt. She had taken no more than half-a-dozen paces before he caught her.

Swinging Fanny against the wall, he knocked the breath from her. By the time she recovered he had pulled her inside a doorway. Still holding her in a grip that squeezed the breath from her body, he kicked out at the door behind her and it crashed open.

She was struggling desperately now, but he dragged her inside.

'Stop! Stop it – do you hear me!' Fanny was angry, but she was frightened too, fully realising the danger she was in.

Momentarily, he released her, but any hopes she entertained that he had come to his senses were brutally dashed. A back-handed swipe caught her across the face and knocked her to the floor.

As she lay there, dazed, he dropped to his knees beside her. It took him only a moment to rip her light, cotton dress from neck to hem. Then his hand was between her legs, touching her.

Next, his knee pressed down painfully on the inside of her thigh, forcing her legs apart.

She was struggling desperately now and suddenly she

could hear voices, passing along the alleyway. Opening her mouth she began screaming for the first time in her life.

'Shut up! You hear me?' He aimed another blow at her but she moved her head and the blow did nothing more than graze her cheek. She continued screaming.

There were voices in the doorway now, but she was aware that it was only children, 'Help! Fetch help – quickly!' Her cries brought another blow from her assailant and she only partly avoided this one.

Then a voice in the doorway said, 'That's Miss Tennant's voice!' She recognised the speaker as one of her more troublesome pupils. He had almost been expelled on more than one occasion for fighting.

'Charlie! Fetch help . . . Hurry!'

Instead of running off, the children crowded in through the doorway and the man straddling her turned his head towards them.

'Clear off, the lot of you . . . agh!' The shout of pain came as Charlie lashed out with his boot, kicking the kneeling man in the back. A moment later a whole avalanche of children fell upon Fanny's assailant, kicking, punching – and biting too when he momentarily secured a grip on one of the smaller boys.

The man's weight was off her now and Fanny scrambled to her feet. Before she could call on the children to flee, the battle came to an abrupt end. With kicks and punches coming at him from all angles, the would-be rapist stumbled out through the doorway and ran away.

'You all right, Miss Tennant?'

Charlie's anxious question came back to her from the doorway. She pulled her dress together as best she could as he and the others entered the derelict house.

'Yes, Charlie. Thanks to you and the others, I am very well, thank you. Now, if you would like to come with me to the ragged school, I think I might find something you will find somewhat more substantial than my gratitude.'

Chapter 7

Fanny would have lied to her father about the source of her bruised face had Ivor Primrose not been in the ragged school when she returned there with her rescuers.

Against all the odds and despite the mistrust that was inherent in the Lewin's Mead children, Ivor had gained the respect of most of the pupils who attended the school. They also liked him. When the children who had helped Fanny saw him, they eagerly poured out all that had happened to her and related their part in rescuing her.

Ivor was full of praise for the youngsters and declared the day would come when he would be welcoming some of their number into the Bristol Police Force. He grinned at the hoots of derision that greeted his prediction.

However, he was much more serious when he spoke to Fanny, after she had rewarded each of them with a shilling and a pocketful of sweets and sent them on their way.

'You were very, very lucky this time, Miss Fanny. Had those children not happened along you would not have escaped with your life, there can be little doubt about that.'

'You don't need to tell *me* that, Ivor. I am fully aware they saved my life. I'm finding it difficult not to shake just thinking about it. But it's over now. I'll do my best to forget it. I trust you will do the same?'

Ivor shook his head. 'I'd be failing in my duty if it ended here, Miss Fanny. I'd like a full description of the man from you and a statement of exactly what happened. I know all the Lewin's Mead men who have been released from prison in the past few weeks and I already have a very good idea of who this man might be. I must report the incident. After this, and the murder of our two constables, I feel it's time determined action was taken against the villains who are using Lewin's Mead as a refuge from arrest.'

Ivor Primrose had correctly judged the reaction of his Chief Constable to the attack upon Fanny. A week later, the 'determined action' he had forecast was carried out in the early morning, at an hour when only those in lawful employment were abroad.

No fewer than a hundred policemen, almost half the total Bristol force, entered Lewin's Mead from two different directions. Each party was headed by a senior superintendent, and each had a separate objective.

One would hopefully arrest the murderer of the two constables. The other was given the task of taking the man who had tried to rape Fanny Tennant.

The policemen knew exactly where to go. No policeman had entered Lewin's Mead prior to the raid, but Ivor Primrose had carefully built a wide net of informers who lived in the Bristol slum. One such man told him the name of the slayer of the two policemen. Another revealed the identity of the man who had attacked Fanny.

The murderer lived in Back Lane, in the house next to the one owned by Ida Stokes. The noise and shouting as the constables broke into the house woke Becky.

By leaning far out of the attic window she could just make out the uniformed men milling about in the narrow lane outside the house.

Dressing hurriedly, she rushed downstairs, pausing briefly to explain to a sleepy Simon what was happening in the lane beneath his window. Leaving him standing in the doorway to his room still thoroughly bewildered, Becky hurried down to the ground-floor passageway.

At the front door she found Ida arguing with a policeman.

'The cheek of it!' she said to Becky, indignantly. 'He's telling me I can't go outside my own front door. This is what things would be like if we had constables walking about Lewin's Mead *all* the time. Our lives wouldn't be our

320

own. We'd have them telling us what we should or shouldn't be doing every minute of the day and night.'

'What *is* happening?' Becky addressed her question to the constable who seemed more amused than offended by Ida's indignation. He also seemed more inclined to give an explanation to the young mother than to the elderly landlady.

'We've come in to make a couple of arrests, miss. You've been living next-door to the man who murdered two of our constables. Ah! There he is now, being brought to the lane, so there's nothing more for you to worry about. I only hope the other arrest was carried out as successfully.'

'Who would the other arrested man be?'

'He's the one who attacked Miss Tennant, from the ragged school.'

His reply took Becky by surprise. She had heard nothing of such an attack.

'When did this happen?'

'About a week ago, when she was foolishly walking through Lewin's Mead on her own.'

A week ago was when Fanny Tennant had come to visit her. Could it have happened when she was on her way back to the ragged school from Back Lane? Now she thought about it, Becky recalled Simon saying she appeared to be the only one to have seen Fanny since her return from London. She had not put in an appearance at the ragged school.

'Was Miss Tennant badly hurt?' She put the question to the talkative constable.

'That I couldn't say, miss. All I *can* say is what I've heard from others. They say that if it hadn't been for some of her children from the school we'd likely have had another murder on our hands. Well, I must go now, but you'll sleep more soundly in your beds for having these two villains safely behind bars.'

'Did you ever hear such nonsense?' asked Ida, as she closed the door on the bustle outside. 'Why should I sleep more soundly for knowing some poor soul's been locked up and will be hung at the next Assize? It wasn't *him* who woke me up. It was them constables with all their shouting and hollering.'

Becky was not listening. She was thinking of what the constable had said about Fanny Tennant. She had not always been in agreement with the principal of the ragged school. Becky felt she interfered far too much in other people's lives. Nevertheless, Fanny had done a great deal for the children of Lewin's Mead, all of it with no thought of reward. She had earned Becky's grudging respect for this.

There was also the nagging suspicion that if Fanny had not come to Back Lane to tell Becky what she knew of Fergus, she would not have been attacked.

She would speak to Simon and tell him what she had heard. Then she would ask him to take her to Clifton, to visit Fanny Tennant there.

The Bristol Chief Constable was determined that never again would Lewin's Mead be an area where his men could not carry out their duties. When the bulk of the large force left the slum, a number remained behind.

They patrolled the narrow alleyways in pairs, each in sight of another, so that in the event of trouble they could call for help.

It spelled the end of Lewin's Mead as an inviolate sanctuary for the criminal fraternity. They, and older residents like Ida Stokes, would complain bitterly about this infringement upon their 'freedom'. Becky grudgingly agreed with Simon that it was probably a good thing to have happened.

When Becky and Simon, together with Lucy, reached the Tennant house, Simon was delighted to find Catherine there. She had been away from the ragged school for a couple of weeks. Sarah Cunningham, to whom she had been a nanny for so long, had been on holiday from school. Her grandparents had written to Catherine, suggesting she might like to spend the holiday period looking after Sarah. She had returned to Bristol only the previous evening.

Watching her face when Catherine greeted Simon, Becky recognised that, whatever doubts *he* might have about their relationship, Catherine had none. She quite obviously adored him.

But it was Fanny they were here to see. The bruising on her face had faded somewhat now, but it was evident she had been violently assaulted. As the constable had told Becky, she was lucky to have escaped with her life.

Fanny was delighted to learn the police had arrested the man responsible for her injuries, but felt a certain apprehension too. It meant she would be obliged to attend court and tell of what had happened. Only the thought that if he were not convicted there would undoubtedly be other victims, made her steel herself for the inevitable.

When Becky apologised for unwittingly being the reason for Fanny's being in Lewin's Mead, the ragged school's teacher cut her protest short.

'It certainly wasn't your fault, Becky. Why, I must have visited Lewin's Mead a hundred times or more, in the interests of the children of the school. Never before have I even *felt* threatened. Unfortunately, the character of the place has been gradually changing over the past year or so. I think the time has come for you seriously to consider moving out with Lucy – and thank you for bringing her here to see me. She really is a darling, isn't she, Catherine?'

'She certainly is,' agreed Catherine. 'But there's another reason why you should be thinking of leaving Lewin's Mead, Becky. Fanny has told me what she said to you about Fergus, and her belief that he survived the sinking of the *Venus*. I can add another piece of information to that. While I was with Sarah a package arrived for her. A rather sad package. It was sent by the same Lieutenant Callington about whom Fanny has spoken and it contained some sketches of Captain Cunningham, drawn by Fergus. The lieutenant thought Sarah would like to have them. Lieutenant Callington didn't actually say anything about Fergus, but he must have given them to him to send. He's alive, Becky, I'm certain of it. When he returns he'll want you and Lucy to be living somewhere other than Lewin's Mead.'

Becky made no direct reply, but she would think about

what both women had said to her. Fergus had wanted her to leave Lewin's Mead soon after they were married. She had refused then. Now there was Lucy to think about. Becky conceded that the Bristol slum was not the place she would choose to bring up her daughter.

However, so much depended upon Fergus himself. What he would want when he returned. She was in no doubt of how he would feel about Lucy. He would love her, as Becky herself did. But how would he feel about *her* after all this time? It was a question that put a cloud over her joy as the odds increased that he had survived the sinking of the *Venus*.

Chapter 8

It had been a lonely day for Becky, as were most days since Maude had gone from the Back Lane house.

She had intended taking Lucy for a walk as far as Bristol Bridge, but teeming rain and strong winds had kept them indoors. It was a pity. Lucy enjoyed going to the bridge where there were usually swans and ducks to feed. Afterwards she would watch the horses passing across the bridge, pulling a wide variety of carts, wagons and carriages.

Horses delighted Lucy and she showed no fear of them. Eight months old now, she took a lively interest in everything about her. In a couple of weeks' time she would be celebrating her first Christmas.

For as long as Becky could remember before meeting Fergus, she had hated Christmas. It was a time when others had a family about them and were given presents. Becky had neither.

She was determined that Christmas would not be the same for Lucy and was already planning what she would do, what she would buy to make her baby's eyes light up with pleasure.

It was the sort of thing Becky might once have chatted about with Maude. The other girl would probably not have listened very carefully, but just being able to discuss Lucy and Christmas would have made Becky happy.

She had spoken to no one other than Lucy all day. For more than an hour now she had been listening for Simon to return home. When she heard him climbing the stairs to his room she would call out to him and make some tea. She might even cook him a meal if he had not eaten.

She would be able to talk to him and hold a sensible conversation. Learn what was happening at the ragged school – and in the world that existed beyond the Back Lane attic.

Becky waited for a very long while, until it was quite late. Lucy had dropped off to sleep and Becky was thinking of going to bed herself.

Then she began to wonder whether Simon was all right. Despite the presence of constables throughout the day, Lewin's Mead was not the safest place to have to pass through at night.

Many vagrants tramped the countryside in summer, seeking work or, more usually, looking for anything they might steal. In winter these same men and women made for the shelter of the towns. In Bristol, Lewin's Mead was one of their favourite haunts. Hitherto, there had been no inquisitive policemen or borough officials to make life difficult for them.

A great many Irish men, women and children had found their way here too in recent weeks. There had been another potato crop failure in Ireland and they had crossed the water to England, seeking food and shelter.

The Irish were desperate to find the means to stay alive. Yet, in the main they committed fewer crimes than the vagrants. However, they were in poor health and had little idea of hygiene. As a result they carried with them disease and sickness that affected many of those with whom they came into contact.

Eventually, Becky heard Simon's footsteps on the stairs. When he reached the landing off which his room was situated, Becky called down to him.

'There's a cup of tea up here if you would like one, Simon.'

'Thank you. I have a couple of things to put in my room then I'll be right up. I was hoping I might find you awake. I want to talk to you.'

When Simon entered the attic room, Becky thought he looked tired, yet not unhappy. Placing a cup of tea in his hand she said, 'Here, get this down and I'll make you another. It's cold and wet outside. A real winter's night. The sort of night when I'm glad I don't have to sleep outside.'

Raking the ashes from the fire, she said, 'Would you like me to cook something for you? I've got a nice piece of bacon. It's already boiled and just needs heating up.'

'No thanks, Becky, I've already eaten. Catherine stayed on late at the school and we sent out for something from the tripe and trotter shop in the square.'

Becky was disappointed. She had looked forward to cooking something for the blind man and chatting with him while he ate.

'Well, you were in good company, but you should have taken her somewhere special. Just the two of you.'

'In truth, I wanted us to be somewhere where there was no one else around at all, so we could talk. It was her idea to send out for some food.'

It seemed to Becky that Simon was trying very hard to contain an excitement that kept threatening to bubble over. Suddenly, he blurted out, 'I've asked Catherine to marry me, Becky.'

'I knew you would one day, Simon. Well, what did she say? She accepted you, of course?'

'Yes . . . Yes, she did, although I don't know why. She's an intelligent girl, with independent means. I can offer her nothing. When I look back on it I wonder I had the nerve to ask her!'

'You have a great deal to offer any girl. *She's* the lucky one. I've very, very happy for you, Simon. I really am.'

Becky crossed the room and gave him a warm hug. 'I've always thought how wonderful it would have been to have a brother. You're the closest I'll ever come to having one and I couldn't be more thrilled for you.'

'I take that as a great compliment, Becky – and I shall miss you very much.'

Sensing her bewilderment, Simon said, 'Of course, it will mean leaving Back Lane.'

Becky had known this would happen one day, but she had always managed to push it to the back of her mind.

She had come to rely upon Simon far more than was good for her.

'I know that, but it won't be until you and Catherine marry. Have you fixed a date yet?'

'We hope to marry next summer, but I'll be leaving here long before then. Possibly as early as next week.'

'Oh!' Becky was genuinely dismayed. 'But . . . why? You'll be all right here until you're married. I'll take good care of you for Catherine.'

'I'm quite certain you would, Becky.' Simon had learned to recognise people's feelings by the tone of their voices. Right now he knew that Becky was very unhappy.

Reaching out, he found her hands and grasped them tightly. 'I'm going to miss you and Lucy very much, but I have an opportunity that's far too good to miss. Mary Carpenter has bought all the houses in the close behind the ragged school. She's offered to let me live in one of them rent free for as long as I am working at the school.'

Mary Carpenter was the woman who had founded the ragged school. She had also opened homes for boys and girls who fell foul of the law, and was a controversial but ardent reformer.

'. . . Catherine will also live there when we're married. Fanny is talking of giving her far more responsibility at the school. Catherine is looking forward to the challenge as much as I am.'

Becky squeezed his hands affectionately. 'I'm very happy for you, Simon. For both of you. There's no one I know more deserving of happiness.'

'Thank you, Becky. I was worried how you would take the news that I would be moving out of Lewin's Mead. You should do the same, you know.'

When Becky made no reply, Simon leaned forward and kissed her. 'I feel that right now I'm probably the happiest man in the world, Becky. The only thing that worries me is the feeling that I'm deserting you. I know it's not true, but that's the way I feel. The only consolation I give to myself is the belief that things are going to come right for you too. They will, Becky. Believe me.'

Chapter 9

Simon moved out of the Back Lane house the following week. His departure made it seem emptier than Becky had ever known it before.

She saw Iris only infrequently. Becky's baby, and Iris's way of life, resulted in their keeping very different hours.

Ida Stokes also missed Simon, but for a different reason. She complained that there was not enough money coming in to maintain her usual high standards in the house and hinted that if no new lodgers were forthcoming, she would need to raise the rents paid by Iris and Becky.

Ida's problems were solved when, only a week before Christmas, she rented out both rooms on the second floor to a large Irish family. In common with so many fellow countrymen and their families, they had fled their homeland to avoid the latest famine. However, Seamus McCabe was one of the few lucky Irishmen who had managed to obtain work in England. He was employed on the construction of the Clifton suspension bridge, which would one day span the gorge above the River Avon.

For Becky, it was like having the O'Ryan family in residence once more, except that the McCabes seemed to be more numerous. They were certainly noisier.

On the first day they were in the house, Becky made excuses to herself for their noisiness. They had only just moved in. The children were bound to be excited about moving in to a new house in a new country. They would soon settle down.

Such thoughts were hard to hold on to when the sound

of their shouting and banging kept her awake long after midnight.

The second night saw no improvement. Indeed, shortly before midnight there was a violent argument between husband and wife.

Eventually, when the sound had twice caused Lucy to wake in fright, Becky went downstairs to the McCabe rooms. The bulk of the noise was coming from the room that had been occupied by Simon.

It was now their living-room-cum-kitchen. The sparse 'furniture' consisted of nothing more than wooden boxes of varying sizes. Dirty plates, mugs and spoons were littered here and there and already they had managed to make more mess than Becky would have believed possible.

The door was open and husband and wife were standing on opposite sides of the room, shouting angry accusations and counter-accusations at each other. The basis of the argument seemed to be that Seamus McCabe had gone straight to a gin-parlour after receiving his first week's wages. There he had spent much of the money with which his wife, Bridget, had intended buying food for their many children.

Seamus's excuse was that he had brought the family safely to England from Ireland. Against all the odds he had found work and given them a home. He had earned the right to spend the evening enjoying a drink.

There were many counters to such an argument and Bridget McCabe used them all . . . repeatedly. Becky stood in the doorway for some minutes trying to attract the attention of the quarrelling couple. Eventually, she was forced to resort to their tactics and shout in order to make herself heard.

Temporarily silenced, they and the children looked at her in surprise.

'That's better,' said Becky. 'Do you mind not making so much noise? I've got a baby upstairs trying to sleep. You've woken her twice already. I've never heard such a din.'

'What we do in our own home is none of your business,' said Seamus McCabe, belligerently.

'That's right,' said his wife. 'We'll make as much noise as we like just so long as we're paying our rent.'

'At least you can agree on *something*,' retorted Becky, laconically. 'But paying rent doesn't give you the right to upset everyone else. You keep this noise up and the rest of us in the house will give notice to Ida Stokes and move out. Rather than let that happen, she'll put you out on the streets again.'

'Don't you come in here threatening me and my family!' Bridget McCabe was a big, raw-boned woman and took a step towards Becky, menacingly.

'Ma! For God's sake listen to the woman. Don't you think we're as sick as she is of listening to youse two fighting each other all the time? She's only been listening to it for two days. I've had to put up with it for thirteen years – and I've just about had enough of it!'

Becky's unexpected ally was an undersized young girl who had been squatting on the bare floor in a corner of the room, her chin resting on her knees.

She rose to her feet as she spoke, adding, 'You keep it up and we'll be thrown out of here – the same as we were from the last place. Yes, and half-a-dozen more in Ireland.'

Without any warning, Seamus McCabe gave the girl a backhanded swipe that knocked her back to the floor once more.

'You keep your tongue between your teeth where it belongs, young Meg. If you don't, you'll find yourself biting it off one day. I'll have no daughter of mine speaking to her mother that way. No, nor me, neither.'

'I'm not *your* daughter, thank the Lord,' said the girl, moving along the floor on her backside away from Seamus. 'Except when it suits you, or when I bring some money into the house.'

'And when was the last time you did that?' demanded the Irishman. 'Here's me working all the hours that God made to feed youse all and there's not one of you raising a hand to help me.'

'You're working all hours to keep yourself in drink!' retorted his wife. '*I'm* the one who's left to feed a family

331

with not enough money to buy a loaf of bread to share between them. It seems to me the only way I'll get any money is by going out with her who has a room downstairs and bringing a man back here for the night.'

'It wouldn't be the first time, would it?' retorted Seamus. 'Here, you want money, take this.'

Reaching in his pocket he took out a fistful of coins and threw them to the floor. There was far more copper than silver among the coins, but all the children dived to retrieve them while Bridget screamed at them to hand the money over.

Meanwhile, Seamus pushed Becky out of his way as he left the room, saying, 'You wanted quiet. Well, now you've got it.'

Jerking a thumb in the direction of the room he had just left, he said, 'You can tell her that if she wants me before morning she can find me down at the gin-parlour. I intend staying there until I'm in a state where I'll need to be carried home.'

As the Irishman clattered heavily down the stairs, Becky backed out of the room before Bridget McCabe turned on her and blamed her for driving her husband from the house.

The young girl who had angered Seamus followed her out. Becky said, 'I'm sorry. I didn't mean to drive him from the house.'

'You did us all a favour,' was the surprising reply. 'It was building up to a big fight before you came down. When that happens he loses his temper and gives Ma a good thumping. Then he blames us and we get it too. Now he'll do exactly what he said. He'll drink until he drops and we'll all enjoy a quiet night. I'm sorry he woke your baby, though. Can I come up to your room and see her some time tomorrow?'

'Of course you can – but right now you'd better go off and do something with your lip. It's split. You'll have blood all over your clothes if you're not careful.'

'It's all right. I got off lightly tonight. Sometimes he won't stop until he's beaten me senseless. He's got a dreadful temper on him and he's never been fussy about whether he's hitting a man or a woman. I'm warning you so you don't cross him when there's none of us around.'

'Thank you. Now I'd better go up and make sure Lucy is still asleep.'

Becky made her way back to her room thoughtfully. She wondered what life was going to be like having the McCabe family living on the floor below her. She hoped it would be better than the first two days – but she somehow doubted it would be.

Chapter 10

Becky did not hear Seamus McCabe return to Back Lane, but he was certainly at home early the following morning. It was Sunday, but it was not a day of rest for Bridget McCabe's tongue.

She began using it as a weapon with which to lash her husband at an hour when Lewin's Mead was normally at its quietest.

It brought Becky awake and startled Lucy for a moment. Fortunately, the baby was far more interested in some sparrows eating crumbs on the sill of the attic window than in the latest argument going on downstairs.

On this occasion the McCabes' noise disturbed Iris. The prostitute had not returned home until the early hours of the morning. She was not amused at being woken by the Irish family.

Becky heard her voice raised above all the others and felt a moment's satisfaction. Iris was the match for any woman in an argument – and most men too.

She had dressed and was changing Lucy when there was a light knock on the door.

'Come in!'

The door opened and Meg McCabe came into the attic room.

'I wasn't sure whether or not I should come up. I thought you might still be asleep.'

'There's not much chance of that with your family in the house, is there?'

'I'm sorry. Ma found Seamus lying on the floor on the landing when she got up, and laid into him something awful. When the woman came up from the first floor I thought I'd get on out of it. She's got a tongue on her worse than Ma's. Some of the words she uses I've never even *heard* before!'

Becky smiled. 'Iris can outswear a sailor. When she speaks her mind, she leaves no one in any doubt about what she's telling them.'

She looked at her visitor. Dark-eyed, the girl was painfully thin with black hair framing a pinched face. 'I gather that Seamus isn't your father?'

'No. He says my real pa was shot when he and some of his friends attacked a party of English soldiers. Ma won't say anything about him at all. She and Seamus were married when I was about four. All the rest of the children are his.'

'Have you had any breakfast?'

'We don't have breakfast – nor dinner most days. Just one meal, when Seamus comes home. Before he got this job, working on the bridge, we were lucky if we got that.'

'Well, me and Lucy are having breakfast. As you're here, see if you can breathe some life into that fire while I finish dressing her.'

'What are you having for breakfast?'

In spite of her assertion that she never ate it, Meg could not hide her interest as Becky dealt with Lucy, placed her on the floor and turned to the meat-safe.

'Some ham, an egg and a slice or two of fried bread. Lucy will probably only have the fried bread and an egg.'

'Jesus! That's more than we'd have in a whole week before we got out of Ireland. It's a feast.'

'Do you want some? There's plenty here.'

Meg hesitated for only a moment before nodding eagerly.

'Then get to work on that fire so it's soon ready for cooking on.'

Meg added a couple of pieces of wood to the fire. Minutes later it was crackling away. As she added coals, she chatted happily to Becky.

'How long have you lived here?'

'As long as I can remember. There was another Irish family staying here for some years. I lived with them when they'd have me. For the rest of the time I lived on the streets. I must have slept in just about every doorway in Lewin's Mead.'

Meg looked sceptical. 'You seem to be doing all right now.'

'Yes.'

'Have you ever been married?'

'I still am.'

The scepticism showed again as Meg asked, 'Where is he then? I haven't seen him since we've lived here.'

'I hope he's safe in India. He was on a ship that was sunk. At first everyone feared he'd been lost with it. But we've had news he was probably one of those who was saved.'

'Is he a sailor?'

'No, he's an artist.' Becky picked up Lucy who was trying to claw her way towards the fireplace. Cross at being thwarted, she complained vociferously, at the same time stiffening arms, legs and body.

'Here, let me have her.'

Meg took the baby from Becky and bounced her in her arms until she relaxed and stopped protesting. Carrying her across to the portrait of Becky on the wall, she asked, 'Did he do this?'

'Yes.'

Meg nodded her approval. 'It's good. I wish there was someone who'd paint me like that.'

When Becky made no immediate comment, Meg said, 'Has he gone off and left youse for good?'

'He'll be back. He hasn't seen Lucy yet.'

'Does he send you money to buy food and things?'

'That's right.' As Becky spoke she began heating fat in a heavy frying pan placed on the fire.

Meg knew enough of people to ask no further questions right now. Holding Lucy up so she could see out of the window, she said, 'I wish Seamus would go off and just send us money now and again.'

'Don't you like him?' Becky threw the young Irish girl a quick glance.

'I *hate* him.'

It was said with such vehemence that Becky asked, 'Is there any particular reason?'

'Lots of reasons. He thinks I should be on the game and bringing money home. Perhaps he's right.'

'He's not right,' declared Becky. 'No girl should *have* to do that to earn a living. Anyway, you're too young to be thinking about things like that.'

'I'm thirteen,' said Meg, indignantly. 'Although I wasn't when he first wanted me to go out on the streets – and let me know what it would be like.'

'He did *that* to you?' Becky was more angry than shocked. There were few things that happened in the world outside that she had not already experienced herself in Lewin's Mead. 'Does your mother know anything of this?'

Meg shrugged. 'She wouldn't *want* to know. Seamus is the man in her life. She's scared of losing him.'

'Has this happened just the once?'

'No. It happens when he has too much to drink. It was easy for him when we were living rough. It might be more difficult now we're living in a house.'

Becky remembered the times when Mary O'Ryan's men had tried the same thing with her, even when Mary herself was sleeping in the same room.

'You don't have to put up with it from him, Meg. If he tries anything, you either scream or come up here with me. No one's going to do anything to you while you're under the same roof as me. Is that understood?'

'Yes . . . Thank you, Becky.'

'Right, now move over and let me get to that frying pan. I'm hungry. Any minute now Lucy is going to let us know in no uncertain terms that she is too.'

Chapter 11

Meg remained with Becky in the attic room for the whole of the morning. She proved to be a great inconsequential chatterer. However, there was no malice in her chatter – unless the subject happened to be her stepfather.

When Becky said it was time to produce a midday meal for Lucy, Meg said she would have to go back to her own rooms. She had promised to take two of her youngest half-sisters for a walk on the Clifton Downs. She hoped they might catch a glimpse of some of the animals kept in the zoological gardens there.

She had been gone for perhaps half-an-hour when Becky heard someone coming up the stairs to the attic. She at first thought it was Meg returning, but decided the step was too heavy.

There was a knock at the door, but before she could call out to ask who it was, the door was pushed open and Seamus McCabe entered the room.

Startled, Becky demanded, 'What do you want?'

'I've come to see if our Meg is here. I've just woken up and I've got to go up to the bridge this afternoon. Her mother's not in and I want something to eat.'

'Meg's taken two of the other children to the Downs. They probably went about half-an-hour ago.'

'Oh! She might have waited until I got up. I thought I'd likely find her here.'

'Well, you haven't. Close the door on your way out. I want to change Lucy and there's a draught.'

Becky had not liked Seamus McCabe even before Meg told her about him. She liked him even less now.

'Now, is that a friendly thing to say, I ask you? We're neighbours. We should at least make the effort to get to know each other.'

'I can hear all I want to know of you during the night hours when you're arguing with your wife – or when you come home drunk on a Sunday morning.'

'It doesn't mean anything. Bridget doesn't understand that a man needs to go out and have a little fun at the end of a hard day's work, that's all.'

'I don't understand, either – and I don't want to. Now, I've got things to do. Goodbye, Mr McCabe.'

'The name is Seamus.' He showed no intention of leaving. Leaning against the door frame, he added, 'If there's anything you need done, you have only to ask. I mean, you not having a man of your own around.'

'I *do* have a man, and if there's anything I can't do for myself I have lots of friends I can call upon. Now, will you leave, or shall I call out of the window to the two constables standing out in the lane?'

'There's no need for such talk. I came up here to be neighbourly, that's all.'

'I've told you, if you want to be neighbourly you'll have some consideration for others when we're trying to sleep. What's more, I don't want you coming up here again, unless you're invited – and I can't see *that* happening.'

'And why not? Do you think you're too high-and-mighty for the likes of me? Or is it that Meg's been telling you things about her family? You want to be careful about believing anything that girl says. She's got a dangerous imagination. It'll get her into serious trouble one of these days, for sure.'

'I choose my own friends, Mr McCabe. I also choose who I do, or don't, believe. Now, I've asked you to go and you're still here. I told you what I'd do.'

Becky walked determinedly to the window and flung it open.

'All right! All right! I'm on my way.'

Seamus McCabe paused at the top of the stairs only long enough to say, 'I'm disappointed in you. Very disappointed. I was hoping you and I might become good friends, you being up here with no one but a small baby for company. I thought you might get lonely.'

Becky leaned far out of the window and Seamus McCabe went clattering noisily down the narrow and rickety staircase.

Almost immediately, there was the sound of someone coming up the stairs once more. Believing it to be the Irishman again, Becky hurried to the door intending to bolt it.

As she reached out for the bolt the door opened and Fanny Tennant entered the room. Behind her was Simon.

Unsmiling, Fanny said, 'You seem to have a surfeit of visitors today, Becky. I was almost knocked over by your last guest. He seemed to be in a great hurry.'

'That's the man who's taken Simon's old room – and the one next to it as well. He and his family make more noise between them than the whole of the rest of Lewin's Mead. He was hurrying downstairs because I'd threatened to call out of the window to the police if he didn't leave my room. I wish you were still living here, Simon . . .'

Becky had a sudden frightening thought. It was unusual for Fanny to come to her room unless she had some money to give to her – and why was Simon with her. 'Why are you both here? Is there bad news of Fergus?'

'No, Becky, there's nothing new – and no news is good news. We're here for the happiest of reasons. I've just come from my church and they're going to put up some money for us to have a party at the ragged school for Christmas. I told Simon about it and he suggested we have a concert to go with it. I know Lucy is only a baby, but we thought you might like to bring her along? The concert is open for anyone, but the party will be just for the children.'

'You'll enjoy it, Becky, I promise you.' Simon was enthusiastic. 'There will be carols and Christmas songs, as well as music from my little band.'

'It sounds a lovely idea,' she said. 'Can I bring one of the young Irish girls from downstairs? Meg is the stepdaughter of the man who almost knocked you over. She's a bright little girl, but she hates her stepfather – and with just cause if what she tells me of him is true. I'd like to show her there's more to life in Lewin's Mead than poverty and abuse. She might even be persuaded to come to the ragged school for lessons.'

'Bring her along by all means.' Fanny gave Becky a searching look. 'I'm always delighted to help someone improve their lot in life. Speaking of which . . . with this man and his family causing problems for you, perhaps this might be a good time for you to leave Lewin's Mead?'

Fanny was aware that such a suggestion from her had always brought an automatic rejection from Becky in the past. She added quickly, 'If Fergus returns home soon – and I strongly suspect he will – think how much nicer it would be if he were to find you living elsewhere. In one of the houses in St James's Court, for instance, with Simon and Catherine as your neighbours.'

Becky had given much thought to the prospect of leaving Lewin's Mead, but she did not want to be beholden to Fanny Tennant. Nor would she let her think that she might be acting upon *her* suggestion.

'I'm quite happy here, for the moment, but I'll give it some thought – for Lucy's sake.'

'I'm delighted to hear it, Becky. Now, let me hold her for a while while we talk about our Christmas concert and the party. I think it's going to be a wonderful evening . . .'

Chapter 12

Seamus and Bridget McCabe managed to maintain a truce with each other for no more than three days. Then the night-time peace of the house was shattered by yet another dispute, this time accompanied by violence.

Becky was awakened by the sound of loud voices and screaming. It was followed immediately by the sound of splintering wood. It sounded as though someone, or something, had broken one of the wooden boxes that passed for 'furniture' in the McCabe rooms.

The Irishman could be heard bellowing at his wife and she screamed yet again as Becky heard what sounded like the thud of a heavy blow.

Foolishly, perhaps, Becky decided she would go down to try to bring the altercation to an end. Putting on a dress, she had opened the door of her room when she heard yet another voice. This one was heavy with a Scandinavian accent.

Moments later there was the sound of another blow being struck. Now Iris's shrill voice was added to the din.

At the bottom of the attic stairs, Becky came across a number of small figures huddled together.

'Who's that?'

Immediately, four pale and frightened faces were turned towards her.

'It's me . . . Meg. I've got the three youngest with me.'

'What's going on?'

'I can't be sure, but with any luck Seamus is taking a pasting from Iris's man.'

'Take the youngsters up to my room – but be quiet when

342

you get there and close the door behind you. I don't want Lucy woken up.'

The children hurried up the stairs. As they went up to her room Becky saw there was a candle burning in the McCabe bedroom. Its light, escaping through a half-open door, was the only illumination on this floor.

The fight, for such it was now, was being carried on in the semi-darkness of the McCabes' living-room and had become a free-for-all.

The Scandinavian seaman Iris had brought home with her from a ship moored in the docks had come up to take Seamus McCabe to task about the noise he was making. McCabe had told the man to mind his own business and the seaman had swung a punch at him, knocking him to the ground. Bridget had immediately attacked her husband's assailant with nails and considerable venom.

This was too much for Iris. She jumped on the back of the Irishwoman, knocking her to the ground. All four were fighting now, with some of the older McCabes throwing a punch or aiming a kick whenever they saw an opportunity to help their parents.

Becky had second thoughts about getting involved and was about to return to the attic when Ida came puffing up the stairs from the ground floor, grasping a stout, hard broom in her hands.

Pausing for only a moment to regain some of her elusive breath, she advanced into the McCabes' living-room, wielding the broom indiscriminately, with immediate effect.

Because of the poor light, Becky could not see who was taking the majority of the blows. Then Iris fled from the room, both arms shielding her head.

Less than a minute later it was Bridget McCabe's turn. Staggering from the room, she shrieked, with painful accuracy, 'Me nose is broken! She's broken me bloody nose!'

With only two of the recent combatants remaining, Ida made short work of them. Iris's Scandinavian 'friend' exited the room on hands and knees. Seamus McCabe remained where he was, flat on his back on the floor, taking no further interest in anything going on about him.

Meanwhile, the McCabe children had either fled the room, or were spreadeagled against the walls of the living room, terrified by the broom-wielding landlady.

Ida left the room carrying her broom in the manner of a triumphant Britannia. Ignoring Bridget McCabe's wailing about her nose, she waved the hard bristles of her broom only inches from the Irishwoman's face.

'You'll have far more than a bloody nose to worry about if I have any more trouble from you, or any one of your family. You'll be nursing your aches and pains out on the streets. I'll not have any more of your troublesome Irish ways in this house. You behave like ordinary civilised human beings, or you'll go. If I had any sense I'd throw you out tonight. I'm too soft, that's my trouble.'

In view of the results achieved by Ida's onslaught, Becky felt the elderly landlady's description of herself fell rather wide of the truth.

Upstairs, in the attic room, Becky found Meg and her three half-sisters squatting on the floor in front of the fire. She recalled there had been no hint of a fire in either of the McCabe rooms.

A question from her brought confirmation that the family had no heating. As a consequence, they had no cooking facilities.

'Does that mean you had no hot food yesterday?' she asked the girls.

'We had nothing to eat at all,' replied Meg. 'There was half a loaf and a bit of cheese left from the day before, but Seamus took it to work with him.'

'My belly was grumbling all day,' complained one of the little girls. 'It was louder than Meg's.'

'I'm not going to start cooking at this time of night,' declared Becky, 'but I've got some bread and plenty of good dripping. Would you like some of that?'

After she had silenced their enthusiasm for fear it would wake Lucy, Becky produced half a loaf of bread. She spread a generous layer of dripping on thick wedges for each of them.

As they ate, she cut second slices. Between mouthfuls,

Meg asked, 'Who won the fight down there?'

'Ida.' Becky told Meg what had happened, adding, 'What caused tonight's fight? Did Seamus come in drunk again?'

'He does most nights,' replied Meg, bitterly, 'but it wasn't just that. He got under my blanket instead of Ma's. I wasn't having any of him and the noise woke Ma. She blamed me, but when she began using her fists, it was him she hit.'

'You'd better stay up here for the rest of the night,' said Becky, as she handed out second slices of bread and dripping to the younger girls.

'Can I?' Meg asked the question eagerly.

'Of course you can.' As the girls ate, Becky told of the time when she too had sought sanctuary in this same attic room. It had been at a time when she was living with the O'Ryan family.

She had witnessed a brutal beating and the drunken perpetrator had come seeking her to ensure she never gave evidence against him.

'I got away from him that time,' Becky said, 'but he caught up with me later and I took an awful beating from him.'

'It's like Ma's always telling me,' Meg sighed. 'There's no escaping from what's set out for us in life. We're born to suffer and it'll happen to us no matter what we try to do about it.'

'Your ma is talking nonsense,' declared Becky. 'Look at me, for instance. You're always saying how well off I am. How you envy what I've got. There was a time when I was far worse off than you. I never had any family at all. When I met Fergus I wanted him more than I'd ever wanted anything in my life. I wanted him so much that it hurt – and in the end I got him.'

'If you wanted him so badly, then why did you let him go? Why isn't he here with you now?'

Meg spoke with genuine puzzlement and Becky found replying to the question painful.

'I let him go because . . . because I didn't believe enough in what I'd got, Meg. Perhaps I listened too much to people like your ma, saying that we can't escape from what we are. It was only after he'd gone and Lucy was born that I realised I *had* escaped. I have everything anyone could possibly want.'

Becky brushed crumbs from the table to the palm of her hand and put them outside the window for the birds to find in the morning. 'When Fergus comes back I'll tell him so. I won't let him go away from me again. Never!'

Meg remained thoughtful for a few minutes, then she said, 'I hope he comes back soon, Becky. When I see you two together then I'll know that you're right and Ma's wrong. I might begin to believe then that I won't always need to live like this.'

Chapter 13

The concert and party at the ragged school were a huge success, even though far more Lewin's Mead children turned up than ever attended the ragged school.

A surprise member of the concert audience was Ida Stokes.

Becky and she had been discussing the peace that had fallen upon the Back Lane house since Ida's dramatic intervention in the McCabe family's argument. The talk turned to the changes occurring in Lewin's Mead and Becky mentioned the ragged school concert and party.

Ida remembered wistfully the only concert she had ever attended. It had been when she was a small girl and a military band had held a concert down at the dockside. It had been part of a campaign to recruit men for the army fighting in Spain against Napoleon's army.

'Beautiful, it was,' she said, wistfully. 'All that lovely music and the men in their smart uniforms. I can remember it as though it was yesterday. That must have been near Christmas too, because I remember us all singing carols there. At least, them as knew the words was singing. I was happy enough just to be listening.'

'There will be carols at the ragged school concert,' said Becky. 'And music from the children and from Simon. Why don't you come? I'm sure you'd enjoy it.'

'Me go to a concert? At my age?' It was a radical idea. Nevertheless, Ida did not dismiss it out of hand. 'I've got nothing to wear that'd be good enough for a *concert*.'

'You've got better clothes on right now than most will be wearing there,' said Becky. 'Come along with Lucy and me.

You'll enjoy it and it'll do you good to get out for a while.'

Much to Becky's surprise, Ida said, 'You know, Becky, I think you're right. I *will* come to the concert with you.'

Ida was less enthusiastic when the evening arrived and she learned that Meg was to accompany them. Her misgivings ended the moment she stepped inside the ragged school building. Catherine saw them standing hesitantly in the doorway and hurried to greet them. She led them to the front of the classroom. Here they were given seats among those reserved for ragged school teachers, a few members of the Bristol City Corporation, and members of the church which had funded the party.

There were a number of Ida's contemporaries in the audience. She relished the shock it would give them to see her being given such special treatment.

Meg was less enthusiastic about the dubious honour, but she was very proud of the dress Becky had bought for her at a shop in St James's that sold secondhand clothes. She had even washed her bare feet without having to be told of the need for taking such an unusual step.

Fanny did not improve Meg's nervousness when she came across to greet Becky. She spoke as though it had already been decided that Meg should attend the ragged school when lessons resumed after Christmas.

Catherine saved the day when she said that Becky had told her so much about Meg that she felt she knew her already.

Fanny and Catherine left them when a party of city Aldermen arrived in something of a state. One of them had just discovered he was no longer wearing the watch and chain with which he had left home.

However, before he could carry out his threat to call in the police and disrupt both concert and party, Simon appeared on the scene. He was dangling a watch and chain from his fingers. Sightless, he regretted he was unable to identify the culprit, but was able to tell the indignant Alderman he had been assured it was taken 'by mistake'.

The evening was a great success for everyone. Even the Alderman left in a happy frame of mind – although he ensured his watch and chain were buttoned inside a pocket and not on display when he left the school.

Ida so enjoyed the concert that before leaving she pressed a half guinea into Simon's hand with the instruction that he was to use it to buy something for the children who had 'made such lovely music, and sung like little angels'.

After the adults had left it was the children's turn to enjoy themselves. They sang carols and Christmas songs, led by Simon. Then they played a number of increasingly rowdy games before Fanny ordered that the food be brought in.

Meg believed the games were beneath her dignity and were only for children. She was, however, thrilled to be told by Simon that she had a very attractive singing voice. He promised that if she attended the ragged school, he would offer her an immediate place in the school choir.

The highlight of the evening came when a 'Father Christmas' entered the schoolroom to a chorus of jeers from some of the older children. Dressed in a long smock, with a crown of holly, he carried a huge sack on his back.

The jeering ceased abruptly when Father Christmas lowered his sack to the ground and began distributing presents to the children who crowded about him.

The younger children were given toys, but the older ones had items of clothing.

Meg had not expected to be given a present as she was not on the ragged school attendance roll. To her surprise and delight she was one of the first called forward. She was told she could select a pair of shoes from the many pairs brought in and placed on display.

She had no idea of sizes and would have chosen a gaudy but far too small pair had Becky not come to her aid.

The pair chosen for her were not quite as eye-catching, but they were reasonably smart. Meg insisted upon putting them on, there and then.

By the time the party came to a close it was obvious to Becky that the unaccustomed shoes were hurting Meg's feet. However, the young Irish girl refused to admit it and doggedly wore them all the way home to Back Lane.

'It was a lovely party, Becky. Thanks for taking me. I

would like to go to the ragged school, but I don't think Seamus will let me. He's on at me every day to go out and earn some money.'

'I'll speak to Fanny about it. She's very good at coming up with ideas to help anyone who really wants to go to her school.'

'I *do* want to go. I want to grow up to be as clever as you.'

Her words startled Becky and she said carefully, 'I'm not at all certain you should try to be like *me*, Meg.' She laughed. 'I'm flattered, all the same.'

They had reached the house by now and Becky said, 'Just you remember, if things don't go right for you with Seamus, you're always welcome to come up to my room.'

'I'll remember, Becky.'

Ida had apparently been watching for them from her room. As they entered the house she came out. 'Becky, I'd like to have a little talk to you.'

'Will it wait, Ida? I'd like to take Lucy upstairs and change her. We've been out for a long time.'

'I won't keep you a few minutes, dearie.' Jabbing a finger at Meg, she said, 'You get on up to your rooms. I heard that drunken father of yours falling up the stairs not ten minutes ago. You can tell him – and your ma – it'll be the broom again if I hear so much as a raised voice from either of them tonight.'

'He's my *stepfather*, not my real pa.' Meg grinned suddenly. 'I'll tell him for you – much as I'd like to see him get another dose of what you gave him the other night.'

Smiling at Becky, she said, 'Goodnight, Becky. Goodnight, Lucy. I'll see you both tomorrow.'

'She's a nice young girl, that one,' said Becky, when Meg had gone beyond hearing. 'She deserves a lot more from life than she's got.'

'Probably,' said Ida. 'She reminds me a lot of you, when you were that age.'

'I hope that, like me, she can find a Fergus,' said Becky, without thinking. When she realised what she had said, she added, 'And I hope I can find him again.'

'So do I,' said Ida, unexpectedly. 'I've always felt guilty about that night when he came back here. After he'd gone out looking for you.'

'You saw Fergus that night?'

'That's right, dearie. It was the night we'd had poor Irish Molly murdered and the house was full of constables, remember? No, of course you don't remember. You was out somewhere. I wasn't myself that night at all. I can't remember when I've ever been more upset. I told your Fergus that nothing like it had happened in the house before he came to Lewin's Mead. I said there was no place for him here any more.'

'You told him *that*?'

As she listened, the blood drained from Becky's face. She tried hard to prevent herself from shaking.

'That's right – but he must have known I didn't mean it. I wasn't myself. But I still wish it had been unsaid.'

'That's what you told him? That he wasn't wanted, here in Lewin's Mead?'

Becky's face was contorted with agonised dismay. 'And I thought he'd come back to me. Come back here. He *won't*. He won't never come back now!'

'Of course he will, dearie. He must have known it was only silly old Ida talking. Besides, he's your husband, isn't he? And you've got that lovely baby . . .'

'No, he won't be back.' Becky had remembered some words he had once repeated to her. Words that had been told to him by a man who had been Fergus's best friend throughout his life. The man for whom he had taken on his crusade to bring the plight of the slum-dwellers of Lewin's Mead to public notice.

'. . . In a slum an artist must observe the rules of the people who live there. *Their* code. Break it and he might as well pack up his things and leave.'

Fergus had taken the words very much to heart. It was the code by which he had lived his life in Lewin's Mead. If he had seen Becky in the Cabot Arms with other men and come back here to have Ida tell him that . . .

Suddenly, she wanted to cry. She had been fooling herself

351

that Fergus would one day return to her. Now she knew he
would not.

Chapter 14

When Meg went to Becky's room the next morning, she found that her friend had not been to bed all night. The attic room was cold and Becky was sitting huddled in front of a dead fire.

Lucy lay on the bed, alternating between complaining quietly and playing with her toes.

'Becky! What's the matter? What's happened? You were so happy when I left you last night.'

She merely shook her head, not replying.

'Come on, move over. I'll light the fire and change Lucy, then I'll make you a nice cup of tea.'

When a hot cup of tea had been placed before Becky, Meg set about finding out what had happened to change her mood of the previous evening.

She was persistent and eventually Becky said, 'It's Fergus. I don't think he's going to come back to me after all.'

'What are you talking about? Of course he is! From what you've told me about him, there's nothing will keep him away once he hears about Lucy.'

'We don't even know if the letter telling him about her ever reached him. If he doesn't know, then he *won't* be coming back. Not after what Ida told him.'

'What's she got to do with it?' Meg snorted. 'I can't see Fergus, or anyone else, letting anything Ida says change their life.'

'You don't understand, Meg. Fergus is more than a husband and a father. More than just a painter. He'd set himself a mission in life. To show the world what life was like here, in Lewin's Mead. In a slum. He wanted people to be shocked by the things he saw every day and painted. He wanted to change things so that everyone who lives here – especially the children – has as much of a chance in life as those who live outside Lewin's Mead. Ida as good as told him that everything he had done was wrong. That the people here don't agree with the changes he's tried to make in their lives. He would have taken it very much to heart because it was something he was concerned about. He knew that what he was doing might take everything away from them without putting anything back. Having Ida say that to him on that night, on top of what I was doing to him, must have left him thinking everything he'd done with his life had been wasted.'

'But . . . if he loves you, he'll come back . . . You said he would.'

Even while wallowing in her own distress, Becky recognised the plaintive despair in Meg's voice. Somehow, having Fergus return really mattered to her. Becky tried to remember what it was she had told Meg that could be so important to her.

She was not thinking very clearly this morning. Nevertheless, she tried to take a grip on herself. 'Yes. Yes, Meg. You're right. I'm just so upset after speaking to Ida, that's all. It's all going to be all right. It's a good job I've got you around to cheer me up.'

They might have been empty words, but Becky felt better for having said them. She felt able to cope with her life once more.

Meg remained with her all day. Her constant irrelevant chatter helped Becky to put her problems to one side, at least, for the time being. She tried to ignore the numbness that returned whenever she thought of Fergus.

Early on the afternoon of Christmas Eve, Simon found his way to the Back Lane attic room. He sat for a while warming his hands before the fire as he chatted to Becky and Meg.

It was cold outside, with a hint that there would be at least a sprinkling of snow for Christmas Day. The prospect excited Meg although neither of her companions shared her enthusiasm.

'How will you be spending your Christmas Day, Becky?' Simon put the question to her.

'Much like any other day, except that I've bought a couple of toys for Lucy.'

'Would you consider coming to have your Christmas dinner at my house, in St James's Court, with Catherine and me?'

'You two don't need my company when you have an opportunity to be on your own.'

'But we *do*, Becky. I'm expecting a visit from Mary Carpenter as I'm one of her tenants. She'd be scandalised if she were to find Catherine and me there alone together. You would be our chaperone.'

Becky was not quite certain what being a 'chaperone' entailed, but she said, 'Are you quite sure? Have you said anything to Catherine about it?'

'Yes. In fact, it was her idea. She doesn't want to spend Christmas Day with Fanny. There are a whole lot of relatives staying in the Tennant house and Catherine feels she would be intruding. Besides, I've bought a big goose. It's being cooked for me in the bakery. There's far more of it than two could eat.'

'All right. Thanks. I could do with some company tomorrow.'

'Good! I have a feeling this is going to be a wonderful Christmas. I'm really looking forward to it.'

'If you're going off for the day, I'd better bring Lucy's present up to you sometime tonight,' said Meg. She tried not to show she was unhappy because Becky was not going to be around for Christmas Day, but did not quite succeed.

'You've got a present for Lucy?' Becky was taken by surprise. She had not even thought of the possibility that Meg would be able to give presents to anyone.

'It's all right, I never pinched it or nothing,' declared Meg, offended because she had correctly guessed the reason for Becky's question. 'I've been helping the butcher and his wife pluck some geese and chickens. Anyway, it's not a very expensive present.'

'I'm sure Lucy will love it, whatever it is,' said Becky, warmly.

'What will you be doing tomorrow, Meg?' asked Simon.

'The same as the rest of the family, I suppose. Trying to keep out of Seamus's way. He's got the whole day off, so he'll be drunk before noon. What he does after that will depend on his mood – and how much money he's got left. If he's in a really good mood he might bring a bottle back to share with us. There again, he might not.'

'Why don't *you* come to St James's Court with us, too?'

'Could I? Honest?'

'Of course. We'd all love to have you there. You could come with Becky and bring Lucy's present with you then. I can see it's going to be quite a party. Now that's all settled, I'll hurry back to the ragged school and tell Catherine. She'll be absolutely delighted, I know.'

When Simon had gone, Meg asked Becky anxiously, 'You don't mind me coming with you tomorrow, do you, Becky?'

'Mind? I'm delighted. I would have felt I was playing gooseberry being with Catherine and Simon on my own. Now you're going to be there they won't feel they have to be including me in their talk all the time. They can talk to each other.'

Meg was seated on the floor beside Lucy, her chin resting on drawn up knees. Hugging her legs, she said, 'I'm *really* looking forward to tomorrow, Becky. I think it's going to be one of my best ever Christmases.'

Meg asked if she could stay with Becky that night. Seamus had finished work early and gone straight to a Lewin's Mead gin-parlour. She was apprehensive about what might happen when he returned.

Her concern was well-founded.

Later that night, Becky was in bed with Lucy and Meg was wrapped in a blanket on the floor in an alcove beside the fire. They had been talking about many things – but mostly about the Christmas Day they were to spend at Simon's house.

They stopped talking when they heard sounds on the stairs leading up from the street. It sounded as though someone was having trouble with their footing. When a swearword was heard, they knew it was Seamus.

Eventually, the sounds ceased and they knew he had reached the second-floor landing. When no more sounds were heard, Becky realised she had been holding her breath and she relaxed.

There was none of the immediate crashing and banging which often preceded arguments between husbands and wives.

Then Becky heard the creaking of the stairs leading to the attic. Seamus was coming up to her room!

Becky tried to remember whether she had put the bolt across on the door. It was doubtful, she did not usually bother.

She swung her legs from the bed slowly so as not to wake Lucy who lay beside her.

'Be careful, Becky,' whispered Meg, who had seen her movements in the firelight. 'He's dangerous when he's been drinking.'

'It's all right, I'm just going to put the bolt on,' was the whispered reply – but she was already too late. Her feet had hardly touched the floor when both girls heard fingers fumbling at the latch. Then it lifted and Seamus stumbled inside the room.

As he picked himself up, Becky demanded, 'What are you doing in my room?'

'Ah! You're still awake. That's good. I've come to wish you a happy Christmas – and I've brought a drink with me. A whole bottle of gin. I thought it was time you and I got to know each other a little better.'

'If I wanted to get to know you better I'd do it in the daytime, not in the dead of night. You go back to your own rooms and share the gin with your wife.'

'Now that would be a waste of good gin. It just puts her in the mood for a fight and I'm not feeling that way at all

357

tonight. Let's you and me enjoy it. You must get lonely up here with no man to keep you company, and you a fine, healthy young girl and all.'

'I *don't* get lonely, but if you're not going to leave then I'd better find three glasses – no, we'll make it four. Meg, you'll have a drink, won't you? But before we start pouring you'd better go and fetch your ma. Tell her that Seamus has just arrived in my room with a bottle of gin. Say I'd like her up here to help us all drink it.'

'Meg's here with you . . .? I don't believe you. You're not going to fool me like that.'

'Meg, perhaps you should say hello to Seamus.'

'Why? I've come up here to get away from him. But you're right. I ought to go downstairs and tell Ma what's happening. She'd want to know.'

'Damn youse! Damn you both! I came up here to be neighbourly. If you don't want to have a drop of gin with me, I'll go.'

'I know exactly why you came here. Goodbye, Mr McCabe – and a happy Christmas to you.'

Seamus left the attic room muttering angrily to himself. Halfway down the stairs he missed his footing and crashed the remainder of the way to the second floor landing.

The fall broke the tension in the attic and suddenly Becky began to laugh.

Meg joined in then said, 'I wish it had been light enough to have seen his face when you said I should go down and fetch my Ma. If she'd come up here she'd have broken the bottle of gin over his head.'

'I thought the suggestion might cool his ardour,' agreed Becky, 'but I'm very glad you were here with me, Meg. If you hadn't been, I doubt if I'd be laughing now. I'm going to get a new bolt for that door too – and I'll make sure it's put on every night from now on.'

358

Chapter 15

Christmas Day was all that both Becky and Meg hoped it would be. Carrying Lucy, they walked along pavements sprinkled with a light covering of snow and arrived at the small St James's Court house soon after eleven o'clock in the morning.

Catherine was already there and the house was decorated for Christmas in a manner that neither Becky nor Meg had ever known before.

When Becky expressed her delight, Catherine said, 'This was the way we always did things at Captain Cunningham's house. Christmas was always the most special day of the year. It was even better on the rare occasions he was home, of course. Somehow the members of the household and the servants became part of one large and happy Christian family on that day. We all felt we belonged.'

Meg frowned and Catherine asked, 'Is something wrong?'

'Not really . . . but I'm a Catholic and you're Protestant. Ma has always said that we're different from the English.'

'That's not entirely true, Meg. We may worship in different ways, but we both celebrate Christmas for the same reason. It's a time to be happy – but now you're here let's open the presents. I'm dying to know what Simon has bought for me . . .'

Simon and Catherine had thought about their presents very carefully. They had bought only small presents for Lucy so that they would not detract from the tiny doll Meg had bought for her.

They were still opening the presents when, as expected,

Mary Carpenter arrived at the door accompanied by Fanny.

Mary possessed a formidable personality. Unswerving in her views on a more enlightened approach to juvenile offenders against the law, she had won reforms in the face of daunting opposition. She was a woman of legendary energy and achievement.

She was also thoughtful and perceptive. During the ten minutes she was at Simon's house she managed to make Meg feel that her present to Lucy was the most wonderful the baby would have that Christmas.

There was also a comforting word about Fergus for Becky, who had once been in Mary's girls' reformatory at the Red Lodge, in Bristol.

Lucy was declared to be one of the 'bonniest babies' she had ever seen. There were congratulations too for Catherine and Simon on their forthcoming marriage. Mary suggested that he should come to the Red Lodge with a view of teaching music to her girls there.

Then she had gone. Outside, in the square, a coach was waiting to whisk her off to nearby Kingswood and the reformatory she had founded there some years before. Fanny went with her, after telling Becky she would be calling on her during the next few days. She wanted to give her some money, as she thought she might well be away from Bristol for a week or two.

Later that day, after everyone had gorged themselves on goose and vegetables, they sat around the fire, enjoying drinks. Simon and Catherine chose this moment to announce they were to be married at Easter. Becky and Meg were the first to be told the exciting news and it was hoped they would both take some part in the ceremony.

The news served to remind Becky how lonely her life had been since Fergus went away from her. Putting the thought behind her, she did not allow it to detract from the genuine delight she felt for Catherine and the blind musician.

The day passed all too quickly, especially for Meg. That evening, when she and Becky were returning to Back Lane, she confessed that it had been a very special Christmas Day for her. The first she had celebrated in such a manner.

As they approached Back Lane, through streets that somehow looked even dingier tonight, they met Maude and her young brother, Albert.

Maude looked pale and cold. Her head was bowed against the wind and she would have passed by without noticing Becky had not her brother nudged her.

Becky was the first to speak. 'Hello, Maude. I'm surprised to see you in Lewin's Mead. Especially today. I thought you'd left us for good.'

'I've just been to Back Lane hoping to see you, but that old cow of a landlady wouldn't let me in the house.'

'You can hardly blame her after all you and your brother have done there. Every time you get anywhere near the place something is pinched.'

'I don't feel like going home just yet,' said Meg hastily, anticipating an argument. 'I think I'll take a walk down to the arcades to have a look at the shops.'

As she hurried away, Maude said to her brother, 'You can clear off too. I want to have a private talk with Becky.'

As Albert slouched off after Meg, Maude said, 'I thought you and me were friends, Becky Vincent. I didn't expect you to take Ida's side against me.'

'I've known you a long time, Maude. Being friends didn't stop you from taking my money along with that of the others. True, it was only a few shillings – but that was only because I had no more in the house. Still, it's Christmas, we'll leave all that in the past. Why did you go to Back Lane to try to see me?'

'Like you say, it's Christmas. I wanted to see how you were keeping.'

Lucy had gone to sleep. Shifting her to a more comfortable position in her arms, Becky looked at Maude sceptically. 'I don't believe you. What's the real reason?'

For a few moments it seemed Maude might protest at Becky's scepticism, then she shrugged. 'I came to see if you would lend me some money.'

'That sounds more like it! But why do you need to borrow money? The last time I spoke to Iris she said you were taking on twice as many men as any other girl working the docks. Don't tell me you've given it all away – for Christmas?'

Maude looked disconsolate. 'I might just as well have. I . . . I found myself a man.'

'You mean a pimp? You let yourself get hooked by a pimp? I would have thought that you, of all people, would know better.'

'You're right, I should have known better, but I didn't know he was a pimp when I first met him. He was just . . . well . . . just someone I enjoyed being with.'

'You gave him all your money – just because you liked being with him?' Becky looked at Maude with undisguised disbelief.

'Not at first. He spent money on me – although when I look back on it I realise it wasn't very much. Then one day he didn't have any money on him and he borrowed some from me. The next day he said he needed more money, urgently. He owed someone and they'd sent a couple of blokes for it. They wouldn't take no for an answer, he said. He promised to pay me back. Said he had some coming in from a couple of stalls he owned. I believed him. Trouble was, it was a long time coming and soon we were both broke. He told me I ought to be earning more on the docks than I was . . . and started taking everything I earned.'

'You're a fool, Maude.'

She nodded, unhappily. 'Yes. I should have known all along. But I fell for him and wanted to believe him, I suppose.'

'Where is he now?'

Maude shrugged. 'I don't know. We had that week of bad weather when no ships came upriver. There were no seamen in the inns around the docks – at least, none with money to spend. We had an argument because I was bringing no money in. He gave me a good hiding and left.'

'You've disappointed me, Maude. I thought you were a girl who could take care of herself, if anyone could. But why do you need to borrow money now? There are ships in the docks today. Why aren't you working them?'

'I haven't done much work since he left me. I haven't felt too well.'

'What's the matter with you?' Becky asked, suspiciously. 'Don't tell me you're pining away for a pimp?'

'No . . . I'm expecting again, Becky. I'm nearly six months gone and this one's playing me up even before it arrives.'

Becky's suspicion increased. Maude was showing no discernible bulge.

As if she knew what Becky was thinking, Maude said, 'I'm wearing stays. They're pulled in so tight I swear that one of these days I'm likely to spit the little brat out if I so much as cough. I certainly couldn't hide it from any man sober enough to want to do anything in bed.'

Maude shrugged helplessly. 'I'm desperate, Becky. I've got no money and no likelihood of making any until after this one's born. If you could lend me something I promise I'll pay it all back to you as soon as I can – cross me heart and hope to die, I will.'

Becky had little faith in Maude's promises, and no cause at all to feel sorry for her, but she did. She knew that Maude would need to be desperate to ask her for money.

'I haven't got very much of my own. It's a long time since Fanny Tennant gave me any and I've spent a lot this Christmas.'

'Can't you ask her to give you some more?' Realising she had overstepped the mark, she added, plaintively. 'Anything will do, Becky. Even a couple of shillings.'

'If I ask Fanny Tennant for more money it certainly won't be so I can give it to *you*.'

Even as she was talking, Becky produced a number of coins and counted them out. The total came to a little over two shillings and she handed it to the other girl, saying, 'This isn't going to go far if you have to buy food for that family of yours.'

Maude looked at the money in her hand. 'It's better than nothing, I suppose. If they want something they'll need to go out and earn more for themselves.'

She turned and hurried away, heading not in the direction of her Broadmead home but towards the docks.

Becky shook her head. Maude would drink the money away before the evening was over. But no doubt she would find another gullible 'friend' when it was gone.

Chapter 16

Meg was looking in a shop window in Broadmead's lower arcade when she saw Albert sauntering along towards her. When he reached her, he stopped.

'You're one of the Irish girls who's moved into the room our Maude used to have, ain't you? What's your name?'

'Meg – but I don't see what business it is of yours.' She glared belligerently at him before resuming her perusal of the items in the shop window.

'Are you on the game? You won't find much business here today. All the men are at home with their families. The only place you'll find business is down at the docks. Some of the ships' officers would pay good money for a young girl like you, 'specially today. They'll most of 'em be feeling a bit lonely, being away from home. I know where a lot of 'em go drinking. I'll show you, if you like?'

'If that's what I was doing I wouldn't need the likes of you to show me anything.' Meg gave Albert another glare and moved on to the next shop.

Here she studied the wide variety of footwear offered for sale. It gave her considerable pleasure to observe that her shoes compared very favourably with those on display here.

Slightly puzzled, Albert had moved along the arcade with her. 'If you're thinking of picking a few pockets, I'll show you where you'll find the nobs tonight. The easiest touch will be those coming out of the cathedral with their families. I'd be there myself, except I haven't been able to move my fingers properly since they was broken – but I could still attract their attention for you while you did the dipping . . .'

Meg rounded on him angrily. 'Do you think the whole world's like you and your sister? Either a thief or a whore? Well, I'm *not*. I never have been, and I never will be. Now, run off and be a nuisance to someone else. I've had a lovely day and I don't want you spoiling it.'

Albert looked genuinely bemused. 'But . . . if that's not what you're up to, what are you doing out here on your own at this time of the day?'

'What time of the day? It hasn't long got dark.'

'Even so . . .' Albert had a sudden thought. 'You're Irish, ain't you? How long you been in England?'

'What's that got to do with anything? Aren't Irish girls allowed to be out at this time of the day unless they're up to something they shouldn't be doing?'

'*No* girl should be out on her own in this part of the town when the shops are closed. The only ones who do that are trying to pick up a man.'

'What sort of city is this?' Meg was angrier than she might otherwise have been, because she was embarrassed at having made such a mistake. 'In Ireland a girl can go out where she likes, when she likes, and nobody thinks any the worse of her for it.'

'Well, this isn't Ireland – and you're living in Lewin's Mead now. If you want to survive you'd better learn these things.'

Albert felt very worldly-wise in the company of this young Irish girl. 'You've got a lot to learn about living in Bristol. I'd better walk around with you for a while. You'll be all right with me. What sort of shops do you want to look at? I know where they all are.'

Meg shrugged. 'I'm not looking at anything special. Just looking at them all.'

'Well, I'll come with you anyway. You're lucky you met up with me. Bristol's one of the toughest places in the country, my pa says. If you live here you've got to look after yourself and not give a damn about anyone else.'

'Oh? What makes him an expert on living in Bristol? How does he earn his living?'

'Any way he can – but he's in prison right now.'

Meg made a derisive sound in the back of her throat. 'So much for his ideas on getting on in the world. I suppose he taught your sister all about life, too? I believe she's been in prison herself, once or twice. Well you can forget your ideas on how to get on in Bristol. You're not going to get *me* in prison.'

'No one *wants* to go there, but it isn't always easy to stay outside. Tell any copper you're from Lewin's Mead and he'll lock you up first, and decide what you've done afterwards.'

Albert was genuinely puzzled by Meg's attitude. Never before had he met anyone from Lewin's Mead with her stand against dishonesty. Not everyone in the Bristol slum had a full-time criminal career, but he had never heard of anyone who would not steal if the opportunity presented itself.

'How do you get your money, then?'

'My Ma feeds me and I find what work I can,' said Meg. 'I didn't do too bad before Christmas. I expect I'll find something else to do, now it's over. What I'd really like is to go to the ragged school.'

She surprised herself by telling this to Albert. In view of his outlook on life, he was hardly likely to have any interest in what *she* wanted.

Interested or not, her words provoked a reaction in him. 'What do you want to go *there* for? No one in their right senses *wants* to go to the ragged school. Besides, you're a girl. What good would learning things do for you?'

'Because I'm a girl doesn't mean I can't learn about things.'

'Well, what good is learning going to do for you, that's what I'd like to know?'

'It makes you a more interesting person, like Becky.'

'Ha! A fat lot of good it's done for *her*! Her husband's gone off and left her and she's still living in Lewin's Mead. No one with any sense lives there.'

Meg leaped to Becky's defence immediately. 'Becky *chooses* to live there – and her husband will come back to her one day, you just wait and see. Besides, she has more to talk

367

about than "going on the game", or picking someone's pocket.'

Meg glared at Albert belligerently. 'You can push off home now. I'll be all right looking in shop windows by myself.'

'No, you won't . . . I'll tell you what . . . I know a shop that has a basketful of kittens in the window. I'll show them to you, if you like?'

Meg was about to tell Albert scornfully that she was not a small child. She could not be won over by the promise of seeing a kitten – but, the more she thought about it, the more she realised she *did* want to see the kittens.

'All right. I'll come with you to see them, if that's what you'd like.'

The kittens were in the window of a pet shop – and the woman owner was inside, feeding the animals. When she looked up, she saw them looking in through the window.

She had enjoyed a happy family Christmas with daughters, and granddaughters – and she came to the door.

Both children immediately went on the defensive, ready to argue that they were not hurting anyone by looking in the pet-shop window.

Instead of telling them to go away, the woman asked if they had kittens of their own.

Albert replied that his father would not have a cat in the house, while Meg said, 'We live upstairs in two rooms. The landlady wouldn't let us have one.'

'Would you like to come in and hold one for a few minutes?'

Meg could hardly contain her delight at the offer and the woman said, 'Come on in then – but keep away from that old parrot in the cage. He's a vicious old devil. If I hadn't known he'd be tough I'd have had him in the oven for Christmas.'

The woman smiled when she saw that Albert had taken her words seriously. 'I got him from the widow of a sailor who'd bought him in one of those foreign countries. He can swear better than a drunken tinker.'

They were in the shop now and the woman reached into

the box that was in the window. 'Here you are, love, you hold this one.' She put a small, fluffy kitten in Meg's hands.

She held it close to her and began stroking the little creature. 'It's so soft! It's lovely!'

The kitten looked up at her, happy at the attention being paid to it, and miaowed.

'What's the matter with it?' said Meg, alarmed.

'There's nothing the matter. It's just pleased to have someone make a fuss of it.'

The woman caught a momentary unguarded expression on Albert's face. Picking up another of the kittens, she thrust it upon him before he could refuse to take it, saying, 'Here, you can hold this one.'

Had any of Albert's friends been with him, he would have scoffed at holding a *kitten*. Anyone who did so would have been forever branded as something less than manly.

But he was holding the kitten before he could protest and as he held it he was aware of its small size and helplessness. He too stroked the kitten automatically until he said, suddenly alarmed, 'What's that noise it's making?'

The woman smiled. 'It's purring, dear. It means it's happy. It likes you.'

Standing holding the kitten, Albert gave way to a feeling he had never experienced before. All too soon the woman said, 'Well, I must finish up in here and get back to my family. Put the kittens back in their box, luvvies. It must be time you went back to your families, too. But if you ever want a pet, this is the place to come. I've always got something interesting around.'

Meg put her kitten back with very real reluctance. When they left the shop, she and Albert stood outside until the light inside was extinguished and it was no longer possible to see the kittens in their box.

As they walked away, Meg said, 'That was a lovely end to the best Christmas I've ever had.'

'We can come and see them again if you like,' said Albert. 'I don't suppose she'll let us hold 'em again, but we could look at 'em through the window,'

'When?'

369

'How about tomorrow afternoon?'

'All right.'

Albert managed to hide the delight he felt at the thought of meeting up with Meg again, saying nonchalantly, 'I'll be waiting for you just outside Back Lane at about two o'clock – that's if nothing important comes up, of course.'

Chapter 17

As Meg climbed the stairs of the Back Lane house, she could hear an argument going on between Seamus and her mother. In the same room she could hear one of the children crying softly but persistently.

The door to the room was closed, no doubt in a bid to keep the sound of the argument from reaching the ears of Ida. Going inside and becoming embroiled in their dispute was not what Meg wanted at the end of such a very enjoyable day.

Passing across the landing quietly, she went up to the attic.

As the young Irish girl entered the room, Becky smiled at her sympathetically. 'You don't need to ask me. I heard the arguing as I came upstairs. You'd better stay up here with me, but I hope they're not going to keep it up all night.'

'They won't,' declared Meg, confidently. 'The fact that they've closed the door is a good sign. It means Seamus is sober enough to care about disturbing Ida.'

'Good, we can do without them causing any trouble tonight. Lucy's tired out.'

As she prepared the baby for bed, Becky asked, 'Where did you go when I began talking to Maude?'

'I looked around the shops and met up with Maude's brother. He showed me a shop that had some kittens in the window. The woman was in the shop feeding them. She let us go in and hold 'em. They were lovely!'

'You be careful of young Albert. He's trouble.'

'Oh, he's all right,' declared Meg, airily. 'He's never had anyone to teach him the difference between right and wrong, that's all. But he's very gentle with animals.'

Meg told Becky of the great pleasure he had derived from holding the small kitten.

'Well, perhaps there's some hope for him yet,' said Becky as she kissed Lucy. Laying her down on the bed, she covered her over. 'But don't let him lead you into any of his bad ways.'

'He won't,' said Meg, positively. 'I think I might even be able to persuade him to come with me to the ragged school – but he doesn't know that yet.'

This was a new, self-assured Meg. Becky did not know what had brought it about, but she hoped that if it had anything to do with Albert Garrett, Meg's confidence would not be misplaced.

A few days into the new year of 1858, Becky was going out shopping with Lucy when she heard a great deal of noise coming from Ida's room. She listened for a while until, increasingly alarmed, she knocked on the door.

'Are you all right, Ida?'

There was no immediate reply, but the noises continued. Eventually, Becky lifted the latch and peered inside the room. The furniture was in disarray and Ida was prodding beneath a sideboard with the handle of the broom she had once used with such effect upon Seamus McCabe.

'Is everything all right, Ida?'

'No, it's not all right.' The landlady was red-faced and out of breath. 'Give Lucy here for a minute and you get down and look under this sideboard for me.'

Handing over Lucy, Becky crouched down on her hands and knees before asking, 'What is it I'm supposed to be looking for?'

'A mouse. It's the third time I've seen it this week. If I don't catch it we'll have the house overrun with the horrible little creatures in no time at all.'

A little more uncertainly now, Becky crouched lower until her cheek was against the cold stone of the floor. 'I can't see a mouse, but I can see where he's gone. There's a hole in the skirting-board.'

'That settles it. I'm going to have to get myself a cat. They're horrible smelly, scratchy things, but we can't have mice in the house. Before you know it they'll be rats!'

Becky could not quite follow the logic of Ida's argument, but she remembered the Christmas Day conversation she had held with Meg.

'If you're serious about getting a cat, I'll speak to Meg. She was telling me about a couple of young kittens for sale in a Broadmead shop. She was very taken with them.'

'If I buy a cat it'll be for me, not to please anyone else. Besides, a kitten would be no good. I'd have to waste good money on food for months before it would be big enough to catch a mouse.'

'Get a full-grown cat in and it would be out through the door the very first time you opened it,' countered Becky. 'Anyway, just the smell of a kitten will be enough to keep the mouse away for a while. By the time it's got used to it enough to come out again, the kitten will be big enough to have it.'

'Um! How much would one of these kittens cost me? I'm not going to pay the earth for one.'

'I don't know. If you like, I'll get Meg to come and speak to you about it.'

Ida thought about it for some moments as Becky rose to her feet. Then, handing back Lucy, she looked down at the broom, and said, 'All right. I'll speak to her about it – but I might change my mind.'

Meg walked back from the pet shop with Albert. He had declined her offer to allow him to carry the kitten, for fear he might be seen by some of his mates.

At the entrance to Back Lane, he said goodbye to Becky and, after a moment's hesitation, reached out and stroked the kitten for a final time.

They were not far enough from Ida's house to have escaped the notice of the landlady, who was looking out for Meg's return.

When she reached the house, Ida's first question was not of the kitten, but of Albert Garrett.

'I saw you on the corner with that Garrett boy. What were you two doing together?' she demanded.

'He was the one who showed me the kittens on Christmas Day,' replied Meg. 'He came with me to buy it today.'

'Oh? And put you up to doubling the price too, I've no doubt?' Ida had given Meg a shilling and told her she expected to see some change from it.

'No. The woman wanted a shilling, but I knocked the price down to tenpence. I've got a receipt here from her and tuppence change.'

Only slightly mollified, Ida said, 'Well, you can keep that boy away from my house. He's tried to steal my money twice before. No doubt he's only waiting his chance to do it again.'

'I don't think so,' said Meg, more calmly than she felt. 'Like I told Becky, I believe he only pinches things because no one's ever told him that it's wrong. I have now, and he's never tried to take anything while I've been with him.'

'Is that so?' Ida looked at Meg and saw that she was serious. 'Well, I've never heard tell of a miracle happening in Lewin's Mead before, but I suppose there's always a first time for everything. Now, let's look at this kitten you've bought – and I hope it's not just a load of trouble.'

Reluctantly, Meg handed the kitten over to its new owner. Ida held it out and scrutinised it from every possible angle.

'There's not much of it for tenpence, is there?'

'It'll grow quickly enough if it's fed properly,' said Meg. 'And it'll be company for you.'

'I've never said I needed any company,' retorted Ida. 'All I want is something that's going to keep the place free from mice.'

'It'll do that all right,' said Meg. 'At least, it will when it's just a bit bigger.' She would have liked to have stroked the kitten one last time, but did not want to ask Ida if she might.

'Here's your tuppence change.' Meg held out the money.

To her surprise, Ida said, 'You can keep that for your trouble. I expected to pay a shilling, and that's what I can spare. Now, off you go, while I give this animal a drop of milk and get it settled down – and make sure you close the door properly after you. I don't intend to lose a shillings-worth of anything within minutes of buying it.'

At the door, Meg turned to look back. Ida had her head down towards the kitten and was gently stroking it.

Meg smiled. It seemed that Back Lane's latest resident had the ability to charm even the tough old landlady.

Outside, in the hall, Meg stayed close to the door for some minutes. Long enough to hear Ida talking to the kitten much as a young mother might talk to a new baby. She knew that, in spite of all her earlier misgivings, the small black kitten would enjoy a happy life with Ida Stokes.

Chapter 18

Some days after the arrival of the kitten, Becky was on her way to a nearby shop when she saw Maude sitting on the ground in a doorway around the corner from Back Lane.

In all probability she had been waiting for Becky to come this way – but this was not the same Maude who earned a living enticing seamen in the inns and taverns around the city's docks.

Unkempt and dirty, her appearance shocked Becky. 'What's happened to you, Maude? I've never before seen you looking like this!'

Her reaction to Becky's question was as lackadaisical as her appearance. 'I've had enough, Becky. I just don't feel like carrying on any longer.'

'But why? You've never let things get you down like this before. What's happened?'

'Just look at me! I'm as big as a barge horse. I can't work because I feel that if I got on my back for anyone I'd never get up again. As if that's not enough, the landlord's threatening to chuck the whole family out on the street because the rent's behind. I'm at my wits' end, Becky. I don't know what I can do.'

Over the years, Becky had learned not to put any trust in Maude who was dishonest in almost everything she said or did. But she remembered what Meg had said about Albert never having learned what was wrong and what was right.

Doubtless Maude was the same. Certainly, Becky had never seen her in such a low state as she was right now.

'How much rent is owing?'

'I don't know. It's not been paid for weeks. It might even be months.'

'I have no intention of paying off all the Garrett debts, but I can let you have a couple of pounds. Give it to the landlord and tell him you'll pay him the rest as soon as you can.'

Becky's offer seemed to put some life back in Maude. Snatching the money as though afraid Becky might change her mind, she struggled awkwardly to her feet.

When she was facing Becky, she said, 'You couldn't come up with another couple of bob, could you, Becky? So I can buy something for the kids to eat? They haven't had a scrap to eat for a couple of days . . .'

'You're the limit, Maude Garrett, you really are! I've left myself short as it is.'

'I know, Becky. It's all right. At least I'll be able to keep a roof over their heads. God bless you!'

'Oh, here you are!' Becky weakened and held out another three shillings. It was money she could ill afford at the moment and she questioned her own foolishness as Maude scurried away, still clutching the money in her hand. Becky doubted whether the plight of the Garrett family was really as dire as Maude had made it out to be.

Nevertheless, she did look dreadful, she was pregnant, and her father was in prison. Things could not be any easier for her than for the remainder of the Garrett family.

Becky saw nothing of Maude during the ensuing week, although she thought of her more than once. Then Meg came to the Back Lane attic to speak to her.

Meg was attending the ragged school on a more or less regular basis at the moment. She was also working for three hours each afternoon, sweeping up in a cardboard box factory, for which she was paid sixpence a day.

The money went home to her mother, who was also working part-time in the same factory.

Meg played with Lucy for a while, then made a cup of tea at Becky's request before coming to the point of her visit.

'Becky? You know Miss Tennant pretty well. How kind-hearted would you say she is?'

'Probably as kindhearted as anyone I know. Why do you want to know?'

'Would you ask her for a favour?'

'That depends,' said Becky, cautiously. 'What sort of favour?'

'Well, I know she gives a bowl of soup to all those who come to the ragged school. For those who can afford to pay she charges a penny. If they haven't got a penny she gives it to them anyway. Sometimes she'll give soup to their young brothers and sisters too.'

'That's right. She won't see any child going hungry.' Becky was still puzzled at Meg's line of questioning. 'But what's this got to do with you? Seamus is working regularly and you and your ma are both in part-time work and bringing money into the house. I doubt very much whether Fanny Tennant would give free soup to your young brothers and sisters.'

'I don't want it for us. It's for Albert and his family. They were thrown out of their rooms nearly a week ago. Since then they've all been living rough down by the river and begging for food during the day. Some days they're lucky, others they're not. I'd like to see they all had something to eat every day at least.'

'They've been thrown out!' Becky exclaimed angrily. 'Less than a week ago I gave Maude two pounds towards what was owing in back rent on their place in Broadmead. Not only that, I gave her another couple of shillings to buy food for the children. What did she do with it?'

'I can't answer that. She certainly didn't give any of it to Albert or the others. He says they're all close to starving. I'm worried for him in particular, Becky.'

Meg looked anxiously at her. 'Albert's stealing for them. If he's caught he'll go to prison – and he doesn't deserve that. Besides, I don't know what will happen to the others if he's put away. He says there's no other way he can get food for them. Will you speak to Miss Tennant? Please, Becky?'

'Of course I will, but I know Fanny. The first thing she'll

want to do is go and see the place where they're living. Do you know where it is?'

Meg nodded vigorously. 'Yes – and it's absolutely awful. It's even worse than some of the places where we've stayed in the past.'

'All right, we'll go and see Fanny now. Even if she can't help she might be able to give me some more of my money. With that we can do *something* for them, at least.'

wanted to begin and see the place where they're living. Do you know where it is?

Meg nodded vigorously. 'Yes — no, it's absolutely awful. It's worse than some of the places where we've stayed in the past.'

'Nothing will help our Fanny now. Even if she can't hold me much longer as to a few pounds more of my money. Whatever we can do for them now, at least ...'

Chapter 19

In the ragged school's office, Fanny listened to what Meg had to say, making no comment until she had finished speaking. Then she asked, 'Where is the place where the Garrett family is staying?'

'Down by the river, in the ruins of some old houses.'

'I know the place you mean. I thought all those houses had been pulled down after a group of your people moved in there and brought cholera to the city. That was some years ago.'

'That's the place,' agreed Meg. 'I've heard some of the Lewin's Mead kids talk about the cholera. That's why they won't go near the place. The houses were knocked down, but there are still one or two cellars left. Albert and the others are living in one of them.'

Fanny's expression was one of stern disapproval. 'We'll all go down there and see exactly what is going on.'

Handing some money to Becky, she said, 'Here's five pounds to help you along for a while. It's all I have with me. I'm keeping your money at home now. The ragged school has been broken into twice in the past month. One day soon I will bring you some more. It is possible I will be going away for a while. I want to make quite certain you are left with enough money to live on until my return.'

Becky tried not to read too much into Fanny's words. The school teacher knew well how Becky had earned a living when short of money in the past. She hoped she would never have to do the same again. However, if there was ever a danger of Lucy's going short of anything, she would put her before any other consideration.

Fanny was talking once more. 'May I suggest you leave Lucy here while we are visiting the Garrett family? It's most unhealthy down there by the river. Catherine will love taking care of her while we are away.'

When the small party reached the riverside, Becky wrinkled her nose in distaste at the smell hanging on the air. At first, she thought Meg must have made a mistake in the place where they would find Albert and the younger members of his family. All that could be seen was a pile of rubble on which many of the Lewin's Mead residents seemed to have discarded much of their household rubbish.

'This *is* the place,' insisted Meg, when Becky queried it. 'Albert found a way in to the cellar. Perhaps it might be better if you and Miss Tennant were to stay here while I go and see if I can find him.'

'No,' said Fanny firmly. 'I want to see for myself the place where they are living – and I am as capable of climbing over rubble as you, young lady. I am twenty-eight, not eighty-eight.'

In spite of her bold words, she found it difficult to clamber over some of the larger piles of rubble. Both she and Becky were grateful for the help offered to them by Meg.

'We're nearly there now,' said Meg. At that moment Becky trod on a loose stone. Fanny grabbed her in time to prevent her from falling, but the movement started an avalanche of stones. Some of them bounced inside a tiny opening, seemingly too small to allow even a medium-sized dog to pass through.

There were muffled shouts from somewhere inside. Moments later Albert's hand came through the hole followed by the upper half of his thin young body. In his hands he grasped half a pickaxe handle.

Blinded by the light, he reminded Fanny of a mole emerging from an underground tunnel.

'It's me, Albert,' said Meg, reassuringly. 'I've brought Becky and Miss Tennant with me. They wanted to come and see where you and the others were staying.'

381

Albert's eyes had grown accustomed to the light and he could see more clearly now. Lowering the makeshift cudgel so it was out of view, he said self-consciously, 'I heard a noise and thought it was one of them men come back again.'

'What men, Albert?' Becky put the question.

'Oh, a couple of tramps. They'd been drinking, most likely. They saw young Florrie climbing over the rubble and tried to grab her. She only just managed to get back in the cellar in time. One of them put his arm inside and felt around for her. I gave him a good whack with this.'

There was another momentary glimpse of the piece of wood before Albert continued his story. 'He yelled for a bit, then shouted down at Florrie not to think she'd got away from him. He said she'd have to come out sometime. When she did, he said he'd be waiting for her. She was so scared she hasn't left the cellar since.'

Becky looked around her. There was no one in sight and on their way here they had seen nobody near the ruins.

'How old is Florrie?' asked Fanny.

'Either nine or ten,' replied Albert. 'I'm not sure, exactly.'

'I see.' Fanny's expression gave away nothing of her thoughts. 'Well, you can tell her there are no men waiting out here for her now. She can come outside. The others can come up from there too. I want to see them.'

'What you going to do with us?' The demand was made aggressively by Albert. 'We're not going to no workhouse.'

'Why not? You'd be looked after there. Fed, cleaned up, and have somewhere to sleep that would be a sight more comfortable than a damp, stinking cellar alongside the river. You'd be safer too – not only from vagrants, but from the river itself. It floods frequently down here. If it were to happen again it would fill the cellar with water before you could get out and you'd all drown.'

'I'd rather that than for all of us to go to a workhouse. They'd break the family up in there. Boys in one place, girls in another. Those of us old enough to work would be sent away. We'd never see each other again. Never.'

Albert lowered himself farther inside the hole and glared accusingly at Fanny. 'None of us are coming out unless you promise you won't put any of us in the workhouse. We'd rather die here, all together.'

Fanny was reluctant to make such a rash promise to Albert. However, she realised that if she did not she would never rescue the children from their unsavoury hideaway.

'All right, Albert. I won't put anyone in the workhouse, but I want all of you to come out of that cellar at once, so I can see just what needs doing for you.'

'You promise?'

Containing her growing impatience, Fanny said, 'Yes, I promise. Now, come out of there, all of you.'

Some minutes later five children stood self-consciously amidst the rubble of the riverside houses. Albert was much older than the other four, whose ages ranged from about five to ten years old. Three of them were girls, the other was a boy who must have been about seven.

The skin of their faces, arms and legs was as filthy as their ragged clothes. Evidence that they had been living in darkness was apparent. Buttons were fastened through wrong buttonholes and some were not fastened at all.

They all stood before Fanny looking ill-at-ease and Becky's heart went out to them. She felt she wanted to hug each and every one of them.

Fanny's feelings were less evident as she stood in silence, looking from one to the other. Eventually, she shook her head in despair. 'What *am* I going to do with you?'

The smallest of the girls said, 'Albert said you was going to feed us.'

'Then I suppose that's what we had better do,' said Fanny. 'Albert seems to have very firm ideas of what is best for you all. We must not disappoint him.'

'Why does she talk so funny?' The second oldest of the girls put the question to Albert.

''Cos she's posh, silly,' said the oldest girl, scornfully. '*All* posh people talk like that. They can't help it.'

Despite the appalling condition of the children, Becky had difficulty holding back a smile. Indeed, it was a relief from the despair she felt at the plight of the Garrett family. A sidelong glance at Fanny confirmed that she felt the same.

'Well, I think you are going to have to accompany this "posh" lady to the ragged school,' said Fanny. 'When we arrive there you'll be fed, we'll clean you up and see if we can find something clean for you to wear while we decide what we're going to do with you.'

'That's all right,' said Albert. 'But remember, none of us are going to the workhouse.'

'I have already made that promise to you,' confirmed Fanny. 'Now, let's get away from this disgusting place as quickly as we can.'

Chapter 20

At the ragged school, every available member of staff rallied around to help feed and clean up the Garrett family. They ate ravenously. 'Like little animals', was the comment of one sympathetic helper. But they were not yet ready to join the other pupils.

When they had all eaten as much as their bellies would hold, the four smaller children huddled together seated on the floor in a corner of Fanny's office, all strangely silent in their unfamiliar surroundings.

'They look much better than when we took them out of the cellar,' said Fanny, viewing them with some satisfaction. 'But what do we do with them now?'

'I've been thinking about that,' said Becky. 'I might have a solution. Mind you, it depends very much on whether I can appeal to Ida Stokes's better nature. She has an empty room on the first floor of the house. It's where Irish Molly used to be.'

She had no need to amplify her bald statement. Irish Molly was the prostitute who had been murdered in the Back Lane house. Her death had led indirectly to Ida's telling Fergus to leave Lewin's Mead.

'The room's never been let out since. It's bound to be in a bit of a state, but Meg and I can set to and clean it up.'

'Ida Stokes would never let me stay in her house,' declared Albert, immediately.

His words puzzled Becky for a moment, then she remembered the incident with the gin trap. 'No, you're probably right. We'll need to think of something else. It's a pity though. It would have solved a great many problems and you'd have been close enough for me to keep an eye on you all.'

'I'll go and speak to her,' said Fanny. 'It may do no good, but we won't know unless we try. If she won't take Albert we may persuade her to allow the others to live in her house.'

He looked from Becky to Fanny, suspiciously. Meg realised he was fearful that by splitting them up, Fanny might be planning to take the younger children away from him.

'It's all right, Albert. You stay here with the others, I'll go with them to speak to Ida. She's not as hard-hearted as she likes people to believe. I might be able to help persuade her to take you all.'

Ida Stokes threw up her hands in horror at the idea of having more children in her house.

Stabbing a chubby finger at Meg, she said, 'Don't you think I have noise and trouble enough in the house with her lot – and they're on the second floor! These others would be right above my head. Oh no! I wouldn't dream of having any more staying here. Especially children who have no mother to keep them in hand.'

'It wouldn't be as bad as all that, Ida,' said Becky. 'They've all agreed to attend the ragged school during the day, and I'd keep a close eye on them in the evening.'

'No! I wouldn't have that oldest Garrett boy in here, for a start. He's a thief. He's tried to steal my money twice before. I wouldn't feel safe in my bed with him in the house.'

'He's not such a bad boy really, Ida. I suspect Maude had a great deal to do with the trouble he got into while she was around.'

'Let's forget about Albert for the moment,' said Fanny. 'I might be able to fix him up with a bed somewhere else – but I can't think of anywhere else I could put the small girls.'

'Albert wouldn't allow the others to be taken from him,' said Becky. 'He's trying desperately to keep the family together.'

'He might do it if I said *I'd* stay with 'em to take care of 'em the way he does,' said Meg, unexpectedly. She added, meaningfully, 'Besides, it'd get me out of Seamus's way. He's up to his old tricks with me again.'

Ida realised what she was saying and exclaimed, 'God bless me! What's the world coming to? And her his own daughter, too!'

'I'm *not* his daughter! He's my *step*father.' Pleading with the landlady, she added, 'You'd be doing me a big favour, Ida.'

She was trading on the fact that Ida seemed to have taken to her in recent weeks. She believed the future of the Garrett children to be important – especially to Albert.

It seemed she had misjudged the landlady. 'Don't you try to appeal to my better nature, young lady. I weakened once before and let their sister into my house. I lived to regret it. This isn't the poor house, you know. I'm not paid to look after them as can't look out for themselves.'

Despite Ida's words, Fanny sensed a weakening of her stance, albeit only a slight one. 'I would, of course, guarantee the rent for the children.'

Talking with Meg afterwards, Becky suggested this was the argument that persuaded Ida to change her mind. Meg disagreed. She believed it merely gave the Lewin's Mead landlady a means of solving the plight of the Garrett children without its being thought she had 'gone soft'.

'That's a good room, that is,' said Ida in response to Fanny's offer. 'Anyone who takes it only has to go up the one flight of stairs. I could ask five shilling a week if a working girl came along looking for a place.'

'You could ask *fifty* shillings a week,' retorted Fanny, 'but you wouldn't get that either. I'll give you two shillings a week and no more.'

'Well! That's gratitude for you,' Ida protested. 'There's me trying to do you a favour and you insult me with an offer like that. But, seeing as how you do a lot of good work for the kids of Lewin's Mead, I'll let you have it for four shillings.'

Fanny stood firm. 'Two shillings a week is what I am offering – with a month's rent paid in advance.'

'Make it two-and-six with a month paid in advance and the room's yours,' countered Ida, hopefully.

'Two-and-threepence,' said Fanny firmly. 'And that is my final offer. If it's not enough for you then the children will have to be lodged in the workhouse. Now, I can't waste more of the ragged school's time and I can't spend any more of their money. I have other needy children too.'

Ida let out an exaggerated sigh. 'You strike a very hard bargain, Miss Tennant. But I'd never be able to live with myself if I let a poor motherless family go to the poorhouse for the sake of only threepence a week. All right, they can have the room – but remember, I'm not having that Albert in this house. No, nor Maude Garrett, neither.'

Chapter 21

Albert was less than happy at the prospect of being separated from the younger members of the Garrett family. However, Meg was able to assure him that she would move in with the children and take good care of them.

'Anyway, you'll be able to see them every day at the ragged school,' she added, when he still seemed unenthusiastic over the idea.

'I don't know whether I'm going to go to the ragged school. Not every day, anyway,' he declared sulkily.

'Why not? Don't you want to learn about things? You'll have to if you want to go out and get a decent job one day.'

'No amount of learning's going to make any difference. As soon as they know I got my learning at a ragged school, no boss will want to know me.'

'He will if Fanny Tennant tells him to,' said Meg, confidently. 'People do what she tells them.'

'Only because her father's an Alderman and is in charge of the police or something. Anyway, he's not going to be in charge for very much longer. I heard someone saying they're having some sort of voting soon. When they do he won't be in charge of nothing. At least, that's what they said.'

'I don't know where you've heard such stupid talk, Albert Garrett. Miss Tennant and her father are important people – and they always will be. I bet they're a sight more important than anyone who's doing this old voting.'

Meg had no idea at all what 'voting' meant, but she would not allow anyone to put down Fanny Tennant's father. Especially if it meant that Albert would not go to school because of it.

Meg attended the ragged school every morning. She worked in the box factory in the afternoon and returned to the ragged school to meet the Garrett children afterwards. Sometimes she found Becky waiting for her and they would walk to Back Lane together.

Today was one such day. As they waited outside the school for the children to come out, Meg spoke to Becky about Albert, adding, 'He's missing the others, Becky. He's missing them a lot.'

'I'm sure he is, but he sees them when they're all at school together.'

'Not really,' said Meg, and explained. 'They're in different classes. Even if they weren't, they wouldn't be allowed to talk to each other during lessons. They're together for a while when they're having their soup, but it's far too noisy for them to be able to talk properly. Albert says it's a waste of time him going to school if he can't get to talk to them.'

'Where's he staying, Meg?'

The young Irish girl looked unhappy. 'He hasn't told me – but I believe he's sleeping rough. That means he'll be mixing with some of them who hang around the pubs down by the docks. None of 'em know anything but thieving. He'll have to do the same if he's to stay alive. Sooner or later he's going to get caught.'

'What do you suggest we do for him, Meg? If he was living in Back Lane he'd still want money. Fanny's paying rent for the rest of the kids and giving all the Garretts one meal a day. I'm cooking more food than me and Lucy need, so I can send some down to the youngsters each night, but it can't go on forever. Albert will need to find work if he's ever going to take care of them himself. To tell you the truth, I can't see him sticking at a job, even if he found one.'

'He *would*, Becky, I know it. He'd do anything to keep the family together – and he *can* work. You ought to have seen how clean he kept the place the family had in Broadmead. He even painted it – although he wouldn't tell me where the paint came from.'

Meg pleaded Albert's cause vehemently. More despondently, she added, 'But he won't ever get a job if he has no proper place to sleep each night.'

Meg's passionate pleas on Albert's behalf laid bare the young Irish girl's feelings for him. Becky's immediate reaction was that she was far too young to become emotionally involved with anyone. Then she recalled her own first meeting with Fergus. She had been no older than Meg, yet she had known immediately that he was what she wanted.

Putting a comforting arm across Meg's thin shoulders, she said, 'I'll have a word with Ida, if you like. I doubt if it will do any good, but if we *can* persuade her to change her mind and allow Albert to stay with the others, I'm sure everything else can be sorted out.'

Later that night, it seemed to Becky that her efforts at changing Ida's mind were doomed to failure.

'You're asking me to have that boy in my house, after what he did? You must believe I'm some senile old fool, Becky. I thought you knew me better.'

'I think he suffered more than anyone else for what he did, Ida – and I'm still convinced he was put up to it by Maude.'

'I don't doubt it, but nothing's changed. He's still her brother.'

'There's nothing he can do about that. Mind you, I don't think her influence counts for a lot since she went off. A caring sister wouldn't have gone away leaving them with no food and owing so much rent they were all put out on the street.'

Ida maintained a tight-lipped silence but Becky tried once more. 'I know he's done a few things in the past that he shouldn't have done, but so have we all. He *does* think the world of those kids – and they of him. Meg has lots of time for him too. She seems to think all he needs is a chance to prove himself. For what it's worth, I think so too, Ida. I remember all too well what I was like when *I* was his age. If I hadn't had some good people looking out for me I'd have probably been shipped off to Australia years ago. Give Albert a chance, eh?'

'I don't see why I should. I've done my Christian duty by letting the rest of the Garrett family live in my house for a rent that would make me a laughing-stock if it got about.'

'You've had no cause to regret it, Ida. Those kids are so well-behaved you would hardly know they're upstairs. They are like that because every day at the ragged school Albert tells them they're lucky to have a roof over their heads. He makes them promise to behave themselves. He's a *good* influence, Ida, but living the way he is right now, he doesn't stand a hope of staying out of trouble himself.'

Ida had been born and brought up in Lewin's Mead. As a young woman she had been no better and no worse than any of her contemporaries. Only a lucky marriage had raised her above their level and given her ownership of a house. She knew as well as anyone the pitfalls of life in Lewin's Mead.

'I'm not saying I *will* let him live under my roof – and I must be getting senile even to consider it – but tell him to come and see me. I'll have a chat with him.'

Becky was so delighted with this unexpected concession that she gave her a warm hug. 'Bless you, Ida! You won't regret it, I promise you.'

'Don't go making promises that someone else may break for you, young lady,' said Ida, as Becky hurried from the room.

When she was alone, Ida gazed into the low-burning flames of the fire and wondered why she was becoming so soft-hearted in her old age. She decided it must be because suddenly she had a houseful of children, and those who were barely out of their childhood.

She also tried to remember the last time anyone had hugged her.

Chapter 22

Becky went straight upstairs to tell Meg of her conversation with Ida. Then she sent the young Irish girl out to find Albert and bring him to the house.

It was late-evening now and Meg was not at all certain where he might be. She tried the dock area first, but drew a blank until she met up with one of the boys she had seen in the class at ragged school with him.

When she asked after Albert, the other boy, who was big for his age, said, 'What do you want him for? Won't I do instead?'

'Not unless you're willing to take care of four young brothers and sisters.'

'I can do without that,' retorted the boy. 'You'll most likely find Albert somewhere near the Drawbridge pub with a few of his mates. They hang about there hoping some seaman with a pocketful of money is going to fall out of the door too drunk to stand up.'

Becky made her way to the Drawbridge public house. Just before she reached it, walking along an unlit part of the dockside, there was a sudden commotion. Among the shouting she thought she recognised Albert's voice.

As she ran towards the disturbance she heard the strident sound of a policeman's whistle. Then there was the noise of running feet and she ran headlong into a crowd of unseen boys.

'Albert? Is that you?'

'Shut up, you silly cow!' It was a voice she did not recognise. 'We don't mention names here.'

A moment later the boys were running away once more,

but she saw the shadowy outline of one who had not gone with them. It was Albert.

Taking her arm, he pulled her into a nearby alleyway as two much larger figures pounded past in pursuit of Albert's late companions.

'What's going on? Why were you being chased?'

'Someone's been robbed,' hissed Albert. 'It was nothing to do with any of us, but we were too close for comfort when it was discovered. What are you doing here? Is something wrong with the kids?'

She could not see his face, but she recognised the concern in his voice. 'No, there's nothing wrong. I've got some *good* news. Becky spoke to Ida Stokes about having you living in Back Lane with Florrie and the others. Ida wants you to come to the house and speak to her.'

Albert's hand tightened on her arm. 'After what I did? I don't believe it. It's a trick to have me arrested.'

'After all this time?' Meg spoke scornfully. 'She could have done that when your hand was bad, if she'd wanted to. I've told you, Becky's been talking to her. Ida doesn't promise anything, though. What happens will depend on what you say to her, but it's a chance – and the only one you're likely to get, so let's not waste any more time.'

Albert said very little as they walked to the house in Back Lane. When they reached the door, Meg sensed the nervousness in him.

'Would you like me to come in with you to see Ida? I'd speak up for you.'

'No, it's something I have to do on my own – but thanks.'

Taking him by surprise in the darkness of the hall, Meg leaned towards him and kissed him. 'Good luck, Albert.' Then she was gone.

Albert knocked at the door, hoping that Ida might be out but knowing she was not.

'Come in!'

He entered the room and found Ida seated by the fire, holding the kitten on her lap. She was seated in such a position that she could see through the window. Back Lane was illuminated only by the lights from the house's window, but he knew she would have seen him arrive with Meg.

Ida's glance went first to his badly scarred fingers, and then to his face. 'This isn't the first time you've been in my room, is it, Albert Garrett?'

'No.'

'Oh! So you don't deny it? It was you who came here hoping to steal my money?'

'Not much use me saying it wasn't me, is it? All I can say now is . . . I'm sorry.'

'I've no doubt you are. Got more than you bargained for, didn't you?'

In truth, Ida was taken aback by Albert's honest admission. She had expected him to deny all knowledge of the attempt to burgle her room. She certainly had not expected him to apologise to her.

'Well, you can think yourself lucky I didn't report you to the police. They'd have had no trouble proving it was you, would they?'

'No.'

When he did not amplify his reply, Ida said, 'Becky tells me you'd like to come and live here, with the rest of your family. What guarantee do I have that you won't rob everyone in the house and disappear again?'

'I wouldn't do that!'

'Oh? Why not?'

'You gave the others a place to stay when they needed it. I owe you a favour. A very big favour. I wouldn't try to take anything from you again.'

Ida sniffed her disbelief. 'I don't know why I should believe you, I'm sure, but Becky and Meg seem to think you're to be trusted. Becky says you're a worker, too. If I let you stay would you show your gratitude by limewashing through the whole house?'

'Yes,' said Albert, eagerly. 'It'd take me some time but I wouldn't slack and I'd do the job properly, an' all. I could start with this room . . .'

'You'll start where I tell you. All right, you can share the room with your brother and sisters – but the first bit of nonsense from you and you're out. Not only that, the others will go out with you. Is that understood?'

'Yes.' He nodded vigorously. 'Can I move in right away? Tonight?'

'You can, but you'll start the limewashing tomorrow.'

'That's all right. I'll make a start on it as soon as I get home from the ragged school. I'll work every day until it's finished.'

After making a couple of false starts, he said, 'Thank you, Mrs Stokes. Thanks for letting me stay – and especially for trusting me. I won't let you down, I promise.'

'Promises come easy, young man, as I told Becky earlier this evening. Say it again in a month and I might believe you then.'

When Albert had hurried excitedly from the room, to find Meg and the others and tell them the good news, Ida thought of all that had been said in her room that evening.

Despite her earlier misgivings, she had to admit to herself that she liked what she had seen of the boy. She thought Becky might have been right about him. There was a lot of good in Albert Garrett.

Brought up properly he would have been a son of whom any mother would have been proud. The sort of son Ida had once hoped she might have . . .

Chapter 23

Albert settled in well in the Back Lane house. He fulfilled his promise to limewash the inside of the house and also carried out a number of odd jobs for Ida.

She and he got on increasingly well together. She even began to pay him for the work he did for her. It was not much but, again on Becky's recommendation, he had been taken on by Fanny Tennant to carry out various small projects at the ragged school.

The additional income, albeit small, ensured that the Garrett children never went to bed hungry. It also gave Albert a sense of independence. All who came to know him agreed this was important.

Another result of his living in the Back Lane house was a blossoming of the relationship he already had with Meg. Everyone in the house was aware of it.

Meg's mother protested that her daughter was far too young for such a romance to be taken seriously, but Becky thought otherwise. She had fallen in love with Fergus when she was no more than Meg's age. In addition, both were street-wise in sexual matters. This was an age when girls of thirteen were considered old enough to marry and know their own minds.

There were, however, two matters which threatened the somewhat fragile stability of life in the Back Lane house. The first was Maude Garrett. After disappearing from the scene for some time, she had been seen once or twice recently. Heavily pregnant, she was reported to be in the company of some tinkers and vagrants, camped out on Horfield Common, just beyond the city limits.

There had also been reports that Maude had visited Lewin's Mead on at least one occasion. However, none of her family had seen her there.

The second problem was Seamus McCabe. He too objected to Meg's friendship with Albert, but his interest in the matter was far from paternal.

Meg's mother had finally faced up to Seamus's unhealthy preoccupation with his stepdaughter and it had increased the friction between husband and wife.

It made a return to the second-floor rooms well-nigh impossible for Meg. Becky solved this difficulty by allowing the young Irish girl to move in with her and Lucy.

One evening, when Becky and Meg were washing some of Lucy's clothes and hanging them about the fire to dry, Becky said, 'It looks as though things are beginning to work out quite satisfactorily for everyone at last.'

'For everyone except you,' pointed out Meg. 'I wish I could wave a magic wand and bring Fergus back to you.'

'I'm beginning to believe it's going to take a miracle to do that,' she said, wistfully. She glanced up at the wall, to the portrait Fergus had painted of her. 'He's probably found some other girl to sketch now. Someone with a lot more sense than me. After what Ida said to him, and all I did, why should he want to come back to us?'

'Because of Lucy – and because you love each other, that's why.'

'No one can say for sure that he knows of Lucy,' said Becky, sadly. 'He might never know. We're not even certain he's still alive!'

The thought that Fergus might be dead still brought her awake in a cold sweat in the darkness of the night.

'Have you ever thought of finding yourself another man?' Meg gave Becky a sidelong glance. 'I mean, one to live with you, here?'

'No. I came very close to it with Simon, but it could never have been the same as it was with Fergus. I couldn't look on him as anything but a brother – although I am still very fond of him. I suppose the truth of it is that I'll never think of anyone in quite the same way as I do of Fergus.'

'That's a bit the way I feel about Albert,' admitted Meg, seriously. 'I believe that one day he'll feel the same about me too. I think he does now, really, but boys don't mature as quickly as girls do.'

'So boys don't "mature" quickly, eh? That's a fine word, Meg, and a very grown-up observation. Fanny would be proud to know you're not wasting her time at the ragged school.'

Meg accepted Becky's praise with a certain amount of pride. It was a remark she had overheard Fanny herself making to one of the ragged school teachers. Meg had been waiting for an opportunity such as this to repeat it.

They were still talking together when they heard someone coming up the stairs to the attic room. There was a knock at the door. It was opened immediately and Fanny stepped inside.

Nodding to Meg, she crossed the room and bent down to lift Lucy from the floor. Giving her a kiss, she turned with the baby in her arms and spoke to Becky. 'I've just been talking to Ida. I must congratulate you, Becky. I never believed she would ever allow Albert to enter her house. Yet I have had to stand in the hall for ten minutes, listening to her singing his praises!'

'Oh, Ida's all right, really. You just need to understand her funny little ways, that's all.' Becky hesitated for a moment before asking fearfully, 'You . . . you haven't come here with bad news of Fergus?'

'No, Becky. I've had no news at all. I'm here because I would like to have a chat with you. I also wanted to look in on the Garrett children. They look a whole lot better than when I first saw them.'

'You must give Meg credit for that. She's been just like a little mother to them.'

'Good girl!' Fanny took out a purse and handed sixpence to Meg. 'They won't be used to treats. Go off and buy some sweets for them.'

Meg realised it was merely a ruse to get her out of the attic room, but it was a generous one and she left happily.

'Your praise means a lot to her,' said Becky. 'She's had precious little of it in her lifetime.'

'The ragged school is filled with children like her and I've yet to find one who doesn't thrive on a little encouragement. But I wanted her out of the way because I have some money to give you. A considerable sum.'

Becky's expression changed to one of disapproval and Fanny added, hastily, 'I'm not for a moment implying she's not to be trusted. Indeed, I think she's one of the most instinctively honest children we've ever had at the school. However, she's still a child. It's possible she might say something in an unguarded moment that could be overheard by less scrupulous persons.'

Fanny pulled a heavy purse from inside her coat and handed it to Becky. 'Keep it safe. It contains fifty pounds.'

Becky gasped. There were many in Lewin's Mead who would kill for far less. 'Why are you giving me so much?'

'I am going away from Bristol for a while. I shall be staying with an aunt in London. It is quite possible I shall then go on to visit ragged schools in other parts of the country. I have been asked by Mary Carpenter to write a book about the ragged schools. I shall probably agree, but it means I must carry out some research. As I don't know how long I will be away, I wanted you to have sufficient money for your needs. I would also like you to pay the rent for the Garrett family and help them in any way that might be needed. I will reimburse you for that upon my return, of course. While I am in London I intend visiting the Admiralty and try gleaning any information they might have about Fergus. If I learn anything, I will write to the ragged school and ask Catherine to send Simon to tell you.'

'Thank you. I'll keep this money in a bag around my neck, inside my dress. It'll be safe enough there. When are you leaving?'

'Most probably the day after tomorrow. The date is fairly flexible but I can't go tomorrow. My father is launching a ship at the Hillhouse yard. He wants me to accompany him to the ceremonies.'

'That sounds exciting. I might bring Lucy down there to watch.'

'The launch of a ship is always a great occasion. I am sure she will enjoy it – but I really must go now. I have a great deal to do.' Fanny kissed Lucy once again and placed her on the floor, saying, 'Goodbye, young lady. I wish I could take you with me.'

Returning her attention to Becky, she said once more, 'Take care of the money.' At the door she paused. 'I wish you and Lucy would move to somewhere outside Lewin's Mead. I really would feel very much happier.'

Becky smiled wanly. She had been awaiting the comment. There was seldom a meeting with Fanny when the same suggestion was not made. She repeated the reply she always made: 'We're quite all right here.'

'You really should think about it, Becky. If . . . *when* Fergus returns he'll want far more for little Lucy than there is here.'

When Fanny had gone, Becky thought yet again of what she had said. She was right, of course. Becky herself wanted more for her daughter – but she could not take such a step alone.

Becky had never known anywhere but Lewin's Mead. Yet, if Fergus returned to her, she knew she would be willing to move then. She believed that with his help she could make such a change in her life.

However, if he wanted nothing more to do with her, she would need to have the familiar cocoon of Lewin's Mead about her.

Chapter 24

The ship to be launched at Hillhouse's shipyard was a very large steam-powered liner, built with the Atlantic passenger trade in mind.

It was one of the largest ships ever to be launched from the shipyard and a large crowd had gathered to witness the occasion. Latecomers and the younger elements in the crowd climbed on walls and roofs in order to gain a vantage point.

All the nearby buildings were draped with bunting, and a gaily uniformed band was playing on the dockside. On the fringe of the crowd, vendors were offering a wide variety of foodstuffs and sweets.

The party of Aldermen and Councillors, together with their families, occupied a raised platform hung with drapes. In front of them was the dry-dock in which the great liner had been constructed.

After a speech by the shipyard owner, praising his workers and painting a rosy future for Bristol shipbuilders, Alderman Tennant gave a very brief address before announcing that the ship was to be called the *Bristol Prince* and calling for the Lord's blessing upon all who sailed in her.

He tugged on a white cord and the nameplate was unveiled on the stern of the vessel. At the same time, two teams of men strained on the capstan levers that worked the gates of the dry-dock and water gushed in to fill it. Not many minutes after the conclusion of the ceremony, the ship was afloat for the first time. As the newly completed vessel was moved from the dock, the music of the band was lost amidst the cheers of the spectators.

A reception followed, held in the offices of the ship-builders, close to the now empty dry-dock. Much food and drink was consumed and more speeches given before the official party left, its pleasant duty completed.

As Alderman Tennant and his daughter left in their carriage, he was in a jovial mood. This had been an important occasion for him.

During many years spent helping to manage the affairs of the city in which he lived, he had made enemies as well as friends. Some were men who were strongly opposed to Fanny's dedication to the poor of Lewin's Mead.

Alderman Tennant supported his daughter's activities. When he also backed the Chief Constable's decision to maintain a heavy police presence in Lewin's Mead, his opponents seized upon it as a means to discredit him. He had long been an advocate for demolishing the slum, now he was wasting money policing it.

A great many Councillors and Aldermen were undecided as to which side they should support. Today, Alderman Tennant had shown them he possessed the confidence of the shipbuilders, a very influential section of the community. It would bring a number of those who were still undecided over to his side. Indeed, they had already made their intentions clear at the reception he and Fanny had just left. His survival was assured.

As they passed through the busy dock area, Alderman Tennant suddenly pointed through the open window. A frenzy of activity was taking place alongside a black-funnelled vessel. 'That's a sight you won't often see, Fanny. An East Indiaman disembarking passengers in Bristol's docks.'

She looked out at the crowded dockside scene. Carriages, carts and people were milling around heaps of cargo and luggage. Laden vehicles trundled from the scene . . .

Suddenly, Fanny's mouth dropped open in utter amazement. For a moment her bewildered father thought she was about to scream.

'What is it, Fanny? What's the matter?'

'Stop the carriage!'

Bewildered, her father repeated, 'What is it?'

Instead of replying, Fanny jumped to her feet and leaned out of the window to shout an order to the carriage driver.

'STOP THE CARRIAGE!'

The startled driver pulled the horses to such a sudden halt that the driver of a following hansom cab had to swerve violently in order to avoid a collision. He cursed the carriage driver roundly, using choice language as his vehicle overtook the now stationary larger vehicle.

Fanny was aware of none of this. Not pausing to give an explanation to her thoroughly confused father, she threw the door open. With her skirts held high, she leaped to the ground.

As she ran towards the East Indiaman, she began shouting.

'Fergus! Fergus!'

Diving in among the crowd at the quayside, she was suddenly hugging him while Lewis looked on, somewhat bemused.

'Fergus! Fergus . . . It *is* you!'

'What are you doing here?'

The immediate excitement of the meeting over, Fergus and Fanny asked the question in unison, and both laughed together.

Remembering Lewis, who stood with his wounded arm supported by a sling, Fergus said, 'Fanny, I would like you to meet Lewis Callington – Lord Callington. Lewis, this is Fanny Tennant. I have spoken of her many times.'

'Of course. Delighted to meet you, Miss Tennant.'

The introductions over, she said, 'You still haven't told me what you are doing here now . . . in Bristol?'

'We've just arrived from India.' Fergus pointed to his companion's protected arm. 'Lewis was wounded there and it's still giving him a great deal of trouble.'

Fanny looked at him sympathetically before continuing her questioning of Fergus. 'We have all been frantic with worry. We learned that the *Venus* had been sunk but could not find out whether you were dead or alive.'

'If it hadn't been for Fergus's sketching there would

have been no survivors,' declared Lewis, adding, 'I was a lieutenant on the *Venus*.'

Before his friend could explain, Fergus said, 'It's a very long story. You'll learn it in due course, but I was on my way from Lucknow to Calcutta when I was given your letter. I made for home straightaway. How are Becky – and the baby?'

Fanny smiled. 'Both are well, Fergus. Lucy is absolutely adorable. You'll love her, as we all do. I was with them only yesterday.'

'Are they still living in Lewin's Mead?'

'Yes, unfortunately. I've tried to persuade Becky to move, but she's very reluctant to make the change. Now you're home, we might be able to do something about it.'

Fergus's happy expression left his face. 'Do you think I'll be able to persuade her to do anything? After all, *I* walked out on *her*.'

'She misses you a great deal, Fergus. The thought that you might have died brought her to her knees. Only Lucy's needs kept her going.'

There was a question that had been troubling him even before he left India. He expressed it now. 'How has Becky been managing? The money I left for her won't have lasted this long.'

'I have been giving her money. I said it was coming from you. We will talk about it later. But this really calls for a celebration. We'll go back to the house and discuss what we are going to do. Where is your luggage? We'll have it taken to the carriage. My father will be wondering what on earth is going on. He has just launched a ship from the Hillhouse yard. We were on our way home from the launching ceremony when I saw you. I really thought I must be imagining things!'

'But . . . I must go to see Becky . . .'

'Of course. We'll talk about it in the carriage.'

With the help of the carriage driver, the luggage was quickly loaded. Once he realised the identity of his unexpected guests, Alderman Tennant said, 'What a fortuitous meeting! You must both stay with us at Clifton.'

405

When Lewis protested that he needed to go home, Alderman Tennant said, 'Of course – but not today.' Nodding at the arm, carried in its sling, he asked, 'Were you wounded in India?'

'Yes. I received a wound to my elbow when a shell fell too close. It's rather reluctant to heal.'

'That settles it!' Alderman Tennant clapped his hands in delight. 'You'll stay at the house. We are having a small dinner party tonight. One of my guests is Sir Ephraim Stern. He is the country's foremost surgeon – and an expert on war wounds. He was knighted for his work in the Crimea. You couldn't ask the opinion of a better man. I will make absolutely certain he gives your arm a thorough examination.'

Lewis readily agreed. He had become increasingly concerned by the failure of his wound to heal. Now it seemed that fate had placed him in the path of a man he might otherwise have had difficulty in meeting.

'I am extremely grateful to you, Mr Tennant. It is an opportunity I cannot pass up.'

Fergus was delighted with his friend's good fortune, but had been thinking hard about his meeting with Becky. 'Fanny, do you think I should go on my own to Back Lane to see Becky? Or do you think it might be best to find an excuse to bring her out of Lewin's Mead to meet me somewhere else?'

'I don't know. Suddenly meeting up with you like this has scrambled my brain. Let me think about it.'

'Don't think about it for too long. I'm desperate to see Becky and the baby.'

'Of course you are, but you've been away for sixteen months. A few more hours will make no difference to anyone. It is important that we do things the right way.'

Fergus was impatient to see both Becky and his new daughter, but he knew that Fanny was speaking sense. It had always been very important to have things right for Becky the first time.

As they rode in the carriage up the hill to Clifton, Fanny waxed lyrical about Lucy. She also gave him an outline of what was happening in Lewin's Mead. He was relieved to hear that Maude Garrett seemed to have disappeared from Becky's life. She had always been a bad influence.

Fanny also said how impressed she was with the way Becky was bringing up Lucy. Despite Fanny's earlier misgivings, Becky had proved to be a loving and responsible mother. She felt certain that Fergus would approve of her way of life since the baby was born.

The only fault Fanny could possibly find was Becky's refusal to leave Lewin's Mead. However, she believed she had sensed a weakening in this stand in recent weeks. She hoped the return of Fergus might persuade Becky finally to leave the Bristol slum.

While Fanny was talking to Fergus, Alderman Tennant was holding a conversation with Lewis. He learned of his title and landholdings and a little of the war in India.

Fanny was occasionally drawn into this conversation, despite Fergus's impatience to learn every possible detail of his wife and unknown daughter.

It was a happy and excited party which arrived at the Tennants' Clifton home – but the joy was short-lived.

The coach had hardly drawn up at the door when Catherine Bell ran from the house. Standing behind her in the doorway was Simon.

When Catherine saw Fergus it looked for a moment as though she might faint. Thinking it was the shock of seeing him, he said, 'It's all right, Catherine. I'm no ghost. I'm very much alive, I can assure you.'

There was a stricken expression on her face as she looked from Fergus to Fanny. Belatedly, he realised that all was not well.

So did Fanny. 'What is it, Catherine? What's the matter?'

Uncertainly, casting an agonised look at Fergus, she said, 'It . . . It's Becky.'

'What's happened to her? Has there been an accident?' Fergus felt his stomach contract.

'No . . . It's even worse than that. She was arrested last night. She's being held in gaol. Lucy's with her.'

'Why? What has she done? We must go and get her out.'

'It's no good. Simon's tried to see her. They won't allow him in.'

'What's she charged with?' Fanny put the practical question.

Catherine seemed to have difficulty in formulating her reply. Then she uttered a single word.

'Murder.'

The word brought gasps from all those who heard it.

'I don't believe it,' said Fergus. 'Who is she supposed to have murdered?'

'Her landlady,' replied the tearful Catherine. 'They say she killed Ida Stokes.'

Chapter 25

The remainder of that afternoon passed in a frenzy of activity for Fergus and the others. Occasionally frantic, it was always frustrating.

It was particularly so for Fergus. He wanted to throw himself wholeheartedly into the efforts being made to free Becky, but Fanny advised him strongly against it, supported by Simon.

At first, Fergus was inclined to resent Simon's part in the discussions. He was overly suspicious of the detailed knowledge he seemed to have of Becky and her way of life. However, when Fanny told him of the part he had played in saving her life, Fergus's resentment became gratitude. The final barrier between the two men was removed when Fergus learned that Simon was to marry Catherine.

It was Simon who patiently explained why he did not think it would be a good idea for Becky to know, at this stage, that Fergus had returned to England and was working for her release from prison.

'Having you return to her and getting to know Lucy has been something she has longed for with all her heart. She is very aware of what she has done wrong in the past and is deeply contrite. She wanted your reunion to be something very, very special. She sees it as a new start together as a family. Something she has never known for herself. It is important for her that everything is done in the right way. To have your reunion take place in a prison cell would desolate her. It would be the worst thing that could possibly happen.'

Reluctantly, Fergus accepted Simon's assessment of how

Becky would react. 'Then we need to find out what this ridiculous charge is about and get her out of custody as quickly as possible.'

'Leave that to me for the moment,' said Fanny, firmly. 'You settle in here while I go down to the police station and speak to Ivor. He'll soon sort this out, I have no doubt.'

Alderman Tennant had been listening to the conversation and now he said, 'Unfortunately, Ivor is not in Bristol at the moment, Fanny. He's in London, at Scotland Yard. Newly promoted to inspector, he's there to learn of the latest methods being employed by the London Criminal Investigation Department. I believe he's due back some time next week. Of course, if you care to leave things until then . . .'

He had serious misgivings about the part Fanny was playing in this whole unhappy affair. It would not help politically if the daughter of the chairman of the Watch Committee were seen to be taking vigorous action on behalf of a woman who had been arrested on a murder charge.

'Oh!' This was a severe setback to Fanny's plans. Pre-empting Fergus's protest, she added, 'I hope to have Becky released long before then. Even if I can't do it immediately I will at least bring Lucy back here. Prison is no place for any baby. I'll go to the police station right away.'

'I'll come with you,' said Fergus.

'No!' Once again, Fanny was adamant. 'It can do no good – only harm. It is best for Becky to know nothing at all of your presence in Bristol. All I will tell her is that it has been confirmed that you are alive. That will give her some cheer, at least.'

'I'll come with you,' said Lewis, unexpectedly. 'I have listened with great interest to what you have both said. I must admit I am both appalled and intrigued by the whole situation. I haven't had my title for long enough to make much use of it. It may possibly – and quite literally – open a few doors for you. It will certainly not do any harm for the authorities to know that a peer of the realm is taking a personal interest in Becky's well-being.'

Fanny hesitated for only a moment. She was fully aware

of the fight her father was having to retain his position within the Bristol City Corporation. There were some who said that if he went then the Chief Constable would have to leave too. There were politics even within the police force. Lewis's title might possibly help everyone.

It was unfortunate that the detective sergeant who had arrested Becky was one of those who believed Alderman Tennant's days on the Watch Committee were numbered. The plain-clothes policeman confirmed that Becky had been arrested for the murder of Ida Stokes. He would volunteer little further information.

Becky was being held in the police cells, but he refused permission for Fanny to visit her. No one could visit her.

'This whole business is quite preposterous,' fumed Fanny. 'Becky has killed no one. You are going to look ridiculous when her innocence is proven.'

'I doubt very much whether that is likely to happen,' said the sergeant, smugly. 'I have both evidence and witnesses to prove her guilt beyond any reasonable doubt.'

'What evidence?' demanded Fanny.

'Well now, Miss Tennant, I think that is purely a police matter, don't you?'

'Such information will be made available to Mrs Vincent's legal representative, I presume?' asked Lewis.

His accent and bearing impressed the detective sergeant in spite of his determination not to be influenced by Fanny's connections.

'I doubt very much whether she will be represented in court. Such people rarely are.'

'I can assure you she *will* be defended, Sergeant – and as early as can be arranged.'

'Begging your pardon, sir, but are you acquainted with the prisoner?'

'I am Lord Callington, a friend of Mrs Vincent's husband. When will she be committed for trial?'

'She'll be coming before the magistrate in a couple of day's time, my lord.'

Observing Fanny's shock, the sergeant shrugged.

'There's no sense in wasting time. Not when everything is cut and dried.'

'You're pushing this through with undue haste, Sergeant,' said Fanny, angrily. 'Would I be right in assuming this is because you are hoping to have Becky convicted before Inspector Primrose returns to Bristol and has an opportunity to carry out a more thorough investigation?'

Detective Sergeant Judd flushed angrily. 'Just what are you insinuating, Miss Tennant?'

'I am *insinuating* nothing. But I would like to point out that having Becky committed for trial before you have carried out adequate enquiries might well rebound on you. This girl is innocent and I intend proving it.'

'You are, of course, free to do whatever you wish, Miss Tennant – just so long as you don't interfere with any police enquiries.'

'Would it be interfering with your enquiries if I were to ask what is happening to Becky's baby?'

'The baby is with its mother at the moment. The magistrate will decide whether it is to remain with her, or be taken into the care of the court.'

'What exactly does "the care of the court" mean?'

'It means it will be lodged in the workhouse, Miss Tennant. That's where it's going to end up anyway, when Mrs Vincent is hung – unless a relative comes forward to claim it.'

'The "it" of which you talk so glibly is a little girl. If you allow me to see Becky I am sure I will be able to persuade her to give Lucy up to me.'

'I am sorry, Miss Tennant. No one will be allowed to speak to the prisoner until she has been seen by the grand jury, tomorrow.'

Fanny was angry. Very angry. However, she knew that nothing would be gained by remaining here, arguing with a detective sergeant. 'Very well, Sergeant Judd. There is nothing more I can do at the moment, but your attitude will not be forgotten, I can assure you.'

Chapter 26

A late-invited guest at the Tennants' dinner table that evening was Bristol's Chief Constable. During the meal he listened patiently to Fanny's carefully phrased but passionate argument that Becky's arrest had been a grave miscarriage of justice.

'I am very sorry, Fanny, I cannot interfere with the investigation at this stage. It will be for a magistrate to decide whether there is a case for this young lady to answer – and I feel there must be. No man in my force would dare make a false arrest on such a serious charge.'

Finding it increasingly difficult to hide the angry frustration she felt, Fanny said, 'If Ivor Primrose had been here such a mistake would never have been made – and I am convinced this *is* a grave error of judgement. If I am proved correct it is going to reflect very badly on the Bristol police force as a whole.'

Impressed as much by Fanny's obvious sincerity as by her words, the Chief Constable looked thoughtful. 'I cannot interfere with the due process of the law – but I can telegraph to London and order Primrose to return to the city tomorrow. Will that help, do you think?'

'That will be *wonderful*!' exclaimed Fanny. 'Ivor will soon discover the truth.'

'I have no doubt he will. Now, have I earned another portion of that delicious goose?'

'You may have a whole goose to yourself if you wish. Thank you for your patience, and kind assistance.'

On the other side of the table, Lewis was having an equally successful conversation with Sir Ephraim Stern.

Alderman Tennant had introduced the two men immediately upon the arrival in the house of the eminent surgeon and his wife.

Less than half-an-hour later, Sir Ephraim examined Lewis's wounded elbow in the privacy of the Alderman's study. It was a very thorough examination. When it was concluded, the surgeon diagnosed that part of the bone had splintered. A section had broken loose and was lodged within the joint.

Alarmed, Lewis asked anxiously whether there was the likelihood that he would lose the arm.

'No,' replied the surgeon, seriously. 'But had you remained in India you would have lost not only an arm, but most probably your life also. That continent is a surgeon's nightmare.'

'What needs to be done to the elbow now?'

'You must have an operation, dear boy. The sooner the better. How long are you remaining in Bristol?'

'I hadn't intended staying here for very long. However, I shall no doubt remain until Fergus's problems are resolved.'

'Good! Come up to the Infirmary early in the morning, the day after tomorrow. I'm spending the day lecturing to students. If you don't mind having them crowding around you while you're under the anaesthetic, I'll carry out the operation then. You'll need to remain in the hospital for a couple of days, at least, but no doubt our host's delightful daughter will pay you a visit or two. There's nothing like a pretty girl to cheer up a wounded man. I saw it at first hand during the Crimean campaign, with Nightingale's girls. Not that they were particularly pretty, you know. They were rather too mature to warrant such a description. But when a man's been fighting a war for a month or two in a foreign land, the sight of the plainest English woman is capable of turning a chap's head.'

'Will the operation mean Lewis will be able to make full use of his arm once more?' Fanny had overheard most of the conversation and she put the question that he had been reluctant to ask.

'I don't see why not. I doubt if he'll ever be able to bowl a

414

devastating over at cricket, but he'll be able to shoot or fish almost as well as the next man.'

The eminent surgeon's prognosis dispelled some of the depression that had been generated by Becky's arrest. Fergus was delighted for his friend. Nevertheless, he felt unable to join in the jubilation engendered by Sir Ephraim's words.

He was aware that his presence did nothing for the celebratory mood about the dinner table. After bringing out the ruby presented to him by Prince Narayan, and telling the story of its acquisition, Fergus agreed to allow Alderman Tennant to place it in his safe.

'What will you do with such a wonderful gem?' asked Fanny.

'I intend having a pendant made from it for Becky. A "thank you" for Lucy.'

It was an idea that had given him much pleasure during the voyage from India. Somehow, with Becky languishing in gaol, much of his enthusiasm had waned.

Soon afterwards, Lewis began regaling the guests with stories of the relief of Lucknow and Fergus took the opportunity quietly to leave the table.

Fanny hurried from the dining-room after him. 'Fergus . . . where are you going?'

'For a walk. You have some very interesting guests in there, Fanny, but I just don't feel like talking. Or listening either, come to that.'

'I am sorry, Fergus. This has been a ghastly homecoming for you.'

'It's far worse for Becky. I feel so frustrated, not being able to do anything for her.'

'We *are* doing something, Fergus. You heard what the Chief Constable said to me. Tomorrow Ivor will be back in Bristol. He will sort things out, you can be certain of that.'

'I'm sure he'll do his best, Fanny, but I can't help thinking about Becky, locked away in a prison cell. If she's tried to live a decent life and be a good mother, this will both hurt and confuse her. As for the charges she has hanging over her . . . she'll be absolutely terrified. I *want* to see her. To be with her.'

'Have patience, Fergus. Everything is going to be all right, I know it. In a few days' time this nightmare will be over. Then you and Becky – and Lucy too – can begin to build your lives again.'

'Thank you, Fanny. Thank you for your sympathy and for your practical help. Go back to your guests now – and take special care of Lewis. He's a good friend and a very brave man.'

Fergus looked at Fanny and saw her as he knew Lewis would. As an intelligent and attractive woman. She had a great deal to offer any man, and he said, 'You're good for Lewis. I know he won't show it to anyone, but he'll be very anxious about the outcome of the operation he's to have. Our military surgeons in India had a very low success rate. However good Sir Ephraim may be, memories of India must be at the back of Lewis's mind.'

'I'll see he doesn't have time to brood over the operation, Fergus, but I wish you'd stay here with us too.'

'I'm not very good company at the moment. This has been a splendid day for your father. It should be a happy time for Lewis too. My presence will only depress everyone. Anyway, I want to take a walk. To savour the land I've missed during the time I've been away. Don't wait up for me, I'll see you in the morning.'

Chapter 27

Fergus had not told Fanny the whole truth. He intended doing rather more than taking a walk. He was going to Lewin's Mead, to Back Lane. He wanted to visit the attic room in the hope he might learn something of what had happened there.

He was dressed rather too well for Lewin's Mead, at the moment. Going to his room, he fished out an old army overcoat. It was one he had worn during the cold nights in India. He had bought it from a wounded infantryman who was being invalided home to England when Fergus was on his way to Lucknow.

The coat was old and extremely tattered, but it had served its purpose in India. It would do the same here.

It was a cold night, but Fergus was too preoccupied to notice. As he walked down the steep hill from Clifton, he marvelled at the extent of the lights stretching out before him. Bristol seemed to have grown while he had been away.

When he eventually reached the dark alleyways and jumbled, close-packed houses of Lewin's Mead, he pulled the coat collar up around his neck.

Hands thrust deep in his pockets, he allowed himself a wry smile. With his limp and tattered coat he could easily pass for a newly returned wounded soldier. As such he would not be expected to be carrying a great deal of money and was unlikely to be a target for any lurking footpad.

Besides, any villain worthy of the name would be out of Lewin's Mead right now, earning a dishonest living.

Passing through the narrow, claustrophobic alleyways, Fergus realised that little had changed since he turned his back on the Bristol slum. There was the same feel to the place – even the same foul odours.

Soon, he reached Back Lane. Nothing had changed here, either. Lights produced chess-board patterns from the windows of houses on either side of the narrow alleyway, where wood and cardboard had been substituted for missing panes of glass.

The first sign that all was not as it had been came when he reached the house where he and Becky had lived. No dim light showed in the downstairs room. This had been where Ida always maintained a vigil, missing nothing that happened in the lane outside.

The rooms on the first floor were in darkness too. Another floor up and an open door revealed a large family, all of whom were strangers to Fergus.

He moved across the landing quietly and no one appeared to notice him. They were intent on a squabble that was going on between two of the children.

Fergus felt a strange feeling in the pit of his stomach as he climbed the rickety stairs leading to the attic. It was in this room that he had spent the most momentous few years of his life. Here he had made his home and had produced work that brought his talents to the attention of the world.

Here he had lived with Becky.

He opened the door to the attic room almost reverently. Stepping inside, he wondered what he should do next. Whether to strike a lucifer match, or retreat from the room before it awoke memories that could only be painful in the present circumstances.

Suddenly he paused. He could hear no sound and could see nothing, but he knew instinctively he was not alone in the room.

He was wondering what he should do when a young and frightened voice said, 'If that's you, Seamus, I've got an iron poker here. You come any closer and I'll use it on you, I swear I will.'

The voice was Irish, but it was not one Fergus recognised.

'It's not Seamus, whoever he is, but who are you? What are you doing here? This is Becky's room.'

'Becky wouldn't mind. I've been staying with her. But you still haven't said who you are.'

'That doesn't matter for now. I'm going to light a lucifer match. Don't you move before I do. If you've really got a poker in your hand you'd better stay right where you are until we can see each other.'

Fergus struck a light and could just make out a small figure crouching in the alcove beside the fireplace. There was a lamp on the table. He lit it, turned down the wick and replaced the pot-bellied glass cover.

Now he could see the girl more clearly and it gave him a shock. He might have been looking at Becky, as she had been when he first met her, some four years before.

The young girl was standing now, and there was indeed a poker in her hand. She looked as though she was quite prepared to use it if the need arose.

Fergus's glance moved to the portrait of Becky, hanging on the wall. It was the best painting he had ever done of her. Temporarily ignoring the girl, he limped across the room to look at it, and a feeling of deep sadness welled up inside him.

After a moment or two he turned to see that the girl had lowered the poker. She was now looking at him with an expression of awe on her face.

'You're Fergus, aren't you?'

'That's right – but who are you?'

She did not answer the question. Still gazing at him as though he had just dropped from the sky, she said, 'I told her you'd come back. I said you would. Everything's going to be all right now, isn't it? You'll get Becky out of prison and you and her will be back together again, with Lucy.'

'I sincerely hope so,' he replied, fervently. 'But you still haven't told me who you are, or what you're doing here.'

'I'm Meg. I live downstairs with my ma, the kids, and my stepfather, but Becky lets me stay up here for much of the time.'

Fergus had a glimmer of understanding of Meg's initial reaction when he had first entered the attic room. 'Is Seamus the name of your stepfather?'

She nodded.

'I see.'

There was a long silence before Meg said, 'Have you come back because of the trouble Becky's in?'

'No. I only returned to England today and learned what had happened.'

'So you were coming back to her anyway?'

'That's right.'

'I knew it! I told her you'd come back to her.'

'Well, as I'm here, why don't you tell me exactly what's been going on? While you're doing it you can light a fire, if there's any wood. It's cold in here.'

He said it more for Meg's sake than his own. He was wearing the old overcoat. She appeared to be wearing only a thin, summer-type dress.

'Becky has some gin in the cupboard in the corner. Pour a drink for yourself – and a small one for me too, while I get the fire going.'

Despite the situation that had brought him back to the Back Lane attic room, Fergus smiled at the cheek of this young Irish girl, even as he did her bidding. She *was* like a young Becky.

When the fire was crackling and spitting sparks in the grate, Fergus handed a small glass of gin to Meg and sat down at a table to watch her.

Her face was decidedly grubby. Because of it, the tear streaks down her cheeks could be seen more clearly. She took a sip of her gin and grimaced. 'You haven't put any sugar in it.'

'Put some in yourself if you want it. I've no doubt you know where it is. Then you can tell me all about Becky's arrest.'

Meg lifted a sugar bowl from a nearby shelf. As she ladled sugar into her glass, she said, 'Becky didn't do it, you know. It wasn't her who killed Ida. The two of 'em got on really well. Becky had no reason to kill her – and she wouldn't have done, even if she had.'

'I don't believe she did it, either,' said Fergus. 'But tell me *exactly* what happened.'

'It was *horrible!*' The sugar dissolved to Meg's satisfaction, she took a large gulp of gin. When her breath returned, she said, 'I went downstairs in the morning and found Ida's kitten playing in the hall, with the door to her room not properly closed. I knew right away that something was wrong. Ida never left her door open. She was very particular about the kitten, you see. Me and Albert got it for her.'

Fergus had no idea who Albert was, but it didn't matter. 'So what did you do?'

Meg began twisting the glass in her hands, agitatedly. 'I knocked at Ida's door, but got no answer. That was strange too, because Ida can ... could hear if you so much as dropped a pin in the hall. I pushed the door open and saw her lying on the floor. I thought at first she must have fallen. It wasn't 'til I got closer to her that I saw all the blood. She'd been bashed about the head. She was dead. Then I started screaming and was heard by two constables who were standing on the corner at the end of the lane. When they came in I took the kitten to Albert's room. It's still there with the kids,' she finished, lamely.

'But ... why did they arrest Becky?'

There was nothing in what Meg had told him to tie Becky in with Ida's death.

'That was the detective bloke. He spoke to everyone in the house, then he and the coppers came up here and searched the room. They found a lot of money and they arrested Becky.'

'How much money did they find?'

'I think it was about fifty pounds – but Becky never pinched it. She had no need to, did she? I mean, not with all the money you was sending to that Miss Tennant for her.'

Fergus remembered what Fanny had said about the money she had given Becky while he was away. He would need to check the amounts with her.

'You've said the police came up here. Did they search any of the other rooms?'

'No.'

'Do you know why?'

Meg looked uncomfortable. 'I think it was probably something Seamus said to them. He told them he'd heard a noise in Ida's room as he went out the night before. Voices. One was a young woman's. He said it sounded like Becky. Then someone came out of the room as he stepped out into the lane. He said she ran upstairs, so it must have been Becky. At least, that's what he said to this detective.'

'But you don't believe him?'

'He might have *thought* he heard Becky. On the other hand, if he believed that's what the detective wanted to hear he'd have said he was certain. Seamus is a bit like that.'

'He's either certain, or he's not. This isn't some game of make-believe he's playing. Becky's life is at stake.'

'He knows that, but I doubt if you'll get him to change his mind. He's told the detective it's what he saw. He probably believes it himself now.'

'Where is Seamus at this moment?'

'Out drinking somewhere, I expect. That's where he usually is at this time of night.'

Fergus remembered Meg's challenge when he first entered the attic room in the darkness. 'You threatened me with the poker when you thought it was Seamus coming in. Why?'

Meg dropped her glance. 'Because of what he does to me when he catches me on my own.'

Fergus knew he should have been shocked, but he was not. He had spent too much of his life in the slums of Edinburgh and Bristol. He felt only sorrow for yet another blighted childhood. 'Isn't there a bolt on the door?'

'There was. Seamus broke it last night.' Meg saw Fergus's expression and added, 'I was lucky. Iris and the bloke she was with heard him and came up here. The bloke threw him downstairs. Then my Ma had a go at him. She got a black eye for her trouble. Seamus is tough enough when he's hitting girls and women. He won't stand up to a man.'

Life in the Back Lane house, as described by Meg, was exactly as it had been at the time Fergus left. The characters had changed, there were new and unfamiliar names, but the violence and the immorality were the same.

This was where Fergus had left Becky to fend for herself. This was where his daughter had spent the first precious months of her life.

Chapter 28

In the uncomfortable silence that followed Meg's description of life in Back Lane during Fergus's absence, both of them heard a noise. It sounded as though a man had stumbled coming up the stairs to the second floor and was cursing his clumsiness.

'It's Seamus!' Meg spoke in an alarmed whisper. 'Quick! Put out the lamp.'

'I want to speak to him . . .'

Ignoring Fergus, Meg hurried to the table and blew down the glass of the lamp, extinguishing the light immediately.

From the darkness, she said, 'It'll be no use trying to talk to him tonight. Perhaps he'll go straight to bed,' she added, hopefully.

'What time will I be able to talk to him tomorrow?' asked Fergus.

'Shh! It sounds as though you might meet him tonight after all,' she said in a tense whisper.

They both heard the stairs creaking beneath the weight of someone climbing to the attic with exaggerated caution.

Fergus looked around for Meg, but she had disappeared. He guessed correctly that she had retreated to the shadows of the alcove – no doubt armed with the poker once more.

The fire had burned low and Fergus sat on the far side of the table from the door, waiting.

The door creaked open and a voice with an Irish accent far stronger than Meg's, said, 'Where are you, Meg? Where are you, me young beauty? I know you're here and there'll be no escape for you tonight. I came home early especially for you.'

'I hope you're not talking to me,' said Fergus, with a calmness he was not feeling.

The shock of hearing an unfamiliar man's voice almost sobered Seamus.

'Who the hell are you?' he demanded, peering through the gloom in the room.

'As you're here, in my room, uninvited, I think that's a question *you* should be answering,' said Fergus.

'Your room? This is Becky's room . . . Oh!' Realisation came to Seamus's drink-dulled mind. 'You'll be her husband, I've no doubt?'

'That's right, but you still haven't told me who *you* are, or what you're doing here.'

'I'm Seamus McCabe, sir, and I beg your pardon for disturbing you. I was on me way home to me own rooms, downstairs. I seem to have got confused and lost me way. No doubt it's the drink I've had tonight. I'm not used to it, you see. What with that and me not having lived here very long.'

'Long enough, it seems, to claim to have recognised my wife coming from Ida Stokes's room on the night she was murdered.'

'Did I say that, sir? No, I didn't. All I said was that it *might* have been her. It was a young woman, certainly. Too young to have been that Iris woman. But, no, I couldn't swear it was your wife, sir, and I didn't say so to the police. Honest to God, I didn't, sir.'

'I hope you'll say exactly the same thing in court, Mr McCabe. For your sake, as well as Becky's. Otherwise I'm going to suggest they have a word with this Meg you've come here looking for. Ask her a few questions about *you* and what you've been up to with her these past few years. How old is she now? Just thirteen, perhaps?'

'If they call on me to give evidence in the court, I'll tell them exactly what I've told you, sir. That I can promise you – and I'll be delighted to do it. She's a fine young girl, that wife of yours, sir. A credit to you. No one in their right mind would believe she could commit a foul murder. No one. I'll bid you good night now, sir. I won't trouble you again.'

'Good. You'll not be welcome up here until this trouble is behind us and Becky is back here with me. Good night, Mr McCabe.'

Meg remained in the alcove until Seamus was heard to fall down the last few attic stairs and arrive in his own room where he was greeted with a tirade of abuse from his wife.

After lighting the lamp, Meg said, 'Fergus, that was marvellous! Becky would be proud of you. You put a flea in Seamus's ear big enough to bother him until Becky gets out of jail. He won't come up here again, that's certain.'

She had a sudden thought. 'But where are *you* staying tonight? Will you want me to move out of your room?'

'No. You're welcome to use it for as long as you please, but before I go I'll fix that bolt. I met Fanny Tennant at the docks. I'll be staying with her until we have Becky out of prison.'

Seeing Meg's instant expression of disapproval, he added, 'I came back from India with a friend who was wounded in the fighting there. He's got to have an operation. He'll need to stay at Fanny's house until he's well enough to go to his own home. I want to be with him.'

Standing by a friend was something Meg could understand – but she had a friend too. 'What's going to happen to Becky?'

'We're going to get her out of jail just as quickly as is possible. We didn't have much success today, but Ivor Primrose should be back tomorrow. We'll try again then.'

'Does Becky know you're home? Have you been to see her?'

'We thought it best to say nothing until she's back home. After the manner in which I went away, we believed she'd want to be at her best when we met again, not locked up in prison. It's probably very important to her. But we're going to try to get Lucy brought out as quickly as we can. Prison is no place for a baby.'

Meg did not like the sound of the 'we', in Fergus's plans. She guessed that it meant Fanny Tennant had a hand in them.

'But you will get Becky out of prison as quickly as you can?'

'That's a promise, Meg. But I want things to be right for us this time.'

'They will be. Becky's the nicest person I've ever met – and she loves you very much.'

'If that's true, then everything *will* be all right. It will mean it's what we both want. Now, let's see what we can do about that bolt – and make quite certain you keep it on when I'm not here. If you have any trouble then go and see Fanny Tennant at the ragged school – or come to Clifton to see me at the Tennant house. I'll leave you the address before I go.'

Chapter 29

The day following Fergus's return to England started reasonably enough, but towards the end of the morning, it erupted in a frenzy of activity.

Word was received from the Chief Constable's office that Ivor Primrose would arrive from London, at about five o'clock in the evening.

Fanny and Fergus were discussing the facts they would present to the detective inspector, when a second policeman called at the house. This man had come from the central police station.

The news he brought threw all their plans into disarray. The information that Ivor would be returning to Bristol that day had been passed on to Detective Sergeant Judd by a friend who worked in the Chief Constable's office.

Judd guessed correctly that the arrest of Becky was behind the decision to recall the detective inspector. However, he thought of a way to prevent his superior officer from interfering with the case. He hurried Becky before the magistrate that morning and she was committed for trial to the next Assizes.

It meant Becky would be sent to prison and could not be released until her case had been considered by a grand jury.

Perhaps as some form of sop to Fanny Tennant, Judd sent the constable with news that he had persuaded Becky to hand over the baby to her. Fanny was to fetch Lucy from the New Gaol, to which Becky had been transferred from the police cells.

Fergus went with Fanny. He waited impatiently in a carriage outside the prison gates while she was inside, completing the necessary formalities for taking charge of baby Lucy.

The 'New' Gaol had, in fact, been in existence for some thirty-seven years. During this time conditions inside had deteriorated alarmingly. An inmate who had tasted life in both this and the earlier prison would have found it difficult to detect any difference between them.

Certainly, the stench in here was as bad as anything Fanny had ever experienced. The unfortunate prisoners reflected the conditions inside the prison. Nevertheless, Fanny was shocked when she saw Becky.

The young mother from Back Lane was dirty and dark-eyed and there was an air about her of just not caring any more.

Fanny tried to put some cheer into her by telling her she would soon be cleared of the charges against her. Release from prison would follow soon afterwards.

After speaking to Becky for a long time without there being any positive response, Fanny realised she was getting nowhere and said, 'You must remain confident, Becky. Do not give up. Everything is going to be all right, I promise you.'

'You weren't in court to hear what Sergeant Judd had to say about me.' Becky spoke despondently. 'If he had his way they'd hang me right away, without bothering about a trial.'

'Fortunately, it doesn't depend entirely upon Detective Sergeant Judd. We have other ideas. We'll have you out of here just as soon as is possible. Ivor Primrose is coming back from London today. He'll soon get at the truth.'

'Will he? If he does he'll be the only one to believe me when I say I didn't kill Ida. I didn't, you know. She could be mean and miserable sometimes, but I was really very fond of her.'

'Well, we'll have no problem explaining about the money, and it seems that Seamus is no longer certain it was you he saw going upstairs at the time of the murder.'

'There's something else that you don't know. The sergeant told the magistrates that Ida had left the house to

429

me in her will. He said I killed her so the house would become mine.'

Fanny was startled. 'When did she decide she'd leave the house to you?'

'I don't know. I never knew she had.'

This was a new and rather alarming aspect of the case Detective Sergeant Judd had built up against Becky. It was a strong enough motive for murder. One that might well impress a jury. But Fanny would not allow Becky to know of her misgivings.

'Don't worry, Becky. I have already spoken to a good lawyer. He's a friend of my father. He'll soon sort all this out. But I'm here now because a constable came to the house saying you wanted me to take Lucy.'

'That's right. This is no place for her. It's no place for any baby. Look over there.'

She pointed to the far side of the communal cell. Here two women were chained to rings in the wall, just beyond reach of each other. One was a toothless old hag, the other was young.

The younger of the two kept laughing, as though at some imagined joke. When she did so she would lift her skirt and throw it over her head.

'That's the dangerous one,' said Becky. 'She'd kill anyone who came within reach of her after dark. Last night a couple of the women amused themselves by saying they'd throw Lucy to her when I dropped off to sleep tonight. I don't know whether they would, or not. I don't intend taking that chance.'

'This is a dreadful place!' exclaimed a horrified Fanny. 'We must get you out of here as quickly as we can.'

'You won't be able to do it,' said Becky, thoroughly defeatist. 'It's all difficult to believe, really. I've tried hard to be a good mother to Lucy. Behaved in the way Fergus would have wanted me to. This is where it's got me. What Maude always said to me was right. There's no escaping what we are or where we come from. I'm a Lewin's Mead waif. It would have been better for me if I'd accepted that from the very beginning. There's no getting away from

430

what I am. What I was born to.'

'That is not true!' Fanny was alarmed at Becky's state, both physically and mentally. She seemed to have given herself up to despair. 'You mustn't talk like this, Becky. You are wrongly imprisoned. You have done nothing and we are going to prove it.'

She had a sudden idea. Perhaps she could use the thought of Fergus to bring some hope back into Becky's life. 'You must try to remain cheerful, Becky. Fergus will have received my letter long ago. He could return any day. When he does, he'll move heaven and earth to secure your release.'

Unfortunately, Fanny's words had the opposite effect to that she had intended.

'I don't want Fergus to find me in here. If he comes back you must make up some story about me. If he saw me in here, like this, I wouldn't want to live. I *couldn't* live. I'd kill myself, I swear it.'

Behind her, the young, insane woman began laughing hysterically. The sound produced a reaction among all the inmates of the cage-like cell. Within minutes the noise had become unbearable and Lucy began to cry.

Becky too was tearful. 'Get the gaoler quickly, Fanny. Take Lucy out of here. But . . . look after her for me. I love her. I love her so very, very much.'

A gaoler arrived at the cell, brought by the din. He shouted for silence, but to no avail. Eventually, Fanny managed to convey to him that she wanted to remove Lucy from the prison as quickly as was possible.

The cage door was opened for no more than a few seconds. It was long enough for Becky to thrust Lucy through the opening, into Fanny's arms.

When she had been relieved of her baby, Becky turned away and hurried to the rear of the cell without looking back. She avoided the mad women who were now both making noises that were only marginally human.

Fanny left the prison cell haunted by the memory of Becky's tortured expression. She was pursued along the corridor by the hysterical laughter of the mad women and a vile stench that would remain with her for a very long time.

Chapter 30

Outside the prison gate, it seemed to Fergus he was waiting in the carriage for a very long time. Catherine was with him and she insisted that Fanny had not been inside overly long.

It did not help that Fergus felt very cold. It would take him some time to get used to the English climate again, after experiencing the heat of India.

Actually, he was unsure whether he was shivering because of the weather, or in anticipation at the thought of seeing his daughter for the first time.

He was talking to Catherine about some of the children he had seen in the villages of India, when they heard the iron gate clang shut. Neither had noticed it opening, but Fergus looked up quickly to see Fanny leaving the prison. She was carrying Lucy.

Before the echoes of the heavy gate's closing had died away, Fergus was out of the carriage and hurrying to meet them.

Lucy was no longer crying, but the tears she had shed were still on her cheeks. He looked down at her with an expression that contained both awe and disbelief.

Eventually, Fanny said, 'Well, take her, Fergus. After all, she is yours.'

Fergus took his daughter from her, holding her uncertainly, as though she was something very fragile.

Lucy looked up at him uncertainly for a few moments. Then she suddenly smiled and captured his heart immediately. It seemed to the two watching women that he would burst into tears.

Instead, he hugged Lucy to him and said huskily, to no

one in particular, 'She's beautiful. Oh, so beautiful!'

'Yes, she is.' Fanny had been so moved by seeing daughter and father together that she could hardly speak. 'And she's yours, Fergus.'

'I never knew it would feel like this.' Hardly able to remove his gaze from her, he asked, 'How is Becky?'

Fanny's face grew suddenly serious. 'She's not doing too well, Fergus. We have to remove her from prison as soon as we can.'

Looking up at her, he asked, 'Do you think I should go in and see her? Let her know I'm here?'

'No!' Fanny's reply was so sharp that she was forced to repeat to him what Becky had said to her.

They discussed Becky's mental state on the journey back to the Tennants' Clifton home and by the time they arrived, Fergus had very mixed emotions about everything.

In his arms he held his baby daughter, who had captivated him from the very first moment of their meeting. Hers was an innocent world in which she had known only love and tenderness.

Behind them was the grim New Gaol, in which the baby's mother languished. Becky's life was everything Lucy's was not. Fanny had reported her to be at a low ebb, harbouring little hope for her own future.

She needed to be rescued as quickly as possible.

Lewis was awaiting the carriage at the front door of the house. He helped the ladies down and then peered dutifully at Lucy. After prompting her to smile at him, he delivered the verdict that she was probably the most delightful baby he had ever seen. Then he stood on the steps and made an announcement.

'Now you have returned to the house with *your* surprise, I have one for you. No, that's not quite correct. I have *two* surprises for you. Look who's come visiting.'

Lewis called, 'You can come out now.'

There were a few moments during which Fergus wondered what all this was about. Then, from the house came Shashi and the effervescent Shirley Buchanan!

Fergus's surprise was so complete he was in grave danger of dropping Lucy, until Catherine relieved him of her.

Shirley advanced upon him and wrapped him in a huge hug that threatened to smother him. She then pounded him on the back as part of her hearty greeting.

When this was over, she stepped to one side to be introduced to Fanny and Catherine.

Fergus was left facing Shashi. She looked even lovelier here, in surroundings far removed from the place where they had first met.

Uncertain at first, he suddenly spread his arms wide and Shashi came into them. As he hugged her close and she clung to him, both Fanny and Catherine looked on in shocked amazement. Such demonstrations of affection in public were virtually unknown.

The initial greeting over, Fergus asked, 'What are you both doing in England? How did you get here so quickly? Lewis and I caught one of the fastest ships sailing out of Calcutta – and you were still there when we left!'

Shirley threw a smile at Shashi before replying. 'We came here the *quick* way. We caught a ship to the Gulf of Suez and made the overland journey to Alexandria. It was very exciting, we rode camels for most of the way. Then we caught another ship to England. We've been in England a week now, haven't we, Shashi?'

'That is right – but is this your daughter, Fergus? Please, may I hold her?'

With some hesitation, Catherine handed Lucy to Shashi. Fanny was glad Becky was not able to see the expression on the Indian girl's face as she held Lucy and looked from the baby to Fergus.

'You must be very, very proud of her,' said Shashi, wistfully. 'She is lovely – but what of your poor Becky? Lewis has told us of what happened. You have not been able to free her, or she would be with you now. Have you seen her?'

'No – but Fanny has. We thought Becky wouldn't want our reunion to take place in a prison. It wouldn't be fair to her. She doesn't even know I'm in Bristol.'

'She gave up her baby not knowing she was coming to

you? Poor Becky, she will be very unhappy.'

Shashi shifted her glance from the baby in her arms to the child's father. 'Poor Fergus too. This should have been such a very happy time for you.'

As Fanny and Catherine followed the others inside the house, their eyes met. Each knew what the other was thinking. They were wondering what part this warm and lovely Indian woman had played in Fergus's life when he was far from home in India.

As the party went in to lunch, every one was talking about the many things that had happened to them during the past weeks and months.

Fergus ate a desultory meal. Afterwards, while the others were still talking, he rose from the table, explaining that he was going to see how Lucy was faring. She had been tired on her return to the house, probably as a result of spending the past twenty-four hours in such insalubrious sur- roundings.

No sooner had he left the room than Shashi said, 'You will excuse me, please. I will go with Fergus to see if there is anything I might to do help him.'

When the two had left the room, Fanny expressed dis- approval. 'I am not at all certain those two should be alone together. She is a very lovely girl. I sense much more than a casual friendship between them.'

'There's much more than friendship, that's for sure,' agreed Shirley, in her booming voice. 'In view of what they have both been through together it would be damned surprising if there wasn't. But it's no more unhealthy than a close brother and sister relationship.'

Seeing that she had the attention of everyone at the table, she amplified her statement.

'Shashi left her heart in India, with poor young Harry Downton. Fergus helped her to get over that tragedy.'

Shirley went on to tell all those at the table the story of the romance between Shashi and Harry Downton and of the subsequent death of the young midshipman.

The tale drew a great deal of sympathy from Fanny and Catherine.

'Fergus helped Shashi recover,' said Shirley. 'In fact, he brought her back when she ran away and convinced her that life was still worth living. Not unnaturally, Shashi would move heaven and earth to repay the debt she feels she owes him.'

'She certainly knows far more about Fergus's relationship with Becky than I ever learned,' said Lewis.

'Of course she does,' said Shirley. 'She offered him a sympathetic ear whenever he felt like talking. There's a great deal in her own life that equates with that of Fergus's wife.'

Shirley went on to tell the listeners something of Shashi's own background and of her life in the Indian temple. 'She is good for Fergus because she knows so much of what poor Becky must be feeling, for all they have been brought up continents apart.'

'That's probably true,' said Lewis. 'Fergus understands Shashi for much the same reason.' He told the story of how Fergus had known where to find Shashi when she left the column and was making her way back to the temple to which she had been given as a young girl. How he had brought her back.

'What an absolutely fascinating story,' said Fanny. 'It makes me realise what an uneventful life I lead here.'

Alderman Tennant almost exploded with indignation. 'Uneventful! If any more happened in your life you would have to find yourself another father. *I* can't keep up with you as it is!'

Looking at Lewis, he added, 'I wish to goodness she would find herself a man and settle down to the sort of life a father expects his daughter to lead. I have friends whose daughters have married good husbands. Every Sunday they bring the grandchildren to see them, they have a pleasant chat, perhaps take a walk and have a picnic somewhere – but not me. If there are ever any children about the house they are usually dressed in rags and need to be searched before they leave because they're likely to have half the silver hidden away in their pockets.'

But the look Alderman Tennant cast in his daughter's direction displayed a pride that belied his words.

436

He sighed. 'Never mind. Perhaps they'll give me a mention when they write the history of all that Fanny has achieved for the children of Lewin's Mead in this ragged school she runs for them. Perhaps she'll be remembered long after folk have forgotten all about Aloysius Tennant, Alderman of the City of Bristol.'

Chapter 31

Lucy was lying awake in her room, kicking her legs vigorously. She was not unhappy, even though, as Shashi was quick to point out, she was wet and needed to have her napkin changed.

As Shashi carried out the task, she said to Fergus, 'You must be very proud of your daughter. She is very beautiful.'

'Yes, she is, but I won't be able to enjoy to the full having her until her mother gets out of prison and this whole nightmare is over.'

'It will not last for very much longer. *Memsahib* Fanny's father says the man who returns to Bristol this afternoon will make everything all right.'

Shashi's use of the Indian prefix to Fanny's name sounded strange here, in a nursery room in Bristol's elite Clifton area.

'You're talking of Ivor? Yes, if anyone can do something for her, it's him. He's known Becky for as many years as I have. Perhaps more. But anything he can do is likely to take time. It's not at all the homecoming I had in mind.'

'Poor Fergus – and poor Becky!'

'Yes, she's the one who's really suffering in all this.'

Thinking of Becky's plight distressed Fergus and he endeavoured to change the subject of their conversation. 'How about you, Shashi? What does the future hold in store for you?'

'I have hope, Fergus. You gave it to me before you left India, do you remember? Shirley is at the heart of that hope. Indeed, she seems to spread it all around her. She has plans for us to take some of ragged school children to America

438

when we leave England. She believes they can have a very good life there. I will help her, of course. It will give me much to do and to think about.'

'I'm very pleased to hear it, but life there won't be successful until you're able to put the past behind you.'

'I have done that.' Shashi secured Lucy's clean napkin and smiled as the baby's legs and arms began to exercise at great speed once more.

'Shirley and I went to see Harry's mother and father soon after we arrived in England. They are very good people. Very sad too. Harry was their only child.'

Shashi handed Lucy back to Fergus before saying, 'I showed them the sketches you made of Harry and I. They thought they were so wonderful I told them they could choose one. I thought they would want to have one of Harry alone. Instead, they chose one of Harry and me together. His mother said Harry looked so happy in the sketch. She thanked me very much for calling on them and wished it might have been in happier circumstances. For the very first time I realised that, had Harry lived, we might have had a future together, had we come back to this country. There will always be a very great sadness that I am not able to share my life with him, but I will always be happy to know that had he lived I would have been accepted by his family.'

Shashi gave Fergus a sad smile. 'So, the answer to your question is "yes". I have put the past where it belongs. I hope you will do the same. If you do there is much in the future for you and Becky – and little Lucy, of course.' As she spoke, she leaned forward and tickled Lucy's tummy and the baby chuckled happily.

Even while Shashi was reminding him of what the future held for Becky and himself when she was free once more, Fergus was thinking of something else she'd said. Of taking some of the children from the ragged school to America for a new start in life. He had one particular young Lewin's Mead resident in mind.

During lunch, Shirley had asked Fanny to draw up a list of those children most likely to benefit from a new start in life in the United States. If ever a young girl deserved an opportunity it was Meg McCabe. He would make certain she was included on her list.

Ivor did not come to the Tennants' Clifton home until after seven o'clock that evening. During the wait for his arrival Fergus had become increasingly agitated. He had half-hoped it might be possible to secure Becky's release before the day was over. However, when he allowed logic to come to the fore he knew this would be virtually impossible.

The detective inspector apologised for his delay. He explained that he had first gone to the Chief Constable's office to learn the reason for his unexpected recall to Bristol.

The Chief Constable had explained the circumstances of Becky's arrest to Ivor and asked him to look into the matter. He also suggested Ivor should proceed with some caution. As a result, he had gone to Central Police Station to discuss the case with Sergeant Judd before making his way to Clifton.

'Sergeant Judd was most upset that his judgement was being questioned,' said Ivor, non-committally. 'I pointed out that no man is infallible. Where someone's life is at stake, every line of inquiry must be pursued. I somehow feel I failed to convince him. However, putting that to one side, he does seem to have a very strong case to present to the court.'

'Nonsense!' exclaimed Fergus, angrily. 'There is absolutely no question of Becky's having killed Ida. She's as innocent as you or I.'

'I mentioned nothing about guilt or innocence,' said Ivor. 'All I said was that Judd has a strong case to present to the court. If you have any evidence that points to her innocence I will be delighted to consider it. Hopefully it will also help me to find the person who *did* kill Widow Stokes.'

Ivor's words made it clear that the big policeman did not believe Becky had killed Ida and Fergus told Ivor of all that Meg had told him.

'It all helps,' was Ivor's comment. 'But Mr McCabe saw *somebody* going upstairs. Even if he's unable to identify Becky positively, his evidence is bound to be considered by the court. They are likely to draw the same conclusions as Sergeant Judd. The thing that concerns me most of all is the fact that Widow Stokes left the house to Becky in her will. It provides a motive strong enough to convince any jury in the land.'

'Becky was not even aware of the bequest,' said Fanny. 'If she didn't know, then she had no motive. I can give evidence that the money found on Becky was from me. Seamus McCabe will say he's not certain the girl he saw – or *half*-saw – was Becky. So what case does that leave against her?'

'The prosecution could argue that, her protests notwithstanding, Becky could have been told by Widow Stokes herself that she would benefit from her will,' pointed out Ivor. 'However, if I can find the solicitor who drew up the will, I'll speak to him tonight. He might be able to throw some light on why Becky was never told she would one day inherit the house.'

He chewed on the end of his pencil, thoughtfully. 'The most likely explanation for the murder – and we have to remember that *someone* killed her – is that it was a stranger who came in off the street and she was a chance victim. If that's the case it's going to be hard to find the guilty party – and equally hard to establish Becky's innocence.'

'But you'll work on it?' pleaded Fergus. 'You've known Becky for as long as any of us. You know she wouldn't kill anyone.'

'I'd contest that statement if she was doing something for you, Fergus,' said Ivor. 'But if, as you say, she doesn't even know you're back in England, then I agree with you. You have my promise that I'll do everything in my power to prove her innocence.'

Ivor shook his head doubtfully. 'As I've already said, the only certain way of doing that is to find whoever it was who *did* kill the unfortunate lady. That, I fear, may not be quite so easy.'

Chapter 32

During breakfast the following morning, Lewis was under-
standably nervous about his operation. Fergus said he
would go with him to the Bristol Infirmary. When Fanny
said she would come too, Lewis protested it was
unnecessary for two of them to accompany him and added
that they both had more than enough to do without having
to think of his needs.

'To be quite truthful,' said Fanny, 'there are a number of
reasons why I should go to the Infirmary. Two of the
children from the ragged school are in there. I like to pay
them a visit whenever I can. I also have a certain amount of
charity money to distribute to some of the older patients.
Today would be a very good day to carry out such duties.'

Lewis was secretly pleased that she would want to find
excuses to be at the Infirmary while the surgeon was operating on him. Nevertheless, he asked, 'What of your other
guests? Shouldn't you be paying them some attention? After
all, they are not familiar with Bristol.'

'I cannot imagine a situation where Shirley would not
be in full command, no matter where she happened to be,'
replied Fanny. 'She and Shashi are going to have a busy
morning. Catherine is taking them to have a look around
the ragged school. But if you would really prefer me to stay
away from the hospital while you are there . . .'

'That's not the impression I intended to convey at all,'
protested Lewis. 'As a matter of fact, I can't think of anyone
I would rather see at my bedside when I come round from
the anaesthetic.'

'This sounds like a cue for me to ask whether you really

want *me* to come with you!' said Fergus. 'I feel I might be intruding.'

'Don't be silly,' said Fanny, her face suddenly a bright pink. 'We'll both go – and bring your sketch pad, Fergus. Not only will it amuse the children, but I don't think anyone has ever recorded life in the Bristol Infirmary. It's something that should be done.'

Shirley and Shashi found their tour of the ragged school extremely interesting, but each looked at it from a very different point of view.

Shirley saw it from the standpoint of one who was a firm believer in giving children such as these a fair start in life. Children whose parents were described in official documents as belonging to 'the dangerous and perishing classes'.

The American woman was not blind to the fact that many of the youngsters – and their parents – took advantage of people who set out to help them. She was aware that whatever was done, the majority would one day stand in the dock in a court of law. The charges against them would range from petty theft and drunkenness, to robbery or murder. However, she would never agree that this was a reason for not trying to help them whenever possible.

Shashi took quite another view of the ragged school. These were European children. Sons and daughters of the white *sahibs* and *memsahibs* who ruled over her own people in India. Who demanded deference and respect from the people of her country, constantly reminding them that they had fewer rights in a world ruled by the Europeans than the animals of their households.

Many of the children here in Lewin's Mead were more ragged, less loved and far more abused than any of the children of India. It was something Shashi had difficulty in coming to terms with.

Shirley had no intention of remaining merely an interested observer. She stopped in each class and questioned the pupils. She asked many questions of them, to judge their standard of knowledge. One of her most frequent questions was, 'What do you know of the United

States of America, the country where I'm from?'

Very few of the children raised their hands to give her an answer. Those who did merely illustrated their ignorance of Shirley Buchanan's country.

A typical reply was, 'It's one of the places where the ships go to from Bristol.'

Another was, 'It's one of the countries we own, a long way from here.'

Perhaps the most illuminating reply was that of a small boy who said, 'It's the place where convicts were sent before they discovered Australia,' adding, 'our ma says that's where her grandpa went.'

In response to her question, 'How many of *you* would like to go to America?' not one pupil felt it might be a good idea.

In the last classroom they visited, Catherine introduced Meg to the two women, saying, 'This young lady is one of our best pupils. She lives in the same house as Becky, Fergus's wife.'

Both visitors to the school took an immediate interest. Shirley said, 'Do you now, Meg? Well, how would you like to take me to have a look at this house of yours?'

'I don't mind.' Meg shrugged a nonchalant agreement, but Catherine was horrified.

'Lewin's Mead is no place for two women to go unescorted. It's a very dangerous place.'

'So was India during the mutiny,' retorted Shirley. 'But I'm still alive to talk about it. Well, Meg. When will you take me there? I'd like to have a look at the place that was Fergus's home.'

'You know him?' Meg's indifference vanished immediately.

'Know him? Shashi and I travelled with him right through India. Through all the fighting too. There's not much you can tell me about Fergus Vincent. I know a bit about Becky too, but I want to know more.'

'When do you want me to take you there?' asked Meg, suddenly eager to please this woman.

Shirley looked at Catherine. 'You'll be breaking for the midday meal soon. Could she take us now? I'll buy something for you to eat,' she added quickly to Meg when she saw her sudden expression of dismay.

'I still don't think it's a good idea,' said Catherine, uncertainly.

'So you've said, but it's my idea, and I'll take full responsibility. Can Meg come with us now?'

'Yes, but . . .'

'Good! Come on, Meg. Lead us to this house of yours. I must say, I've heard so much about Lewin's Mead from Fergus, and seen so many of his sketches, I feel I know it already.'

Even before Shirley had suggested that she guide her to Back Lane, Meg had intended returning there at some time during the midday lunch break. The American woman had merely brought forward the timing of her visit.

Neither Albert nor his brother or sisters had attended the ragged school this morning. Usually they and Meg walked to school together. Only when they were very late would she go to school alone. This morning had been one such occasion, but none of the Garretts had subsequently arrived.

However, on the walk through Lewin's Mead, the talk was mainly of Becky.

'When does Fergus think he'll be able to get Becky released from jail?' Meg asked Shirley.

'Nobody's putting a time scale on it, but that big policeman who's just come back from London was at the Tennants' house for an hour or so last night. As far as I can make out, they've been able to prove that the money they found on Becky is rightfully hers. They hope to disprove the eye-witness account of your stepfather too. Unfortunately, the detective sergeant who arrested Becky is still left with a very good motive for her to kill the landlady of the house. I'd say that right now she has no more than a fifty-fifty chance of proving her innocence.'

'But she *is* innocent,' declared Meg. 'She shouldn't be in prison at all!'

'So everyone says,' agreed Shirley. 'At least, everyone except the man who had her put there. What's needed is for the one who *did* murder that unfortunate woman to be

446

found. That's the only way we can be certain of getting Becky out of jail and back with Fergus.'

Meg was silent for a while. Then she said, 'Do you really think Fergus will go back to her?'

'I am certain of it,' smiled Shashi. 'But do you think Becky will have him back?'

'Of course she will!' Meg spoke scornfully, looking at the Indian girl as though she had asked a thoroughly foolish question. 'She loves him.'

'Then it's going to be all right for them,' agreed Shashi, matching Meg's seriousness.

As they neared Back Lane, Shirley Buchanan looked about her in silent disapproval. She had seen slums before, in many lands, but this was one of the worst. There seemed to have been very little effort either to clean the narrow alleyways, or carry out basic repairs to the decrepit houses on either side.

Suddenly, two men came from the shadows to block the alleyway ahead of them. Dirty and unshaven, both wore tattered overcoats of the type issued to soldiers. They were vagrants of a kind who roamed the country living on what they could find, or steal. Both men had been scavenging among the rubbish in the alleyway.

Meg came to an abrupt halt and held her arms wide to stop the others. 'We'd better go back and try another way.'

'Nonsense!' said Shirley, firmly. 'They won't interfere with us.'

'They will. I know them . . .' She was too late. Brushing past her outstretched arm, Shirley was already advancing along the alleyway towards the two men.

Meg's inclination was to turn and run, but now Shashi was following after the American woman. Meg knew she could not leave them in the maze of Lewin's Mead's alleyways, confronted by two dangerous vagrants.

The two men moved to prevent Shirley from passing. She stopped a couple of paces from them and said politely, 'Do you mind moving, gentlemen? I wish to go past you.'

'D'you hear that?' asked one of the men of his companion. 'She called us "gentlemen". I ain't never been called a "gentleman" before.'

'Well, it's right enough, Ned. We're "gentlemen of the pad", that's what we are. You know what that means, missus?'

'I presume it has something to do with a footpad,' replied Shirley, showing not the slightest vestige of fear.

'You've got it, missus – and Ned here has a fearful reputation for using violence to them as don't cough up their money straightway. I don't hold with it, meself, but I admits that it saves us a whole lot of arguing with people. So if you'll just hand over your purse – yes, and that of the Indian lady too – we'll all be on our way in no time.'

'You talk too much,' growled his companion. 'I could have knocked her down and been off with her purse by now. This is the way you do it.'

He took a pace towards Shirley – but only one. From inside her coat she withdrew a small handgun. It brought the would-be robber to an abrupt halt.

'I see you know what this is,' said the American woman to the man in front of her. 'In case your companion isn't so well informed, I'll explain. It's a six-shot pepperbox pistol – and I'm a damned good shot with it. So I suggest you both retreat along the alley ahead of us. Right now!'

The man in front of her stood his ground, breathing heavily. His glance moved from the gun to her face and Shirley knew he was weighing his chances of tackling her, despite the weapon in her hand.

His companion knew it too. 'Go on, Ben. She won't use it.'

The sound of the shot was amplified in the narrow alleyway and made everyone jump. The most frightened man of all was the would-be footpad who had suggested Shirley would not use the gun. The bullet had hit the wall of the house not a foot from his head and left a scar in the stonework.

He did not wait for a second shot, or to see what would happen to his companion. He turned and ran. Aware that he was now on his own, Ben began to back away from

Shirley, along the alleyway, saying, 'I'm going, missus. I'm going. Keep your finger away from that trigger. I'm going . . .'

When he had retreated for about a dozen paces, he suddenly turned and ran as though he was expecting a shot to come after him at any moment.

Meg looked at Shirley with awed respect. 'You drove 'em both off! I've never seen anything like it.' She gulped before saying, 'Would you *really* have shot him if he hadn't run away?'

'He thought so,' said Shirley enigmatically. 'That's all that mattered.' Tucking the gun back in a pocket inside her coat, she said, 'Now, lead on to Becky's house. The smell of this place is beginning to get to me.'

Chapter 34

At the Back Lane house Shirley and Shashi were first shown the room where Ida Stokes was murdered, then taken upstairs to Becky's attic room. On the way up Meg heard noises coming from the room occupied by Albert and his young family, but the door was closed.

On the next floor Meg was challenged by her mother, who wanted to know why she was not at the ragged school. She accepted with bad grace an explanation that Meg was showing Shirley and Shashi the room occupied by Becky.

'I thought you was supposed to be at school to get some learning,' she grumbled. 'If it's errands you're running I can find some for you to do right here. You needn't think that as you're home you'll be getting something to eat. There's barely enough for the others.'

Shashi looked sympathetically at Meg, but the young girl avoided her glance and led the way up the attic stairs.

Some of Meg's things were strewn on the bed and she explained, 'Becky used to let me stay here with her. When Fergus came up here and found me, he said I could stay here as long as I wanted.'

'Fergus has been back here?' asked Shashi.

'That's right. He came here the first night he got back to England. We had a long chat, about Becky and . . . and things.'

'Who else lives in the house?' asked Shirley.

'Only Iris – and Albert and his brother and sisters. They're all younger than him. Iris isn't always here. She spends a lot of time on the boats.'

'I see.' Shirley thought she understood why Iris spent so

much time 'on the boats'. Her expression showed neither approval nor disapproval. 'Was she in the house on the night of the murder?'

'No. She didn't come back until the night after, but news had got around. She'd heard about it.'

'Then it couldn't have been her your stepfather saw that night. Can we have a word with Albert?'

'He wasn't at school this morning. I'll go down and see if I can find him.'

When Meg had gone, Shirley had a look around the attic room. She was particularly attracted to the portrait of Becky. She knew who it was, having seen many similar sketches in Fergus's pad, in India.

'Poor girl!' she commented.

Turning to Shashi, she said, 'You might well have become romantically involved with Fergus yourself, Shashi. You and Becky have the same look in your eyes. As an artist, Fergus would have been aware of that.'

'Perhaps,' said Shashi, non-committally. She did not add that there had been a time when she herself believed she and Fergus might become lovers. She did not pursue the thought of what the future might have held for both of them had they done so.

Meg came back up the stairs, looking vaguely unhappy.

'Is something wrong?' asked Shirley.

'Not really . . . It's just that Albert usually takes the youngsters to school so they can have some soup there. He hasn't taken them today and the children say he went out early without saying when he'd be back.'

'How many of them are there?'

'Four. One boy and three girls.'

'Do they have any parents?'

'No. There's an older sister, Maude, but she's no good. She's expecting a baby herself. The last I heard, she'd gone off to live with some tinkers, somewhere outside Bristol. There's another sister too, Lisa, I think her name is. Nobody knows where she's gone.'

'Let's go down and visit Albert's young family and see if there's anything we can do for them.'

Shirley and Shashi spent some twenty minutes with the young Garrett family. During this time they both worked at cleaning up the room – and the children too. It was evident that Albert was doing his best for them, but it was more than any young boy could, or should have to, do to take care of them all.

When Shirley was satisfied they had done everything possible for them in the room, she gave Meg some money. 'Go out and buy them something to eat, Meg. When you see this young Albert, tell him I'd like to speak to him. It will probably be better if we meet at the ragged school.'

Meg immediately went on the defensive on Albert's behalf. However, once she was assured that Shirley did not intend to take him to task about the way he was looking after his brother and sisters, she promised she would pass the message on to him.

When Shirley and Shashi had left the alleyways of Lewin's Mead behind, Shirley took in a great breath of air. 'I'm glad to be out of there, Shashi. Can you imagine anyone actually *wanting* to live in a place like that?'

'Fergus did.'

'He set himself a mission in life. Unfortunately, I don't think it could have been successful. Had it been the whole place would have been pulled down immediately. Well, I'll set myself a mission in life too. I'll take what children I can back to America with me. When I get there I'll set up an Association with the aim of bringing other underprivileged youngsters to America. They'll have a better life there, that's certain.'

Shirley suddenly grinned at Shashi. 'What's more, we probably put two would-be robbers off crime for at least a day or two. All in all, I don't think our visit to Lewin's Mead today has been wasted.'

Meg returned to Back Lane with food for the Garrett children and stayed with them to await the return of Albert, hoping he would come back soon. She was concerned he might have gone off and done something silly. He was frustrated by being able to provide for his young family at a level that did no more than keep them alive.

It proved to be a long wait. Albert did not come back to the house until just before eight o'clock that evening. He looked very tired and in his hand carried a turnip which he placed on the table in the room.

'Where have you been?' Meg demanded to know. 'I've been waiting here all day for you to return.'

'I had to go off somewhere,' said Albert, unhelpfully. 'Anyway, nobody asked you to wait for me. I've brought something for the kids' supper. I'll get on and cook it now.'

'They've all eaten,' said Meg. 'An American woman who's staying with Fanny Tennant came here. She gave me some money to buy food for them. It's just as well. One turnip wouldn't have gone far, even made into soup.'

She looked from the vegetable to Albert. 'Where did you get it from?'

'I bought it.'

'Don't lie to me, Albert Garrett. You pinched it. There's still fresh earth on it. You're a fool to risk going to prison for the sake of one measly little turnip.'

Albert said nothing and Meg spoke more sympathetically. 'Have *you* eaten?'

'No. I'm not hungry.'

'Yes, you are. There's some bread left and half a dish of dripping I brought down from Becky's room. It seemed a pity to waste it.'

As she cut a couple of very thick slices from the stale loaf and spread them liberally with dripping, Meg looked at Albert with a worried frown. 'I'm sorry I got on to you when you came in, Albert, but I've been worried about you. It's not like you to go off and leave the others, like you did.'

'I had to go and see someone.'

'Can you tell me about it?'

Albert had bitten off an over-large mouthful of bread and dripping. Gulping it down with difficulty, he seemed to be trying to make up his mind about something. Eventually, he nodded his head.

'Let's go up to Becky's room while the kids are getting ready for bed. I'll tell you there.'

Meg's mother was busy cooking a meal for Seamus. She did not see them pass her rooms and make their way to the attic.

Albert had brought his bread and dripping with him and sat eating it for so long that Meg felt obliged to prompt him. 'Well? You were going to tell me why you and the others didn't come to school today. When you've done that I'll tell you what's been happening *here* today. How Fanny Tennant's friend used a gun to frighten off two men who tried to rob her!'

Such a dramatic statement should have had Albert begging to know more, but he seemed hardly to have taken her words in.

Suddenly putting the bread and dripping down on the table, he said, 'I've found out who killed Ida.'

'You've done WHAT! How . . .? Who is it? Will it get Becky out of jail?'

When Albert did not reply immediately, Meg said, 'Come on, tell me who did it!'

'It was someone named Herbert Sims. He's living rough up on Horfield Common.'

Excitedly, she said, 'Have you told anyone? If we go down to speak to that policeman who's a friend of Fanny Tennant we might be able to get Becky out of jail tonight.'

'I can't tell anyone,' said Albert, unhappily.

Meg looked at him, not understanding. 'What d'you mean? You've got to say what you've found out. You know you have.'

Albert shook his head unhappily. 'I can't, Meg. Our Maude is involved in it.'

Meg could not hide her dismay. 'What do you mean, your Maude is involved? How do you know?' When Albert made no immediate reply, she said, 'I think you'd better tell me everything you know.'

Albert nodded and began to tell his story. It was a brief one, but enough to exonerate Becky entirely from the crime of which she was accused.

Maude had always believed that Ida Stokes had a fortune hidden in the room of her Back Lane house. When she threw in her lot with the tinkers of Horfield Common, she told the man with whom she was living of her belief. On the night of the murder, Maude and Herbert Sims came to Back Lane and forced their way into Ida Stokes's room.

The tinker had demanded to know where Ida kept her money. When she refused to tell him he began to beat her with the heavy cudgel he carried. She still refused to tell and he beat her until she lay dying on the floor.

After a search of the room, Maude and Herbert Sims were almost a hundred pounds richer. Herbert Sims fled from the house immediately. Maude remained long enough to go upstairs to the first-floor room. She left ten pounds with one of her younger sisters, warning her she was to say nothing to Albert about the money until the following day.

When Albert had finished his horrific story, Meg asked, 'What are you going to do about this, Albert?'

'What *can* I do?' he pleaded. 'Maude is my sister.'

'And Becky is our friend,' said Meg. 'A very good friend to both of us. Would you say nothing and see her hung for a murder she had nothing to do with?'

'What else can I do?' Albert was almost in tears. 'I *can't* say anything.'

'How does Maude feel about it?'

'She's frightened. She believes Herbert would kill her if he thought she'd tell anyone about what happened.'

'Would she tell the truth if she knew nothing would happen to her?'

'Of course she would. But she'd be hung, the same as him.'

'No, she wouldn't,' said Meg, firmly. 'Haven't you ever heard of someone giving "Queen's Evidence"? It means that if they say everything of what they know, then they get let off. I thought everyone knew about that. Come on.'

'Come where? I'm not going anywhere.'

'Yes, you are. We're going down to the ragged school to see if Fanny Tennant's there. If she's not then we're going straight down to the Central Police Station to see Ivor Primrose. Your Maude is going to tell the truth about what happened to Ida – and Becky is going to get out of jail. She's been good to both of us. Now we're going to pay her back for all she's done.'

Chapter 35

Lewis was brought back to a small private room in the Infirmary after his operation. The nurses said they believed it to have been successful, but the surgeon had not been able to discuss his recovery with Fergus and Fanny. A wagoner had been brought in with a badly shattered leg. He had fallen from the seat of his laden dray-cart and been run over by the vehicle. The Infirmary's senior surgeon had asked Sir Ephraim Stern if he would take charge of an operation aimed at saving the unfortunate drayman's leg.

When it became increasingly apparent there would be no progress report on Lewis for a while, Fanny and Fergus decided there was little sense in remaining at the Infirmary. One or both of them would return to visit Lewis later in the day.

They walked together to the ragged school, discussing the whirlwind events that had overtaken them during the very brief time since Fergus had returned from India.

The conversation turned to the subject of Shashi and Fanny said, 'She is a most attractive woman, Fergus.'

'Yes. Very beautiful.'

'She also adores both you and Lewis. Was there ever any romantic involvement – I mean, between Shashi and Lewis?'

Fergus looked at Fanny quickly. She had only known Lewis for a couple of days, and yet . . . Only that morning, when he was readying himself to go to the Infirmary, Lewis had asked a similar question about any possible attachments Fanny might have! Nothing would delight Fergus more than for a romance to blossom between the two.

'No, although we both think the world of Shashi. After all, she saved our lives and the lives of the other *Venus* survivors. But she and poor Harry Downton were so wrapped up in each other I doubt if either of them ever seriously looked at anyone else.'

Fergus told Fanny what Shashi had said of the meeting with Harry's parents.

'How very sad,' said Fanny. Even as she uttered the words her thoughts were elsewhere, and were not of such melancholy matters.

Shashi and Shirley were at the ragged school when Fanny and Fergus arrived there. The American woman immediately took Fanny off to discuss with her the idea she had of taking Bristol children to America to begin new lives there.

Left alone with Fergus, Shashi asked, 'Is there anything you can do for Becky today?'

He shook his head. 'Nothing. I have to rely on the solicitor we've engaged for her, and Ivor Primrose's inquiries. Neither can be hurried, unfortunately. All I can do is rage silently that we can't do more.'

'Then, if you are doing nothing else, will you take me to see something of Bristol? Shirley said we would go together if she found the time. Unfortunately, I fear that she and time will always be at war with each other.'

Fergus was amused at such a description of Shirley Buchanan's lifestyle. He was less amused later, when Shashi told him of the confrontation with the would-be robbers that morning.

'You should never have gone there without an escort,' he admonished. 'There's always something happening in Lewin's Mead. It's a very dangerous place.'

'I am quite certain the two men who wanted to rob us thought so,' agreed Shashi. 'But you will take me to look at some nice shops now, please. *Memsahib* Tennant has been very kind to allow us to stay at her house. I would like to buy her a small present.'

Later that night, Fergus and Fanny were concluding a somewhat pessimistic meeting at the Tennant home with the solicitor they had appointed to represent Becky. Unknown to any of them, Ivor Primrose was taking far more positive action to prove her innocence.

Albert had reluctantly accompanied Meg to the Central Police Station. There he had told the story of Maude and Herbert Sims to the detective inspector.

'You only learned of this today?' asked Ivor, fixing Albert with a stern look.

'That's right.'

He nodded, satisfied Albert was telling him the truth. 'You did the right thing in coming here to tell me about it. The right thing for Becky – and for Maude too. Had we learned of it later, in some other way, Sims and Maude would both have been charged with Ida's murder. As it is, if Maude didn't carry out the attack herself and is willing to co-operate with us in convicting young Sims, she'll escape the due process of the law, yet again.'

When Albert did not appear to be fully convinced by Ivor's words, the detective inspector said wearily, 'Don't worry, lad. What I think of your sister's way of life isn't important. You have my word that she'll appear in court as a witness for the prosecution and not as a prisoner. Away you go – here, take this with you.'

Ivor flicked a shilling across the room and it was caught by a puzzled Albert.

'Buy something tasty for yourself and your brother and sisters on the way home. It will help take your mind off what you've just told me.'

For the raid on the tinkers' encampment on Horfield Common, Ivor used a police van in which were hidden twenty uniformed constables.

The vehicle was taken almost up to the tinkers' den before the policemen leaped from the van and took hold of everyone they found there. Among their number was a heavily pregnant Maude and three other women.

Without disclosing the reason for the raid, Ivor went among the men and women being detained by the constables. He asked each of them his or her name. Some he knew. Two of these were already wanted by the police.

By the time the raid was over, Ivor and his men had arrested four men and two of the women.

When Herbert Sims was arrested and told he would be charged with the murder of Ida Stokes, he rounded upon Maude immediately.

'You bitch! It was you who told the coppers about me. I'll see someone gets you for this.'

'I've never said a word to anyone,' cried Maude, genuinely frightened by his threat. Herbert Sims had a number of friends who would not hesitate to murder her on his behalf.

'It must have been you. No one else knew about it.'

'Never mind who told us,' said Ivor. 'We know it was you who did it, so save anything you have to say until we reach the Central Police Station.'

'I'm not going to ride there in the van with him,' said Maude, indicating Sims. 'He'd kill me before we got there.'

'I have no intention of putting you in with him,' said Ivor. 'You and me – and a few constables – are going to enjoy a quiet little walk back to Bristol. On the way we'll have a nice chat. You can explain why you were prepared to let someone who's been a very good friend to you, go to the gallows for something you know very well she hasn't done.'

460

Chapter 36

Detective Inspector Ivor Primrose worked through the night taking statements from Maude and the tinkers who had been brought to the Central Police Station from Horfield Common.

By the time dawn put in a lethargic, grey appearance, he felt he had everything he needed to convict Herbert Sims of the murder of Ida Stokes. It also meant he could set about having Becky released from the New Gaol.

Sims had not actually confessed to killing Ida, but he had admitted robbing her and using a certain amount of violence in the process.

Maude, on the other hand, had made a long and detailed statement. In it she gave details of how her lover had bludgeoned the unfortunate landlady. He had continued the attack long after Ida had collapsed to the floor and ceased to put up resistance.

Her statement tied in with the one Albert had made to Ivor earlier, saying that Maude had gone upstairs in the house and left money with one of the children.

When told of the advantage to be gained by turning Queen's Evidence, Maude was eager to co-operate in every way possible. She did not stop at details of the murder. Ivor learned of many other crimes committed by the Horfield Common tinkers, including a series of highway robberies.

By the time he had finished writing down Maude's numerous statements, Ivor was beginning to feel the effects of a night's lost sleep and the pressure of the past few days. Nevertheless, there was still much to be done.

At nine o'clock he was waiting in the Chief Constable's

461

office when the police chief arrived for work.

He listened while Ivor gave him details of the night's work. Then he said, 'You're confident you have enough evidence to convict Sims?'

'I've never been more certain of anything, sir.'

'So Fanny Tennant was right. This Vincent girl is innocent of the charges against her?'

'That's so, sir.'

'Good work, Primrose. You've handled this sorry business exactly as I would expect my senior detective to investigate a murder case.'

'Thank you, sir. What I would like now is to have Becky Vincent released from prison as quickly as possible. Unfortunately, she was committed from the Magistrates' Court. That complicates things somewhat.'

'That problem is easily solved and in the best possible way, Primrose. A grand jury will be sworn in today for the Quarter Sessions. Have Mrs Vincent's indictment brought before them and formally rejected. It will mean more work for you this morning, I am afraid, but I am fully confident you will have it done in time.'

As Ivor was leaving the office, the Chief Constable called to him, 'By the way . . . will you send Sergeant Judd here to see me. After I've spoken to him I think you should choose another sergeant for your department. Judd will better serve Bristol as a uniformed policeman.'

For Becky, being incarcerated in prison was a nightmare of the worst kind. She was parted from Lucy and had lost her freedom which had always been of paramount importance to her.

She had led a very harsh existence in the Lewin's Mead slum, sometimes an extremely cruel one. Yet there had always been the freedom to go wherever she wished, and do whatever she wanted to. This alone had made her otherwise bleak life bearable.

Now this freedom had been taken from her, along with the one person who was truly hers and whom she loved without reservation – Lucy.

Becky was also living with the knowledge that the punishment for the crime of which she stood accused, was death.

Fortunately, this part of the nightmare was too unreal to cause her the concern it might otherwise have done. She had not committed the crime with which she had been charged, and never seriously doubted that the truth would eventually come out.

'Given your baby away, 'ave you?'

The speaker was a toothless, emaciated old crone who sniffed noisily and unconsciously between every second or third word.

The woman seemed to work to a time-table in the communal cell, drifting from one prisoner to another, rarely receiving a reply to her disinterested questioning.

This morning Becky was being given a few minutes of her time. Her failure to reply to the old hag's question made no difference.

'It's for the best. I should know. Three of 'em I've given away. Three out of seven. The other four died 'afore they was a month old. That was for the best, an' all. I mean, yer can't look after 'em when you're in and out of stir all the time, can yer?'

With no intimation that she was expecting a reply, she continued, 'You're the one as is in 'ere for killing yer landlady, ain't you?'

Looking about her furtively, the woman lowered her voice to say, 'I topped my old man. The second one, it was . . . or was it the first? I dunno, p'raps it was both of 'em. Neither was any better'n the other. Smothered 'im, I did. Lying there drunk, 'e was. Snoring his bleedin' 'ead off after giving me a good 'iding. I wasn't going to let him do that again. "Died by a visitation from God" was wot the coroner said it was.'

The woman cackled in amusement. It was a dry, high-pitched sound that grated on Becky's nerves.

' "Visitation from God!" he said. I ask you, do I look like the Almighty?'

She cackled again. 'Mind you, it makes yer feel like God

when he's lying there dead and yer know it's you who's done it.'

She looked at Becky, slyly. 'But yer don't need me to tell yer about that, d'yer? You being in 'ere for killing an old woman. What was it for . . . 'er money? 'Ow much did yer get?'

Rounding on the old crone, Becky said angrily, 'I did it for fun, because I enjoy doing it and because she talked too much. So you'd better watch your step. I've got my eye on you too.'

The woman scuttled away to the far side of the cell and promptly repeated the one-sided conversation to a small group of fellow prisoners.

There was a great deal of muttering among the women, but none of them came near Becky.

She was thankful for the respite her outburst had given her. However, it was to have unexpected repercussions.

When a gaoler entered the communal cell, the women crowded around him and repeated what Becky had said. The gaoler left the cell, only to return some fifteen minutes later. This time he had two companions with him. All three were carrying chains.

Without any warning, the three men pounced on Becky. She struggled violently and screamed until a back-handed blow from one of the gaolers dazed her.

By the time she recovered her senses she was shackled hand and foot, with a short chain linking the two. She could only shuffle along, bent almost double.

Moving in this awkward and painful way she was led from the cell. When she fell over, as she frequently did, the gaoler who had struck her pulled her violently to her feet, using the chains.

In tears, as much from anger as from pain, Becky soon left the cat-calls and jeers of the other prisoners behind. She was led to a small, narrow, windowless cell and thrown inside. When the solid door slammed shut behind her, Becky was left lying helpless on the floor.

Through a small grille in the door, the bullying gaoler said, 'You'll be comfortable enough there, but in case you

464

get lonely I'll come and pay you a friendly visit when I'm next on duty. Make sure you're bathed and perfumed for me.' He then went away, chuckling and joking with the other gaolers.

The only ventilation in the small cell came through the tiny grille in the door. It let in just enough light for Becky to see that the tiny punishment cell had not been cleaned since it was occupied by the previous unfortunate prisoner, who had probably been secured in a similar fashion.

It was a struggle for her to raise herself to a sitting position. When she was eventually successful she sat against the wall, hunched forward, her arms wrapped about her knees.

Becky did not know how long she was locked in the cell. Indeed, it was impossible to tell night from day. When she was brought meals they tasted as bad as they smelled and she was not sure whether she had three or four of them.

Only twice during her stay in the cell was she taken out to perform bodily functions and allowed to shuffle back and forth in the narrow corridor outside her cell.

For these brief excursions the chain linking wrists to ankles was removed and she was able to straighten up, stiffly and painfully. She begged to be allowed to have the short chain removed altogether, but it was always replaced when she was put back inside the punishment cell.

Her only consolation was that the bullying warder did not return to torment her.

During the long hours between exercise and meals, Becky crouched in the filthy cell, suffering her degradation, thankful that she had allowed Fanny to take Lucy away from such appalling surroundings.

Chapter 37

Becky was dozing, lying on her side on the filthy straw-strewn floor of her cell, when she was awoken by the sound of a key being turned in the unoiled lever lock.

She struggled to sit upright but had not succeeded when the cell doorway swung open. A gaoler entered, followed by Ivor Primrose.

The prison official stood just inside the cell door, watching Becky's unsuccessful efforts to raise herself from the floor. Angrily, Ivor roughly brushed the man aside and helped her to a sitting position.

Turning to the gaoler, he said, 'I want these chains taken off – now!'

'She's a dangerous criminal,' protested the gaoler. 'A murderess. We had her in a cell with the others until she threatened to kill one of them. We had to put her in chains and place her in solitary for their sakes.'

'I don't give a damn for any of the others you have in here.' Ivor looked at the gaoler with undisguised distaste. 'Becky poses no threat to anyone, and never has. She's going before a grand jury this morning to have her innocence formally recognised. I've arrested the man who committed the murder for which she was blamed.'

The big policeman rose to his feet and towered menacingly over the gaoler. 'If these chains aren't taken off immediately, I'll take her before the grand jury as she is, and make an official complaint about the way the staff in the New Gaol treat prisoners who haven't had their guilt proven before a court of law.'

The chains were removed in a matter of a few minutes.

As Becky rubbed her chafed wrists, Ivor said, 'You'll want to clean yourself up before you appear before the grand jury . . .'

'No!' She spoke belligerently. 'I'll go just as I am. You said you've arrested someone for Ida's murder. Does that mean I'm definitely going to be freed?'

'That's right. Having the grand jury find you have no case to answer is a mere formality. You'll be free by noon.'

'Then I'll not waste any time cleaning myself up. I can do that when I'm out of here.'

'Are you quite sure, Becky?' Ivor was appalled by her filthy condition. 'It wouldn't take very long.'

'I don't want to spend one minute more in this place than I have to. Just get me out of here.'

Half-an-hour later, as Becky waited in the cells beneath the courtroom, she was able to peer out through a small barred window at pavement level. Watching people passing by in the street, she gave a brief shiver of anticipation. Out there was a world of free people. Soon she would be one of them. Able to walk without chains . . . Able to hold Lucy once more!

This thought made her doubly impatient at having to wait for the grand jury to send for her.

When Ivor came down to the cell, he said, 'It won't be long now. They're going to take you next.'

'Who have you arrested for the murder of poor Ida?' It was a question Becky should have asked before.

'A man named Herbert Sims. He's a tinker – and Maude Garrett's lover.'

The information startled Becky momentarily, then she shrugged. 'I should have guessed she'd be mixed up in it somewhere. Did she know about what he was doing?'

'Yes. She's turned Queen's Evidence and will be giving evidence for the prosecution.'

'Does that mean she'll walk off scot-free?'

'I'm afraid so, Becky. I don't like it very much either, but that's the price we have had to pay for your freedom.'

Becky thought about it for a while before saying, 'I'd like

467

to thank you for all you've done, Mr Primrose. I know I owe my freedom to you.'

Ivor almost suggested that she owed it to Fergus and Fanny, but he had been sworn to secrecy about Fergus's return to England. Instead, he said, 'You have more people who care about you than you realise, Becky. But I think we're being called to go upstairs and face the grand jury . . .'

Upstairs in the high-ceilinged court room, the well-dressed gentlemen of the jury viewed Becky's filthy appearance with distaste.

The foreman expressed their views when he asked if she might not have been cleaned up before being brought before them.

'Regrettably, Mrs Vincent has been held in solitary confinement in a cell, chained hand and foot, sir. This in spite of being convicted of no crime. Indeed, I am bringing her before you now to tell you the police will be offering no evidence against her. She was wrongly charged and committed for trial. I have arrested another for the crime with which she was charged – and I have witnesses to prove the case against him.'

The foreman of the jury frowned. 'This is a most disturbing state of affairs, Inspector Primrose. Most disturbing. You are saying this unfortunate young woman has been held in such appalling conditions yet is entirely innocent of the charges brought against her?'

'That is so, sir – but I would add that it was the Chief Constable himself who became very perturbed about the matter. So much so that he had me brought back from London to investigate the case.'

'I see.' Somewhat mollified, the jury foreman said, 'Well, let's get on with the formalities in order that this young woman can go off and take up her life once more.'

Twenty minutes later, Becky was standing outside the court, blinking in the bright light of the sun and soaking up the warmth that freedom brought with it.

'Well, that's all over and done with now, Becky. You can

go back to Lewin's Mead, clean yourself up and then go and fetch Lucy.'

She nodded. 'I never realised how much I would miss her. But I'm very, very glad she wasn't with me in that last cell. There was a rat came in there that was as bold as a dog . . .' Becky shuddered at the memory.

Resting a hand on her shoulder, Ivor said, 'It's all over now, Becky. I have an idea that life will improve for you very soon. You're also the owner of a house. Who'd have thought *that* a few years ago when you were just another Lewin's Mead urchin?'

Becky managed a wan grin. 'You mean, just like I am now? Goodbye, Mr Primrose – and thanks again for all you've done.'

Ivor watched her hurry away and wondered what would happen when she discovered Fergus had returned. He hoped things would work out exactly as everyone wanted.

Unfortunately, very little that was associated with Lewin's Mead seemed to work out according to plan.

Chapter 38

Once Becky left Ivor outside the Assize Courts, she changed her mind about going straight home to Back Lane. More than anything else, she wanted to have Lucy back with her. She decided she would go to Clifton first and collect her from Fanny Tennant.

Becky realised she was in a filthy state. Had there not been the evidence of her own eyes, it would have been apparent from the disapproving looks she received from passers-by. Indeed, two women walking with young children actually crossed the street to avoid passing close to her.

Becky did not care. She was a free woman once again.

On the way to Clifton, she stopped at a conduit, from which there was a constant flow of fresh spring water. Here she washed her face and arms and the lower part of her legs. She thought of washing her hair, but decided she would look worse, not better, until it had dried.

There was little she could do about the filthy state of her dress. Defiantly, she decided that if anyone at the Tennant house commented upon it, she could point out that it owed its condition to the deplorable state of the city's gaol. She would suggest that Alderman Tennant use his influence to improve conditions there.

The walk to Clifton was uphill and it took Becky longer than she would have liked. When it started drizzling the cold rain did nothing to improve her already bedraggled appearance.

Concerned about taking Lucy back to Lewin's Mead in the rain, she consoled herself with the thought that Fanny might send her off in the Tennant carriage.

If she did not, there was fifty pounds in the bag she carried about her neck, attached to a thong. It had been returned to her by Ivor upon her release from prison. She would use some of that to take a hansom cab.

By the time she reached the Tennants' house, Becky was in a state of high excitement and anticipation. She ran up the steps to the front door and tugged on the bell-pull.

She waited impatiently until the door eventually opened and a smartly dressed maid stood before her.

The maid had been working in the Tennant household for only a week. Prior to this she had been in service with a dowager countess. This formidable lady would not even allow the bishop of the diocese to cross her front doorstep if he arrived with mud on his shoes.

The maid looked at Becky in utter disbelief. Her first thought was that she was begging. Or perhaps she was a gipsy, offering to tell fortunes, or something . . .

'You've come to the wrong door. Go round to the back of the house.'

Startled, Becky began, 'I've not . . .'

'I don't care what you've *not*,' interrupted the maid, rudely. 'Round the back.'

With this, she slammed the door before Becky had a chance to explain further.

Becky's initial reaction was one of anger. Then she looked down at herself and smiled wryly. She must look an awful mess to anyone who worked in a house such as this.

In order to reach the back door of the Tennant house, she needed to walk out of the gateway and down a narrow lane at the side of the house.

As she went down the lane, Becky heard a carriage come along the road. It turned in at the gate to the Tennant house.

The wall here was almost as tall as she was, but by standing on tip-toe she could see over it. The carriage pulled up at the front steps. A moment later the door to the house was flung open and Fanny came out and stood at the top of the steps.

Becky was watching her and did not look at the man who left the carriage until he too was at the top of the steps with Fanny.

When she did, Becky received such a shock that she felt certain her cry of astonishment must have carried to the two people outside the Tennants' front door.

However, they seemed to be oblivious of anyone except each other. The man said something to Fanny. She replied and then flung her arms around him and they hugged each other warmly.

At this stage, Becky's disbelief became dismay. The man holding Fanny in his arms was – Fergus! Her husband!

Becky crouched at the foot of the wall, unable to watch what was happening at the front door.

Her thoughts were in utter turmoil. Fergus, the husband she had believed to be far away in India, if indeed he was alive at all, was here. In Bristol. She had seen him. In Fanny Tennant's house.

She tried to make some sense of her feelings, but failed miserably. How long had he been here? Why had he not come to see her in Lewin's Mead? Why had he done nothing to help her during her time in prison, when she needed him most of all?

Indeed, had he been out of the country at all? Or had everything been no more than an elaborate ruse to prevent her from finding him?

Becky was unable to put everything together and make sense of it. The only thing that eventually crystallised in her thinking was that she was out here, while Fanny and Fergus were inside – with Lucy.

Crouched in the lane, out of sight of Fergus and Fanny, not wanting to look at them, Becky contemplated her next move.

It was difficult to think straight any more. She was hurt. Desperately hurt. More hurt than she had ever been in her whole miserable life. She felt utterly and totally betrayed by those whom she loved and trusted implicitly.

* * *

472

Becky remained in the lane until well after it was dark. By now she had decided upon her course of action. She could not go to the house. Fanny and Fergus would never give up Lucy to her. She would need to take her baby from them.

Becky waited until the lights began to go out and she was certain that most of the household and the servants were in bed.

During the time she was waiting, a hansom cab arrived at the house and Catherine hurried inside. It only made the deception worse. Becky had trusted Catherine as much as she had Fanny. It seemed her trust in everyone had been betrayed.

There was much coming and going from the house, but Becky did not move from her hiding place to find out what was going on. She was not aware that Fergus, Fanny and Catherine had all left the house at different times.

When the Tennant household seemed to have settled down for the night, Becky put the plan she had formulated into action.

She made her way to the side of the house farthest from the lane. Here there was a window that led to a ground-floor corridor. Checking there were no lights showing in the near vicinity, Becky broke one of the panes of glass in the window with her shoe. Reaching inside, she released the catch.

Sliding the sash window up, she climbed over the windowsill and was then inside the house. She knew exactly where she was going. Lucy had been kept here before while she, Becky, was ill. She would no doubt have the same room.

Halfway up the stairs to the nursery, Becky heard someone talking and hid in a nearby cupboard. Two women, unknown to her, passed down the stairs. Most probably they were servants who had been to Lucy's room.

Vindictively, Becky thought it would be the last time either of them would see Lucy. When she had taken her back she would go out of their lives for ever. Out of Fergus's life too, though Becky did not dwell upon this. The thought was too painful.

As Becky had anticipated, Lucy was in the room she had previously occupied. It was the work of only a moment to lift her from the cot and carry her from the room.

Lucy hardly stirred as Becky hugged her daughter to her and made her way back down the stairs. She stepped out through the window to the garden. Moments later and she was clear of the house.

The drizzle had become a more persistent rain now, but Becky pulled the blanket in which Lucy was wrapped higher around her face and sheltered her daughter from the rain with her own body.

As she hurried through the Clifton roads, a carriage passed by. It turned in through the Tennant gate and came to a halt at the foot of the steps.

By now Becky had disappeared from view. She never saw Fergus leap from the carriage and limp up the steps to the house, as quickly as his lame leg would allow.

Chapter 39

Fergus had spent much of the day at the Bristol Infirmary with Lewis Callington. His friend had succeeded in shaking off the effects of the anaesthetic administered to him, but was still awaiting a visit from Sir Ephraim Stern.

The distinguished surgeon had been kept far busier than he had anticipated during his brief visit to the Bristol hospital. Not until late-afternoon was he able to pay a visit to Lewis, in his private ward.

A nurse removed the bandages to allow the surgeon to examine the results of his operation. After inspecting it, he nodded his approval.

'Good! Good! It's one of my better efforts, although perhaps I shouldn't say so.'

'Will it heal now?' asked Lewis, anxiously.

'Heal? My dear chap, give it a couple of months and, unless it's a cold, damp day, you'll never know you've had anything wrong with it. You'll be a bit slow bringing up your sporting gun, perhaps, and you should favour the other arm when you're reining in a lively horse. Apart from that you're as good as new.'

This was very encouraging news and Fergus had passed it on to Fanny when she met him at the door of the Tennant house that evening.

'That is *wonderful*,' she'd said happily. 'I'll go and see him first thing in the morning. No . . . no I won't, I'll go and see him right away – but first, I have some marvellous news for you too. Becky is free! Ivor has arrested Ida Stokes's murderer.'

Fergus fought to control the sudden surge of emotion he

felt. Then, suddenly, he hugged Fanny to him.

When he released her, he said, 'I . . . I don't know what to say . . . Where is she now?'

'I don't know – but let's go inside and talk about it. We'll get wet out here. It's beginning to drizzle quite hard.'

They entered the house, where Shashi and Shirley were waiting in the hallway. None of them glimpsed the stricken face peering from the other side of the garden wall.

Inside the house, Fanny said, 'I expect Becky's gone to Lewin's Mead. Once she's cleaned herself up she'll probably come here. It will be a wonderful reunion for both of you. We must have some sort of celebration.'

'No, Fanny, this isn't the place for our reunion. That should take place in Lewin's Mead. In the attic room in Back Lane.'

'But . . .' Fanny bit off the protest she was about to make. 'You know best, Fergus. It's your life. Yours and Becky's – Lucy's too now. You'll not be taking her with you? The servant who's looking after her is preparing her bath right now.'

'Lucy will be better off here for the time being. I'm hoping to be able to persuade Becky to leave Lewin's Mead this time. But I don't intend making a big issue of it.'

'She is going to have to leave, Fergus – and quite soon. Nothing has been officially announced yet but the City Corporation have decided to demolish much of Lewin's Mead. It has become a serious health risk and the Corporation is making plans to change the character of the area. Back Lane will be among the first streets to go. The houses are to be bought up by the Corporation. Becky will receive money for the house left to her in Ida Stokes's will.'

'I'd like her to agree to move before she learns about it,' said Fergus. Suddenly, he said, 'I can't just sit around here waiting for her to arrive, Fanny. I'm going to Back Lane, to see if she's there.'

'Do you think that's a good idea?' queried Fanny doubtfully. She knew Fergus would be absolutely devastated were he to find Becky in the room with 'a friend', as she once had. But she could not explain this to him. Instead, she said, 'After all, you'll not be remembered by everyone as you walk through Lewin's Mead.'

'I'll be all right.'

'Well, go and see Lucy first. She'll be in bed by the time you return. In the meantime I'll have a room prepared for Becky, in case she arrives while you're out. Remember, if you do find her, she might need time to think about things, Fergus. Be prepared for such an eventuality. On the other hand, you might decide you prefer to remain in Lewin's Mead for the night. Either way, I think it will be best for Lucy to remain where she is, for tonight at least. It would disturb her far too much to be shifted at this time of day. Now, I must make ready to go to the Infirmary.'

She looked up in time to catch the expression on his face and coloured up unexpectedly.

Fergus smiled at her affectionately. 'He's a good man, Fanny. He deserves someone like you.'

'There's nothing like that between us, Fergus . . . although I do find him very personable. But I have only known him a very short time.'

'He's attracted to you too,' replied Fergus. 'You were the first person he asked for when I visited him. Go and see him and pass on the good news about Becky.'

He left the house, to be followed no more than half-an-hour later by Fanny.

Fergus reached Back Lane without incident and climbed the stairs to the attic. He was seen by Meg as he passed the McCabe rooms and she hurried after him.

The attic was disappointingly empty. He turned to Meg. 'Have you seen anything of Becky?'

The questions she posed in return gave him his answer.

'Is she out of prison? When?'

'She was released some time today. It seems that Ivor Primrose has arrested the real murderer.'

'That'll be because of what Albert told him.' Meg explained the part the boy had played in securing Becky's release.

'Is Albert in the house now?'

'Yes, he's with the children, downstairs.'

'I'd like to speak to him, to thank him for what he did.'

Meg looked suddenly anxious. 'You won't say anything that might make him change his mind tomorrow?'

When Fergus looked blank, she explained, 'We're meeting the American woman at the ragged school. She wants to talk about taking us to America. We can begin a new life there, she says. I've spoken to Albert about it lots. It's what we both want. But if he thinks anything's likely to happen to Maude, he might change his mind.'

'I won't say anything to turn him against it, Meg. I think it's a wonderful opportunity for you to begin a new life, in a new place. Perhaps that's what Becky and I should have done.'

Suddenly eager, she said, 'It's not too late. You can come to America too!'

Fergus smiled at her youthful enthusiasm. 'I've tried in the past, but couldn't even persuade Becky to leave Lewin's Mead and move as far as Clifton.'

'You'll find she's changed a lot since then,' said Meg. 'I think that's because she really cares about what will happen to Lucy in the future.' Suddenly her thoughts took a new direction. 'Do you think Miss Buchanan will let me take a kitten to America?'

'Why would you want to take a kitten there? I'm sure you can find plenty of cats there, if you want one.'

Meg explained how she had come by the kitten that had belonged to Ida Stokes.

'I doubt if you'll be allowed to take him with you, but don't worry, I'll find a good home for him. As a matter of fact, Fanny Tennant was telling me they're troubled with mice in the ragged school. The kitten would have a good home there. Now, go and fetch Albert for me.'

He came to the attic room reluctantly, but after speaking to him for only a few minutes, Fergus had taken a great liking to him, even though he was Maude Garrett's brother.

There was no doubt that Albert felt guilty for telling Ivor Primrose about Maude's part in the killing of Ida. Fergus did his best to reassure him that Maude would not suffer for what she had done, although privately he felt she probably deserved to be punished.

'Then why's she being kept in prison?' asked the boy.

'The main reason is to ensure that she'll give evidence for the prosecution when the time comes. It's also to prevent any of the murderer's friends from threatening her. She'll be released as soon as the case is over.'

When he was certain that Albert accepted what he had been told, Fergus said, 'I'll see you again before you go to America with Shirley. I'll give her some money for you. Then, when you find the place where you want to settle down, it will help to give you a good start to your new life.'

'Fergus and Becky might come there too,' said Meg, and Albert's face lit up almost as much as had her own at the suggestion.

'I only said it might be a good idea,' corrected Fergus. 'But, talking of Becky . . .'

He pulled out a watch and frowned. 'It doesn't look as though she's going to put in an appearance tonight. She must have gone somewhere. Probably she's having a celebratory drink with her friends.'

'Becky wouldn't do that,' declared Meg. 'I tried to get her to go out sometimes, to have a drink or two and enjoy herself. She always said she'd rather stay here, with Lucy. I expect *that's* where she's gone now. To collect Lucy. That would be the first thing she'd think of as soon as she got out of prison.'

Exactly as Meg had intended, Fergus was building up a picture of a new and more responsible Becky. He was also aware that she had a loyal friend in Meg.

'In that case I ought to return to Clifton and wait for her there. That's the place where I can be certain of seeing her. As long as Lucy's at the Tennants' house I'll know Becky will come there sooner or later.'

Fergus took a guinea from his pocket and handed it to Meg. 'I'm fairly certain Becky has some money. Just in case she hasn't, use this to pay for a cab to take her to Clifton if she does come here first.'

He shrugged off his disappointment. 'I had wanted to

surprise her with my return, but perhaps that wouldn't be altogether fair. *You* tell her I've come back, Meg. You can also tell her that I know now I should never have gone away.'

Chapter 40

Clutching Lucy in her arms, Becky made her way from Clifton, through the heart of the city to Lewin's Mead. She was desolated and thoroughly confused by what she had just witnessed.

Fergus, the husband she had feared dead, was not only alive, but *here*, in Bristol!

How long had he been here? Had he ever been away? She was particularly deeply wounded that he had made no attempt to see her when she was locked up in gaol with the threat of execution hanging over her.

If he had been in Bristol *before* her imprisonment, why had he made no attempt to visit her in order to see their daughter?

The questions were many, and unanswerable, but there was one thing about which there could be no argument. He had used Fanny Tennant as a means of taking Lucy from her. She had also seen clear evidence of a close relationship between Fergus and the principal of the ragged school.

Hugging Lucy closer to her, Becky determined he would not get her baby again. She would take her away from Bristol, if necessary.

All these thoughts and many, many more passed confusingly through Becky's mind as she made her way to Back Lane.

When she reached the house she was cold and shivering. Lucy too was beginning to complain now.

The McCabe family were still awake when Becky passed through their landing, but the door to the attic room was bolted. It was a few minutes before there was any response to her increasingly insistent knocking.

'Who is it?' The sound of Meg's sleepy voice came to her through the door.

'It's Becky, and I've got Lucy here with me. Open up.'

Moments later the door swung open and Becky went inside the room. There was a low red glow in the fireplace. Becky made for it immediately, to warm herself and Lucy.

Behind her the lamp flared into life and Meg said excitedly. 'I expected you back before this. Fergus said . . .'

'Fergus has been here? When?' Becky was alarmed. Had he come looking for Lucy already? If so she would need to leave Back Lane again, quickly.

'Earlier this evening. He said you were out of prison. He waited for more than an hour thinking you'd come back here. Then we decided you must have gone to Clifton, to collect Lucy, so he left. I thought he must have found you.' Meg sounded disappointed.

'He'll be back again when they find I've taken Lucy. I must get away from here, Meg. You must help me.'

Meg looked at her with a total lack of understanding. 'Why? He wants to find you, to make things up with you. I thought that was what you wanted too? It *is* what you want. You've said so lots of times.' She was confused by Becky's apparent change of heart.

'Things have changed. It isn't me he wants at all. He wants to get Lucy so he and Fanny can have her, that's all. Well, he's not getting her.'

'That isn't true, Becky. I know. He told me . . .'

'I don't care what he told you. I know what I've seen with my own two eyes. Now, are you going to help me, or are you going to get out of my way so I can do things for myself?'

'I'm your friend, Becky. I always will be, I hope. I'll do whatever you want me to . . . but I think you're doing all the wrong things – all right, what is it you want me to do?' she added as she saw Becky's lips tighten angrily.

'Gather some of Lucy's things together while I change out of this filthy dress and get a few of my own things.'

'Where are you going?'

Becky rounded on the young girl. 'How far can I trust

you not to say anything to Fergus or Fanny Tennant?'

'I won't say anything . . . cross my heart! But where are you going? Are you leaving Lewin's Mead?'

'I might have to, but not just yet. I'm going to ask Simon to take me in for a while, until I've decided. Will you help me to take my stuff there?'

Meg nodded, but she was very unhappy. Things were going all wrong. She had spoken to Fergus. She *knew* how excited he had been at the thought of being with Becky once more. She had been happy for him. For both of them.

'I'll help you, Becky, of course I will – but I wish you'd let me talk to you about Fergus.'

'There's nothing to talk about, I've already told you that. Now, let me clean up a bit and give Lucy something to eat, then we'll be on our way.'

Simon was also brought from his bed by Becky. He was every bit as reluctant to go along with her arrangement as Meg had been. 'It puts me in an impossible position, Becky, you must see that. I'm engaged to be married to Catherine. She's working for Fanny, who's also her best friend. It's a web of deceit that I'd rather not get involved in.'

'Very well, I'll find somewhere else to go. Somewhere as far from Bristol as possible.'

'No! Now let's sit down and talk about this. Meg, put the kettle on, will you? We'll have a cup of tea and sort something out. The best solution would be for you and Fergus to meet and talk this over, face-to-face. But I can see that right now might not be the best time to discuss anything. You and Lucy can stay here tonight and I promise I won't say anything to anyone while you're here – but we *will* have a serious talk about it tomorrow. For now we'll just be happy that you're out of prison and are no longer facing a charge of murder.'

Becky was greatly relieved. She had been relying upon Simon to help her. Had he refused, she would have been at a loss as to what she could do next. It might be only a temporary arrangement, but she felt certain he would help her to do whatever needed to be done.

'Now, as we've said, we'll leave talking about all this until tomorrow. While we're having our tea we'll discuss something entirely different. Has Meg told you that she and young Albert Garrett are having a chat with Shirley Buchanan tomorrow? It's more in the nature of an interview really, to discuss the young Garrett family – and Meg too – being taken to live in America. Doesn't that sound to you as though it's an absolutely wonderful opportunity for them all?'

Chapter 41

Fergus was deeply disappointed when he reached the Tennant house. He had convinced himself he would find Becky here. He now began to be seriously concerned for her. From all he had been told, Becky thought so much of Lucy that she had changed her way of life because of her. Yet she had been out of prison for many hours now but had made no attempt to see her. What was almost equally worrying was that she had apparently been seen by nobody since the time she left the New Gaol.

It was very difficult to convey to Fanny the sense of unease he felt. She was in a very happy frame of mind. She had spent an hour with Lewis and also had a conversation with Sir Ephraim Stern.

The doctor had agreed Lewis could leave the Infirmary the following day and return to her house in Clifton. However, he would need to remain in Bristol for at least another ten days in order that he might receive daily treatment at the Infirmary.

It meant Fanny would be able to show Lewis around Bristol and introduce him to her friends. It would also be ten days during which they could really get to know each other.

Fergus was aware that this was all very important to Fanny, and he was pleased for her, but he had other matters on his mind. He would not settle until he had been reunited with Becky.

'You must try not to worry too much about her, Fergus,' said Fanny. 'She will want to get that dreadful place out of her system. I can't say I blame her at all. It is an absolutely *horrible* place. A disgrace to the city.'

'You're probably right,' said Fergus, 'but Meg seemed to think Becky would be far more interested in being with Lucy than in enjoying any form of celebration. I'm very surprised she hasn't come here.'

'Well, I doubt whether she'll come now. The best thing you can do is go to bed. Resume your search for her in the morning.'

'There's very little else I *can* do,' he agreed, reluctantly. 'But I am worried about where she might have gone. Becky has always hated being locked up. She's such a free spirit I fear prison might have turned her mind.'

'You worry too much, Fergus. Go to bed. We'll organise everyone in the morning – and we'll find her, you can be certain of that. Oh, and don't look in on Lucy, you might disturb her. She's teething and took a while to go to sleep tonight.'

Fergus came awake aware of an unusual noise. As he shook sleep off, he realised someone was banging on his door.

'Come in! It's not locked.'

The door opened and a wide-eyed servant practically fell inside the room. 'Mr Vincent. Come quickly, sir. We've just been into Miss Lucy's room. She's gone. Been taken from her bed. There's a window smashed too. Someone got into the house from the garden . . .'

The servant turned away as Fergus flung the bedclothes from him and put his feet to the floor.

'Does Miss Fanny know?'

'Yes, sir. She's in Miss Lucy's room right now.'

Fergus arrived at the room where Lucy had been, to find Fanny with a crowd of servants and house guests there. The servant whose duty it had been to take care of Lucy was in hysterics.

'What's going on?' Fergus demanded of Fanny.

'Someone broke into the house during the night,' she said, grimly. 'They've taken Lucy. It must have been Becky. No one else would have done such a thing.'

'But *why*?' Fergus was horrified. 'Why would she want to

486

take her away? Why didn't she just come to the house and speak to someone?'

'I don't know,' said Fanny who did not appear to be fully awake yet in spite of the high drama. 'It seems no one saw anything. It's a complete mystery.'

'Begging your pardon, Miss Fanny.' The new maid who had opened the front door to Becky and sent her to the back of the house, spoke now. 'I don't know whether it might have anything to do with what's happened, but I opened the front door to a young woman yesterday afternoon. She was filthy dirty. Not the sort of person you'd have calling at the front door. I sent her round the back, but she didn't go there and no one else saw her.'

'What time was this?' asked Fergus.

'It would be just a few minutes before you came back from seeing Lord Callington at the Infirmary, sir. As a matter of fact, I'm surprised you didn't see her for yourself. She could hardly have left the garden when you arrived.'

Fergus cast his mind back to the previous day. He remembered coming back to the house and passing on the news of Lewis's progress to Fanny. It was then when she had told him of Becky's release from prison. Suddenly he remembered how he had reacted. He had hugged Fanny. If Becky had been watching . . . The shock of realising he was in Bristol and of seeing him show such affection to Fanny could explain her action in taking Lucy – and be the reason why no one had seen her.

Fanny had reached the same conclusion. Although she too was alarmed, she said, 'Don't worry, Fergus. We'll find her and explain exactly what happened.'

'We'll need to find her very quickly,' he said. 'Becky has always been so uncertain of herself that she's likely to jump to the wrong conclusion and do something she'll bitterly regret later. Why didn't she just come out of hiding and speak to me?'

'We'll get dressed and talk about it over some breakfast . . . No, I realise you won't feel like eating, but there's nothing more we can do right now. I suspect that Lucy was taken from her room earlier than we realise last night. Possibly before we'd even gone to bed. By now Becky will have had lots of time to do whatever she intended doing. I'll go to the ragged school and you can go to Back Lane. Between us we might find out something. If she was going away she wouldn't do it until she'd been home and collected some things.'

'Is there anything we can do?' Shirley had been standing in the background with Shashi, listening to all that was being said, but remaining uncharacteristically silent.

'Not at the moment,' said Fanny. 'But you'll be talking to Meg and Albert later. I doubt if they would say anything to us because of a misplaced sense of loyalty to Becky – but you can bring considerable pressure to bear upon them if you feel they know anything. Meg, in particular, is desperate to go to America with you – and I don't doubt you'll *want* to take her once you have spoken to her. But she does not need to know that immediately.'

Fanny turned her attention to the servants. 'Off you go and speed breakfast up. No one is doing any good standing around here crying about what's too late to mend. If everyone goes about their business we'll have things put to rights far more quickly.'

Chapter 42

Fergus walked to the nearest hansom cab rank and rode to Lewin's Mead. He then hurried through the quiet, early-morning alleyways to Back Lane.

The house was as silent as the remainder of the slum. He made his way up the stairs to the attic, hoping he might find Becky here, but the room was empty.

Returning to the second floor he could hear no sound or movement from either of the two rooms occupied by the McCabe family. However, the thought of disturbing people did not trouble Fergus today.

After banging loudly on each of the two closed doors in turn, he was rewarded when one of them opened. A bleary-eyed Mrs McCabe opened it no more than three or four inches.

Behind her, light from outside entered the room through an uncurtained window. Fergus could see a number of small children lying or sitting on two tattered mattresses. They seemed no wider awake than their mother.

'Who are you? What are you wanting at this hour of the morning? If it's Seamus, you're too late. He went to work more than an hour ago.'

'I'm Fergus Vincent. I'm looking for Becky. Have you seen her?'

'You woke me from a well-earned sleep to ask me that? The girl doesn't even live on this floor. Try her room upstairs.'

'I've already been there.'

'Well, I can't help you. I haven't seen her since the police came and took her away for killing our poor landlady, God

489

rest her saintly soul.' The woman's hand made the sign of the cross, in the vicinity of her left bosom.

Before Fergus could correct her version of the murder of Ida Stokes, one of the small boys in the room behind her, said, 'I saw her. I saw her last night. She went upstairs to her room carrying the baby.'

'Now how could you have seen her when none of the rest of us did? You were all asleep long before me and your pa came to bed. I swear she hadn't come into the house before then.'

'It was after that,' insisted the small boy. 'I'd got out of bed and gone to the other room to pee out of the window into the lane. She came up the stairs while I was doing it.'

'You can't be believing anything young Connor says,' said Mrs McCabe, apologetically. 'He'd be no doubt dreaming and never got up at all.'

'Yes he did,' confirmed a girl, smaller than her brother. 'He trod on me and woke me up when he was coming back.'

Fergus knew it was no use asking any of them what time it was when Becky came to the house. Instead, he asked, 'Has anyone seen Meg this morning?'

'We've seen no one this morning but you,' said Mrs McCabe. 'And you'd have been a sight more welcome had you come an hour or two later.'

'Meg went out with Becky,' said the young girl who had complained of being trodden on by her brother. 'I heard them going downstairs together. I couldn't sleep after Connor trod on me,' she explained. 'He trod on my arm and it hurt.'

'Thank you,' said Fergus. 'I'll see if Meg is downstairs in Albert's room.'

'She'd better not be!' exclaimed her mother. 'Those two are far friendlier than any girl and boy of their age ought to be. I'll be glad when this American woman takes 'em off and they become *her* responsibility – 'though I'd have thanked her more had she done it when there was good food going inside her belly for no return. Now she's big enough to earn a penny or two to help with feeding the rest of the family, she's thinking of going off to America.'

Leaving the Irishwoman still grumbling at the door to her room, Fergus made his way down to the first floor and the room occupied by Albert and his young brother and sisters. He had no need to knock at the door. It stood open. Inside, Albert was inspecting the hands and faces of the young family. In one hand he held a wet cloth which he used to wipe excess dirt from faces and hands.

This was a big day for the youngsters. Albert had no intention of having it go wrong for want of a quick rub with a wet rag, however strong the protests against such a radical measure.

'Have you seen Meg this morning?' Fergus asked the question over the complaints of the youngest member of the family.

'Isn't she upstairs?'

'No.'

'I hope she hasn't gone off somewhere and forgotten what we're supposed to be doing this morning,' Albert seemed genuinely concerned.

'Does she often go off unexpectedly?'

'Only when Seamus has had a go at her and she's run off somewhere to get away from him,' said Albert, bitterly.

An alarming thought crossed Fergus's mind. What if Seamus had come home drunk and surprised *Becky* in the attic room?

He dismissed the thought as being a most unlikely explanation. He felt certain that Becky's intention was to hide herself and Lucy from the world. Unfortunately, such a plan was all too easy to carry out in Lewin's Mead.

For more than an hour after he left the Back Lane house, Fergus tramped the narrow lanes and alleyways of Lewin's Mead, entertaining a vain hope that he might catch an unexpected glimpse of his wife and child.

Eventually he was forced to admit to himself that he would never find them in Lewin's Mead if they did not want to be found. No one here would tell him, even if they knew their whereabouts.

Leaving the alleyways behind him, he made his despondent way to the ragged school. Meg was the only hope he had now of finding Becky. He hoped the young Irish girl was at the school.

Fergus met Fanny coming out of a classroom. Her immediate question about his success or otherwise in finding Becky dashed what faint hope he had entertained that she might have learned of her whereabouts.

'She's not in Back Lane,' he said. 'But there's a faint chance that Meg McCabe might know something. Have you seen her this morning?'

'She's in my office with Albert. They're talking to Shirley and Shashi.'

'How long are they likely to be?'

'Probably quite some time, but that doesn't matter. I asked Shirley to find out what she could from Meg, but I think it's time I had a few words with her myself.'

Chapter 43

When Fergus and Fanny entered the office, both Meg and Albert turned around to see who it was. When Meg saw Fergus an expression crossed her face that came close to panic.

'Meg, I want to speak to you,' he said.

'I . . . I've got your guinea here.' She scrabbled in a deep pocket on the front of her dress and her hand came out clutching the golden coin.

'Never mind the money. Have you seen Becky?'

'I . . . No . . . Please, Miss Buchanan, can I go to the privy?'

'Not yet, Meg. Mr Vincent asked you a question. Answer him.'

'Please . . . I . . .'

'You heard me. Answer him this minute.' The order was issued by Fanny at her sternest.

'You must tell him, child.' This from Shirley Buchanan. 'It's very important.'

'Meg! If you know where Becky is, you *have* to tell me.'

She was looking from one to the other as though seeking a means of escape, when Shashi spoke for the first time. 'Do you mind if I take Meg into another room and have a word with her?' she asked Fanny.

'Why?' Fanny was angry. 'If she knows something she must tell us.'

'Please, I think I understand why she cannot say anything to you. I would like to speak to her alone.'

Fanny was about to protest once more and *demand* that Meg tell them what she knew. Fergus interrupted. 'Let

Shashi speak to her, Fanny. I think I know what's in her mind. May we use the spare classroom?'

Fanny was angry with Meg for her stubbornness. For a moment Fergus thought she would refuse his request. Instead, she nodded, without speaking.

'Come!' Shashi put an arm about Meg's shoulders and led her from the room.

'Such defiance!' Fanny was still angry. 'I don't know what you must think of her, I really don't, Shirley.'

'I'm quite sure that Shirley realises she's dealing with an extraordinarily honourable young girl,' declared Fergus. 'Unless I'm mistaken, Meg has given her word to Becky that she'll say nothing of her whereabouts to you or me. Despite all the pressure we put her under she hasn't broken her promise. But I doubt if she's made any promises about speaking to Shashi.'

Fergus's assessment of the situation was an accurate one. In the empty classroom, Shashi was talking softly to Meg and drawing the story of the previous evening from the young Irish girl who was by now very close to tears.

'I *couldn't* tell anyone in there,' she said for the third time. 'I promised Becky I wouldn't.'

'Did Becky say anything to you about not telling me?' asked Shashi.

'No, of course not. I don't suppose she even knows of you.'

'Well then, there is no reason why you can't tell me what you are unable to say to Fergus.'

'But you'd go straight back to the office and tell him what I'd told you. That would be just the same as if I'd told him myself.'

'Not necessarily. Tell me, do you know where Becky is at this moment?'

After only a moment's hesitation, Meg nodded.

'Good. But you have made a promise that you will not tell Fergus.'

'Or Fanny Tennant, either.'

'Or Fanny Tennant,' agreed Shashi. 'And you are afraid

494

that if you tell me I will return to the office and tell them. This is so?'

Again Meg nodded.

'Why does Becky not want you to tell them? Is it because she no longer loves Fergus?'

'No! She thinks the world of him.'

'And he of her! Why does she not want to meet him? He has returned from India to be with her once more. I do not understand.'

'She thinks there's something going on between Fanny and Fergus. That all he really wants is to take Lucy from her, so he and Fanny can have her.'

'I see. She is, of course, very mistaken. She will need to be told and made to believe what is the truth.' Shashi looked thoughtful. 'So, you must not tell Fanny or Fergus where she is, and you will not tell me because you believe I will tell them?'

Meg nodded again, but somewhat less emphatically this time.

'Yet I believe you and I want the same thing. To see two people who love each other back where they belong. Together. Am I not right once again?'

'Yes.'

'Very well. Then I *must* talk to Becky. I do not ask you to tell me where she is, only to take me to her. You will do this?'

Meg thought about it for a while, and then said, 'If I do will you really be able to persuade her and Fergus to get back together?'

'I have no need to persuade Fergus. I already know what he wants. He has told me so many times. I need only to persuade Becky. I think perhaps I might be able to do this more easily than anyone else. Will you take me to her?'

Once again Meg thought about it for a while, before saying quietly, 'All right – but you don't think Miss Buchanan will stop me going to America because I wouldn't say anything back there?'

'I think I know Shirley Buchanan as well as anyone does. I promise you she will admire you greatly for not breaking

495

your word. Come, we will speak to them first.'

Back in the office, Fanny said, 'Have you agreed to tell Mr Vincent what he wants to know, Meg?'

'No,' said Shashi. 'She made a promise to Becky and a promise is not something to be easily broken, even though she feels she *should* tell Fergus. However, we have reached an honourable agreement. Meg will tell no one, but she will take me to the place where Becky is staying. I will talk to her there.'

This time it was Fergus who protested strongly until Shashi raised her hand in a gesture that silenced him.

'Fergus. We have spoken many times about your Becky, and you know a great deal of me too. I understand all your hopes and fears for the future. Can you think of anyone better able to speak on your behalf? To tell of how you feel about Becky? Anyone, also, more able to understand the way she thinks?'

It seemed for a moment that Fergus might argue with her but she held his gaze unflinchingly. After a few moments, he shook his head. 'No, Shashi. If she won't talk to me then I can't think of anyone more capable of speaking to her on my behalf.'

'You trust me to speak to her? To try to make things right for both of you?'

'Yes, Shashi. I trust you.'

'I thank you for that, Fergus. It is a great honour. I will not fail you. I promise.'

Chapter 44

As she walked away from the ragged school, in company with Shashi, Meg was constantly glancing over her shoulder. Eventually, the Indian girl said, 'Why do you keep looking back? Are you afraid someone is going to follow us?'

'No, but I want to be sure no one's watching.'

Shashi was not certain she fully understood, but she said, 'How far do we have to go?'

Looking back once more, Meg suddenly slowed her pace. 'We're here.'

Shashi was startled. 'Here?' They were still in full view of the ragged school. 'You mean . . .? Fergus and Becky are so close to each other, yet he doesn't know it?'

Meg nodded. 'Come in here quickly, before someone sees us.' She pulled Shashi into the doorway of a small house and knocked at the door.

Glancing back towards the ragged school once more, she repeated the knock, more urgently this time.

'Who is it?'

A woman's voice called from the other side of the door.

'It's Meg. Let me in quickly.'

When the door opened, she pushed Shashi inside and followed her in.

'Who's this?' Becky demanded to know.

'She's an Indian friend of Fergus's.'

'You promised!'

'Meg has not broken her promise. She refused to say anything to Fergus. She brought me here only because I convinced her it is very important I should speak to you.'

'I have nothing to talk about with Fergus, or with any of his friends.'

'You are wrong, Becky. There is much to talk about. Of your future, and that of your baby, Lucy. Where is she? Perhaps Meg will go and look after her while we talk.'

'I expect she's in the bedroom,' said Meg. 'I'll go and find her.' She was anxious to escape from Becky's accusing glare, but before she went, she asked, 'Is Simon in?'

Shashi looked at Becky sharply. 'There is a man in this house?'

'This is his house, yes, although he's not in at the moment. He is a very good friend who saved my life when I was ill, even though he's blind. He is also engaged to marry Catherine.'

'The Catherine who works at the ragged school? She knows you are here?'

'No, but Simon says he will tell her tonight if I haven't gone somewhere else by then.'

'Your friends are very good at keeping your secrets, Becky.'

'I have good friends, yes – but you said you came here because you have something important to say to me. What is it?'

'First, may I ask you a question?' Without awaiting a reply, Shashi asked, 'Why are you hiding from your husband? Have you done something of which you are ashamed?'

'Me? It was Fergus who left me! I didn't even know he was back in the country. If he is as eager to see me as everyone says, he'd have come to see me before this. When I was in prison, for instance. No, all he wants is to take Lucy from me. Then he'll go off with that Fanny Tennant and I'll be left with no one.'

Shashi realised there was more to untangle in this situation than she'd realised. 'None of this is true, Becky. Fergus only returned from India a few days ago – when you were already in prison. He very much wanted to come and see you there. It was *Memsahib* – Miss Tennant who said he should not come to see you there.'

'She would!' declared Becky, bitterly. 'She didn't care what happened to me once she'd got hold of Lucy. Well, she's not going to have her again.'

'You are wrong, Becky. Miss Fanny is a very good friend. It was she who spoke to the head of the police here and had the inspector brought back from London to help you. As for stopping Fergus from seeing you . . . Did you not tell her you would kill yourself if he returned and saw you as you were in prison?'

'Yes . . .' Becky admitted, grudgingly. 'But I didn't think it would ever happen. I didn't know he was back in Bristol then.'

'He came back because he learned that you had his baby. The news made him very happy.'

Suddenly suspicious of this woman who knew so much about Fergus, Becky asked, 'Did you come back from India with him?'

'No, but I came to know him very well there.'

'Has he made love to you?' Becky put the question bluntly.

Shashi replied in a similar manner. 'No. Had he wanted to I would have let him, but his thoughts were always of you.'

Hiding the surprise she felt at this woman's unexpected honesty, Becky made a derisive sound. 'If he thought so much about me, why did he go away and leave me?'

'We did not discuss his reasons for leaving you – but I think in your heart you already know.'

Suddenly, Shashi reached out a hand and grasped Becky's arm. 'Don't let foolish feelings of bitterness stand in the way of your happiness with Fergus, Becky, or one day you will regret it very much. Will you sit down, please? I want to tell you something of India, of myself, and of Fergus's part in my life.'

The two women sat for a very long time in the room in the small house in St James's Square. Shashi told of her first meeting with Fergus and the survivors of the *Venus*. She told of the long journey from Calcutta to Lucknow. Of the fighting. Of her love for Midshipman Harry Downton and of his death. Then she told of how, when she was on her way to the temple to return to the unhappy way of life she had formerly known, Fergus came after her and persuaded her to return with him.

'There is much, much more I could tell you,' said Shashi, to the now silent Becky. 'I once had a child, a girl child, but she died. Had Fergus not called me back when I was returning to the temple, I too would have died in here.' Shashi touched her breast. 'I did not die and I owe this to Fergus. I would do anything for him. Anything. I have come to speak to you today because I know that more than anything else he wants you and Lucy. It would be the greatest gift I could give to him. Please, do not throw away the thing you both have that is so very precious.'

Becky had been moved far more than she would admit by Shashi's story, but she said, 'I wish I could believe you, but I can't think he really wants me back. When I went to Fanny Tennant's house to fetch Lucy, I saw him and Fanny kissing and cuddling together.'

Shashi could not conceal her shock. 'I do not believe this.'

'It's true. I saw it. He arrived back from somewhere in a carriage and she came out to meet him. It was then they kissed and hugged each other.'

'It was for this you broke into the house to take back Lucy? Your reason for hiding from Fergus?'

'Isn't it enough? You didn't see them . . .'

Becky was taken aback when Shashi greeted her statement with a broad smile.

'But I *did* see them and I heard what was said, too. I was standing in the hallway of the house when Fergus arrived. He gave Miss Fanny some good news. The wounded friend with whom he returned from India – and of whom she has grown very fond – had just had a successful operation. Then she told him that *you* had been released from prison and someone else charged with the murder. Both were so excited to have such good news that they hugged each other in sheer delight. Then Fergus said he must rush to Lewin's

Mead, to see you. No doubt you saw him leave a few minutes later?'

Feeling discomfited, Becky admitted that she had not seen him leave, but added, 'I know he went to Lewin's Mead. Meg told me.'

'Miss Fanny went out too. She went to the hospital, to see Fergus's friend – the man whom I think she hopes she might marry one day.'

Becky remained silent for a long time, staring down at her lap. Eventually, Shashi said softly, 'There has been much unnecessary foolishness. But now we have put it right, you and I. There is no reason at all why you cannot be a happy family now. You, Fergus and Lucy.'

'It's not quite as simple as all that. There *was* a reason why Fergus left me. A very good reason. He won't have forgotten.'

'Perhaps he will not have forgotten. But I think he will not reproach you if you do nothing again to remind him.'

Shashi leaned forward and took both Becky's hands in hers. 'There was much that Fergus never told me about you, yet he spoke of you so often I feel I have known you for a very long time. I built a picture of you in my mind – and this picture is of someone very like me. For a long time I lived a life I did not enjoy, only because I knew of no other. Things were very different when I found a better way – especially after I met Harry. Yet there came a time when there was very little food and Harry was very ill. He was dying. It was then I once more became what I was before – but only for Harry's sake. I gave my body to another man in exchange for food. Fergus learned of this and it distressed him very much. When he spoke of it I asked him whether I should love my body more than I loved Harry. Even if he were to find out, keeping him alive mattered more to me than my happiness. Fergus showed great understanding towards me. Should he show less to you, whom he loves more than anyone else?'

Fergus had in fact told Shashi far more about Becky than she had revealed, but she felt there was no reason for her to say anything of this.

'I *do* love him, Shashi. I love him in the way you loved Harry.' Becky was having great difficulty in holding back her tears.

'I know you do. I also know how much Fergus loves you. You both have so much to give each other – and now there is Lucy too. There is so much happiness in the future for you all.'

Becky squeezed Shashi's hands gratefully, 'Thank you, Shashi. I . . . I would like to see Fergus now.'

'I am so very glad. Would you like to meet him in your own home? Shall I tell him . . .?'

'No. I don't want to go back to Lewin's Mead. Ever. I want us to start a new life somewhere else. Somewhere far away.'

Standing up, Becky said, 'Will you take Meg with you and go to Fergus? Ask him to come here. Tell him . . . tell him . . . No, I'll tell him all that needs to be said. Just ask him to come here. Lucy and I will be waiting.'

E V Thompson

His exotic new saga

Blue Dress Girl

A stirring tale of adventure and a moving and tender love story played out against the exotic background of China at one of the most turbulent periods in its history.

Fleeing from the busy port of Canton to avoid scandal and danger, blue dress girl She-she is caught in crossfire and rescued by Second Lieutenant Kernow Keats of the Royal Marines. Instantly moved by her fragile beauty, the young man takes She-she to Hong Kong, to the home of missionaries Hugh and Hannah Jefferies, where she can regain her strength. As she comes to know the handsome hero, the girl's gratitude becomes love – and her feelings are returned.

But a love affair between a Chinese peasant girl and an English officer seems unthinkable in 1857. And as the Taiping rebellion gets underway, Kernow is torn from She-she's side to do his patriotic duty. Can their great love cross the chasm of race, class and background that divides them?

'Thompson enjoys working his backdrop – lots of chaps fighting on boats, warlords, pirate raids, skirmishes and bloodshed . . .' *The Sunday Times*

'It will keep you turning the pages and certainly appeal to the vast readership who enjoy top quality historical novels.' *Sunday Independent*

FICTION / SAGA 0 7472 4136 8

MARGARET BARD

The Changing Room

Step into its seductive world of ambition, secrets and betrayal . . .

Welcome to the Changing Room – where lives are transformed, hearts are broken, and careers are made or destroyed – all in the time it takes to switch TV channels.

For ambitious young producer Julia Hudlow, assembling the cast of her first ever network TV show – a sitcom that follows the fortunes of a revolutionary beauty salon named the Changing Room – is a fantasy come true. But she quickly discovers her stars – from every woman's heart-throb Brandon Tate to housewife-turned-overnight-star Debra Jo Fawcett to child actress Melissa McKimmie – are all too palpably flesh and blood: volatile, vulnerable and with personal crises that spill into their on-screen lives. And, as the show climbs the ratings and Julia struggles to juggle the demands of her marriage with the pressures and behind-the-scenes passions of her show, she quickly realises that swimming in the sea of sharks that is network TV you can find yourself being eaten alive . . .

FICTION / GENERAL 0 7472 4173 2

A selection of bestsellers from Headline